CITY OF
A THOUSAND
GATES

CITY OF
A THOUSAND
GATES

A Novel

REBECCA SACKS

HARPER

An Imprint of HarperCollins*Publishers*

CITY OF A THOUSAND GATES. Copyright © 2021 by Rebecca Sacks. All rights reserved. Printed in the United States of America. No part of this book may be used or reproduced in any manner whatsoever without written permission except in the case of brief quotations embodied in critical articles and reviews. For information, address HarperCollins Publishers, 195 Broadway, New York, NY 10007.

In Canada, address HarperCollins Publishers Ltd, Bay Adelaide Centre, East Tower, 22 Adelaide Street West, 41st Floor, Toronto, Ontario, M5H 4E3, Canada.

HarperCollins books may be purchased for educational, business, or sales promotional use. For information, please email the Special Markets Department in the U.S. at SPsales@harpercollins.com or in Canada at HCOrder@harpercollins.com.

FIRST EDITION

Library of Congress Cataloging-in-Publication Data has been applied for.

Library and Archives Canada Cataloguing in Publication information is available upon request.

ISBN 978-0-06-301147-2

ISBN 978-1-4434-6218-1 (Canada)

21 22 23 24 25   LSC   10 9 8 7 6 5 4 3 2 1

"It seemed—even though outside in the world the high drama of history might be going on—that this, for all its painful aspects, was one of the moments for the sake of which God had created the earth."

—Robert Musil, *The Man Without Qualities*
(trans. Eithne Wilkins & Ernst Kaiser)

Contents

Cast of Characters

IDO: professional animator, reservist in the Israeli army, originally from Tel Aviv

MAYAN: their newborn daughter

ORI LEV: enlisted soldier whose family lives in the Israeli settlement of Gush Etzion

MIRIAM: Ori's mother, a religious instructor for young brides

YUVAL: Ori's father

TOVAH and **AVITAL**: Ori's younger sisters

MEIR KLAUSMAN: professional soccer player, Ori's childhood friend, Amir's teammate

DANNY: a unit-mate of Ori's

PROFESSOR SAMAR FARHA: PhD in comparative literature, teaches at Bethlehem University, lives with her mother in Bethlehem

FATIMA: Samar's sister-in-law

SHIBI HASSIN: professional soccer player, teammate of Meir and Amir, Palestinian resident of Jerusalem with Israeli residency

AMAL: Shibi's wife

NASIR: their young son

MAI: university student at Bethlehem University, classmate of Hamid, Palestinian resident of Jerusalem with Israeli residency

LEILA: Mai's sister

TARIQ: Leila's husband, Mai's brother-in-law

MUHAMMED AND FAROUQ: Mai's younger brothers

NOOR: student at Bethlehem University, classmate and friend of Mai, resident of Bethlehem

HUSSEIN: Noor's brother, interned in an Israeli prison

WINTER

Crossings: Hamid, Vera, Ori, Samar

Hamid is fucked. He knows it now. If he hadn't let his boss convince him to stay an extra hour to finish installing the last air conditioner. If he hadn't stayed to work inside Israel for nearly a month already—all that pay carefully folded into his wallet and, for good measure, his socks. If he wasn't rattled and jumpy, hearing about the boy the Jews beat half to death in a settlement parking lot last night. If he actually had a permit to be here. If, if, if.

By the time Hamid got to the bus stop, it was midmorning. He was supposed to wait for a bus that would take him in the general direction of Jerusalem. From there, he could get home to Bethlehem. He waited at an overhang by a highway, cars rushing by. On the other side of the road were a gas station and an "American-style" waffle place. A few Jews were waiting for buses—women with their hair covered tending to babies, guys maybe his own age talking over a cell phone that blasted the latest Israeli pop song to rip off Palestinian music. *My beloved, my beloved, my beloved*, the singer trilled in Arabic. Hamid's real phone doesn't get service this far inside the Jewish areas, so he used his shitty phone—the one with an Israeli SIM card—to read about Salem Abu-Khdeir. Someone posted what looked like security footage of the beating, but his phone wouldn't load it. At the bus stop, Hamid began noticing how the Jews his own age seemed to be drifting closer to him, saying something among themselves that made them laugh, and then looking at Hamid again. He wondered if they had seen the video. He wondered if they were in it. Fuck this, he decided, and the next bus that stopped, he got on, not even bothering to ask the driver where it was heading. Anything was better than being beaten half to death in some suburban bus stop. Right?

Wrong. Because now he is so spectacularly fucked. Ever since the bus flew by the junction and continued down the highway, he has known that he is fucked. Because this bus will not take him to the outskirts of Jerusalem, to a place where nobody checks your hawiyya to see if it's green or blue, to see if you're from the West Bank, to see if you're allowed to be here without a permit. No, this bus will take him—he's sure now—deep inside, all the way to Tel Aviv, all the way to the Central Station, a place where every hawiyya is checked as they funnel you out of the exits, a place where he'll be caught. Fucked.

On the highway, they speed deep into the interior of the Jewish state, past fields of brown grass. In the distance, dystopian-looking power plants vibrate. Signs for Tel Aviv begin to appear. Hamid presses a hand up to the glass. Breathe, he tells himself. There are probably a lot of bus stations in Tel Aviv. He doesn't actually know this to be true but it stands to reason. There are a lot of stations, so who's to say that this bus is going to the one station that he absolutely, absolutely cannot enter?

Ask someone, he begs himself. It might not be too late. He might be able to get out before they pull into the Central Station, before he's forced to show his hawiyya and his expired permit to the soldiers there. But he doesn't move. The bus's seats have soft fabric that was probably itchy once, long since worn away. He's sitting near the back, and there's nobody immediately next to him, but there are people around. A tourist-looking white lady, European maybe, writes in a journal. A couple speaks Hebrew a few places up. In the back, some tired, refugee-looking black guys watch something on a cell phone held between four hands.

There are two soldiers on the bus, but they are sitting closer to the front, and anyway, as he's recently learned, outside of checkpoints most soldiers aren't working. They take buses from this place to that place; they wander around in little packs waiting for some train; they eat falafel. When he first began to come into Israeli territory without papers, he was shocked to see off-duty soldiers—like an action movie showing the villains making coffee or taking a shit—but the more times he comes inside the Wall (the fucking Wall) the less bewildering it is. They are dangerous only contextually. They don't ask you to produce your hawiyya—match the picture to your face, call in the ID number on a walkie-talkie—they don't do all that unless it's their job. Unless they're manning, oh, say, one of the countless security checks at the big bus station in Tel Aviv. Even when he has the right papers, he doesn't go near that big central station. Everyone avoids it if they can. What's to stop one of them from pocketing the document, or tearing it up, or finding some otherwise unnoticed flaw? Because really, their job isn't to check for the right anything. Their job is to catch him.

He thinks about texting Mama, but what would he even text to her? *Don't wait up. They got me*? He rolls his head to face the window, lets out a whimper. What is Mama doing now? She must be home from work. Cooking, probably. Cooking in Teta's kitchen while Teta has her late-afternoon lie-down. He hopes it's something simple, something comforting. His favorite meals are the ones she makes in a rush. Macaroni and cheese, baked with strips of chicken. His empty stomach clenches acidly. Whenever he comes back from working inside, Mama and Teta lament how skinny he's gotten. Will he spend tonight in jail? Will they shoot him on the spot?

His elbows rest on his thighs, his face in his hands. It was supposed to be easy today. Just a few final air conditioners to install before he went home. Cash and no questions from the boss, Segev. He's a decent guy, a Jew, but not a real Jew—a Russian with Hebrew worse than Hamid's. The work was brilliant all summer and fall, the pay so good that Hamid enrolled in university for the winter. But now he's fucked. "Fucked" means going to jail, of course, but it means more than that. This will be the third time. The first two times, it's just a day lost in handcuffs and getting printed at some station. But the third time is jail time. How much is impossible to say. How much do they feel like giving you? Are you on any lists? Do you want to find out? Jail means being taken inside, far inside—an inside so deep that nobody, not even God, can reach him. Once they have him, Hamid feels in his heart that they will never let him go.

He knows the bus is pulling into the Central Station because it slows to ascend a ramp. The closer he gets, the calmer he gets. None of this is intuitive. He's never terrified when he should be terrified. The first time Hamid came inside without papers, he was stupid about it, and so of course got tear canisters shot at him. This was before he had the job with Segev. Before he knew how it worked— the early-morning rides down south to spots where you can slip through, the waiting cars—before it was all a routine. He had seen a rope that someone else had used. He took his chance, hoisted himself over the cement slabs like a mountain climber. His palms, not yet hardened with working blisters, tore. Before his feet hit the ground, the live canisters were coming, and, from the guard tower, the voices shouted in Hebrew. Even then, he was calm. He knew what to do, the way to run, to zigzag, only later stopping in a side alley to puke.

The bus brakes squeak to a stop. People begin to move, bags crinkle, sweaters are unfolded. He closes his eyes. Come on. He doesn't move. *Come on.* Then, aloud to himself: "Yalla." And he gets up, takes his backpack from the seat next to him, and descends from the bus.

⤳⤳

They're posted just outside the exit so that you have to pass them to get out, which he needs to do if he wants to catch a shared van going southeast. If he can make it to East Jerusalem, getting to Bethlehem from there won't be so bad. Gray uniforms of the border police, each with a handgun and a semiautomatic, a pair of silver handcuffs dangling from a pocket. They are standing in the sun. Another weird thing Hamid has almost gotten used to: a lot of them are girls, the soldiers in gray who get in guys' faces to check their papers and pat them down. Teenage girls his own age—crazy humiliating, that it's a woman who does it to you. A woman treating you like a woman.

Hamid is under the fluorescents of the bus complex. There is nowhere to run. Inside the station is a labyrinth of cheap clothing shops and closed storefronts, Filipino grocers, and, he's heard, a complex of clubs and abandoned movie theaters underneath.

His skin is prickly. What he needs is to buy himself some time. The corridor leading outside, leading past the soldiers, has a few shops. Who would come here to buy anything? Who would come here voluntarily? There's a rip-off cell phone kiosk and next to that, a guy with a little falafel stand. The falafel guy—a heavyset Jew, with signs saying the food is kosher; Hamid can read enough Hebrew to tell—is sweaty and unshaven and putting on a little show, flipping around his spreading knife, throwing falafel into the deep fryer then opening up a pita, each movement marked by a tap of the knife. His stall is decorated by a string of palm-sized Zionist flags. Somehow, a gray dove has gotten inside. It mills around the exit like a tiny businessman.

From where he's standing, Hamid can watch the soldiers at the exit checking papers and try to divine some kind of pattern. They check almost everyone, almost. Sometimes they let someone pass, but without any detectable reason. Of the two soldiers, one is unsettlingly pretty: long hair, small waist pinched in by a belt. It makes it worse, somehow. The falafel guy is still moving, bobbing, smacking out rhythms with his dull spreading knife. Knife in her face, slashing her fucking face. *Shut up, focus.*

"*Im hakol?*" the falafel man says in Hebrew, calling to someone down the hallway, to the guy who ordered. Hamid hears the Arabic in the Jew's accent—always an odd sensation to know that the man's family came from Iraq or Morocco, came here to invent Israel. Hamid stays focused on the exit, which is quiet for a moment. Not a good time to go. He leans against the falafel stand's display glass. There are piles of chopped cucumber and tomato, cabbage pickled purple—a landscape of plenty. A few more people pass him where he stands, must be another bus just got in. One of the soldiers pulls aside an elderly man, someone's grandfather, in from a southern village. Yaa haaj, what are you doing here? The soldier talks into her radio while the haaj tries to explain something to her. He points to a document that she holds in her hand now. She doesn't acknowledge that she hears him. The man is stooped with age, thin in a cheap striped T-shirt, which is clean; it is the necessity and fragility of his dignity, of the clean T-shirt's dignity, that makes it so hard to watch. And Hamid knows that it has to be now. If he's going to make it through, it will have to be now, while they are dealing with someone else but before the situation escalates and the soldiers go crazy, before they arrest the old man or he starts crying. Hamid feels like a bastard, but what can he do? Twelve steps and he's out. Twelve steps.

He walks toward the exit, two steps, four, seven. He is looking past the soldiers as if he were already outside, as if he had momentum. Hawiyya out of his pocket. Nine steps, almost there. He feels a freezing-cold dread rise up from the deepest part of his gut as the soldiers turn at the same time to look at him, and he knows he will not make it. He will not make it. They are going to get him.

Then a voice behind him.

"*Achi!*"

He stops.

"*Achi!*" The falafel guy comes out from behind the counter, carrying a falafel in bread. The Jew laughs, says a jumble of words in Hebrew. They filter toward Hamid: *Forgot, you forgot, didn't you forget, aren't you forgetting something?* An olive-colored man, swarthy and glistening. An Arab in another life. He's speaking in Hebrew, but Hamid has been working with Segev long enough to understand him.

Information reorganizes itself; the situation appears to him in separate parts being fit back together, him in it and all the other little pieces. This man has confused Hamid with someone else. With whoever ordered. But how? The soldiers are still watching. Is this a joke? A trick? A dream? Does it matter? Hamid adjusts. He is focused. He is present. Now he knows what to do.

In Hebrew, he says, "*Ken, ken, shakhakhti,*" And takes the bread, heavy with falafel and salads and sauce. It is warm in his hand. The smell is overwhelming. He thanks him: *Todah.*

Something about this exchange, the normalcy of this exchange, has opened a door, has created a moment. Now, now, it has to be now. Hamid has the green plastic case of his ID in one hand and a dripping pita in the other. The soldiers have returned their attention to the short man whom Hamid cannot bring himself to look at. He smiles like a clown, a little sauce dripping down his hand. Warm sesame. He's young, and he looks younger, a skinny guy in fashionable sneakers with a pita the size of his own head. He's moving, expired permit held up to the sexy soldier, who nods without bothering to inspect it. She wrinkles her nose as if the falafel stinks—it probably does. Hamid walks out into the acute angle of a midday sun. He keeps walking, as if he has any idea where he is going, keeping his pace even, not breaking into the run that is itching up his legs. Behind him, a man is being harassed, maybe arrested. Somewhere else, a young man—a boy named Salem—has been chewed up by the Jewish machine and lies nearly lifeless in an East Jerusalem hospital. Above Hamid, a dove has taken flight into the filthy sky. But Hamid is walking up a crowded sidewalk still holding the uneaten falafel, his hawiyya back in his pocket, and to the God he is no longer sure he believes in, he is whispering, "Thank you, thank you, thank you."

⤙⤙⤚⤚

Vera nearly bumps into the dazed-looking guy holding the overstuffed pita as she hurries around the corner. "*Slicha*," she says in Hebrew, and then, for good measure, "*Asfa*" in Arabic. She's never sure which language to speak to people in Tel Aviv, but anyway, he doesn't respond to either. She hurries toward the lot of shared taxi-vans— *monit sherut*, she's heard Israelis call them—that ferry people back and forth between Tel Aviv and Jerusalem. She gets the last available seat, which means as soon as she gets in, the driver closes the sliding van door behind her and they are off. She checks the time on her phone: still morning, technically.

It's been a week of tit-for-tat violence in Jerusalem that started when the Israelis announced the expansion of several settlements. That night, a fourteen-year-old Jewish girl, a settler, was stabbed to death in her bedroom. The Palestinian who did it was shot but survived; he's probably being interrogated (tortured) right now. Then last night, a mob of Jewish teenagers beat up a Palestinian kid—also fourteen—so badly that he's now in a coma. A revenge attack, people are saying. It happened in a Jerusalem parking lot. But, of course, Vera is not rushing into Jerusalem to write about cycles of violence or cultures of revenge. Oh, no. She has received an assignment from an in-flight magazine that wants a mindless, fluffy write-up of a newly opened hotel. Already, cheesy descriptors float around in her head: "a stately property" that "oozes Levantine charm." This is the bullshit that pays her bills.

On the radio, a man is singing in a style Vera has recently learned to call Mizrahi. *Habibti, habibti, habibti*, he sings. My beloved, my beloved, my beloved. Vera is the only white woman in the van. The other passengers are Asian tourists—Korean, if she is not mistaken, from the round sound of their whispered words—and a few Palestinians who will probably catch an Arab bus from Jerusalem to the West Bank. The first time she heard someone refer to an "Arab bus," she was taken aback. Which Arabs? Meaning the buses were owned by Gulf states? Or Palestinians weren't allowed on Israeli buses? The truth was at once more boring and more horrifying. Buses that serve the West Bank were called "Arab buses" by Israelis, in keeping with the general aversion to referring to the Palestinians of Jerusalem as Palestinians. "Arab" meant Palestinian, but it also suggested a statelessness. The way they said "Arab" made her think, she couldn't help it, of the way her grandparents might have said "Jew." Of all the wars waged here, the ones in language were the hardest to detect. Should she write about that? She's thought about a potential story angle: something about the violence of language, something about how the language itself conditions you to ignore the "other." But her ideas remain too vague, too theoretical. This is what the editor at *Der Spiegel* says every time she pitches an article idea to him. "Where are the characters?" he asks. "What is the story?" He hasn't published a thing of hers since the gimmicky profile she wrote of Jerusalem's only tattoo artist: a man who has set up shop in the Armenian Quarter of the Old City, practicing the forbidden art on the bodies of Christian pilgrims who come for elaborate crosses as tokens of their journey. She suspects her editor published the story mostly because he liked the headline he could give it: *Holy Ink*.

The air in the *monit sherut* is stuffy for the first half hour of the journey, but it cools the closer they get to Jerusalem. Non-native pine trees line the highways, planted by refugee Zionists in the last century. Elsewhere, the ghosts of Palestinian villages.

The Israeli that Vera is currently fucking—this absolutely ripped futballer with horrible tattoos—told her that in Hebrew one literally "ascends" to Jerusalem, a reflection both of the city's hilly location and its holiness. As if people didn't throw garbage onto the streets of Jerusalem, didn't let their toddlers squat and shit on the sidewalk. The entire place has an oppressive and—she'd never used this word aloud, but she thinks it—primitive air. Every woman's body angrily obscured by various orthodoxies. No wonder all the secular Israelis end up in Berlin. Long before she came to Israel to try her hand at journalism, she'd met more Israelis than she could count: she'd snorted coke with them at four a.m. clubs, sat in their chilly Graefekiez flats drinking instant coffee. She understands why they come to Berlin—to rid themselves of some weight, to escape the demands of their ideology into a city that purports to be allergic to any national ideology. The question is, why did she decide to come to their country, armed only with a few press contacts and a conversational ability in Arabic? What does she want? When anybody asks her, she tells them she wants to write stories that matter. It sounds true, or at least plausible.

The taxi-van winds up and around until they crest into the city. A wooden sign by the side of the highway: WELCOME TO JERUSALEM. Welcome to Jerusalem, city of graves. The hills of the city tower above them, covered in graves like broken teeth. Orthodox Jewish men daven and tremble among the markers, their black coats in the early noonday sun flapping like crows.

Vera shifts her weight from foot to foot. She is on a private terrace—perk of this particular class of hotel suite—as an Israeli PR woman in a pencil skirt and sensible flats talks to her about the thread count of the sheets on the bed inside. She writes down the number 500 in her notebook. The woman and Vera speak English, the shared language between them. "Many guests, they enjoy room service on their private patios," the woman says as she waves a gray mourning dove off the balcony. The dove takes flight in a murmur of wings. The woman has a bit of lipstick on her teeth. Vera can imagine her commuting each morning from some suburban settlement—her bus crossing the old armistice line without anyone noticing as she texts with her husband about whether or not to buy a rice steamer.

She looks out over the sun-drenched city. White stone, new construction. On the sidewalk below, women with their hair covered pull market baskets on wheels. An Israeli soldier—red boots, green uniform—leaves a convenience store, his rifle swung casually over his shoulder. Two priests pass in front of him, kicking up their robes as they ascend the steep hill toward the Old City. The hotel—a prominent stone building erected under the Ottomans—is angled with its back, as it were, toward the Old City, instead facing Western Jerusalem. Everything that happens in Jerusalem happens to the east, which is, technically, where the West Bank begins. Somewhere out there, ideology is unfolding in violent, consequential ways. The Israeli settlements continue their steady takeover of Area C. A monstrous, eight-meter-high wall snakes around the city of Jerusalem, with entrances monitored carefully by a series of checkpoints. And in a hospital, high above the city, is the body of a fourteen-year-old hooked up to wires and tubes, alive but barely.

"Do you have any questions?" the woman asks as they walk back into the hotel room.

The hotel bed is huge, pristine. Vera, for a moment, thinks of the weight of her Israeli lover on top of her—the way he collapses when he orgasms, almost convulsing into the back of her neck. No matter how loud he groans, she always needs to be louder. Always, it's the sounds of her own pleasure that make her come.

Because of course she knows what she is doing here. She came to take note of how plastic bags shudder and shred on all the ubiquitous barbed wire; she came to conduct interviews in stuffy rooms where mothers weep for their sacrificed sons; she came to cross checkpoints armed by teenage soldiers, baby-faced and lethal. She came to watch the beast of this place choke on its own tail; she came to write about it, to narrate it, to publish article after article until her voice—Vera's voice—becomes a kind of soundtrack that brings poignancy, maybe even beauty, to the most divisive conflict in the whole world. And yet, here is Vera, listening to a woman with a topknot talk about the unconventional light switches in this hotel that costs over four hundred euros a night, more than she will get paid for the review she writes for the in-flight magazine.

"Please excuse me," Vera says, stuffing her notebook into her leather backpack. "I must leave."

"But the tour," the woman in flats says, her eyebrows contorting in alarm. "You haven't seen the spa yet."

"Send photos," she cries over her shoulder as she rushes out of the room and down the hallways of identical doors. She is through the marble lobby, and then she is out. She is going east.

The hotel is not far from the Old City, which is perfect because it will only take her ten or so minutes to run up past Jaffa Gate then down Sultan Suleiman Road and catch a bus—yes, an Arab bus—at one of the bus depots outside Damascus Gate.

She runs. The sun hot on her head. Her sandals smack-smacking against the sidewalk. Her lungs are tight. She runs in the direction of the depot—just a parking lot, really—where she'll catch her bus. It's late enough that the crush of morning workers from the villages and city outskirts—herded in through the checkpoints, hours given over to waiting in line each morning—will be long gone.

When she spots a gap in the traffic, she makes a dash across the street, knowing it's stupid even as she does it, and yes, a car probably almost hits but manages the sudden stop, the driver—Vera turns to see it is a man and his wife—too shocked to even honk. Sorry, sorry, she thinks, still running, her blue scarf loose around her neck, her black backpack smacking against her.

At the ornate mouth of Damascus Gate, she slows to a walk, the drum of her heart in her ears. Here begins the filth of East Jerusalem: garbage rotting in the strengthening sun, black bile accumulating in the gutters, where old village women with their dresses spread over their knees sell bags of herbs that Vera can't distinguish. Everything looks more or less like mint to her. In the shade of delicate trees, young Palestinian men lean against blocks of ancient white stone and watch her. She adjusts the straps of her backpack, carefully touches her lower back to make sure her shirt hasn't ridden up to reveal her body. She tugs her scarf—bright blue, bought in Bethlehem—over her shoulders. Although perhaps the young men aren't watching her at all, but rather the three border police posted at the small traffic island by Damascus Gate, each one facing a different direction. Gray uniforms and green berets. Three men this time, although often there will be a girl, all of them in reflective sunglasses, free hand resting in their combat vests.

She catches her bus just before the door closes, pays the driver in change, then finds a seat next to an elderly woman whose lap is spread with groceries—at least a dozen plastic bags heavy with cucumbers, tomatoes, peppers, cheeses. Nobody in East Jerusalem seems particularly interested in reusable shopping bags. The bus maneuvers through the market area—over collapsed and rotten produce boxes, stopping and honking for pedestrians who pay it no mind. They pass a boy in jeans pushing a cart of dead goats, skinned whole. The goats' pink, exposed bodies wag perversely as the cart rumbles over the stones. Vera turns to stare. Their eyes remain but without eyelids, like the goats are all horrified by what they see and cannot look away.

❧

The bus drops her near Augusta Victoria Hospital. She's read about it, but never been here. It's often described as an "oasis" of Europe in East Jerusalem, looking more like a cathedral than a hospital. Its most famous feature is the stately bell tower—a grand witness to the entire city below it. The grounds are quiet. Families eat picnics on benches. All the women in hijabs. All the men sit spread across the benches. Vera has read how families from the West Bank— from Gaza, even—bring their children here for treatment, although only if the Israelis give them permission. Somewhere in this hospital is the body of Salem Abu-Khdeir. A boy who is neither alive nor dead.

She picks at her cuticles, a bad habit she can't quite shake. She has no plan now that she's arrived at the hospital. Surely, she can't go inside and run around looking for the dying boy. But she wants to be here. She wants to be where it is happening—whatever it is.

She walks among the picnicking families, the frail and unwell children. She walks toward the hospital. Olive trees and white stone. The grand architecture makes a promise—something about order and decency, something about God and empire. It is the kind of promise that white people, her people, truly believed a hundred years ago. She looks up at the windows, all of them shapely like a woman's upper lip. Where are you? Vera thinks. Where am I?

❧

Ido hasn't slept more than two consecutive hours since the baby came home, so when Emily rushes into their bathroom holding the tiny poop machine they named Mayan, and says, "I can't find her sun hat," he doesn't hear the English right and finds himself saying, "Son what?" before his brain processes her words. Sun hat. "Doesn't she have more than one sun hat?" he asks, finishing up his shaving in the mirror.

Emily gets free stuff all the time from her weirdly successful online presence. Baby gear, mommy gear, organic face serums, activated charcoal everything, crystals. She's dressed already for the wedding in a startlingly blue floor-length dress, which ripples proteanly as she rushes out of the bathroom and around the bedroom, baby Mayan tucked under one arm, her head at maybe a not-great angle as she wails. Opening drawers, closing drawers. "But this one has SPF in it."

"Is she hungry?" he asks from the bathroom threshold.

Emily doesn't answer as she kneels to look under the bed. That silk dress costs as much as Ido makes in, like, three days at the animation studio. Not that it really matters—they don't pay rent on the Jerusalem house his parents let him use, and they don't have car payments to make, because his parents gave them that, too—but there is something insulting in it. Earlier today, he diligently photographed Emily in their garden, wearing this blue dress and her own floppy sun hat, holding their newborn in the crook of her arm. He must admit that he admires how his wife walks a line between creating an aspirational life—Turkish tiles and copper basins in their bathroom, lemon trees in their yard—and using a tone that is self-deprecating enough for other women to celebrate her for being "brave." The caption for this most recent photo: *Can you tell I'm wearing an actual adult diaper? #postpartum.*

There's no doubt that it's working. Since Mayan was born, Emily's follower count has edged into the six digits, and she's making real money.

"Here," he says, striding across the room to his bedside table, where he opens a drawer to pull out the faded olive-green bucket hat he got in the army and still keeps around, keeping it handy for reserve duty.

Emily staggers up from kneeling to look under the bed. Mayan is now moaning more than wailing, her useless little hands moving in agitation like a tiny, enraged prophet.

Ido puts his old army hat over Mayan's head, fuzzy with black hair. Blue eyes, black hair, and a unibrow that makes her seem a little skeptical at all times. Mayan disappears under the cloth hat, faded from the sun. On the side of that hat is the logo of his old unit, bat wings stitched roughly. He was twenty years old when he got this hat. He wore it in the Negev, in Gaza, in Nepal. For a moment, in the dark, Mayan is silent. Ido watches a gray dove land on their bedroom window ledge, cooing softly. Then Mayan's screaming snaps him back. The sound claws at the nerves in Ido's neck.

"Ew," Emily says, plucking the hat off Mayan and handing it back to him. "No."

"What do you mean, 'Ew. No'?"

"Our baby is not wearing army paraphernalia."

"Oh, come on," he says, keeping his tone light as he takes Mayan from Emily. He holds her close as he sways the way she likes, his body like a ship. "Shh," he says. "Shh, shh.

"Mayan is going to be a sniper." He uses his baby voice. "Aren't you? Mayan the marksman?" He's aware of a kind of chasm widening, one that exists in his peripheral vision, that he can't quite bear to think about—the ideological chasm between him and his foreigner wife.

"Come on," she says, pulling the sun hat out of her own underwear drawer, "we're already late for the wedding."

They've been in the car less than ten minutes, and Emily is already insisting that Ido pull over so she can nurse Mayan. He's inching onto Highway 60 near the Old City, the rush-hour traffic into the settlements beginning already. "Nu, Emily." He turns back to face her in the back seat, where she's leaning over Mayan's car seat. Their baby screams at a pitch that may in fact be evolutionarily perfected to make him want to crash this car right into the taxi in front of him. "Ido, I don't think," she begins, but before she can say what he knows she will say—that she doesn't want to take Mayan out of the car seat when they are driving—there is a horrible flash across Ido's windshield, and he brakes as fast as he can, screaming in English, "Shit! Shit! Shit!" because he's sure he's about to hit the body that just stepped in front of the car. The car stops sharply.

For a long second, silence. The girl—a tourist, with a black backpack and one of those exotically blue shawls that all Europeans seem to wear—glances at him but gives not even an apologetic wave as she continues across the street. Then Mayan is screaming again, twice as loud, and Emily is shouting over the baby's screams, "Ido!" Mayan's ridiculously floppy sun hat has fallen over her face. Thank God she's buckled. "Ido! I told you!" She says it in Hebrew. "I told you to be careful!" Her American accent flattens out the words.

"Beseder," he shouts. Both of them are delirious with lack of sleep. It was stupid to think that, three weeks after Emily came home from the hospital, they could make it to a wedding. "At least let me get through the tunnels." They are moving now in the flow of traffic on Highway 60, soon to be carried through the tunnels that lead them under the Arab villages and out of the Jerusalem periphery.

A few minutes out of Jerusalem, they pull into a gas station on Highway 60. Emily sits in the back of the car, blanket over their nursing baby, while Ido leans against the hood of the car. "Is that nice?" she coos. "Were you hungry? You're a hungry girl."

Emily looks up at him. Freckles, golden hair. His blond, American Jew. His heart grows full and tender. "She's hungry, ah?"

"Always hungry!" Emily laughs. She checks on Mayan, peeking under the organic cotton eyelet breastfeeding blanket that she received for free from some hopeful company.

"Let's try to time her puking until after the chuppah." In about an hour, no doubt, Mayan will begin voiding the contents of her tiny, greedy belly.

The sun is harsh. All around them, families are fueling up. Somewhere, a child yells out, "Mama, I have to go pee-pee." Down the highway—not far from here at all, but in a world hidden from Emily and their baby—teenagers, kids really, are working checkpoints, bored in the almost-winter sun.

It was on a settlement not much deeper in that a girl, just fourteen years old, was killed when the fucking terrorist climbed in her bedroom window. The photos he saw on Facebook were horrific. What did that girl, Yael Salomon, do to hurt anyone? Just a girl. Someone's daughter. "Let's go," he says, needing his wife and his baby to be enclosed in the car, needing to get them away from these anxious points of contact from which so much violence springs. Nervous but unwilling to admit that he's nervous. "Let's go."

⋙⋘

When Ori's shift at Checkpoint 300 is over, the first thing he's going to do is message his mom to ask if he can get a new phone for his birthday this year. No. Okay, first, he'll check to see if he's gotten any comments on the photo he posted—his boots and the muzzle of his Tavor looking out at the view from a guard tower. Caption: *Boker tov, Bethlehem*. Perfect. Then he'll message Ima about the phone. Unless he should eat a granola bar first? No, shut up, stick with the plan.

Ori is waving Arabs through the turnstile where they funnel out of the caged corridor, narrow and barred to help control the crowds. Danny the gingie is waving them through the X-ray machine, one by one. It's such a dumbass arrangement. Anyone can do this—the border patrol girls can do this; a fucking jobnik could do this. It's stupid and boring and, today, it's Ori and Danny's job.

An old Arab is taking forever to put his belt back on after going through the X-ray machine. "Yalla, yalla, yaa Allah," Danny moans, all red hair and not giving a fuck. Ori looks down the line of Arabs— hijabis with strollers, huge grandmothers with a million plastic grocery bags, which Ori never gets—like, what? They don't have grocery stores you can go to in Jerusalem? At least he didn't have to be here early in the morning, when it's all shabaab coming through— proud and honor-sore—cramming themselves through the cages at four a.m. to go work construction. Someone is always getting trampled and passing out. A total mess. At this time of day it's more about establishing a presence. That's what their commander told them. It's past noon now, but you'd never know it from the fluorescent lights in here.

Ori rolls his shoulders against his combat vest. He's so tired he could dream on his feet, and he hasn't had a shit in two days. He's almost-almost a third of the way through his service. Then it's India, Thailand, Peru—literally anywhere but here. Anywhere but Checkpoint 300, where the Arabs trickle their way through the turnstiles and the X-ray machine, then bring their paperwork—entry permit, the ID card they call a *hawiyya*—up to the girls behind the glass. That's it. Then they're free to waltz into Jerusalem and steal a car or blow up a bus or sneak into a fourteen-year-old's bedroom with a knife. *That's not funny.* He hears the rebuke in Ima's voice. That's not funny. He is here because that's not funny.

It was Ima's idea for him to go to the mall last night with Meir and Liran. The three of them go all the way back to grade four, but since Ori and Liran recruited, it's hard to find time. Meir has it lucky— drafted into one of the Premier League teams for Jerusalem just after high school graduation. Who the fuck becomes an actual professional athlete? Meir, apparently. The army will grant him special athlete's status. Meir won't serve combat, but will be a jobnik—sitting behind a desk, working with office girls. Anyway, Ima is always pushing Ori to spend time with Meir—"What about Meir? You boys haven't hung out in ages!"—because Meir still wears his kippa. It hurts her, Ori knows, that he's stopped wearing it. He wears it at home: a compromise that neither of them finds particularly satisfactory. Ima's logic is that Meir—who still wears his kippa despite playing with secular teammates who have tattoos and foreign girlfriends—must be a good influence. A good influence. Given what went down last night, that's almost funny.

Anyway, Ori might have ignored Ima's suggestion to invite Meir, but she's been so sad since the funeral for Yael. The funeral was in Jerusalem, and Ima went with little Tovah and Avital. School was canceled that day. Ori knows they feel everything, his mother and his sisters. All the grief and rage and terror that Ori won't let himself feel—they feel it, almost as if they feel it for him. Is that what it means to be a woman? The last funeral that Ori went to was like maybe a month ago when a guy from his old yeshiva was stabbed to death while napping on the bus. Because he was in his uniform when the terrorist got him, he was promoted to staff sergeant. It was a huge funeral. Flag on the coffin, his ima throwing herself over it, screaming. If Ori dies in uniform, he'll get promoted, too. So perhaps Ori wanted to make his mother happy when he said that sure, he'd see if Meir—Meir and his kippa—wanted to hang out at the mall.

Ori watches a small, gray bird fly in the barred window, across the heads of the Arabs in line, and then out another window. Danny is shouting to the girls behind the glass, "Do I have to put on his belt for him?" The old guy with the shaky hands isn't through yet. He looks up from his belt, not that he can understand most of what Danny is saying.

"*Shu?*" the old man asks. He's wearing a dress shirt tucked into slacks.

Danny fucks with the Arabs a bit sometimes. Nothing crazy, nothing physical—just pretending not to understand what someone is saying or making one of them go through the X-ray machine a bunch of times for no reason. "*Shu? Shu?*" Danny imitates the Arab.

"*Shu shu,*" Ori answers. His stomach grumbles. Okay. New plan:

First thing when his shift ends, he'll eat his granola bar. Then he'll check in with Ima. Finally—best for last—he'll check to see if anyone's left any comments on his *Boker tov, Bethlehem* photo.

Don't check your watch, he tells himself. But of course, Ori checks his watch. Forty-nine more minutes left in his guarding shift.

On the car ride home from the mall, only Meir spoke. He kept calling what happened a "fight." But it wasn't a fight. There were, like, twenty of them and one Arab. Ori doesn't want to think about it. He doesn't want to think about how Meir walked toward the crowd that had the Arab trapped at their center. He doesn't want to see photos of the Arab in the hospital, now in a coma. All morning—since Ima dropped him off at the bus, since he got to his base, since he was assigned to spend a few hours guarding Checkpoint 300 before they go patrol the camps—he's been determined not to think about it. There is a lot not to think about.

"Bravo!" Daniel calls out to the old man. "I knew you could do it!"

Ori laughs and shakes his head, tries to resist the urge to check his watch again.

⤜⤛⤚

At the crossing into Jerusalem, Samar tries to hold on to herself. She edges into the cages of Checkpoint 300—single file in a line of people with permits to cross. She knows she is lucky that she did not have to travel in the morning, when the men arrive as early as four a.m. to cram themselves into the winding walkway of cement and bars. Even now, early afternoon, she has waited over an hour to get to the head of the line. Bodies push against Samar, everyone pushing up to the front, pushing their way to the soldiers—a mass of people constantly at risk of trampling themselves. Nearby, someone's festering sweat is giving off the overpowering smell of onions. Samar has her hawiyya ready, her entry permit carefully folded. There are only five people ahead of her. Each person waits until the turnstile beeps green. Then you must awkwardly sidestep through the turnstile, never mind if you have a stroller, crutches, a wheelchair. In the autumn, she read a brilliant article in *Qui Parle* about the nature of the turnstiles at the Israeli checkpoints, how they are specifically designed to be difficult to maneuver—that what seems like a malfunction is in fact a form of tactical degradation.

Samar herself has written about checkpoints. Papers in Arabic, English, German. As an academic, she has read the checkpoint through a variety of theoretical lenses that, if they don't make the experience mean something, at least communicate the senselessness of her life within the Israeli system. But at the checkpoint itself, it doesn't matter, does it? It doesn't matter that she has a brilliant mind, that she is on her way to pick up a visa that will allow her to attend an academic conference in Chicago and present a paper there. It doesn't matter that her articles on the violence of bureaucracy, memorial, and nation-states are widely cited. It doesn't matter from inside the moment what she will do later to narrativize the moment. What matters is that she breathes, that she does not panic in the cage of the checkpoint, that she does not turn around and yell at the person behind her, *Get your hands off me.*

Samar stands tiptoe to see over a large woman carrying her groceries, two teenage girls with books—high school students, maybe—and a middle-aged man her own age. At the X-ray machine, an elderly man is having trouble with his belt. One of the soldiers keeps asking him the same pointless question. "What?" he asks, one hand on his weapon. "What? What?"

When Samar found out her paper had been accepted by the conference in Chicago, she felt not gratification but a panic that was only made worse by the organizers' enthusiastic phone calls ensuring her that all expenses would be covered. A nightmare of logistics ensued: an entry permit into Jerusalem to secure an entry visa from the Americans, a transit visa from the Jordanians. Too much approval, too many forms. Not for you, she coaxed herself, but for The Work, trying to imagine it as a separate entity. In measures of minutes and sentences, Samar has tried to build a life for her mind. She tends to The Work; they sustain one another, like a garden, or maybe, like a child.

Of course, Mother does not want Samar to go present her paper at the conference in Chicago. "I almost lost you once," she says, referring to the years of graduate work in England, as if Samar were leaving not for a few days, but for years, and as if Samar did not come home, come back—back in time to see her father die and the Wall completed, the checkpoints formalized. Now Samar gets by on the scraps of the English department at Bethlehem University—teaching lower-level composition that nobody else wants. It leaves little time for her own research on nationalism and erasure. She pushes her work to the side; she apologizes for it, when a cousin of her mother's, for instance, eyes her to ask, "And what exactly is 'comparative literature'?" assessing why she remains unmarried, the excuse of her father's death long expired, and her eligible years evaporated. Now the men they suggest are divorced, widowed—men who want help with the children they already have.

Samar watches a gray dove fly in the barred window of the long, narrow, caged corridor where she and dozens of others are wedged like livestock to be slaughtered. The bird flies in one window and out another. She closes her eyes and tries to breathe.

When it is her turn, the blond soldier waves her through, and Samar wedges herself through the turnstile. The red-haired soldier watches Samar as she puts her purse on the machine. They are all standing on a concrete floor under harsh lights. Once she passes through this machine, she will bring her papers to the girl soldiers behind the glass up ahead, who will ask her where she lives (Bethlehem), where she is going (Jerusalem, for an appointment regarding her travel visa to America). But when she steps through the body scanner, it beeps.

Samar freezes. She looks at the red-haired soldier. He is as young as the students she teaches at the university. He has his hand on his weapon now as he waves at her to walk through again. The machine must be broken. When she dressed this morning, Samar was careful, not wearing so much as a belt—nothing that would set off these machines. She walks back around to the body scanner. The woman behind her in line—large, with two little girls—sighs with impatience. Samar steps through again. It beeps.

The red-haired soldier motions her to stop. He says something to the blond soldier standing behind Samar, closer to the turnstiles. The blond soldier laughs, says something back. Samar is not moving. She is careful not to move her hands too quickly, not to give either of them a reason to shoot.

The red-haired soldier makes a circular motion with his pointer finger: again.

Samar walks through again. This time, it does not beep. He should let her through, but instead he motions her to stop. "*Shuv pa'am*," he says. He makes the circular motion with his finger: again. Samar walks through again. Again, it does not beep. He motions her to stop. She stands in front of him. He is very young, with large, awkward hands. He's not even looking at her, as he talks to the blond soldier. He's holding his rifle up. It is pointing at her.

Samar can hear the large woman behind her in line—and all the people farther back, the mothers and grandmothers, sons and uncles—shifting with annoyance, mumbling at her, about her, everyone waiting their turn to go through the screening, to get to the other side of the checkpoint where they will catch a bus, a ride, or simply walk along the highway where the Jewish cars will be speeding by, not stopped, never stopped. Samar breathes. She remembers to breathe. She watches a fly land on her shirtsleeve. She doesn't move to swat it. She does not ask herself why this teenager is making her stand here because the answer is too monstrous and simple to let herself think: because he can.

What matters, right now, is that Samar does not move her hands suddenly, that she does not swat away the fly rubbing its filthy little legs together, that she does not get shot, does not collapse on this cement floor, does not turn around and scream at the people waiting behind her, her fellow countrymen tsking with impatience—more annoyed with her for holding up the line than at the Jews for training them to accept this ceaseless humiliation, day after day after day after day. What matters is that Samar holds on to herself, just a little longer.

"Go through again," the soldier says at last, his rifle still pointed at her.

She goes through the white portal of the body scanner again. It does not beep.

Reserve Duty

Ido wiggles forward on his belly to get better leverage, then takes a few more shots at the terrorist. Pop, pop, pop. The target is a paper cutout on a stick. It shudders with direct hits. Not bad, this time. Ido finds he's getting used to the trigger weight of the Tavor. The shooting trainer, a girl of eighteen, leans over to yell, "Much better," and when she does, her long, straight hair tickles his ears. They're advancing as a group of three—he, Yitzi, and Gil—with the trainer following close behind. The three oldest guys in the reserve unit.

It's day two of reserve duty. Morning in the desert: cold and dry. No work yesterday, no work today, no work tomorrow. "Advance!" Gil cries.

And they all get up, heaving from their bellies to their knees to their feet, then run through the arid field, firing as they go. Down again to their bellies. Time to reload.

"One reloading!" Gil yells out from ten paces away.

"Number two reloading!" Yitzi is between Ido and Gil, about five paces. Out of all the slightly ragtag reserve unit, it's only Yitzi that Ido has known since they were enlisted soldiers. Nineteen years old. Now they're both dads. Yitzi is the head coder at some start-up in Herzliya and has the frameless glasses to prove it.

"Number three reloading!" Ido cries out as he fumbles with the new magazine. All around him are the cheerful pops of live fire. He can't remember the last time he was this happy. When Mayan was born, sure. But that was less happiness than it was wonder and terror—nothing like the simple clarity of reserve duty. Last night, he slept in a tent, and he slept all night. All night! He has changed exactly zero diapers in the last twenty-four hours, smoked half a cigarette, eaten two cans of tuna (straight out of the can). And the best part? Today is war. After they finish the shooting drills, they'll head over to the fake Arab city for a little more action.

It's about nine in the morning. Usually, Ido would be at the animation studio now, hunched over his desk and clicking around in Maya, ZBrush, or Houdini—who names this software?—for the Disney contract his boss recently landed. The studio specializes in work that can be consumed by both children and adult stoners, which means its output is saccharine in a way that also manages to be self-referential. Three years working there now. Three years of drawing a sardonic unicorn that shits actual rainbows and turns to the "camera" with an expression that says, Can you fucking believe this? Ido cannot believe it: three years. It's an impressive job, coveted by graduates of his program, but it's a job. Real success comes from striking out on your own, subsisting on freelance work while you try to get your shorts into festivals. Working for an impressive studio was like having a rich father, or husband maybe, in that the prestige lent you value but it wasn't your own.

The three men—all of them in hiking boots, all of them a little heavier this year than they were last year—squat around the portable gas burner that Ido has set up, sipping Turkish coffee from tiny paper cups. Coffee break. "Not bad with the coffee, Abuya," Yitzi says. Since yesterday the guys are calling him *Abuya*, in honor of his firstborn. First it was Aba, but then someone switched to Arabic, and that stuck. "*Abuya, Abu-yaya*," they coo over pictures of the baby on his phone. "She doesn't look like you, *alhamdulillah*, *Abuya*." Ido knows what Emily would say about the way they use Arabic; she calls it *casual othering*, which sounds to him like a clothing brand.

Nearby, the younger reservists are inspecting one another's Tavors. The new rifles are fun.

"We're headed to the urban combat drill?" Ido asks Gil.

"Soon, yes." Gil runs a hand over his shaved head. Now in his forties, he's been Ido's reserve commander for about three years. Every year he balded a little more, until last year, when he shaved it all off. "But listen, the problem is . . ." Gil says, typing hurriedly into his phone—every commander seems to live on their cell phone these days—"The problem is that we have to walk there." Then almost immediately, he's speaking into his phone. "Beseder. I got it," he says flatly, recording a voice memo for whomever is on the other end.

"But why?" Yitzi says. "We already signed out our weapons."

Ido uses his finger to draw a single line in the dirt. Forehead, nose, lips, chin. Emily's profile. He wipes it away.

"Nothing to be done." Gil takes another sip of coffee.

Yitzi is right about this pointlessly complicated, time-consuming arrangement: They'll walk all the way to the armory. Two k, at least, and from there somehow get to the fake Arab city for the simulation. It makes no sense. Why can't they go from here? What's the point of such wasted time? When he was young, this was the part about the army that made Ido want to smash his head into a wall—the lack of coherent explanations for anything. But these days, he loves it. He craves the nonsensical chain of command, not having to think, just to do what someone tells you to do. It makes him feel like a child.

From the day that he and Emily brought Mayan home from the hospital, he had been secretly hoping to get that text message from Gil, telling him to pack a bag and drive south from Jerusalem into the desert for training. He knows that it makes him a hopeless trope—the newly minted father looking to the past to escape a beautiful if exacting wife—but he can't help it. When Gil's text message finally came, it was apologetic—congratulating him and Emily on their little girl, offering assurances that, if necessary, Ido could skip this round of reserve duty. It wasn't a huge deal, Gil said, just some training on the new rifles. Which is, of course, not how Ido relayed it to Emily. "Baby, you know I wouldn't go if I didn't have to," he said in English, almost always in English. She was holding their baby like a prop, as if Mayan were somehow part of the argument.

Ido crossed the bedroom to her—sweet Emily, scented by the organic rosewater she sprays on her face throughout the day; little Emily, in mismatched wool socks and with her still-soft belly, which embarrasses her so much but which he wants to squeeze and kiss. He took her hand, knowing that she would pull it free—the pattern of her rejecting his touch was exhausting and, frankly, unoriginal—and she did.

"Are they sending you into the West Bank?" An annoying question, but not a stupid one: reserve units often work the checkpoints, sometimes deeper in. It takes a lot of manpower, "oppressing a civilian population" (Emily's words in his head).

"They are not," he told her.

"But if they ordered you to, you would go." The baby rested over her shoulder in a little striped onesie Emily's mom had sent over from the States. He knew without seeing that their daughter was grasping for Emily's hair, the gold of it fallen loose from what she calls a *messy bun*, which always makes Ido think of German pastries.

"They haven't ordered me to." He rose from the bed and walked over to her; the room lit softly by the small fairy-style lights Emily had used to frame the doorway and the bed's headboard. They stood in a room filled with framed photographs of them smiling alongside framed prayers and mantras scribed by Emily with a quill—real feather and ink, a brief fixation of hers—to yield a shaky, imprecise

Hebrew. This is Emily, his American Jew, hanging the feathers of birds of prey in their windows.

"But you would go," she insisted, trying to catch his gaze as he looked away.

Once, when it seemed like it would never happen, he'd told her he would refuse to serve if they tried to send him to the West Bank; he'd go to jail before he let them use him that way. But that was never true. They'd tell him a place to show up, and he'd show up, same as always.

"That's not what my reserve unit is for," he said, needing to force her out of the question she was trying to ask, needing to shut down the insane, hysterical morality test she was attempting. He took the baby, her weight in his arms a precise calculation. He knew Emily was struggling with herself in that moment. He knew that she would give in, that deep down, she likes to give in to him. He felt the scratch of his cheek against the baby's soft head, wispy hairs. He knew before it would happen that the baby would make an adorable, helpless grab for his caterpillar eyebrows, and Emily would try not to laugh, and that would be it. The question about his reserve duty—about his participation in the military and what it meant and who it hurt—would once again dissolve.

Ido and Yitzi are trudging side by side while Yitzi takes selfies to send to his wife. So begins their two-k trek along the unpaved road toward the base's center. Always familiar: the weight of the packs pinning you to the earth, fixing you to the rhythm of your stride, a stride somehow matched by everyone else's. When did it become so miraculous to Ido, the unity between bodies?

It's been about a year since he and Yitzi caught up; Yitzi didn't make it to the last training. They're all connected on social media, but you know how that goes—you mean to look at other people's lives and just end up clicking backward through your own photos, watching yourself dissolve into a young man. Or is that just Ido?

Over a decade ago—cus emek, well over a decade now—he had been in basic. His father waited with him at the bus stop that would take him to the base, Ido with his high school backpack and a buzz cut, one he'd done himself; it made him look like a penis. Other families turned out in big numbers to see off their own—Mizrahi mothers with tan arms stacked with clacking bracelets, crying out in deep, exotic accents, pressing their sons into giant tits. His father, stiff and uncomfortable, leaned against the bus stop; they were in some southern neighborhood of Tel Aviv where all the roofs were tin.

"Why are you doing this?" his father asked. He was a fleshy man who ate unsalted food and read Bialik in leather-bound volumes, wore pastel polo shirts bought in America. "We don't have to do this," he said. He meant, people like us aren't cannon fodder. At that time, boys were still dying in southern Lebanon, and in a few months, the Second Intifada would rear its head. It was unusual for someone from Ido's neighborhood to choose to go to infantry. Most of his classmates—kids of lawyers, architects—would go serve in desk jobs, even the guys. One or two might ascend to the ranks of the air force demigods. But Ido had been set on infantry.

He and his father stood under a tree with large, oily leaves that cast shadows like hands on his father's face. Ido answered. He said, "I'm doing this because it's mine to do." And then the bus pulled up and he got on, feeling bigger than himself, bigger than his father—a jobnik who had spent the Yom Kippur War on a telephone in the Kirya base in central Tel Aviv. Now Ido can't imagine using a line like that—*it's mine to do*—and keeping a straight face. Some things you can only say when you're eighteen.

"How old is your boy now?" Ido asks Yitzi between breaths.

"Shilo, the little prince, he just turned four," Yitzi says. He makes some quick movements with his thumb over the screen then holds it out to Ido: a naked child with a garden hose. He's lighter than Yitzi.

"What a cutie," Ido obliges. "And the cold war?" This is how

Yitzi refers to relations between the mothers-in-law. Ido remembers when Yitzi first got married to that Ashkenazi girl. "It's hard to say whose mother considers this a bigger tragedy," he said at the time.

"You know how it goes, Abuya," Yitzi says, breathing through his mouth as he adjusts his pack. "Now that they have a grandkid to fuss over, they don't worry about us."

Ido knows if he checks his own phone there will be messages from Emily and photos from yesterday's visit to his parents' condo—his father holding the baby, grinning up at the camera or staring down at her in terror and wonder, as they are all prone to do. Emily gets along too well with his parents, who are delighted with the enhanced credibility—of the educated, Ashkenazi, upper-middle-class persuasion—brought by this pretty, American leftist. She is a kind of ornament that confirms their worldliness, their good taste, as if they weren't invested in the status quo and all it has given them. And yet, a sudden memory of Yitzi at, cus emek, nineteen years old, coming over for Shabbat dinner. The relief to find that it was easy, fun even—Yitzi making his parents laugh with Arabic expressions he learned from his ancient safta come over from Yemen, his father breaking out some great stories Ido had never heard before about bartering cigarettes for Adidas track pants back when everyone was on rations. Even sixteen years ago, it had mattered more, much more than now, what kind of Jew you were: your last name, your skin tone. So maybe he's being unfair, or underestimating them.

"Yitzi, how long . . ." Ido hesitates. "How long, I mean, after the baby, how long did it take for things to go back to normal?"

"Between you two, yanni?"

"Between us, yeah." He's embarrassed. He doesn't look at Yitzi.

"Give her time. It's been what, five weeks?"

Ido nods. "Yeah." Although it's been only three.

"So tell her she's beautiful and be the big spoon. The rest will come, Abuya."

Emily and Ido were in their twenties when they met by chance in a claustrophobic bar favored by Jerusalem art students. This bar—did it still exist?—always played the right music from the wrong place: '80s hardcore out of Jamaica, '60s girl groups from Sri Lanka. There, among the braless and dull-eyed, was Emily, soft-haired and open-faced, so unlike Israeli girls, who treated dating like a hostage negotiation. He sketched her on the back of a coaster. In those days, halfway through his animation degree, he was always drawing. Even seeing was a kind of drawing. That's how they trained you in the sketching courses—bodies moving broke down in his vision into cones and squares, triangles and arcs, always arcs, in the pelvis, in the neck, in the hair. He wouldn't give her the coaster with her portrait until she gave him her phone number. It seemed like what an American girl would expect an Israeli to do.

She was visiting Jerusalem from Tel Aviv, visiting Tel Aviv from Michigan, or not really visiting, she said, doing her master's degree in "conflict resolution." The way she described the degree, it sounded vaguely recreational—mostly guest speakers, all in English—but anyway, she said, she planned to have a career in something more creative, working with brands, maybe. What he noticed was that her lips touched between words.

The best part about being with an American Jew was how sad you could make her. Ido remembers them sitting together on his narrow bed, the chill seeping out of the bloodless Jerusalem stone, while he told her about the Second Intifada—the fire and the mobs, the bodies in the street, the haunting echo of their call to prayer. She was almost in tears when she said, "But you were just babies." He told her the only Arabic he knew was *Show me your ID. Stop or I'll shoot.*

"How do you say, 'My name is Emily'?" she asked.

He laughed, delighted to have been set up so perfectly. "Emily, we don't introduce ourselves."

At that, her face had contorted into a tragic mask that, later, he would connect to the expression she made as she orgasmed, fighting off something inside herself as she kicked against his legs and he repeated in her ear what she had begged him to say, "You're mine, you're mine, you're mine."

Should he have been paying more attention to the divide? Until the baby, their political differences had never seemed to be more than a kind of elaborate foreplay, a site of difference that excited them both, like the weight of his body against her smallness, the smoothness of her tummy and arms against the monstrosity of the little black hairs that cover him like a pelt. But now, those differences are taking on concrete significance.

Any day, Emily is going to begin insisting that they look into some mixed "hand in hand" day school where all the students learn to write their names in Hebrew and Arabic. A school like that is a natural target for right-wing hard-liners with firebombs, probably Hamasniks, too. And for what? So his daughter can have friends who live in East Jerusalem neighborhoods he won't let her go to? And every time there is a terrorist attack—a stabbing, a car ramming, who knows what else—Ido will have to wave at women in hijabs dropping off their kids, wondering if they were among those celebrating in the streets, ululating like animals at the news of spilled Israeli blood.

The armory is a busted yellow trailer, draped half-heartedly in camo netting. By the time they get there, it's nearly noon and the sun is harsh. The others wait outside, eating the candy bars and protein drinks they brought from home. Ido goes in hoping to escape the too-bright sun. Inside, the air is stale. The counter is strewn with broken staplers (Ido just knows, broken) and coffee-sogged paper cups. On the wall, a hand-drawn poster wishes some departing officer well—*Good luck, Gabi!*—with cutout photos of smiling girls and jobniks chasing one another with staplers. Behind the counter, the oily jobnik who signs out the weapons looks up.

"No air conditioning?" Ido asks.

He could swear the kid rolls his eyes. Shithead. He looks like the kind of guy that girls talk to when they are having trouble with their boyfriends, the kind you worried about while you were out in the field. Fucking jobnik. *Calm down*, Ido catches himself. What's wrong with you? He's a kid. They're all kids. He goes back outside.

Outside the armory, Gil is using his shoulder to talk on his cell phone so he can pick at his fingernails, while around him, the guys lean against one another or squat in the red earth. The scene looks oddly composed, like a Renaissance painting of early martyrs. Yitzi in quiet conversation with Erez, who is now in real estate, while Tal and Tal—both young, both in their twenties, both studying at the Technion, both Tal—lean against the pile of packs and stare somewhere off canvas. The sun passes behind a cloud. "Beseder, okay, no problem, beseder, achi." Gil puts his phone in his cargo pocket and addresses the group. "So Golani is lending us a few young ones," he says, "for the drill."

Ido and Yitzi sit in a beat-up desert jeep on either side of an enlisted soldier who has, no joke, the kind of features you'd hand-select if you were custom-ordering a baby boy: a strong chin, jawline like a model, blue eyes like a Swede. Beautiful kid. The jeep bounces across packed red earth, shifting all of them on the hard seats of the open vehicle.

"What's your name?" Ido asks, keeping his voice low so it travels. His hair is a little in his eyes, the dirt and sand are everywhere—it's great.

"I'm Ori," the beautiful kid says. He's affected the glazed eyes of an overworked warrior, but his half smile reveals a dimple. Pretty boy. The guys in his unit must give him shit. "You?"

"I'm Ido, and he's Yitzi," Ido says, gesturing to Yitzi, who's on his cell phone, bouncing with the motion of the jeep as he types away.

"What?" Yitzi looks up from his phone and yells across Ori to Ido, into the wind of the moving vehicle, the dust stirred up by the treads.

"I said you are Yitzi," Ido yells. "Yitzi!"

"What?" Yitzi yells.

This embarrasses Ido more than it should, his friend's inability to hear what's going on.

After a couple more attempts to get them to repeat stuff—"What? Nu, what?"—Yitzi gestures to his ears to say, *Can't hear you*, and begins filming the ride on his phone, the bleak desert flashing by. Videos to send home, to say, Here I am.

But sitting as close as he is to Ori, Ido finds that his voice carries, he doesn't even have to yell when he gestures down at Ori's rifle and asks, "So, how do you like the Tavor?" Then, immediately, he hates himself for asking.

Ori glances at him, already bored, probably. "You know, beseder."

"When I was a soldier"—Ido can't believe he's starting a sentence like this—"when I was a soldier, we were on the M16s."

"Some units still use them," Ori says flatly.

"The trigger on the Tavor is a little heavy, you know?" He wants to stop but doesn't know how, so he keeps talking. "But great firepower."

"Sure," Ori says, and Ido decides to leave it at that. On the hilltop opposite them, a Bedouin ignores his scattered goats and talks into a cell phone. Ido knows from Emily how the army is dispossessing them of their land, village by village, to create more firing ranges. Someone will have to chase this man out of this area one day soon. Someone else.

After Ido finished basic, his father pretty much gave in. He said something like, "Well, if someone has to be doing it, at least it's you and not some extremist." At the time, Ido found this inspiring, but now he's not sure. Was he any more gentle than the next guy when it came to putting a teenager's wrists in zip ties?

The training facility rises out of the desert in the not-too-far distance. Ido has trained here twice before and he still can't get over the size of it. Hundreds of buildings, they say, six kilometers all told, and he believes it. The army did an amazing job, right down to the burnt-out Mercedes stuck in the dirt, the posters of martyrs, the hurried graffiti over the three- or four-story buildings. No smell of rotting trash, though, no burning rubber, no human shit, and of course, no Palestinians.

The jeep stops outside the city's perimeter. The road is asphalt here; they paved it and everything. Where it enters the city, the road forks into two almost immediately, but not before creating an anxious little bottleneck where they'll be running the drills. Ugly cement buildings regard them—perfectly spaced windows and doorways like eyeless sockets, like toothless mouths. No curtains, no glass, just holes. From across the city comes the barking of dogs, which must be the K9 units.

Their small group gathers around Gil, who explains the exercise. "Listen," he says, "we'll warm up with a sweep." Gil no longer seems goofy but impressive, capable. He nods a chin toward the enlisted soldiers. "You guys, too." Already, Ido feels embarrassed about how rusty he'll be, how heavy his equipment will feel.

Gil says that after an hour, they'll switch to an enemy sniper drill. He holds up a few kaffiyeh scarves—authentic ones with the white and black checkers. Ido sees Ori nudge another enlisted soldier his age, and he knows they are hoping they'll get to be Arabs for the drill. Soon they'll begin a simulation of combat that feels more real than anything that's happened to Ido in the last year. Ido will crouch in the thresholds of houses that have never been homes and hunt the gray and empty city for Ori the blue-eyed terrorist. Gil won't be filming anymore. Instead the entire thing will be caught on the closed-circuit cameras that monitor every inch of the city. It's all there, being recorded so that afterward they can do a play-by-play: *See, you wouldn't have died there if you'd been paying more attention to the upper floors.*

"Yalla," Gil says.

Ori is already tying a kaffiyeh over his face.

Yitzi is on his belly, waiting for his shot. Gil is kneeling by Yitzi. There's dust all around them, and everyone is sweating. Ido and both of the Tals are providing cover, angled up against the alley wall, their rifles held close. Ido kneels, thankful for his knee pads.

"That's it, achi," Gil says to Yitzi, pointing up at the third-story window where they're waiting out a terrorist. "Wait for your shot."

Ido glances back to see the target move into the window. There it is. A full view of the terrorist in the window.

"Permission to fire," Yitzi shouts, but just as he does, the fucking call to prayer whines through the fake city. *Allahu Akbar,* trills the voice that Yitzi is shouting over now. "Permission to fire!" he screams, and then fires into the open window.

When Ido's mind stays out of the way, his body knows what to do. When to crouch, when to roll. No need for thinking, no need for a decision. He rolls through the dirt through a doorway, lands on one knee—primed, ready. He knows where all his unit-mates are. They call out to one another. Their voices, his voice, their voices, his voice. Nothing in the world is this simple, this true. Nothing feels this good.

Ido and Ori are dead. Ido was taken out by friendly fire, cus emek, Erez; Ori was taken out by one of the Tals. All day, Ido had been looking forward to the urban combat drill, and now here he is—dead in a room with a dirt floor. Outside, he can hear Gil telling someone to move faster. Ori is on his phone, leaning against a once-white wall, kaffiyeh draped around his shoulders. His notifications are on, and every second the phone makes a jarring bell sound at apparently the highest possible volume setting. From across the room, Ido uses all his restraint to not tell the kid to put his phone on silent. That would make him look old. Wouldn't it?

Tentatively, Ido asks, "Girlfriend?" hoping it sounds casual.

Ori looks up. "What?"

"Is there a girlfriend?"

Ori runs a hand over his buzz cut. It's a gesture of agitation that Ido remembers from the days of his own buzz cuts. "Girls don't want a combat soldier who comes back horny and smelly once every two weeks," he says, sounding like he's quoting someone. "They want a jobnik." Outside, maybe a block away, there is a crash as a door is smashed in. Neither of them gets up to look.

Ori's phone dings three times in rapid succession. He rolls his eyes, moans a little, then leaves a voice recording for someone on the other end. "Beseder, achi, I'll fix it when I get back," he says into his phone. He makes an impatient gesture at Ido, as if to say, *This idiot, am I right?*

"Your commander?" Ido asks after Ori has put down his phone.

"When will it end?" Ori responds, a kind of answer. It's a phrase the enlisted repeat again and again. When will it end? When will it end? Implied answer: the day they finish their mandatory service. The day they cut up their army ID cards. The day they go free. Or that's what they think. Maybe this is what Ido envies about Ori: he envies that Ori can envy him. A young soldier believes the factors that trap him are conditional. When he gets out of the army, he'll be free; he'll be himself. Ido envies anyone who can talk to himself this way, who can say, *Just a little bit longer*, and really believe it. He doesn't envy the young guys he sees at the airport sometimes—fresh out of the army, growing out their hair, using their standard-issue packs to make that six-month trip around Nepal or Peru or Thailand. Even them he pities already, pities what they are about to find out: that you can go halfway around the world to a town with a population of twenty-two, including the goats, and you will still find an Israeli who says to you, "Where did you serve in the army, achi?" Israelis everywhere. Israelis in all the hostels, the bus stops. Israelis holding illegal raves in UNESCO ruins. Sherpas who speak Hebrew. All over the world, Israelis looking for something that was never there. He pities the kids he sees in the airport because of the futile years they are going to spend lost, and some of them never come back. You'll find them washed up and vague on mountains all over India. But in the army, they are waiting for the moment—it's coming, it's finally coming—they can feel it coming, and when you are with them, you almost believe it, too. You almost believe that there is a version of yourself—of each of us—a true version, waiting to be found, and as soon as the army lets you go, as soon as your life begins, you'll find him. You'll find your true self. He's out there; he's waiting for you.

It was that day in the hospital that taught Ido otherwise, that showed Ido all that he was not. When the bloody head emerged from his wife's body, Emily wasn't his wife, wasn't a woman. In that moment, he had understood that these words—wife, woman—were invented to trap Emily, to trick her into believing that she needed Ido, that she was a lesser version of him, drawn out from his body. It's a bit of etymology that any Hebrew speaker knows, that Emily learned in Hebrew school. *Woman*: "ishah" is so-called because from "ish" (*man*) she was made, that fateful rib. But it's a lie; he saw it in that hospital room. The truth is the reverse. He came from her. Even the word "ish" fits inside "ishah." His whole purpose was born and extinguished on the night, whatever night it was, or a Saturday afternoon on the kitchen floor, his hand gripping her hair and she pressing up into his weight, turning away from him as she came and the sound of her coming made him come. He remembers God's curse to Eve in the garden, remembers that the husband himself is the curse: *Your desire will be for your husband, and he will rule over you.* But Emily doesn't need him anymore, doesn't crave his control anymore. And now, Ido knows, he has to decide whether he wants to spend the coming years trying to be a person that Emily could need, or whether he will hide from the truth he saw in the perfection of Emily's daughter emerging from Emily's body.

Gil appears in the door frame, his face a little red. He's got a handgun with blanks. "Yalla," he says, nodding at Ori and at Ido. "We're starting up again."

Ido rises to his feet, heads back out into the late-afternoon sun, a chill in the air now, detectable in the long shadows cast by empty buildings. Ori is taking a selfie with the kaffiyeh covering most of his face, black and white squares, like some Ashkenazi jihadi. Somewhere, a dog is barking. Somewhere, the percussive shudder of a door blown off. Somewhere, a CCTV camera is filming him. Here he is. Here is Ido, a grainy image on the black-and-white footage, below him, the date and time, the seconds whirling by.

Daughters

It's nearly Shabbat, and Miriam is still fussing with her salad dressing.

"Ima, are you almost ready?" asks little Tovah, sitting at one of the kitchen counter stools while Avital stands behind her to fix her hair, freckled face scrunched in concentration.

"Another minute, just another minute," Miriam says, as if she were the daughter and little Tovah the impatient mother. But she wants to get the dressing just right. It calls for, of all things, curry powder—an adventurous choice for Miriam. Ori would love it, but it's another weekend on base for her son, another Shabbat without him.

Yuval comes rushing down the stairs, hair wet from the shower and dripping onto his nice Friday-night dress shirt. "Are we almost ready?"

Avital finishes with Tovah's hair—a diadem of small braids and the rest of her wild, curly hair down. Daughters of Jerusalem. "We're ready," Avital says, that charming gap between her front teeth flashing.

"Are your phones off?" Yuval asks, powering his down and putting it in the bookcase where all their phones go until Shabbat is over.

"Ima," Avital asks, with false severity.

Miriam tastes the dressing again. Is it too spicy? It's probably fine. Maybe a little more lemon? No, it's fine, it's probably fine. "Coming, coming," she exclaims, checking her messages from Ori one last time. (*Shabbat shalom, Ima*, he wrote earlier today and nothing since.) She checks the fridge to make sure the salads are covered, she checks the hot plate to make sure it is turned on, she opens the dishwasher to be sure it's on the automatic setting.

"Yalla," Yuval says, "it's time to light."

After Miriam and the girls light the candles—their warmth and glow illuminating her fingers held over her eyes—everyone hugs. "Shabbat shalom," they say, "Shabbat shalom."

They had planned to all walk to services together, but now Miriam finds herself unwilling to leave the glow of the kitchen, the closed doors. "You go ahead," she says to Yuval and the girls, who are already slipping on jackets and heading for the open door.

Yuval hesitates. "Are you sure?" he asks. His hair is still wet.

"Wear a hat," Miriam says. "And yes, I'll meet you there."

Yuval crosses the room back to her. Clean smell of his aftershave when he kisses her. "We'll see you soon," he says.

The heavy front door closes behind them, and Miriam is alone in her kitchen.

Now, alone in her house, Miriam goes to each room and checks the windows. Avital's room is its usual mess—sneakers and sports bras thrown all over. The full-length mirror is unusable ever since Avital insisted that all the girls in her scouts troop sign it in permanent marker: *We love you, Avitush!*

Little Tovah's room is also the family bomb shelter, with reinforced walls and only a small high window. They made sure to fill it with lamps and fairy lights. She still keeps stuffed animals on the bunk bed she shared with Avital back when there were more kids at home and the younger girls shared a room. Didn't Yael Salomon have a bunk bed?

Last is Ori's room. Of course, he's always had his own room, the little prince. One window looks out over their neighborhood, another at the security fence protecting the settlement. His room is on the second floor, but she checks the windows anyway. She runs her hand along the little hutch desk she bought so many years ago. How many hours did he spend here, studying for the math tests he barely passed? On the wall, a map of Israel unsullied by international boundaries and armistice agreements. A complete Israel. His twin bed is freshly made, ready for him to come home. Blue flannel sheets, warm for winter.

Just a moment, Miriam thinks. *I'll lie down for just a moment.* And then she is curled up on her son's bed, inhaling what must be the scent of him, but what smells to her more like his deodorant— chemical fruit.

If she doesn't get up now, she'll fall asleep in her son's bed. She knows that Avital and Tovah must be a bit worried, checking the synagogue entrance every time someone else enters for the service—singing and looking back over their shoulders. So Miriam rises from her son's bed, touching the dark blue pillow one last time. She rises and she goes downstairs. She grabs a thick sweater from the couch. It should keep her warm enough. Then she exits her home into the glorious, shimmering light that seems unique to the minutes before sundown on Friday. She walks through her settlement's quiet, carless streets toward the small local synagogue where her family is waiting for her.

She walks in the middle of the street. No reason not to. Silent Shabbat streets. She does not rush. The time for rushing is over. The week is over. What is lovelier than the peace of a community that observes Shabbat together? All over Gush Etzion, there are birds in the olive trees. No cars on the street. Each week, a miracle.

And this is why, in a community not far away, Yael Salomon's mother has paused her seven days of mourning. Not even the most desperate grief overrides Shabbat. A few days ago, the woman was flinging herself over Yael's grave, unleashing horrible cries that seemed to echo deep inside Miriam's twisted gut. But today, Miriam imagines, or really, knows, the grieving mother has bathed for the first time since her daughter was buried; she has dressed carefully, her clothes untorn, and put on lipstick, perhaps also a pair of earrings, perhaps ones belonging to Yael; she is walking to the synagogue arm in arm with her neighbors. For this single day, Yael Salomon's mother must let the world be perfect, because each week, it is indeed perfect—even with Yael not in it. Miriam has heard that for those in profound mourning, Shabbat offers a kind of transcendence. Miriam has seen the mothers of dead sons radiant in their grief. It is possible that pain brings us closer to the Holy One, closer to our own souls. Miriam hopes she never finds out if this is true.

At some point she stopped walking. She is staring out into some distance, unsure if she can keep going.

"Shabbat shalom, Miriam!"

Miriam looks around and realizes she's standing in front of the Klausmans' home. Meir's mother, looking lovely in a vibrant red dress and matching hair covering, is standing at the open door, waving to her.

"Shabbat shalom." Miriam waves back. "How are you?"

"Baruch haShem," Meir's ima says to her, then turns to shout into the house in English, maybe to Meir, "Yalla, are you coming?"

"I'll see you at shul?" Miriam calls, across the lawn.

"Yes, see you there," she shouts back in her charming, British-sounding Hebrew.

Ori and Meir used to be so close. Privately, Miriam has hoped that they might reconnect, that perhaps old friends might bring Ori back to a more robust observance. Her son has pulled away in stages: choosing not to enlist in a religious unit, wearing his kippa only when he's home, sleeping through services on Saturday mornings.

The first time she buzzed his hair, it was the night before she took him to the bus that would take him to basic training. That was over a year ago. How is this possible? But it's true, over a year ago that he sat before her in a plastic chair on their cement patio, where they keep the washer and dryer under a tarp. Miriam had laid down a garbage bag to catch the honeyed ash of her son's hair. After, it had pained her to throw it all away. Scraps of his boyhood, gone. How young he looked without his blond hair. How exposed his sweet skull without his kippa.

And, look, Miriam understands the need to leave childhood behind. She was the first of her family born in Israel. She grew up with Holocaust grandparents living in the basement, dreaming of starvation, sneaking potatoes under their pillows. Even her own mother had been weird about food, weird about watching Miriam eat. She was the only child in a silent house filled with women watching her eat. Lace and the smell of rotting apples. They spoke to her in Yiddish, but she would only answer in Hebrew. She hated Yiddish—its nasal, shtetl kvetch. She wanted strong babies born from the land. So yes, she understands the need to separate, but couldn't her son do it in some other way?

Because if Ori walks away from all that they have taught him, from the life they have built for him, then what is the point? What is the point of all of this? This is not a question Miriam asks herself often, but tonight, Yael Salomon's mother has made blessings over candles without her daughter, and Miriam is asking herself, What is the point of the locked doors and the locked windows, the walls and the barbed wire, the grief, the rocks, the knives, and all the ways there are to die in these territories? These are sacrifices, this is labor—it is the work of a whole life to keep the commandments, to love and tend to this land, the only inheritance that matters. She has tried to give her children a beautiful life, meaning one with purpose and ideals. This life has horrible risks. Nobody needs to tell Miriam that. She is not stupid. But if Ori falls away from them, then what was the point? They might as well live in Tel Aviv. In Berlin, for that matter.

Stop that, she chides herself. Many people fall off and find their way back again. Many a twisted road can lead to a good life. And anyway, there's nowhere on earth you can't be killed for being a Jew. Like being a woman, in that way.

She has arrived at the modest house of prayer—single-story, white cinder block with a small garden out front. For Torah services on Saturday morning, they go to the big, new shul, built with South African money, all glass and sculpted metal. But for Friday night, the family keeps it local—just a few minutes' walk away. "Shabbat shalom," she greets the handful of people lingering on the sidewalk outside. Kisses on cheeks for the women, everyone holding a baby or a prayer book. When she opens the doors, it's to a flood of voices harmonizing songs of praise. *It is good to give thanks; it is good.* She spots her daughters on the women's side of the room. Her girls in bright skirts and gold hoop earrings. Little Tovah, giggling at something Avital has whispered to her. Miriam slips beside them, whispering hellos and giving little squeezes and smiles. She has come right on time. The congregation turns to face the doors of the synagogue. "Boi b'shalom," they sing. "Come in peace." She can hear the sweet, harmonizing strands of her daughters' voices above the melody of the hymn. Sanctify us, Miriam sings. Sanctify us with the seventh day, again and again, a taste of the world to come, again and again. Somewhere, Yael Salomon's mother is lifting up her voice. "Boi kallah," they sing. "Come, bride," and as they do, they bow. Miriam and her daughters, her husband, her neighbors— to Shabbat, to the Holy One Blessed Be He, and to creation itself. They bow. In a room with almost everyone they love, all of them together. They bow.

Salem Abu-Something

Meir throws his weight into the kick. The long ball he sends flying toward Shibi's end of the field looks like it's going to land exactly where you want it—inside the eighteen, outside the six. The promised land, Coach calls it. But there's no time to wait and find out, because the drill calls for a series of push-ups. So it's down into the grass, still damp from last night's rain—a smell of life and decay together. Today, Meir is practicing with the starting lineup. If he keeps his head in it, he may get some playing time this week—his first Premier League game, which means being on TV, and everyone seeing him, Liran and Ori for sure. He's focused. Yet even while he focuses, part of him is remembering the night at the mall, the way the Arab's face split on the asphalt.

"Fast feet," Coach yells, at no one in particular. "Yalla, pick it up."

They're practicing in the Jerusalem stadium today. Last year, when Meir went pro, the stadiums had felt, well, holy. He had wanted to kiss the grass each time he ran onto the field, the announcer calling his name. He wanted to kneel or something, like the players in Brazil and Portugal do, all those goyim with glints of gold crosses on their open chests. Now he understands that it's not the stadium on its own that is holy. The stadium is only the stadium when it's full, when barbarian fans with faces painted red hoist their sons on their shoulders and scream until their eyes bulge. It's only the stadium when the loudspeaker voice is trembling across grass cast greener than green in the nightmare of white lights.

Cradle, touch, tap. Meir is gentle with his feet as he maneuvers around the cones, aware of Coach watching with his clipboard resting on his belly. Meir whales into a cross that, fuck, swings way out past Shibi. Cus emek.

"Oy va voy, Klausman," Coach cries out, his hands on the back of his head, a fat, frustrated old mermaid.

It's a miserable ball. Anyone else would let it fly out, but Shibi—that Arab psycho—books it, one leg extending out of bounds in a freakishly effortless-looking limbo move that flattens out his torso. He could be in a Gatorade ad, cus emek. The moment is suspended, airless. Someone whistles in admiration. Shut up, Meir thinks.

For a while after getting called up to the Premier League—eighteen when he got the call last year, one of the youngest—all Meir could talk about was Shibi Hassin. At dinner, in the family group chat, walking home from services on Saturday. Shibi the playmaker, the true number ten. Shibi the broad-shouldered Arab with a shaved head like a bullet, the cleft-chin Arab who was bulky but somehow agile, accelerating like a guy half his size. An Arab, yes, but different from the Arabs who came to work on the settlement, guys from Palestinian villages who did construction and got paid in cash. Shibi was different.

Aba listened when Meir talked about Shibi, listened and nodded his head. He sat at the head of a Shabbat table that was covered in disposable tinny lasagna dishes and half-empty soda bottles. Gray hairs sprouted out his nose. He said to Meir in Hebrew, always in Hebrew—Talk to me in English, Meir wanted to say. Talk to me in your mother tongue. But always in Hebrew, his father said,

"Remember, they only look like you." There is a Jewish soul and there is an animal soul, and nothing in between.

In the yeshiva, debates were ongoing about whether Meir would be desecrating Shabbat by playing on Saturdays when the games started before sundown. For a while, it seemed that every observant Israeli had an opinion on whether this was permissible, everyone knowing that of course it was basically not, but enough people wanting it to be permissible that they finagled an interpretation of the commandments. *Kula v'Khumra*, the lenient and the strict. What it comes down to, really, is how far you have to push the boundaries of the issue to protect its heart. How many hours to put between eating meat and dairy? Or, maybe better to say, how close can you cut to the heart while still preserving the heart? How late in the day can you pray the shema? There are times for Kula and times for Khumra. This is what Meir's aba said when he gave the lengthy explanation that concluded, as everyone in the room knew it would, with the decision that Meir could play on Shabbat. The real reason, in Meir's opinion, is that he's the youngest—the blessing of his father's old age. Aba already has a son to be proud of—one who served with combat engineers, studied Torah with his M16 resting under the yeshiva bench. His father already has eight grandkids by Meir's two sisters—one in Jerusalem and another way out beyond the safety of the settlement gates, in a trailer encampment on a hill that one day soon will either be recognized by the State or evacuated by it, protected by a husband who goes every morning to shacharit services with a handgun tucked into his jeans. What could Meir give his father that he doesn't already have? Let the boy play, Aba must have said.

On TV this morning, there was a photo of the Arab from the mall. At least on the UK news that his mum streams at home. She had it on while she packed Meir the lunch he'd bring to practice. "The sandwich wraps are corn flour, so say Shehakol on them, not Hamotzi," Ima said, fussing with Tupperware at the kitchen island next to the dairy sink. "Hello-o, Merush, do you copy?" She said it in English. She talks to him in English except around Aba.

"Beseder, Ima." He knew he should answer in English—he needs the practice—but it takes too much effort.

He always tells himself that he won't bother with the blessings over food when he's at practice; if he's eating bread, won't bother to go to the bathroom and rinse his hands with the two-handled jug, the one that Coach himself—after meeting with a rabbi about how to accommodate Meir—made sure to put in there so that Meir could fulfill the commandment. He tells himself he won't bother, won't bother to step out of the bathroom before he says the words he's been saying his whole life, *Blessed be thou, oh Lord our G-d, king of the universe, who has sanctified us with your commandments and commanded us on the washing of hands.* But he always does. Maybe that's how it is, growing up the way he did—it's easier to keep going than to stop.

The image on TV was the Arab in a hospital bed. His face, what you could see of it, was ballooned. Hard to tell where the eye was supposed to be. Blood-damp bandages, neck splint, arm in a cast. An older woman was holding up his face for the photographer, so you could see the dark wound of his mouth. Maybe teeth missing, hard to tell.

Meir was eating cornflakes that had a picture of Shibi on the box. Every few months it's a different futbal star, and this month it's Shibi—the first time they chose an Arab. Meir doesn't stand a chance to end up on a box unless he's starting.

The news anchor said something about internal organs. They cut to a video, security footage from the mall parking lot. The news anchor said the Arab's name: Salem Abu-Something. Ima muted the TV, but the CCTV footage didn't have sound anyway, just the date and time on the bottom of the screen.

What the video showed began before Meir had gotten there, when it was just a few guys outside Burger Ranch, waiting for the Arab to come out. Four then five guys. Later, he'd found out that the initial group had planned it—not to get this Arab in particular, but to get one of the Arabs that hung around the mall, to wait outside the burger place until they got one alone. Revenge, they said, for Yael Salomon. Fourteen years old when she was stabbed to death in her bedroom. Everyone had seen the photos on Facebook—blood smears on the floor. But at the time, Meir didn't know it had been planned; all he knew was that he was part of something. The video pauses when the scrawny Arab comes out of the burger place. Red circle on the screen. He's the only one who doesn't know what's about to happen. Then the video jumps ahead again. The crowd is a teardrop now, maybe ten or so guys, not quite encircling him yet. You can see the Arab trying to get away without breaking into a run. Someone hits him with something. Meir wasn't there for that either. It's blurry on the screen, shot from above in black-and-white by a camera mounted on a streetlamp or roof, but it seems like maybe they hit him with a stick or a baton or something, hitting the Arab's back. You can see that he staggers. But it hasn't really started yet. Something is holding the guys back. A few of them run up and shove the Arab, then return into the crowd. The video jumps forward again. He's on the ground now, and you can't see him anymore, just the bodies pressed around him, jerking, jerking—something is making them convulse.

Meir couldn't pick himself out in the video. That's you in there, somewhere in there. He tried to make himself know it, but it all seemed so far away somehow.

Certain things you can't see at all in the video. You can't tell that by now, he'd wet himself. Meir remembers someone yelling, "He's pissed himself, the Arab pissed himself." You can't hear that. And you can't hear the groans—not from the Arab, he stopped making noise after a while, but from each guy who kicked him in the back or balls, or stomped down on his fucking head. That's not in the video either.

Another jump in the footage. This last part Meir hadn't seen: the crowd gone, the Arab lying in the street. You can't tell it's a person, just looks like an old towel or something. People walk by.

Ima turned off the TV. She didn't ask if Meir was there when it happened. On the cereal box, Shibi is holding the ball under his elbow. He's not smiling but looking intensely out at Meir, like, *Game on, motherfucker*.

Meir resumed eating his cereal, though he wasn't aware that he had stopped. A familiar swell of frustration grew in him. He could just release it, like going into the bathroom to jack off, but Ima would probably start yelling for him to hurry up and get to practice and it would all be ruined.

"Why does the news keep saying the Arab was a *boy*?" Ima asked. "He was in a gang!"

"They come up from East Jerusalem," Meir said. "They bother the girls."

"And it's just a matter of time," she said.

"Through a fence, you mean." Through a window, into a little girl's bedroom. Meir knew that Ima was already making Facebook posts about what happened, writing stuff in English for those back home, or back in England, whatever he should call it—he wasn't born there. Sure, the Western media picks up on this unfortunate event, she'd use those words, "Western media" and "unfortunate event," but where was their coverage of the terrorist attack less than a week ago? What did the *Western media* say about Yael Salomon? What did the *Western media* say about the carnage in her room, the blood on her floor?

"Wall or no wall," she said.

"I know, Ima."

"Fourteen years old." She covered half her face in her hand, like she was praying, but she wasn't. Ima went to Yael's funeral. She knows her mom.

"Ima, I know." He felt the rising panic of knowing his mum might cry.

Meir doesn't ask himself a lot of questions. He has his goals, he has the enormous task of maintaining those goals, maintaining his body in service of his talent. But every now and then, maybe when the World Cup is on TV and Israel hasn't qualified, or when he hears one of the trainers talking about one of their part-time jobs, questions sneak up on Meir. What if his parents had stayed? What if he'd grown up playing on the futbal pitches of England, in their youth clubs? No army, no terrorists—or, well, not as many terrorists. But he can't let himself go any further than that. Something in him folds away from the questions. So he tells himself, Look, you would have been a thin, nervous outsider touching your kippa, okay? How many Jews do you know playing for Man U? Okay? He'd be bruised knees on the Tube. Jew boy with shtetl Hebrew like Aba. He'd miss the league tryouts for Shabbat, since it's different for Jews outside of Israel, how careful they have to be. His parents had left England so they could stop being weak Jews. Aba and Ima wanted Hebrew-speaking babies who ate raw cactus fruits and shot rifles, so here Meir was.

After the drill, the guys cool down by running a few laps. Coach stands at the center of the pitch, slapping his thigh, all yalla yalla, and reading inspirational quotes from this stupid book he loves, *Life Lessons from Athletes*, or something like that. With his inflated-looking belly and stick legs shooting out from his shorts, Coach really does seem like a lollipop, hence his nickname. When the guys use it, as in, "Lollipop was killing me today," they use the Tel Aviv word for lollipop, which matters, as Meir learned recently in the locker rooms, because the word for lollipop in his slang, the Jerusalem-style slang they use on the settlements, actually means blow job in the rest of Israel. It's like the secular are from a whole different country: a different language, a different calendar. Lollipop—currently standing in the middle of the field, yelling about freeing the mind from the body—probably can't even name the Jewish date, the real date.

As he jogs, Meir looks down at his body in motion: the automatic legs, the unmistakable imprint of abs against the snug, sweat-wicking top his aunt sent from England. A warm pleasure rises in him, not the sudden rage of being turned on by some slutty girl posting a photo of her ass for attention, but a quiet, stable gratitude he feels toward his own body, his beauty, really. He thinks of the prayers he has said every morning as long as he can remember. Give thanks that your soul has returned to your body; give thanks for the Torah and the commandments that separate us from them; give thanks you are not one of them, not a goy, not a slave, not a woman.

He pulls back against his instinct to speed up and pass Amir, instead slows down to match his pace. Amir lumbers along, his bulky, overproteined shoulders outweighing his slim waist. Meir and Amir have an understanding because they were both raised religious, even if Amir isn't observant anymore. His forearms are covered in thorny-looking tattoo branches, or maybe they are supposed to be claw marks. Still, he seems close with his family, always complaining about his mother's meddling, his sister's shithead fiancé. In a Mizrahi house, things are less divided, Meir thinks. Half of them keep Shabbat, half of them are using their cell phones under the table, but they all go to Torah services together on Saturday morning, even if half of them drive to the beach after.

Meir nods at Amir, who slaps him on the back a little too hard. Showy guy. "Achi."

"Achi." Call and response. "How's your brother-in-law the shithead?" Meir asks.

"Achi, he's still looking for a job."

"Tell him we need a new goalie," Meir says.

Amir ignores this. "What kind of man? You know what I mean?" His torso is very erect when he jogs. He takes sips of breath between every few words. "I should have known. In the army, he was a fucking jobnik." He looks at Meir. "Nothing personal," he says.

Everyone knows that Meir will serve a desk job in the army. Not a warrior, no, but a jobnik. *Nothing personal.* Fuck you. Later, Meir knows, probably in the shower, he will get trapped in a fantasy version of this conversation where he replies in a way that makes him seem smarter, more powerful than Amir. What he needs is a plan—a line he'll use for the coming years, as he finds himself, again and again, on the wrong side of the warrior-jobnik rivalry.

Meir's army summons came maybe a month ago—deferments all used up—complete with the blessed papers confirming his special athlete's accommodation: a desk job with few hours, no combat, barely any basic training. The only way to do less in the army is to do no army at all, like a black-hatter Charedi supporting twelve kids on unemployment in Bnei Brak, or like an Arab, like Shibi, who will spend his afternoons on the pitch while Meir slouches around in a polyester uniform stapling duplicates together in an office with girls who smell like cheese.

Amir somehow did it all. Before he went pro, he was a warrior. Nothing elite, something to do with tanks, but still, a warrior. During the war in Gaza, not the one last year but one before that, his reserve unit was called in to help with a sweep. A video of Amir filmed by one of his tank-mates got pretty famous: he's shirtless in his army cargo pants and combat helmet, juggling a ball in a makeshift camp outside the Gaza border fence. You can still find it on YouTube. When the video starts, Amir is already talking to the guy filming. "Yalla, achi, let's beat Hamas in futbal instead," he says, eyeing the ball as it bounces from his thigh to his chest down to his feet then back up to his thigh. "Five on five," he says. "Winner takes Gaza." His dog tags smack, smack, smack against his bare chest, smooth and hairless thanks to laser removal, Meir knows. Amir talks about it without shame. He got his hairy ass done, too. In the video, Amir is filthy but in a way that seems kind of glamorous under the harsh desert sun. The whole thing looks like a war movie. In the background, a soldier in boxers pours a bucket of water over another soldier who is in briefs. They wash their armpits, handing a bar of soap back and forth between them. The water reddens the earth where they stand.

They played the video on the news pretty much constantly during the ground invasion. When Amir came back, they put him on a cornflakes box, too.

If you saw Amir on the street you might think he was Arab, his coloring is olive like that. His grandparents walked from Iraq—literally, arrived in Israel by foot. The guys in Amir's family find ways to announce they are Jews: his dad wears a kippa, Amir has his tattoos, his Star of David pendant, his deep-V tee.

Amir gets girls. They like his swagger and indifference. He's talking about his current fuck now—some German girl—how he's driving to Tel Aviv to see her tonight. "She's crazy," Amir says, stretching his arms as he jogs. "Which, you know, has its benefits." Amir's eyes are electric, sensuous. Meir recalls the story about Amir losing his virginity—his dad taking him to a whorehouse when he turned thirteen. Meir didn't tell him how his own father listens outside the bathroom to make sure he isn't jacking off.

Meir asks, "Did you see the video?"

"What video?" Amir pants. "You mean the Arab?"

"Yeah, well, maybe. Which one?"

"You mean the terrorist?" Amir says. "The car ramming?" This is their most recent tactic: mowing people down at bus stops.

"No. Wait, when was the car ramming?"

"I don't know, there's always a car ramming."

"Achi. No."

"You mean the video of that Arab getting beat," Amir says.

"That one, yeah," Meir says as he scouts around him. He spots Shibi, running a few paces ahead. He wants to make sure Shibi doesn't hear. Or no, maybe he wants to make sure Shibi does hear.

"That video is crazy," Amir says.

"Yeah," Meir says. He thinks, *If only you knew.* It feels good.

"That poor kid."

"He wasn't a kid," Meir says. Up ahead, Shibi doesn't turn around.

"He was like, what, fourteen, fifteen," Amir says.

"Look," Meir starts to say, but he stumbles and has to catch up a few steps.

Amir waits, then keeps talking. "But they were all kids, the whole crowd, just teens."

"He didn't die," Meir says.

"Beseder, achi," Amir says, like he's calming Meir down, which makes Meir more annoyed. He looks for Shibi, but he is gone.

"Sprint it in," Coach yells.

No more thinking, just the mechanics of legs pumping. Sprint it in.

The night it happened, Meir didn't see it begin. He was inside the shopping center. He and Liran and Ori used to go to one mall or another every week after Shabbat went out, to wander for a few hours, eat waffles, check out new cell phones. Now that Ori and Liran are in the army, it's different. They're home only once or twice a month, and rarely at the same time. But anyway, this time it worked out, so Liran drove them to the Pisgat Ze'ev mall in his dad's hulking Oldsmobile, which always smells of cigars though his dad swears that he's quit. Each time Meir sees his friends they look different. First they were buzz-cut, then they got skinny, now they're getting strong. He doesn't always understand them anymore, their slang, their complicated opinions on the best way to make black coffee, the most effective method to mop up blood. Meir was young when his brother was in the army. He remembers he slept a lot and never let anyone touch his weapon, no matter how badly Meir wanted to.

At the mall, Ori was carrying around his Tavor because, he said, there were some Arabs in his housing block these days, doing renovations and installing air conditioners, and so his commander told him not to leave it at home. Meir suspected Ori made it up so he'd have an excuse to bring out his weapon. Ori and Liran both wore their own clothes—jeans and a sweatshirt with their unit decals, something with bat wings. Ori stopped wearing his kippa as soon as high school ended. His parents don't mind, he says, as long as he wears his kippa when he's at home. At the mall, Ori leaned against the frozen yogurt display case and looked so bored, looked so good-looking bored—all blue-eyed and armed. He had always been the pretty boy, not as fast as Meir and not as strong as Liran, but he had done this prerecruitment training regime—running the dusty trail around the settlement carrying cinder blocks, and lo and behold, Ori made it into a halfway decent infantry unit. Poor Liran got stuck in a tank.

Ori's hand was resting on his Tavor. "Do you even know how to shoot that thing?" Liran asked Ori as he handed him his frozen yogurt, smothered in gooey strawberries. But of course he did.

Meir didn't know it then, but the guys who led the beating were already out in the parking lot. Four of them, or maybe it was five, circling, waiting for the Arab, for the right Arab, an Arab alone.

In the locker room, Meir finishes his shower first. He grabs his duffel bag and goes to the parking lot to wait for Amir. Outside, there's just one other person, sitting on the bench between the locker room and the parking lot. Meir gets closer to see that it's Shibi, doubled over to untie his cleats. Usually, he's with the two other Arab guys on the team, midfielders both of them. Even among themselves, Meir has noticed, they all speak Hebrew, at least within earshot. But now Shibi is alone.

"Hey," Meir says. He's standing off to the side at a clean angle for a pass, actually, if Shibi ever decides to pass the ball to him. He is stupid and nervous, feeling like a kid, carrying his oversized duffel bag, his cleats tied around his neck, flopping along in dorky shower shoes.

Shibi sits up. The cleft in his chin really does make him look famous.

"Aren't you that guy from the cereal box?" Meir says, pointing his fingers into pistols, awkwardly because he's got his phone in one hand. It's all so lame, but he can't stop himself.

Whatever is the smallest amount of smiling that can pass as a smile, that's what Shibi gives. He says, "Today you don't walk home." Meir is, frankly, flattered that Shibi knows this about him—that when games fall on Saturday evening, he walks to the stadium to avoid travel by car before the end of Shabbat. But that's only on Saturdays.

Meir hears the Arabic shadowing Shibi's Hebrew, a deepening of the sounds at once dangerous and exciting. He gets an image of himself slamming Shibi up against the side of a car to handcuff him, the way you see soldiers making arrests on the highway. "No, not today," Meir says. "I only walk when it's forbidden to drive, *yanni fi yom al-sabt*." He says the last part in Arabic just to see what happens.

What happens is Shibi ignores it. "Today you drive," he says.

"I'll get a ride with Amir, yeah."

Shibi looks right at him when he says, "I could drive you."

Obviously, Shibi is fucking with him, and, like, okay, ha-ha, very funny, like they'd even open the settlement gates for Shibi. Meir says, "No need."

But Shibi won't let it go. "Don't we live pretty close, one to the another?" he asks in his weird Hebrew. When he stands up, he's taller than Meir, but not by much. And it might be the way Shibi angles his shoulders or the way his jaw clenches, but it's obvious to Meir that Shibi heard him talking about the mall, about what happened to that kid, and that even if Shibi doesn't know Meir was there, he may have guessed, or maybe can feel it, smell it, like an animal. Late-day sun breaks through the clouds as if an angel were about to descend. Light glints off the windshields of parked cars. They are both within arm's length. If Meir says the Arab's name, if he says, "Salem," they will fight. It's simple.

Meir says, "I don't know where you live." He once heard that Shibi lives in some shitty village. Is it inside the Wall? Outside the Wall? Meir doesn't know how to ask these kinds of questions. They're not his problem.

Shibi says, "Or would they shoot me?"

"What?"

"At the gates to your settlement, would they shoot me?" And then he laughs in a way that makes his face seem tight.

Shibi thinks he's so smart with his little games. All this talking without saying what they are talking about. Your mum's a whore, Meir wants to say. Talk about that. Of course, he knows, that's a great way to get stabbed. These people. They are so primitive when it comes to their women.

From the locker room door, it's Amir's voice. "Sha-bi-bi sheli!" he cries. "You're making us look bad in those drills." He's got his duffel bag over his shoulder and a towel around his neck, stepping lightly as he surveys the parked cars, flicks his chin toward Meir. "Yalla, habibi, let's go."

Now it's Shibi's turn to make an impatient click with his tongue. "No, achi, I'm driving Meir home." His voice is smoother than a moment ago, without barbs. It's a move Meir recognizes: by being overly friendly to Amir, Shibi can communicate to Meir how much he dislikes him—Meir, that is—while also making it impossible for Meir to bring it up with Amir afterward, because no matter what Meir describes, Amir will say, Oh, weird, but he seemed cool to me.

A defensive play. Even when he's being a dick, Shibi is so tactical about it.

Amir laughs. "Oh yeah? You're going over for dinner?"

"Should I bring my own spices?"

Amir lets out an appreciative howl. "Have you seen this boy's lunches?" He ruffles Meir's hair. Meir throws him off with an elbow. "I ask him, 'Where's the flavor?' He says, 'There's salt.' Salt!"

Meir throws up his hands like, You guys got me. But inside, in- dignation prickles at his chest and up his neck. He feels wronged and excluded with Amir and Shibi laughing at him.

"Yalla," Shibi says. That means they're done.

"Yalla," Amir echoes, and heads toward his car, Meir following after him like a kid.

Shibi and Amir click buttons to make their respective cars chirp. Shibi's sedan—black, European—is not flashy but sturdy, elite. By contrast, Amir drives an absurd luxury car. Its doors open like the wings of a terrible insect. Meir climbs in the passenger side. As soon as Amir turns the ignition, there's a brain-deadening club jam play- ing full blast that Meir dials down to a normal volume. Amir goes to Tel Aviv for parties and comes back with stories about getting sucked off in the bathrooms of clubs, or double-teaming some girl in her apartment after. To hear him tell it, the minute you get into Tel Aviv, they're jumping on your dick, but Meir isn't exactly sure he believes him. It sounds like something you'd make up to shock your religious friend. When Meir goes into Tel Aviv, all he seems to do is walk around for hours and eat overpriced pizza.

"Yalla," Amir says, and they're off.

As they maneuver toward the highway, Amir is talking about practice, but Meir ignores him. Instead he slips into a recurring fantasy—it happens a lot when music is on—where he's the guy performing the song he hears. He's behind a DJ setup, whatever it's called, the record thing with the headphones. He's focused on what he's doing in the dark club with the seizure lights. A crowd is pressing around him, beneath him, bodies he is making move, they move through him. They watch him, but he watches his own hands on those control things, the levers and dials. He's woken up something in them that they didn't know was there, and now they need him.

Amir nudges him. "I said, so you were there?" He's driving with one hand.

"What? Listen." He can feel his heart in his temples.

"You and some preteens . . ." But Amir can't finish the sentence, he's laughing too hard. He tries again. "You and some preteens taught that bad Arab a lesson?"

"Achi, shut up, it wasn't like that."

Amir ruffles his hair. "*Yaa weled*," he says, in a jokey Arabic accent. "Hurry up and go to the army."

"Enough, *yaa* homo." Meir shakes off Amir's hand. "Hey. Where does Shibi live?"

"He'll be harder to beat up, achi."

"Fuck you," he says, in English.

"You think you can take him?" Amir is grinning like a drunk.

"Fuck you." They're on the highway. Soon they'll be driving out past the Wall. For now, they're stopping and starting behind a white truck.

"Originally? He's from some camp," Amir says. "You didn't know?"

"What, like in the territories?"

"No, some East Jerusalem ghetto. But he moved to a luxury condo near the center. A big thing. He took shit from both sides, but he was funny about it, like, 'Fuck it, the Jews have better water pressure.'" Amir does a solid imitation of Shibi's accent.

Meir shifts in the seat, a soft material that passes for leather. Amir spent more than he should have on this ridiculous sports car, especially considering that one day soon it will probably get dented to shit from the stone-throwers who lurk the highways between Arab villages. But maybe Meir would do it, buy something crazy, if he got officially signed to Div One. His Div Two contract gives him enough to, like, maybe buy a fridge. Ima puts it all in savings for him.

On his phone, Meir scrolls through his feeds: pics of food, ad for deodorant, a chubby girl's selfie, and here's a photo of Ori, or at least Ori's boots and the muzzle of his rifle. What did he call those? IDF dick pics. Meir starts to write a comment but erases it. He looks at the comments other people have left. "Achiiiiiiiiiiii" from the guys. Girls wrote stuff like, "Thank you for guarding over us," with little heart icons. It's a great photo—Ori's boots up, his Tavor or whatever resting on his leg, all like *Here's what I'm working with.*

Amir is talking about the goalies he wishes they had, and Meir does his part with a few grunts of agreement. He keeps waiting for Amir to ask him about what happened that night, but he's moved on already, and it seems to Meir that maybe he's been waiting in the creeping-slow days since it happened for someone—Amir or Liran or Ori, or Ima, even—to make a thing out of this, to make it feel like a big deal. He wants someone to ask, "But how did it start? How did you come to do such a thing?"

That night, the night at the mall, there was something electric, something sharp in the air. Nobody talked about Yael or the photos of her room or her mother screaming on TV, but still, you were kind of thinking of it when you held the gaze of the Arab guys who swept the floors or worked the registers, searching for traces of a smirk. Although really, the problem wasn't the ones who came to work, for the most part. It was the Arabs who slunk in from the nearby camp, not to work, but to hang out, to litter empty energy drinks on curbs and whistle at Jewish girls as if they had a right.

Who had said it? Someone running by maybe, running toward the exit. A guy in cargo shorts holding his kippa as he ran. "They've got an Arab." Or something like that. And all of them had followed immediately, pulled by a force, out the turnstile, past the aging security guard leaning against the wall, past the dead fountain filled with wet leaves and Styrofoam cups.

You couldn't see at first what the crowd, maybe twenty guys, was moving around. Later, Meir would learn that the initial group—the few who had planned to get it started—had already more than doubled, more guys jumping in as the energy grew, the energy that tugged at Meir, that pulled him out of those doors. Everything began to seem clear, simple. Girls in long skirts were prowling the perimeter, yelling with their arms crossed, "Terrorist! Go back to Gaza." Meir let his cup of yogurt fall to the ground, strawberries and cream.

The dinosaur security guard was watching, and not far away, a police car was parked. Meir assumed someone, some adult, would come stop them eventually. When did he realize that Liran and Ori had held back? They weren't with him. It was just him, walking into the crowd, the tightness of the guys around the Arab. He was on his knees, a hand held across his ribs. He was wearing jeans in that bleached-out style worn by the especially trashy ones who come up from the camp. Meir couldn't see his face. There was a lull in the action. How did Meir know that's what it was? But he knew, knew that it would pick up again soon, that they were riding out an energy they had created but that was also outside of them. They were working up to it. The Arab let out a low groan that sent an electricity through him, and the crowd pulled closer, drawn in by the sound of it. Meir didn't know the guys here, the mall being pretty far from his settlement, and none of them looked at one another for long. It was kind of understood that you wouldn't make eye contact, that you'd focus on the Arab. Someone said, "No cell phones, boys." The Arab began to crawl, or try to crawl—he sort of lunged forward like maybe he was trying to run away, but instead he fell, awkwardly, back to the ground. And this is what did it. This is what got them going again: watching the Arab get up and struggle. They were at it all at once. Kicking his legs and nuts, his head and back. He was moving a little, trying to cover his face.

Meir was part of it. He shifted his weight. He let the momentum take him forward. He kicked the Arab.

After a while, it was clear he wasn't going to start moving again. Someone spat, a few of them spat. The Arab wasn't moving as they trailed away, as the last of the girls came to take a look. Nobody stopped them.

When Meir got home, he peed first. A long, deep pee that felt like the entire universe was rushing out of him. Then he went upstairs to the only bedroom he has ever had. Took off his shoes and socks, got down to his boxers. He should shower, he knew, but he let himself crawl into bed. The sheets were worn thin and fuzzy with time. Geometric shapes in primary colors, pure '90s stuff. They were bought for some older sibling and had made their way down to him, the only one left in the house. He'd lie there for a minute. Just a minute, he told himself. Just a minute, then I'll get up and get clean.

A Good Arab

They fought again last night. Why wouldn't they? Night after night. Invariably, Shibi says something that annoys his wife. It was just the two of them—Nasir had gone down easily—and Shibi thought that maybe he and Amal might watch a movie, a TV show, really anything but the news, which was showing the same horrifying photo of Salem Abu-Khdeir in his hospital bed. Face swollen, bloodied, all of this on the seventy-seven-inch screen, ultra-high definition, that they have mounted up on the wall in a setup so involved it's not called a TV but a "home theater." Amal was leaning toward the television from the couch. "You want me to change it?" he asked. She turned to him but didn't respond, her eyes glazed over as if she saw Shibi perfectly and was disappointed but not surprised. When did he come to expect this look? When did it start making him so angry? Instead of responding as he once might have—perhaps with gentle teasing—he found his voice rising, so satisfying that it was like scratching a bug bite. "Are you deaf?" he cried. From there, it all went downhill.

Night after night, it goes like this. Is this how it's supposed to be, a marriage? He doesn't know how to formulate this concern into a question he could actually ask anyone.

Shibi wakes first. No light filters through the heavy, sumptuous curtains that Amal has hung in their bedroom, but he rises with the dawn regardless. It's an old habit from the training he put himself through each morning before high school. Those empty-stomach runs—his mother worried the neighbors would think he was crazy—made him the sprinter he is today. His modern wife sleeps late. No matter. There's nothing to cook, because his nutritionist insists that his first meal be a chalky protein shake from a mix. Shibi orders the powder from Germany. Expensive stuff. He'd never tell Baba how much he pays per tub. Shibi finds this atomized intake for most of his nutrients these days—powders, elixirs, capsules—a bit depressing. Doesn't a body need living sustenance? Meat and greens and love? Still, his nutritionist is adamant on this regimen, and the guy gets results. You can see him in promotional videos on his social feeds, doing one-armed push-ups over a plate of sushi. Cheat day.

Some days, Shibi rises as soon as he wakes to mix his breakfast in their splendid marble kitchen. But today, he remains in bed with his sleeping wife and tries to understand where he is, where they are. Her back is toward him. Her breath is even. Their sheets are soft and cool; their duvet is stuffed with real goose feathers—all of this bought at some Israeli store that imports everything from Europe. He shifts to his side, facing her facing away from him. It is stupid, he knows, to compare his life now to when they were young. They are a family now, a real family, with baby Nasir. Before, they were just two people in love. So young. Newlyweds in his parents' home, left to themselves. A half day when he wasn't training became a universe. The soft creases of her elbows, her little sighs. Time, time, time. They wallowed in time. All morning they lay in an unmade bed that sopped up rich sunlight. They were sleepy with pleasure. That's how Nasir was conceived: in a state of sustained, blissful exhaustion. Where are those beautifully squandered hours now? Now, when he reaches for her, it is across a dark water.

Amal, he thinks. *Let's start again.* Her hair is dark and mussed across the pillow. He thinks of last night. She in tears and he with his head in his hands, pacing the room. Nasir awake and clinging to her, sobbing. He tries to remember the last time they went three days in a row without fighting. When did this become the routine? He thinks it may have changed when he moved her to the Jewish part of the city. He can't let himself say, That was a mistake. But he does admit that, yes, there were trade-offs he hadn't foreseen.

On the futbal pitch, there are no surprises. Shibi can dip into the flow of the game, anticipate it and—so naturally! so easily!—alter it, like changing the course of running water. Off the pitch, he's like some mediocre defender, always on his heels and reacting after the fact, unable to foresee or predict. He didn't know. *I didn't know.* He didn't know she would be choked like a flower by weeds in the Jewish neighborhood. Is that how it started? With her isolation? They are close to home. Just a short drive across the light rail tracks to his parents, to her parents. And yet it is also true that now, Shibi and his wife live in a different world. That was part of the appeal. Not the distance from their families but the luxuries of living in a place as expensive and well tended to as this. The neighborhood actually gets garbage collection, has reliable drinking water, parks. But maybe he didn't consider the costs to his wife and their baby boy to spend so much time in the Jews' world. He wonders if part of him wanted to feel less lonely here, in their world—in their futbal arenas, on their talk shows, on their cereal boxes—so he brought Amal and Nasir over to this side, and now they are all paying for it.

Once, it would have been impossible for an East Jerusalemite to play for a Jewish team or to live in a Jewish building. Not so much because of the Jews but because of your own neighborhood—how they would look at your family, at you. For most of Shibi's childhood, the threat of collaborators was everywhere. You never knew who the Jews had gotten, what they had beaten out of him, bribed him into. Shibi was young when he heard about the dog who middlemanned a real estate deal for the Zionists to start spreading past Salah ad-Din Street. After, he hanged himself, or was forced to, maybe. But things are shifting. Nobody can wait forever, not even a city. All his childhood, they were waiting for Palestine to rise up and take them back, take East Jerusalem back into her arms, free them. Now he plays futbal for an Israeli team and there is a Palestinian candidate in the Jerusalem mayoral election. Shibi is not the only one participating in what thinkers call "normalization," but he's one of the most visible. "I can't stand you," a woman yelled at him recently. A young Palestinian woman with the look of an artist, long scarf. "You normalizer!" she screamed. "It is shameless, it is collaboration." They were in his parents' neighborhood, and everyone on the street looked away, including his wife.

On his jersey, his family name is written out in Hebrew letters: HASSIN. That's his name, but also—in the brutal, blocky letters of the Hebrew alphabet—not his name.

At first it had been funny, almost hilarious, to live in the snobby West Jerusalem complex. Every few months, the lobby was decorated for a different Jewish holiday. Little flags, celebrating the capture of Jerusalem, the founding of their state. None of it seemed real. Even greeting their neighbors in friendly Hebrew was a kind of farce. His wife had laughed, too. It was a joke they both were in on. But when the joke wore off, this was still their life, waking up in an apartment complex filled with strangers, no neighbor to come over and help her hollow out zucchini, nobody to talk to (to *really* talk to), and if she is on the phone in the hallway speaking Arabic, the long looks. Nobody says anything. Not the young family who moved from France—father is big in shipping—not the elderly couple whose high-tech son bought them their condo. Nobody says anything but nobody has to say anything. Last night, Amal said not for the first time, "I can feel them watching me." Her hand gripped her chest. Purple-red manicured fingernails, stacks of golden rings, eyeliner smudged. "I can feel them watching us." She was terrifying, Shibi thought in that moment. His own worst fears alive in this woman.

Now that Nasir has become chatty, it is definitely worse. Yet another thing that Shibi failed to anticipate: how much Hebrew his

son will have to speak, day in and day out, even if he goes to a diplomats' school where they learn mostly in English and Arabic, a bit
of German, and minimal Hebrew. There are questions they have not
discussed and that Shibi does not know the answers to. Should they
speak to Nasir in Hebrew when they are in public? When they are
in the hallways of their own apartment building? Will he be safe?
Will he be safer? They are rich, so they are supposed to be safe, but
they worry. They worry. How many were watching while the boy
from Shuafat was beaten? For over five minutes they beat him. Five
minutes. One, two, three, four, five. Nobody stopped them. A kid.
He turned fifteen in a coma, Shibi heard—as a vegetable in Augusta
Victoria Hospital.

In a horrible way, it had been a relief when news broke about
the beating, because in the days after the settler-girl was murdered,
everyone had known that some kind of retribution would be coming. True, the Jews had shot down the man who did it. True, he
had survived and would now spend the rest of his days being tortured in Mejiddo prison. True, the Jews would bulldoze his mother's
house. True, they would expand some settlement in that girl's name,
chase a family off their olive groves. True. But none of that would
be enough. For the Jews, nothing is ever enough. Shibi had known
and Amal had known and everyone they know had known that the
Jews would come for blood. Once they got poor Salem, at least the
wait was over.

But last night when Amal listed these horrible facts—Salem in a
coma, the way everyone watched him being beaten, Nasir speaking
Arabic, how scared she is for him—Shibi found himself carried off
in a wave of frustration, maybe even rage. "Halas, it's nonsense," he
cried, throwing her hand off his arm. He has had those very same
thoughts, but he could not bear to hear her echo his fears. He could
not bear the accusation of it: How can we choose to live among them
when they want to erase us? He said, "I am doing the best I can."
Don't they have two cars? Won't his son go to a private school with

the children of diplomats? Shibi is the starting number ten on a team that has a solid chance at winning the league this year. He is in his midtwenties and has—inshallah—a long career ahead of him. He is giving her a beautiful life. He yelled it—"I'm doing the best I can!"—and then almost immediately caught himself lest the neighbors hear words they didn't understand and call the cops. Angry Arabic.

Amal saw it. She saw the moment of Shibi holding himself back, of Shibi anticipating their Jewish neighbors' response and silencing himself. She saw it and laughed. "What are we doing?" she said. "Can we really go through with it?"

She was referencing the secret that they speak of only in whispers. A secret so big they have not explained it to Nasir, not told their parents. The secret is this: they are in the process of applying for Israeli passports. It is too hard to live like this, to accept the stateless limbo of being an East Jerusalem Palestinian: not an Israeli, not in Palestine, just a symbol buckling under the weight of a million bureaucratic anomalies. Traveling abroad, for example, is insane: driving all the way to Jordan with a slew of laissez-passer documents and visas, no passport, no citizenship. The Israelis will grant his application for a passport, he knows. He is, to them, the model of a good Arab. (He hears a rejoinder here, in the voice of the young artist who yelled at him in the street: *To them, the only good Arab is a dead Arab.*) They'll give him the passport. Under nationality it will say "Israeli." Nasir's will, too. His son, an Israeli. His son, a Palestinian barred from entering Beirut, Baghdad, Damascus, Muscat. But fuck it, Shibi thinks. Fuck the Arab world that has watched the dream of Palestine rot for generations now. Fuck everyone. Israel is haram, they say. Fine, so is America haram? Is it forbidden to get an American passport? Would he be a collaborator if he were applying for an American passport? All his life, outsiders have been piling contradictions upon his back, and now all he wants is to protect what is his. That's what he's doing, isn't it? By moving to this part of the city? By taking their paperwork, accepting their government?

Last night, he didn't answer his wife's question. He left. Out the door of their apartment, the sounds of her crying chasing him down the hallway. He got in his car—his European car, tinted windows—and drove through the Jewish streets. He went north on the empty boulevard, waiting at the interchange while the light-rail—the last one of the night, no doubt—crisscrossed its way north, too. He drove past settlements, past the invisible entrance to Shuafat camp, carefully obscured from view. He didn't realize where he was driving until he got to the mall where they beat Salem. Aldo, American Eagle, Burger King. He idled out front. He watched a settler woman with a stroller—they never seem to sleep—and two young children hurrying home, maybe. The woman glanced at Shibi's car, perhaps nervously. What did she see? Black, luxury vehicle with dark windows. Then he turned around. He headed home. He said to himself, When I get back, she will be gone. She will have taken Nasir and fled.

When he got back, she was not gone. She was in bed, already asleep, her face puffy from crying. She hadn't left. Then again, where would she have to go?

Now, in the dawn, in the silence of their high-ceilinged apartment, in their West Jerusalem palace, where they cannot even hear the muezzin's morning call, Shibi lies in bed with his pointless hypotheticals. He asks himself how far back they would have to go. Back before each interaction was dancing over pain, through pain, in pain. And the ones that aren't—the interactions where they laugh sincerely—feel inordinate in their relief. *We're fine, right? We're fine, we're fine.* Back, back. Back before he guided her through this newly built apartment, making her touch each marble counter. Back before she wept at the threshold of her mother's house. And why not back further? Back before the wedding, her hair huge and her face pale. A gorgeous stranger.

It's not that he regrets coming to know her. Her beauty and her quiet smiles are now substantiated by moments he has seen her in anger, accusing him of not helping enough with Nasir; substantiated by the stories she told him about her childhood: her long walks to school as a girl, the pets she kept in secret, kittens and—she insists this is true—a praying mantis; substantiated by secrets he has learned of her body, how she sleeps with one delicate foot curled into the other, the way a dove hides under its own wing. It's not that he regrets coming to know his wife as a person, no, it's becoming known to her that he regrets—becoming known to her and disappointing her.

He reaches out to touch her. He pulls his hand back.

But did he force her to leave? Did he pull her away from her mother's house screaming? No. They had talked about it. They had talked about the parks, the water, the privacy—not living under the constant watch of neighbors, of relatives, not sucked into the endless petty battles over money, over insults. What a relief it was to walk hand in hand through streets where they did not see a single person they knew. What a relief it was. And now? Now he realizes that he is even more visible here than he ever was back home. More visible and yet invisible. Ignored. The Jews, they look right through you. During the painful, lonely hours he spends in bed as dawn slips away, Shibi goes over it again and again. He can't go back. He can't go on. He can't go back, but he wants to go back. Back before he built her a marble kitchen. Back before those initial anxious meetings at her parents' in their salon. He fidgeting with the cuffs of the dress shirt he had bought with Mama. Back even before the first time he saw her, still in her pleated high school uniform, laughing brilliantly in a group of dowdy friends. Back, maybe, before either of them was born, before their villages were erased, their cities smashed up, before they were herded into the slums that their parents will never, ever leave. How far back is that? How far back is far enough?

Shibi turns away from her, readying himself to get up—to make his protein shake, to head out for his first workout of the day, to continue to provide for this family. He turns away from her, the luxurious bedsheets crinkling softly. They lie back to back, two people facing opposite directions. One facing forward, the other facing back. Which is which? Who is who?

Just as he is about to rise, he feels her shift, and all at once, her small body is surrounding him. She is holding him—her arms pulling his rib cage toward her, her birdlike pelvis pressed into his back. How did someone so tiny bear their son? It is a miracle. Such compact strength. She presses her face into the nape of his neck. He can feel her hair in his ear. He puts his hands over her hands, which are pressed hard against his chest, pressed so hard that he knows she is not sleeping. She has been lying awake, scared as he is, anxious in her own, private ways. She is so warm, so strong. She envelops him, despite the difference in their size. She pulls him into her rhythmically, gently. She is rocking him. Like a child, she is rocking him. "Shh," she whispers, her voice soft and distant, "my love, my man."

Yael's Room

All the furniture is white. Wood and wicker. She said she liked how clean it made the room feel. He remembers the afternoon that she got him to carry that old dresser out back and together they painted it white. He didn't think to put down a tarp. White paint on the lawn.

That's how she was once she got an idea in her head. As a girl, she had insisted on a bunk bed for sleepovers. By fourteen, she had come to regret it, perhaps, but she was stuck with the bunk bed. Now the bottom mattress is missing. Whoever got rid of it must have been the same person to clean up all the blood. Who was it? A neighbor? An EMT? Yael's father never found out. When he got back from the hospital where they told him what he knew, that his daughter was gone, the room had been cleaned, but he still had Yael's blood on his clothes.

For days after, when washing his hands, he found her blood sticking between his nails and cuticles like gold leaf. Each time, he put his fingers in his mouth rather than let these last parts of her disappear down the drain.

Yael's father lies on the top bunk. It still has a mattress, which sags under his weight. His feet hang over the back edge. He is not sure if he will sleep here again tonight. He knows he is hiding from his wife, cannot bear the feeling of his own grief magnified in her. He has spent so much time in this room that he is fairly certain this room lives inside him now, that his own memories have taken its shape—his own childhood of playing in the irrigation sprinklers of the desert is waiting for him in the closet, where, he knows without getting up to look, his daughter's ballet slippers are still hanging. And under the bed, her pink Converse sneakers waiting for spring. He is not sure how long he has been lying in his daughter's bed today.

If he opens the drawers of her dresser, he knows he will find carefully rolled socks and neatly folded T-shirts organized by color. Yael likes order. And yet, she is so creative. Dance class, poetry for school projects, painting a delicate border of flowers around the frame of her mirror. Perhaps that is how it goes. Creativity requires structure.

Everything is here. Hair ribbons tied to the neck of a standing lamp. Picture frames shaped like hearts displaying photos where two, three, or even four girls are cramming their joyful faces into view. Seashells she collected from visits to Tel Aviv and a family trip to Greece last year, lined up along the window. That window. Everything is here, but everything is gone.

He closes his eyes. Sometimes he can feel—or almost feel—Yael there, in the bottom bunk, shifting in sleep or texting furiously on her phone, delighted by one of the dozens of group chats that mapped out her social life. What will happen to Yael's phone number now?

He lies on his side, hugging his belly. His body does not know that Yael is gone. His body still conjures her in dreams, pulls her close, as if that could repair what was ripped away the night the emergency workers lifted her onto a gurney.

If he sleeps, he may wake to the sound of Yael screaming. *Ima*, she screams. She died crying out for her mother. Only sometimes, in his dreams, it's Yael as a baby—crying in the dark hours between night and morning, and he will wake up into the sound and his first thought will be, *She's hungry*, as he shakes awake his wife, who cries and says, "Please, no more, please."

And, oh, the darling sound of Yael's chewing. When she was a toddler—Yael, little Yaeli with those dimples, where did they come from?—he used to listen to the sound of her chewing by bringing an ear up to her cheek. Tiny, determined crunching sounds while she ate spoonfuls of cornflakes. It was intoxicating.

He never told anyone this, but when she was born, he sometimes let himself imagine that Yael had grown inside his belly, that he'd carried her. In his heart of hearts, he has to believe that every father has had the same thought. How could they not?

Flesh of my flesh.

There is a story from Talmud that he has always hated. Two sons die on Shabbat. Their mother covers their bodies behind a closed door, then lies about where they are to their father. Only after Shabbat does the father begin to insist, saying, "Come on now, where are they?"

She answers with a question of her own. She says years ago, a man loaned them something, and that on Friday, this very same man had come by to ask for the return of what they had borrowed. "Should we do as he says?" she asks her husband. "Should we return what we borrowed?"

"Of course," the husband says, not knowing that he is consenting to the loss of his children.

That man was the Holy One Blessed Be He, the woman says. Our sons are gone. Then she pulls back the blanket to reveal to him the bodies. The moral is that all children, all life is on loan from heaven.

An unbearable story. Yael's father is finding that all the familiar texts are haunted with a horror that did not quite communicate itself to him before, the way that certain features of a room announce themselves only in partial darkness. Stories of sages falling on their faces, sages clinging to the ruins of a destroyed ship, sages tortured to death, torn apart by Roman meat hooks, scalped. So much Torah learning, and this is the reward. For what?

Some died in prayer. Dying on the word "one" or the word "holy." As if this was a comfort. How many died screaming for their mothers?

The afternoon is fading. Across the room, Yael's window is open. He has left the window open, the window the Arab came through. He has left the window open, because what does he have to fear now?

At some point, he must have fallen asleep because he wakes in the partial light of early evening. His first thought: *She's here.* She is here. Yael. In the bunk below. He can feel her subtle movement, her breathing. "Yael," he says. Just once. He says her name only once, and please, heavenly father, let him die now, please, die with her still here.

His wife is crying. Not Yael. Of course not Yael. In the bunk below, his wife is crying. She must be lying on the wooden slats of Yael's bunk, the mattress missing, the bloody mattress gone.

Two parents in separate bunks, separate agonies.

And yet.

He wants to tell her that he is sorry. What have I done? he wants to ask. What have I not done?

Without looking, he reaches over the edge of the bed so that his hand is outstretched to his wife in the bunk below. He waits. He waits for her to reach up and take it.

Strangers

It is Ido's idea to pull over for the hitchhiker.

"*Lama*, Ido?" Emily asks. Why? Why now, why this? She wants to get back to the rental cottage to prepare dinner: rinse the wild rice, flash-marinate the mushrooms, get the proofed dough in the oven. Never mind the breast milk she's eager to refrigerate and bring back home tomorrow.

"Because," he says, as he checks the rearview mirror and backs up along the gravel shoulder toward the girl—all leggy in shorts, despite the winter chill. "She's alone."

This is remote area to hitch for a ride—a single road between far-flung northern kibbutzes. A damp, heavy wind rushes in as Ido lowers Emily's window and the girl leans close to the window to say, "English?" in a German accent, or Norwegian, or Danish, one of those. Golden strands of the girl's hair reach into the car, kissing Emily's cheeks. What's odd is how much this girl looks like her, like Emily—fair coloring, cute nose—only younger, so much younger. The radio is still on, playing a Hebrew pop song in the Arab-inflected Mizrahi style. *My beloved, my beloved, my beloved*, the man trills exotically.

Ido turns it off. "English, yes!" he says, leaning across Emily. She can smell his antidandruff shampoo. Unsure of where to look, Emily looks at her own sneakers, still muddy from when they stopped to hike earlier today. She nudges her toe against what must be a baby toy—soft plastic circle in a friendly orange. One of Mayan's, surely, but why doesn't Emily recognize it? "Where to?" Ido asks the hitchhiker. He's straining against his seat belt.

"I have an address," she says, thumbing around her phone. Her cheeks are flushed, her eyelashes long. When she smiles, faint lines appear around her eyes and mouth, smoothed away almost immediately by the elasticity of her young skin. In the late afternoon's weak light, there's something blurred about her face, almost photoshopped. Emily can tell by the way the girl smiles helplessly toward her that it's her presence in the car—a woman in the passenger seat—that makes this safe. "It's near here," she says, "the kibbutz I look for." She hesitates then butchers the name of the very kibbutz where Ido and Emily have rented a cottage for the night.

"That's where we go!" Ido exclaims, and then just like that, he presses a button and the car doors unlock.

The girl glances at Emily again, then nods okay, and gets into the back, tipping in a large pack before her. She sits in the center seat. It's the spot where, usually, Mayan's car seat is.

"*Mah atah oseh*, Ido?" Emily asks softly, assuming the tourist doesn't speak Hebrew. This is to be their first night alone since Mayan was born. It's not quite four p.m., but they'll both be exhausted by nine. Ido is squandering their last hours alone before they go back home tomorrow.

Ido winks at her as he pulls the car back onto the road. The wink says, Don't worry, I got this. Emily breathes in slowly to the count of eight, holds, and releases to the count of ten. A calming technique.

Glancing in the rearview mirror as he drives, Ido asks the German girl where she came from. A city in the south, she says, not far from Switzerland. Ido is laughing. "No, no," he says, "I mean, how did you get here?" She says she took the train from Tel Aviv. "You are visiting to be a kibbutznikit?" Ido asks.

The girl, not quite understanding the question, says, "Yes, it is a beautiful country."

He wants to know how long she's been in Israel ("not too long," a kind of cagey answer, it seems to Emily); where she has gone already (Tel Aviv, of course, yes, and Jerusalem too, but she prefers Tel Aviv). "Ahh, come on!" Ido is smiling goofily. "We love living in Jerusalem." He names a bar they haven't been to in years. "Did you go there?" he asks in the rearview mirror. The girl thinks she did; she's not sure. Her voice has the cheerful competence that seems to come with a German accent.

Emily nursed Mayan this morning before they began the drive north. It was a whole production: arriving the night before to Ido's parents' place, stacking the fridge with too many glass, BPA-free canning jars (four ounces) of expressed breast milk, all so they could wake up early this morning and get up north in time. Really, this should be a two-night trip, but they've condensed it into one—one night is all they are willing to spend away from their baby.

Ido is talking to the German about land mines. He's talking about the Second Lebanon War without naming it, because nobody outside of Israel—well, and Lebanon, presumably—noticed it happening. He says a phrase that Emily recognizes because he has said it to her. "Boredom punctuated by tragedy." That's how Ido describes combat.

She presses her forehead against the cold, damp glass of her window. What is Mayan doing right now? Are you sleeping, my little life? Mayan's hair is dark, like Ido's, but flossy soft. Emily could spend the rest of her life staring at her eyelids, near-translucent and fluttering. Shock of blue eyes, panicked and searching, then closing again, drifting back into . . . what? What do you dream without language? Dream of me, Emily thinks. Please, of me.

All day a mist has lingered. Through it, she can see the summit of the modest mountain they hiked, just a few miles away. *We were there*, she almost whispers. Near the summit, her hand rested on Ido's shoulder as she balanced on an uneven rock, looking out over fields.

All around them were quiet monuments to the war dead. Names of dead boys, engraved in plaques and mounted on boulders, on trees. Up there, everything was green and gray, windswept and dolorous. Emily didn't take any photos.

"And are you a soldier still?" the girl asks.

"Well, in Israel we are always soldiers." He glances at Emily, but she pretends not to notice. Emily's role, if you can call it that, is to express displeasure at Ido's decision to keep serving with his reserve unit. They've cast these parts for each other. Her part requires that she use phrases like "casual dehumanization" when discussing the most recent atrocity—for example, what happened to the Palestinian boy in the mall parking lot. Ido's part is to answer back, "And what about Yael Salomon? What about the terrorist who casual dehumanized that girl in her bedroom?"

Ido continues, "But at my age, I am a soldier only a few times a year. Mostly, I am an animator."

"Oh my gosh!" The girl leans forward so her head is between the two of them. "Like cartoons? You make cartoons?"

Oh, come on, Emily thinks. Grow up.

Ido smiles back at the girl. "Yes, I make cartoons."

He names a cartoon that, yes, it's true, he worked on, but didn't create or write or even storyboard, just provided labor for. It's a cartoon with a sardonic unicorn that hangs out in dive bars and takes large, rainbow-colored bowel movements. The German girl knows this cartoon. "It is amazing!" she says. She says it a few more times.

When Ido and Emily are alone, he only brings up his job to complain about his "bullshit paint-by-numbers" projects, his unappreciative bosses, and the terrible pay. He frets, he dismisses alternatives, as if this is the only way it could be, because (Emily senses this rather than it ever being said aloud) of Emily and the baby. It's because of them that Ido must shelve his dream of being an independent artist. Who cares? she wants to say. Who cares about that job? They could take money from his parents. They could better monetize Emily's already-considerable social media presence. She knows the formula for a marketable, stylized calm set to a background of mix-and-match textiles: a single orange, Mayan's tiny hand clutching a sprig of lavender. But Ido is protective of his dignity, and in a way, Emily is too—scared that he might not be someone who can take care of her, scared that he might be a loser.

At the gates to the kibbutz, Ido waves at the guard booth, where an old husk of a kibbutznik is drinking a paper cup of what must be black coffee, leaning back to accommodate quite the gut. He doesn't bother to open the sliding glass window so that Ido can call out, *Hey, we've rented a cottage*, just nods and presses a button that opens the tinny gates. How is he explaining the arrangement of figures to himself? Does he wonder about the girl in the back seat? Emily looks too young to be the German girl's mother, she hopes. The girl might seem like Emily's much younger sister. Or a younger friend. Or a sex worker they solicited on Craigslist.

The girl is reading directions off her phone. The directions are in German—she met the guy whose place she is crashing at in Berlin, of course, because all Israelis end up in Berlin eventually—so she translates out loud on the spot, slowly yielding words in English. Strange how Emily is the only one in the car speaking in her first language. Strange how vulnerable that makes her feel, like she's the only one who has the burden to tell the truth, the real truth, not just the approximation of the truth you hazard in your non-native tongue.

They drive slowly through a fog that parts for them, the car bumping and dipping with the smoothed stones. They drive slowly because dogs and children abound on a kibbutz. They pass squat, one-story houses built close to the road. From their uniform simplicity, you can tell they belong to the early days of the kibbutz—back when the egalitarian dream was still alive.

"Do you have what to eat?" Emily asks. She talks like this now—

her English inflected by Hebrew syntax. *Where you from?* This is the first question anyone asks when they hear her speak Hebrew. She doesn't know what to say. I am from a series of Midwestern American suburbs, and none of them told me anything about myself.

The girl says, "I'm not too worried about food. I have this onion I brought."

Seriously? But Ido's face lights up, and Emily knows what he's thinking: How pure the unencumbered youth, how unfussy, how unlike Emily, with the complicated food she packed into baskets and coolers: crushed garlic, sliced mushrooms, temperamental bread dough. The list goes on. The quinoa salad heaped with diced peppers, the dressing left on the side so it won't grow soggy. All this packed alongside the accoutrements that sex would require, if they hazarded it—a staggering array of organic, fragrance-free lubes that Ido ordered for her at tremendous cost, because since giving birth, sex has remained difficult. The stitches inside Emily have melted, yes, but all these months later and she still needs to be careful, so careful. Now their sex doesn't follow a narrative arc as it once did—one that starts many ways but always, always ends in penetration.

The mist is rising. Out of it, and quite suddenly, appears a man walking the dirt road. All Emily can see of him is his leather shepherd hat. When he looks over his shoulder at them, Emily sees that he's older than her father, snow-bearded. He raises his hand in greeting as they pass, rumbling over the uneven, rocky way. He's from another time, another era, and even though she knows it is rude, Emily takes a quick photo of him with her phone.

The fog closes like a palm and opens to reveal a kibbutz dog, mangy and enormous, asleep in the middle of the road. Emily touches Ido's arm to make sure he sees it. He slows. He honks. The dog stirs and slowly rises—a heavy-titted bitch with low-hanging dusty nipples and a torn ear. According to the instructions Emily received by email, the cottage they rented should be around here. The German girl says, "I think it is this one on the left."

"Actually," Ido says—*Don't do it*, Emily thinks, *please don't tell her*—"our place is next door."

"Well, bye!" Emily says, trying to sound unbothered.

"You should come by for dinner," Ido continues, and Emily closes her eyes.

"Thank you," the German girl says, opening the car door. "That is so nice."

"Hey," Ido says, and the girl pauses. "What's your name?"

"Vera," the girl says. "My name is Vera."

The car feels empty without Vera. It takes all of Emily's restraint to stop herself from asking Ido, Does she look like me? Her body, her hair? Like me, but younger? They pull into the driveway of their cottage, which, indeed, is next door.

Emily is the first to shower, washing off the grime of the day. After, in the steam of the little white bathroom, over a sink lined with bottles of creams and serums she's not interested in, assuming they have all kinds of artificial fragrances added, Emily wipes away the clouds from the mirror. Of course, she has gained weight, but she looks good, she thinks. The yoga studio she goes to doesn't have mirrors, but the Pilates place does. From certain angles, she admires herself. Other angles she avoids.

She cups her breasts, their denseness still startling. So tender. After dinner, she'll milk herself—strap suction cups affixed to her breasts for the acheful release that has, already, become so familiar.

The first month after Mayan came home, it was what people say it is. Sweet and exhausting—the sweetness somehow deepened by the exhaustion. Nobody slept in Mayan's house, and so the moments when her tiny fist gripped a handful of your hair, for example, could push you over the edge of your delirious exhaustion into something like joy. They tracked all the milestones: Mayan following objects with her eyes, her limbs becoming less jerky in their movements. Recently Mayan has been blessed in sleep. Ten hours a day, fifteen hours! She rolls from her belly to her back, from her back to her belly, and sometimes—this is new!—her voice bubbles and pops in a way that suggests real words might come soon. Slow down, Emily begs silently. Please slow down. She knew it would happen fast, but secretly held herself as an exception, always an exception. During her pregnancy, she had worried that she would not be a good mother, that she lacked some critical giving gene, that she would withhold a love she felt jealous of. Now she sees that this was another way to feel exceptional, the idea that she could resist what her body was designed to do. That first morning in the hospital—early morning after an endless night, when the doula put the slippery, screaming wrinkle of Mayan in her arms—Emily knew that nobody had ever loved like this. All her history and all of human history, its ravages—all of it had been leading to Emily and her baby.

She hesitates before leaving the warmth of the bathroom, then steps out into the chill, wrapped in two towels, one around her body and another for her hair. Ido is squatting over a black box on the floor, presumably the router. "Mami, the Wi-Fi isn't working." It started as a kind of joke, him calling her "mami," which is a thing that Mizrahi couples do. It's a little trashy, but calling it trashy is a little classist. Or racist? Anyway, it's something they do now, unironically, as far as Emily can tell.

"Just a minute," she says, her feet cold on the tile floor. She goes into the bedroom to dress in her loose, drapey clothing—soft blue-greens.

When she comes out of the bedroom, he's sitting on the couch, fiddling around on his phone, clucking to himself. She sits next to him.

Lets herself be pulled into the gravitational field that used to keep her trapped in bed for days, used to make her sleepy the moment he started to touch her, so complete was she. She breathes in the woody smell of his old sweater. The cold water from her hair drips onto her shoulders, dampening her shawl. She kisses his shoulder; he kisses the top of her head, never taking his eyes off his phone. She pulls away and heads to the open kitchen to get the food started.

He calls from the couch, "Let's make a little extra in case Vera comes by."

Flickers of happiness, lit and extinguished, again and again. Is that the story of a marriage? On the hike this morning, Emily tabulated injustices, and knew that Ido was doing the same. Him not waiting for her at the steepest part of the trail, just before the lookout over the sweep of the Galilee to the south. Her finishing the last of the Turkish apricots and raw walnuts before he had a chance to eat any. A quiet war. But then again, he had waited until she caught up, had helped her over those uneven rocks. And she had saved a granola bar for him (a single bite taken—"Tax," she explained, sticking out her tongue as Ido pretended to be outraged).

Emily takes the glass containers out of the fridge, preheats the oven to ready it for the bread, begins stacking things on other things, looking for the right dishes, the right this and that. Futzing. And, yes, fine—she'll put on some extra mushrooms for the girl—for Vera— just in case.

Still on his phone, Ido wanders into the kitchen, leans against the refrigerator. He wants to be close to her, she knows. She becomes the idea of home when she is chopping fragrant rosemary in the kitchen, when she is halving fresh fruits in wool socks. She puts a pale green ceramic bowl in the oven to heat it for the bread dough when it's time.

"Ido," she says as she closes the oven, "would you let her tramp?" That's the word they use for hitchhiking in Israel—*tramp*—

presumably from Yiddish, but who knows. "Mayan, I mean." She begins placing vegetables in a baking dish, clear juices trickling down her wrists.

Ido looks up. "Of course not." Looks back down. "You know what can happen to girls."

"We did it." A decade ago, when Emily first moved to Israel, it was Ido who taught her how to hitchhike. The trick is that the girl thumbs for the ride while the guy hides in the bushes or behind the bus shelter.

"She won't." He gives a grim little laugh. She turns to see a flash of something sharp and possessive in the way his mouth is set. Emily recalls how for weeks after Mayan was born, Ido would lie in bed shirtless with his daughter on his chest as if to make up for the time she lived inside of Emily. Right now, a glint of fear is making itself known to Emily, peeking out from under the folds of cautious thinking where it usually lies hidden. Here, a series of unsettling questions that Ido and Emily have never asked themselves: How possessive is our love? How controlling? How withholding? What will happen as the gap between us widens? Whose body will we stuff in to bridge that gap? Mayan's? What are we going to do to her? What are we going to do to our baby?

And then the thought is gone.

Emily can't remember what she was just thinking about. The German girl, maybe. She wipes off her hands on a dish towel and begins slicing avocados for the salad.

Still up against the fridge, Ido says, "Yalla, finally," which means he's connected to the Wi-Fi. He looks beefy, leaning up against the refrigerator. Her swarthy man, her old man—frowning into his phone. What pulls her in this time, specifically, is the way he plays with his old brown sweater, gripping the fabric at his stomach such that she's watching little flashes of his boxers sitting low, the curve of his obliques, yes, and the coarse hair below his belly button leading down.

Did you know, you can change all the energy in the room by pulling on the top button of his jeans? Yes, it's a fact. Just a little tug and you're both sinking down to the floor of the kitchen; the frying tomatoes need to be stirred every few minutes, but fuck it—it's better like this. Let it all fall apart, let the marinated mushrooms—hours in the making, blooming with rosemary and crushed garlic—let them burn, his jeans unzipped and pulled down, don't even bother to take them off fully, leave them around his knees and go down on him on this stranger's floor. Ido says a single word, "Baby."

She's kneeling over him, balancing her weight on one hand and then another. The floor is hard, and just the faintest bit sticky. He is lying with his head at an awkward angle against the fridge so that he can watch her suck him off, he's tucking her hair behind her ears, he's gently touching the back of her head, but not pressing her down onto his dick, not Ido. The first time he came on her face—in that cold, damp Jerusalem apartment he lived in as an art student—he was so sweet and apologetic and she played along, sitting cross-legged on the bed, sitting still, letting him run back and forth to the bathroom for tissues to gingerly blot the stuff off her lips, her nose, as if his tenderness repaired something, created the necessary safety to make what they had done—this filthy thing, apparently—okay, meaning permissible. But it was all okay. So few things actually disgust or scare her. Emily knew this long before her baby threw up in her actual mouth.

He's at the point where he barely has any words left, just sucking air in at intervals. "Baby." Then, "Fuck." His eyes are closed; his head rolls against the fridge. He's trying to bear it. Every time her head bobs up, she eases a little more to the right, eventually finding a position from which she can catch a glimpse of the frying pan to see if the mushrooms and garlic are burning, if there is smoke. It's a small kitchen, kind of cramped, but the kitchen island—a butcher's block on wheels—does give a decent amount of counter space. She puts the weight on her left hand, her breasts sore where her arm presses into her own chest. Her eyes are leaky and nose runny, the slick of them accumulating. She goes far enough to gag on him, and he says, "Please, baby," and she knows he means about using her hands the way he likes, so she does. It's a motion not unlike grinding pepper. He taught her to do this.

When he comes, the taste is woody and metallic. A taste she has never minded. The first time she swallowed he asked her if it was bad, if she hated it. "No," she said, "no, I love it because it's part of you." She's never been sure if that's true, but she likes the way it sounds.

She kisses his belly. Rises to turn off the burner—mushrooms probably aren't salvageable, but no matter. Pours herself a glass of tap water in a repurposed jam jar. Ido is behind her now, his hand on her stomach, which she tries to remind herself isn't meant to make her feel fat. "*Boei*, mami," he says, tugging her toward the bedroom, just off the kitchen. White walls and a pale blue bedspread.

She lies beneath a ceiling fan turned off. The curtains are closed. He lies next to her, the bed giving under his weight. Into her shoulder, he says, "Do you want to use the stuff?" Meaning, *Do you want to try with me inside you?*

She shakes her head no. No stuff, no lube, no attempts at penetration. "Just from the outside," she says. And he knows what this means. Like her, he knows the formula. He lies on his belly with his head between her knees, and she lifts her hips so he can undress her. And then, the gentle familiar lapping at her, soft circles with his tongue exactly where she wants it. Never too different but always, somehow, always shocking, always a little heartbreaking, always love.

In the weeks before Emily got pregnant, she was aware of a kind of blooming in her. Everything made her wet. Their shoes side by side, the difference in size between them, was enough for her to need him, a need she found impossible to put into words. It's a shyness at odds with the rest of her, she knows, but what can she do. She's scared of vulgarity. Instead she would lead his hand wordlessly under her skirt. That's how she told him what she wanted. And he might laugh, but it was a happy laugh—happy for the burden of fulfilling a hot-bodied wife. What was odd was that other men seemed to be able to tell. They sensed something in her, maybe smelled something. At parties, Ido left her alone when he went to go pee and came back to find her surrounded by Israeli guys, some of them sitting next to her, standing above her, a hand on her shoulder. Surely they know, Emily had thought. They know that I want to be entered again and again. My body is telling them; my body betrays me.

His hands grip her thighs, but not so hard that she couldn't kick him away. Sometimes, for Emily to reach an orgasm, she needs to tell herself a story. It has to be scary to work. In one of them, she and Ido are killing a girl. In another, he's killing the girl and Emily is watching. Although probably, if Emily were to guess, she's both girls in the story. It's okay. This time, the story is that he's fucking her. No, wait, he's fucking Vera the hitchhiker. No, Emily is Vera, Emily is the hitchhiker, and he's telling her she's so young and so tight. When she comes, she cries out in the darkened room.

Emily returns to the kitchen, barefoot this time, to throw out the burnt food and start over. Ido sings from the shower, a song with no words. She scrapes the blackened mushrooms and onions out of the pan to wash it under warm water, scrubs away the burnt bits. It feels right, somehow, to attempt the meal again. A reminder that sometimes you really can start over.

When the doorbell rings, it startles Emily. She'd been zoning out while frying a newly crushed segment of garlic in the avocado oil she brought from home, making mental lists of everything she has to do when they get back to Jerusalem. Please, Emily thinks, let's ignore the doorbell, let's hope she goes away. But Ido, hair still wet and shining, goes to answer the door. Emily holds on to a hope that he might turn Vera away, or that it might not be her at all, but a moment later she's in the kitchen, nervously smiling. She's carrying that sad-looking white onion, of course she is. "Welcome," Emily says.

The kitchen is lit only by the weak bulb that hangs over the gas range hood, the living room by the soy wax candles, scented lightly with organic orange blossoms that Emily has placed at the center of the table. Nobody turns the overhead lights on; perhaps the hush is what they crave. The next half hour passes like this: Emily browns garlic, dresses the quinoa salad, adds newly cut mushrooms—meaty king oysters and heady shiitake—into the saucepan, blanches the greens, quickly kneads the twice-proofed dough and shapes it carefully so that the crust will be thick, then places it into the heated green ceramic bowl, which she returns to the oven. All this while Ido and the German girl occupy the kitchen island, him making a big deal out of teaching her the Israeli way to make a salad. "Vera!" Ido towers over the girl, who is hunched over cucumbers, laughing. "You must cut them finer!"

Emily wonders about dessert. Ido looks up to ask her a question across the island: *"Dibart im ima sheli?"* It takes Emily a full second to process that he's speaking Hebrew. They so rarely speak Hebrew together. Did you talk to my mom? This is what he asks.

The smell of bread fills the kitchen. Mayan's smell, comfort and longing. Emily's back is to the oven. *"Ken,"* she says. Yes. They are excluding Vera, who can't understand them and who continues to stupidly cut cucumbers. Good.

"Mayan kvar nirdema?" Ido asks. Did Mayan go down?

Emily answers him that yes: their baby is already sleeping and she drank all of her milk. She waits for Ido to say more, but he just nods. And, oh, she understands now that it's not to exclude Vera, is it? That's not why they were speaking in Hebrew. It's because Ido doesn't want this beautiful young woman to think of him as a dad, as old, and Emily aided in that dissembling.

◦⁓◦

When they sit to eat—Emily fixing plates and Ido bringing them to the table, which Vera set—they sit across from the girl, like an interview. Her features are soft, lovely in the near dark. Emily glimpses the story the girl is telling herself about this couple who picked her up. A young father (she knows from the baby toys in the car) who is terrified of his wife's body, not just because it has changed, and not just because it is the site of his new responsibilities, but because he uses that body to measure himself, and knows he will be found wanting. Emily knows that Vera sees all this, no matter her age.

The bread is cut into thick slices and sits at the center of the table, swaddled in a pretty, faded dish towel patterned with small, blue flowers, forget-me-nots, maybe.

Ido has a mouthful of something when he says, "So, you fall in love with an Israeli yet?"

What is Ido thinking? Or not thinking, not letting himself think but feeling? Does the animal of his body know that this girl—a teenager with her smooth skin and anxious eyebrows—is a body he can fuck? Usually, Emily finds it tiresome when women talk about sex as "fucking"—trying too hard to sound indifferent. But yes, sometimes she likes how the word sounds when she says it to Ido, softly. It's an old trick: the contrast between what you say and how you say it. The way you'd whisper "I missed you" is how she says, "Fuck me." Or, anyway, it used to be.

"Actually, I'm running away from someone," Vera says. She is pushing around mushrooms on her plate, and Emily has to resist the urge to tell her to finish her food. "I'm in love with someone who is ignoring me."

"An Israeli?" Ido asks, eyebrow up.

Vera nods, picking the cuticle of her thumb, then catching herself and stopping, then doing it again.

"How did you meet?" Ido asks.

Oh, she says, it's quite a story. "Listen," Vera starts, "so I was jogging on the beach."

"You jog?" Emily says, needing to say something.

Yes, she loves to jog, she says. She jogs on the beach in Tel Aviv, up from Jaffa and into the center. What happened was this guy came up to her when she was stretching. He looked not quite Israeli, in her opinion. When she thinks of Israelis, she thinks of guys like Ido, she says, gesturing her fork toward him. But this guy, he was enormous and possibly waxed—hulking, hairless arms covered in these tattoos, like thorns or maybe like claws. At first he didn't say anything. He watched her for a second as she squatted down on her left leg to stretch out the right hamstring then switched, alternating back and forth. Just as she was about to say, *Can I help you?* he said, "Our trainers tell us it's better to rotate your knee upward in that stretch." All this in English.

And so she says to him, she says, "What?" And looks at him, really looks at him for the first time, and that's when—at this point in her telling, Vera covers her entire face in her hands, a gesture that Emily finds a bit overwrought but that Ido evidently finds girlishly charming because he says, quietly, almost to himself, "*Chamudah*," cutie—that's when, she repeats, she recognized him from the stupid cereal box.

"But hold on," Ido says. "What do you mean you recognize him from a cereal box?"

"The place I rent in Tel Aviv," she says, "my roommate has sugary cereal. I don't eat it."

Emily nods in agreement.

Ido is confused now. "Wait, you live here?"

"Well, for the year, yes."

"I thought you were a tourist." By "tourist" he means "teenager."

"I'm a journalist," she says, and for a moment, Emily wonders about her true age. "Anyway, I recognize him from a cereal box,"

Vera continues. "I mean from my roommate's cereal. It's got his picture. Him holding a futbal."

"Like, that's your job?" Ido is stuck on the journalism thing. "But how old are you?"

She laughs, hands girlishly spread across her face again. No answer.

Ido looks at Emily, then at Vera, then down at his plate, which is clean but for the sauce of marinade.

Emily needs her to go back to the story. "So he's a professional athlete?"

"A pro futballer," she says. "You know, your soccer."

"On a cereal box," Emily says.

"Yeah." Vera is picking at her cuticles again. She names the Jerusalem team he plays for.

"Not the Arab!" Ido exclaims, looking up from his plate, where he's using his fork to doodle with sauce.

Emily feels a wave of embarrassment for her small-minded husband.

"No." Vera shakes her head. "Amir. The striker. Amir Oved."

"Let's see." Ido is typing the name into his phone. "Wow, look at those tattoos."

Vera flinches, and Emily intervenes to say, "Forget it. Just keep going. So, you're stretching."

"Yeah," Vera says, she was stretching. And Amir got down in the sand behind her, and very gently, he touched the back of her knee. Emily closes her eyes for a long second. Vera continues, "It really did help to intensify the stretch. Anyway, so we go to get a drink."

"You're still in your sweaty clothes," Emily says.

"Yeah," Vera says, shrugging. "It's Tel Aviv, you know, so whatever." The drinks are what they always are, she says. Him asking her questions and not listening to the answers so much as watching the shape of her mouth, waiting for his turn to tell her what his opinion is on whatever he asked her about. Then back to her place. She doesn't sound embarrassed by this; she says it in a kind of matter-of-fact way, like they're all adults and they've all been there.

Ido scrunches up his face, looking a little lost. "To your place?"

"Yeah, to fool around," Vera says, so matter-of-factly. Her face is shadowed by candlelight.

"Oh," Ido says, sounding taken aback. He goes back to his phone, hunches away from the women.

"So, back at my place," Vera says, she'd barely closed the door when he pulled down her shorts and her underthings in a single motion. He ate her out on the floor outside the bedroom—roommate could have come home at any minute. Sometimes, Vera says, it takes a while for her to come, you know? Emily nods. So she told him, "It may take a while."

Ido stands up. Go away, Emily thinks. He begins to clear the table.

Vera makes a motion to help him, but Emily stills her. "Keep going," she says.

"I was nervous," Vera continues. "You know, embarrassed. But he looks at me, he's holding my thighs, and he says, 'I'm an athlete, mami. We go all night.'"

The women laugh together. Ido, standing, reaches over Emily for her empty plate.

"And he wasn't lying," Vera says. "Do you do this? Is this dumb? I keep score."

"What do you mean?" Emily asks. Ido disappears into the kitchen with a stack of plates.

"Like who gets orgasms. To me it is a score, and the score was one to zero." She goes on: He carried her to the bedroom. He was bigger than anyone she had ever been with, no, not his cock—"Ha, I wish"—but his body: the mass of him, the muscle. All this for me, she thought, and laughed as she kissed him, climbing into his lap. She watched him evenly while he rolled on a condom, but that's not the word Vera uses: "evenly." Instead she says, "I watched him with no expression, like this," and then she turns to Emily with a flat, even gaze, expectant and uninflected. "I do this when men are with the condom," she says. "It makes them nervous."

Emily knows every word this girl is going to say before she says it. Like this story is her own dream. The way they started, Vera says, she was kind of riding him except that he was cradling her, making her move with his enormous, cartoon arms. Absurd arms, with really just the ugliest tattoos. Thorns. Trashy.

"But it was good," she continues. "It was so good, the fucking."

Yes. Emily almost says the word aloud. Ido is in the kitchen clanging around with the dishes in the sink, trying to drown out the story.

"And then it was over." Vera claps her hands, startling Emily.

"What do you mean over? Like, over-over?"

"Yeah he came after, I don't know, two minutes?"

"No, shut up."

But yes, he orgasmed almost as soon as he entered her, one of those subdued, wincing orgasms like he's stubbed his toe. "He's still inside me at this point," Vera says. "I'm straddling him like, Is this for real?"

What would Emily have done? Probably fallen in love with him, she thinks. Probably enlisted herself to the project of his dignity and married him.

"So I told him," Vera says, "'You have more work to do.'"

Emily feels her eyebrows go up. Imagine being able to do this.

"He said to me, 'But, mami, you will taste like condom.' So I push down on his throat, not hard or anything, just to put a little pressure, and I say to him, 'Shut up.'"

Emily touches her own throat at the base—that tender spot where so much feeling is contained. "Then what?" she whispers.

"Then," Vera says, "the score was two to one."

Emily wants to ask her what happened next, if the score kept changing, but before she can, there is a sudden sharpness everywhere. Too much light. Ido must have switched on the dining room lamp—large rectangular fluorescents over the table. It is overwhelmingly bright. The muted evening of the house feels now like an operating theater. All at once, Emily sees that the girl isn't young. Why did she assume? It's as if she has aged twenty years in front of Emily. There are deep laugh lines, crow's-feet around her eyes, an infestation of gray hairs at her part. She has to be thirty. At least thirty, or maybe older, maybe older than Emily. Forty. Fifty. Older, old as Emily's own mother.

"It's late," Emily says, but it comes out too soft.

The woman doesn't seem to notice. She's talking about how this guy hasn't texted her back, how she doesn't know what to do. "He ignores my calls," she says. She gives an unhappy, wild laugh that, surely, must come from a dangerous and unstable person. Emily is searching the woman's face for traces of the girl. And Ido. Where is Ido?

Outside, the kibbutz dogs begin to howl.

Orchards

It's not exactly remembering, the way that Zev thinks about her, about what he wants to call the last time he saw her, but it isn't, couldn't have been the last time, because she didn't pack up and leave the kibbutz that morning—the morning she asked him. He thinks about that morning all the time. All the time. Not exactly an active recollecting, but rather that it's always happening in a part of his mind that is, apparently, reserved exclusively for the memory of the way she asked him on that morning so long ago. How long has it been going on? The looping? He became aware of it only recently, only during his evening walks around the kibbutz, but it seems to him now that he may have been replaying that morning for the past fifty-something years, that most of his life has been spent remembering.

The two of them—two kids, really—used to watch the sheep graze in the gray dark before the day began, fog lifting off the hills like a veil. Her in her boots, those boots, two sizes too big so that they swallowed her freckled calves. Her hair wild, and a perfect drop of moisture suspended from her lovely nose. Once, she asked him a question, in an accent that he wants now to call elfin. She turned to him to ask a question that he did not answer. The last time he saw her, or it feels that way.

He's an old man now, nothing to be done. Every day he tries to get his steps in. His steps. That's what he's learned to call the amount of movement he has done in a day, as tabulated by the thin, rubbery watch-looking thing that a grandson-in-law, the computer programmer, gave him for his eightieth birthday. Zev hadn't expected to use it, but it turns out he's grateful for the reminder on days when he's spent too many hours inside, reading and drinking weak tea, just how he likes it, listening to the rumblings of ceaseless construction on the kibbutz; it seems that everyone is in a constant state of remodeling or tearing down and starting again.

Often, it's twilight by the time he leaves the house. He walks through the near dark after sunset, down the main kibbutz road, which for a long time was the only road you could take a car on, not that any of them had a car back then. He walks until he reaches the hole in the fence—he has spent his entire adult life stepping gingerly through this hole—and into the high grasses that buffer the avocado orchards. Here, he first learned what it means to work the land, to turn soil, to nurture and tend.

He walks with a staff, one he sanded himself, a habit he got into back when he tended the kibbutz sheep. It's a craggly thing with good weight. More than once, he's used it to clock a mangy wild dog that was getting territorial with Sumsum, the ancient bitch with the torn ear that follows him around when she's not napping in a hazardous way that strikes Zev as narcoleptic. If you hear a car horn honking in the kibbutz, it's probably some city person trying to startle napping Sumsum out of the middle of the road.

The orchards are quiet just before the first stars begin to show. Can it really be decades ago that he worked this land with a pocketful of salt? That was all you needed on harvest days: when it was time to break for water and a snack, you took an avocado from the wood shipping crates and halved it in your own hand, sprinkled it with salt, and ate it standing. Creamy, rich, fresh. But now, a private company farms the orchards, and so it's technically illegal for Zev to pick one of the fruit of these trees. He hears that these days, the avocados are exported abroad anyway.

On the radio earlier today: news of a Tel Aviv skyscraper that when completed will be the tallest building in Israel. It could be a dispatch from a foreign country.

Back then, in a country of dirt roads, Zev was falling in love with a girl he did not marry. A freckled gentile who came from Norway to work on the kibbutz. Why did she come to the kibbutz to farm avocados? It was never clear. Something about socialism—sure, why not? He had his own small place then, not exactly a house, but living quarters. No kitchen, no fridge, just a hot plate for the kettle. But he had a bed and a window, a few books on a shelf he built, and a Norwegian girl who would pretend to be mad at him when he pretended to be her mother—a woman he would never meet—reacting to him, to Zev, should this girl ever bring him home to Norway. "*Le juif*," he would say, with a sour expression he imagined an old goy might wear. "For what you bring *le juif*?" His imitation was bad. It all came out like the accents he'd heard in Paris after fleeing Algeria in '54, at the outbreak of the Arabs' revolution. Zev and this girl spoke a broken-winged hybrid of French, English, and Hebrew together. She would turn away from him in bed squealing, "*Ce n'est pas juste!*" And he loved to take her protesting face in his hands and kiss her nose and mouth and ears and cheeks until his kisses subdued her.

You could always tell her from her too-big rubber boots. When she worked in the orchards she looked like a fly-fisher. Zev could spot her goofy silhouette from a distance in the hills as he tended to the modest flock of kibbutz sheep, not a cash flock but subsistence: enough for the kibbutz itself. They scraped by with a little of everything back then, and no one on the kibbutz had a private bank account.

They were always wearing the wrong shoes. All of them. One of the men from the kibbutz—Avi, a simple-minded guy who tended beautifully to the kibbutz gardens, coaxing them into lushness and order—showed up for the Six-Day War in leather sandals. 1967. There had been no time to change before catching a ride to the bus stop that took them to the northern front—an Egged bus, a city bus, the radio playing reserve announcements, messages from families to their sons and fathers, as the men watched the farms disappear and the Arab villages begin.

He can't remember when his own clothing started to feel like a costume. Visitors to the kibbutz, who rent houses for a weekend away, for example, have taken photos of him when they think he's not looking: a rustic figure in jeans and a denim workshirt, the leather shepherd's hat pulled low over his forehead, and Sumsum trailing behind.

What he had loved back then was that if you dreamt it, you really could build it. Everything was new, everything was poised to be re-written. His father had been an accountant in Algiers, then a nobody in Paris. But here was Zev, wandering among the flocks of sheep like King David, an alternative Jewish history springing up under his feet. He loved to awkwardly wade into Hebrew, which he learned only at sixteen when he took a one-way boat ride to the port of Haifa, then a bus inland, until he reached the kibbutz he'd been assigned to. He was always scribbling notes in the journal he'd bought before he left. Stitched pages, creamy and unlined—the journal opened the wrong way, the gentile way, so Zev wrote in it from back to front so that he could write in Hebrew, right to left, the way he'd seen Alge-rians write in the Arabic that he never learned in school. He wrote down new names for ageless plants, either resurrected from the Bible or invented anew. He wrote down the antiquated Hebrew phrases he heard the survivors use, the ones still struggling not to speak Yiddish. They spoke like Moses. "And I spake unto the taxi driver, saying, 'Lo! Do you take me for a proletariat that you have tithed me thusly?'"

Of course, survivors lived on different kibbutzes: rich Ashkenazi

kibbutzes that got more government funding, never mind the repa-
rations the German government threw at them. The Norwegian girl
had been confused by all the distinctions, the hierarchy of Jews. "But
you are all Jews, *non*?" she asked.

"In a few years it won't matter," Zev said. "Soon we'll all be
Israeli."

Most mornings, he left her sleeping when he went off to his sheep
before dawn. But sometimes she would rise with him, and they
would dress silently to spend a dark hour together in the fields. The
sheep munched at the dew-wet grasses while Zev and the Norwegian
girl wordlessly shared an apple. They took turns eating pieces off the
blade of his long, thin pocket knife. Those mornings, Zev treated
himself to a quiet assurance—that anything he dreamt was possible,
and even what he had not.

Over the years they exchanged a few letters. After the Six-Day
War, he wrote to her about the wonder of seeing the Western Wall,
about the horror of watching Arab fathers and sons butted along by
rifles as if they were the fleeing Jews. By then, she and he each had
their own families and, over the years, the letters trickled off. The
last letter she sent came in 1974. Months after he got back from Sinai,
her letter came, asking if he was alive. She said she had watched the
Yom Kippur War unfold on TV. Heard about the Israelis still held in
Sinai, tortured in Egyptian prisons. The letter felt so foreign, so out
of touch—Zev didn't make a decision to not respond to the letter,
so much as he kept not responding to the letter, and in that way, it
became a decision.

He thought of her sometimes, things he wondered if she saw,
when the first skyscraper went up in Tel Aviv, for example; or things
she would never know, like how the kibbutz decided to try out a
collective car. What a disaster, he could imagine telling her. You had
to sign up for the car. The sheet was on the bulletin board near the
dining hall where they all, all of them, ate every meal. The kibbutz
car keys somehow always ended up with pushy Ruti—cunning, that

woman. Now Ruti has got one of the nicest homes on the kibbutz. When the kibbutz privatized—let go of the commune ethos and became something closer to a suburban outpost—Zev wondered if the Norwegian knew, but then again, who would report on that outside of Israel? "Of course we must privatize," Ruti said in the meetings where privatization was first brought up. "We must evolve with the times." And everyone had nodded along. Everyone, it turned out, had some source of income on the side. Even Avi, whom Zev had always looked on with something approaching pity, had invested in real estate in Haifa. Where had the money come from? How had they built their money? Had everyone managed to develop a contingency plan? Yes, apparently. Everyone but Zev, who spent all those decades tending sheep, scribbling in the cloth-bound notebook on the hills around the kibbutz, which shrank every year, more and more land given to the nearby infantry base, to the private developments that crowd the kibbutz lands. He hadn't known there was an alternative future he was supposed to plan for.

He doesn't remember the day she left, or how it ended. He remembers that she was increasingly annoyed with elements of kibbutz life she had initially professed to find endearing, like how everyone knew when she and Zev fought, when they had made up, not necessarily because of someone's gossip, but because the kibbutz members seemed to share a central nervous system, never quite existing apart. In those days, they were still raising kids collectively—all of them sleeping in the children's quarters rather than at home with their own parents. The Norwegian girl claimed she could hear them crying at night. All of this had been increasingly disturbing to her.

She only asked him once. It was dark, and they were sharing an apple. Mist was rising from the fields, Zev's favorite ewe, an oddly affectionate creature, was already covered in burrs. The hours before dawn and the hours after sunset look similar, if reversed. In a photograph, you might not be able to tell which was which, but standing in the field you always feel whether it's the beginning of the day or the end. She asked him once. She said, "Come with me, come back with me."

He hadn't answered, had he? He kissed her forehead, then went to pick the burrs off his wandering ewe. He isn't sure, he still isn't sure, if he's replaying that moment because he wants to know what would have happened if he had answered differently, if he had imagined his own life as separate from a collective future that never materialized anyway. What he means is, he's not sure if he regrets it, wants a chance to try again, or if he simply wants to return back to a time when all decisions were possible, were laid out before him like a feast, waiting for him to choose.

Salem Abu-Khdeir

Salem is not dreaming. No, he is not dreaming. Still, his body pulses with memories. Broken repository. His whole life lives inside a body lying on a hospital bed. What you might call his mind is not there. But his body remembers. His body holds every day of his short life. In the deep center of his right palm, for example, beneath the IV drip needled into the veiny bridge of his hand, is the feeling of the curve in the street just before his block, the curve that always told him, when he was a child walking home from the UN school, that he was almost there, almost home to his mother's bustle and scold. All the days of his childhood the feeling of rounding that curve accumulated inside him, stored itself in his right hand like water drips into a pool. Memory lives in the body, moves through the body, picks a place to house itself and stays there. At the base of Salem's throat—alongside the hospital tubes that now keep him (technically) alive—resides the thrill and wonder that rose up in him on the day a friend's father took the boys up to a rooftop and ripped away a tarp to reveal an enormous cage of electric green parakeets, gorgeous and shrill.

Right shoulder: He is three years old and Mama is shaking him and yelling in her hoarse voice, yelling at him for crying, to stop crying, because he's not a baby. Shaking and shaking. *Stop crying.*

Along his spine between his shoulder blades: The gentle crinkle of the small plastic bags, purple or yellow or black, that Mama carried home by the armful from the vegetable vendor.

Lower down on his spine: The safe and enclosed feeling of pretending to be asleep so Baba would carry him from the couch to his bed.

Tender crease of his left hip: He's maybe twelve and he's just stolen some Jewish bitch's phone right from her open purse on the Jerusalem tram; he's slipping out of the automatic doors as they close and she's realizing it—one second too late, just as the doors are closing, she realizes it and begins to yell and Salem turns back (the doors separate them now) to see the bitch's face, shocked and unbelieving and Salem thinking, *Yes.*

They got him in a parking lot when he was alone. He and a few of the guys from the camp liked to go to the Jewish mall. Walk around a bit. Look at the sneakers, the phones. Groups of nervous Jewish girls would look at them and walk faster. Swish, swish, go the jean skirts. Now and then, Salem or one of the guys might make a little hissing noise to watch the Jews scurry, but mostly they just looked at stuff and then bought chips. The Jews who jumped Salem got right into it. "What are you doing here?" "What do you mean what am I doing here?" A shove, another shove. There were two of them. Settlers his age or maybe a little older, all dressed in hiking boots and sweatshirts. A police car cruised by without stopping. Salem figured he'd get a few hits in before it got broken up. Then there were four of them, six of them.

In Salem's gut, beneath his navel, there is a tangled contradiction: repulsion and attraction, knotted into each other. Times when he felt one or the other, times when he felt both, or felt one disguised as the other—it came from his gut, and then it lived on in his gut. So much has been lost; so much survives. When the mob kicked Salem's stomach, he threw up chips, then later, blood. But inside his body is another body, the body that remembers, and in this body it is the day that Salem went to the sea.

It had been a hot day, too hot, with swampy air. "This is it?" Salem thought. This was Tel Aviv? Low buildings, dirty streets, whores at bus stops. It wasn't his first time coming in on the shared van, but it was his first time since he started middle school. Baba needed to pick up cash from someone, some job he'd worked where the pay had been delayed. Salem and his brother tagged along, all the way from Jerusalem to Tel Aviv—"This is it?"—then south to Jaffa, all with the promise of the beach after.

The three of them walked the streets of Jaffa, Baba on his old cell phone, confirming side streets. Salem's family had never lived in Jaffa—before the Zionist disaster, his great-grandparents had lived in an inland valley—but it felt like he could have been from Jaffa. The villas were almost familiar, reminded him of the rich neighborhood uphill from the camp. Almost familiar. They could not see the sea, not yet, but the streets were filled with tourists wearing shorts, carrying towels. He saw boys his age on bikes—Palestinians with full Israeli citizenship—yelling to each other in a garbled mix of Arabic and Hebrew. Familiar but not familiar at all.

That day, after Baba got the cash, the three of them walked up the boardwalk, north past the port where men fixed fishing nets and tourists ate fried seafood from paper cones, north until they reached steps that took them down to a beach, a small beach, not with umbrellas and lifeguard stands, but just a sandy place you could descend to. They had less time than they'd thought they would have—in a day of buses, each one takes slightly longer than you expect, and the end result is no time at all. But still, they descended down the stairs from an overlook surrounded by people taking photos and a man with puppets performing for change. That was not the first day he saw the sea, and it would not be the last, but it's the time he remembers best because it was the first time he felt he understood what he was seeing: a fucked-up version of history that happened to be true. He looked up the coast to the skyscrapers of Tel Aviv, he looked behind him to the familiar white buildings of Jaffa, and understood that he was in an inverted world where the Jews lived in the grand villas of murdered Palestinians and Salem lived in a camp that was walled off and forgotten by everyone, even their own government, who Baba said were as bad as the Jews and not to repeat that.

Young as Salem's brother was that day, he acted even younger, running toward the water then running away. He wouldn't have done it in front of anyone from home, Salem knew, but they were far away from home. Salem found himself kicking rocks. On the beach, a settler couple pushed a baby stroller in the sand. The husband was not carrying a handgun. Elsewhere, a man was photographing another man with blue hair holding a violin. Gays? Salem kicked a rock. He felt a surge of annoyance, rage. Up north, farther north than they would go that day, he could see the glittering towers of Tel Aviv—the Tel Aviv that people talk about. Blue glass, green glass, balconies. Already, Baba was mounting the steps to go back, to go home. Salem's brother shouted at him, "Baba is leaving," then to Baba, "Baba, wait!" Salem kicked a rock. Seeing that Salem was coming, his brother, scrawny kid, ran after their father, who was already halfway up the stairs to the street. Salem paused. He turned to the sea. He bent down and picked up a stone, a perfectly smooth gray stone that he truly expected to throw as hard as he could into the water. But he didn't. He lingered one more moment on shore, looking out at all the blues of the sea, all the nameless shades of blue churning. His thumb moved over the rock. Now there is nobody on earth who knows how Salem did not throw the stone into the sea, but slipped it into a pocket. He took the small stone home and then almost immediately lost it, of course he did. But he remembers the pull in his gut. Or, better to say, his gut remembers how Salem was pulled between the sea and his father, between disgust and fascination for the glittering Jewish city.

When the beating started, Salem fought back. The news reports don't mention this. They talk about him like he was helpless, but he did fight back, and he made good contact: someone in the face, someone else right in the solar plexus. But after one of the Jews kicked Salem in the nuts, he went down and it got bad. At first the kicks sent something horrible through his whole body, waves of hell. He threw up. They didn't stop. He tried to crawl away. He fell back down in his own vomit. Someone kicked him in the face. He was blacking in and out when his nose broke. Snotty blood down the front of him. When the heavy dark washed over him—a dark that has not lifted even in this hospital room, where Mama holds his hand and cries while a machine goes beep-beep-beep—when it washed over him he was, for one perfect breath, back at the sea, his brother calling after him and Salem half turning, saying, "Hold on, I'll be right there, hold on," the stone unthrown in his pocket, waiting.

SPRING

Augusta Victoria

Vera is hungover in Bethlehem. Any day now, Salem Abu-Khdeir is going to die. The article Vera successfully pitched to *Der Spiegel* promises an intimate account of nationalism and violence, hence this interview with a Palestinian professor at Bethlehem University. Professor Farha—"Call me Samar, please"—is a carefully dressed middle-aged woman. Dress slacks, no hijab. They sit at the professor's desk, which Vera will describe, when the time comes, as buckling under the weight of stacks of papers and books in English, Arabic, German, and French. Her article will not mention that Samar shares her on-campus office with two other instructors, also women, lest it undermine Samar's credibility.

Using each of her fingers in succession, Vera pushes at a torn cuticle on her thumb. So far, she has not gotten the intense, powerful quotes she had hoped for from the professor. "Let me ask you directly," she says. "What do you think will happen when he dies?" Salem has contracted some kind of infection in his breathing tube. He will not emerge from the coma the Jewish mob beat him into.

Samar tugs self-consciously at her dark blue patterned blouse. "As you know," she says, "most likely, if Salem dies, the Israeli army will kidnap his corpse." The woman's German is superb—an effortless Berliner's Hochdeutsch that Vera herself is careful to use, lest she sound like the Swiss milkmaid her classmates used to joke that she was. Outside the office window, pale leaves shimmer in clear light. Spring in Bethlehem, nearly Easter.

Vera fights an urge to check her phone for messages from Amir. She's on airplane mode, not so much to prevent him from reaching her, but so she'll stop hoping that he might. His chat icon is a newspaper photo of him moments after scoring a goal, on his knees, back to the camera, tattooed arms open to the futbal stadium. The icon tells her he's online, that he's seen her messages and is ignoring them.

Samar continues, "That is why you are writing this article, yes? On the assumption that the army will come for his corpse?"

Rather than indulge Samar's rhetorical question—obviously that's why Vera is writing this article, obviously *Der Spiegel* finally accepted her pitch because the boy is going to die and someone must write a grievous, enraged account, and obviously she saw her chance and took it—Vera pushes on. "Why would the Israeli army steal a young man's corpse?" Sometimes, conducting interviews, she feels guilty, as if the interview were an inherently violent, combative practice. And yet, she needs quotes from this Palestinian woman: powerful quotes, ones that will bolster her own ideas about what the violence done to Salem means.

Samar echoes the question. "Why?" She looks tired. Her hair is dyed black. Vera wonders how old she is. Early forties? Everyone knows that the army steals corpses to prevent martyrs' funerals from becoming protests, but that's not what Samar says. "All nations sustain themselves on violence."

That's not bad. Vera writes that down. *All nations sustain themselves on violence.* Does that sound too academic? Her editor at *Der Spiegel* is worried about the article feeling too academic. "When people are killed here, it's like their bodies belong to an ideology," Vera said to him on the phone recently. Think of it: nearly Easter. Christ is about to be executed in accordance with the scriptures. Holy Week. In the story, he is at a Passover seder—the last supper of his life—holding up the ceremonial matzah to say, *Take, this is my body.* On Friday, Christ will die. The son of God, a corpse. And it will be this body— the body nailed up and dying in public, the body carried limp and torn down from the cross, bloodied in its burial shroud—this is the body, behold, this is the body that will inflict millennia of believers with a madness to kill and die. Teenagers are dying, and it is Easter in Jerusalem. At this point, her editor had cut her off. "Fine, fine, fine," he said. "Just don't get too theoretical." She's never met the editor in person. She pictures a neatly dressed man in his thirties— that mystical age of fruition—who wears wire-rimmed glasses.

Vera wonders if she should give up on the professor and pack up. After all, she needs to get to Augusta Victoria Hospital soon in case it happens today. Perhaps the interview was doomed. Samar seemed disappointed right from the start, as Vera used her phone to take photographs for the story and video for the online version. "I thought there might be a photographer," Samar said, tugging at her blouse. All downhill from there.

But just as Vera is about to ask Samar if she'd like to make any final remarks, there is a knock on the office door. Two students, girls in hijabs—one in pink, one in white—lean their heads into the doorway.

"Excuse me," Samar says to Vera in German, then louder, in Arabic, "*Tfaddalen, yaa banat.*"

The girls step into the room. "Professor," the one in the white hijab says in Arabic, "are you busy?" Vera worries that she always sees a woman's hijab as her defining feature. She tries to notice another detail. The girl is very thin.

The one in the pink hijab says, "Oh!" when she sees Vera. "Excuse us," she says in English.

Samar does not seem upset. "Hello, girls." She smiles, speaks warmly. "I am in an interview." She introduces them in English.

"These are two of my favorite students." Noor, skinny in the white hijab; Mai, pretty in the pink.

"I'm interviewing your professor for *Der Spiegel*," Vera says in English. "May I"—she glances at Samar, who nods—"may I ask if you have heard of Salem Abu-Khdeir?"

"Of course," Noor, the thin girl, says, almost derisively, so stupid the question must sound to her. Who hasn't heard of the boy? For months now he has lain in a coma, kicked into a vegetative state by a settler mob. "Mai lives not far from the beating."

"In East Jerusalem? In Shuafat camp?" Vera asks, surprised. It's a rough place, and the girl in pink has a real princess vibe in an expensive-looking floral blouse buttoned all the way to the top.

"Not in the camp," Mai says, touching her sternum elegantly, "in a villa." Then she says something in Arabic to Samar, too fast for Vera to follow.

Samar translates: "Mai says it's no surprise that the Israelis did that to Salem, only surprising that anyone cares."

Once the girls leave, making arrangements to review their essays with Professor Farha in half an hour, Samar and Vera continue the interview. The professor speaks with an increased intensity, which Vera isn't sure how to account for. Perhaps the presence of her students reminded her that she, not just Vera, has something to gain from the article—a certain acclaim. "The Israelis say that we are a 'culture of death,'" she says. Here, Vera makes a note to herself: "Embed footage of Hamas martyr's funeral." (Her editor pushes for this type of "multimodality" for online versions.) They are afraid, Samar continues, of Palestinian pain, Palestinian grief. The Israelis are haunted by the current of despair that accompanies a young man's body through the streets of his village or refugee camp, lifted high and wrapped in a flag, the energy that unfurls into rallies and protests. It terrifies them to the point that they have begun stealing the bodies of the Palestinian dead. You'll get special forces in a hospital—nurses cowering with trays of pudding, unarmed doctors with clipboards standing bravely, uselessly in the doorways of their dead patients. The Israelis come in and they take the bodies. "Who has the culture of death," Samar asks, "if they are the ones stealing corpses?" Then she says—and this is the part that Vera underlines twice in her notebook, with two stars in the margins and the recording's time stamp circled—she says, "And what do we have left? Not even the right to mourn." There it is. This is what she needs, what will probably become the headline. Here are the words that Vera came to extract: *Not even the right to mourn.*

On the bus back from Bethlehem to Jerusalem, Vera finally checks her phone, but her restraint was for nothing. Amir has not responded to the single text she sent from Bethlehem: a poster of a martyr with the caption *Hi from the territories.* She used the Israeli word for Palestine, a shameless attempt to coerce a response from him, maybe a text saying, *Be careful,* along with a few knife emojis in reference to the recent stabbings. But no, nothing.

Amir Oved. Jewish and Jerusalem-born, and yet, not exactly *not* Arab, although he'd freak out if she said that to him. His grandparents fled Iraq. Now here he is, the tattooed and coddled son. What a joke: Vera obsessed with an actual pro futballer.

Over the course of these humiliating months, their sex has developed a deep, ecstatic rhythm. His fingers in her mouth, his slow, agonizing thrusts opening her. Never two nights in a row. Always three days apart, or four, or a week, or once, when she called him too many times and he seemed annoyed, ten miserable days. But when he is inside her again, the wound repairs and deepens, repairs and deepens in the same gesture.

She hardly notices when the bus stops at the checkpoint before the tunnels. There is no need for someone like Vera—white, German passport—to get off the bus, but the Palestinians file down and line up outside to have their identification checked. Vera remains seated, merely holds up her passport open to the visa page with her left hand; with her right hand, she keeps scrolling through her social feeds. People who aren't her have birthdays, stories not written by her are being shared by other journalists. *Here's my take on the most recent stabbing. Here's my take on Hamas beheadings. Here's my take on the finances of the Occupation.*

Two Israeli soldiers board the bus, one of them joking in Arabic to the driver. Sometimes they are friendly; other times, they play tough and bark at tourists for their visas. You never know what you're going to get.

It has only taken a few months for this ethnic sorting to become familiar. At first, it shocked her. When she landed in Israel from Berlin, she went to passport control with her visa and a letter from the editor at the in-flight magazine confirming she wrote for them. A woman, no older than Vera, in a tight bun behind a high desk in customs shuffled through the file. "You Jewish?" the agent asked in English. Vera heard herself gasp. Such a question seemed to emerge from the nightmare of history, a question from Vera's own history, or the one she inherited, haunting her now in the mouth of a woman, a girl her own age. "I am not Jewish," Vera said. Then after a pause, scrambling to say something neutral, "You have a beautiful country." The agent didn't respond to this.

Now Vera looks up when the soldier reaches her seat. The one who seems to be in charge leans forward to inspect her passport photo, matching it to her face. He is a pale teenager with prominent ears. The soldier behind him in a bulletproof vest is black, Ethiopian Jewish, presumably. Vera flashes a tight, brief smile, and the soldier continues down the bus aisle.

After she puts away her passport, she scans a disgustingly popular article about love and violence by a Jewish American journalist named Sara. Vera actually met this woman last fall at a film screening, introduced by a mutual Israeli friend. "It's cool you two meet. You're similar." Vera and Sara, Sara and Vera. The occasion was a documentary screening—a series of frenetic jump cuts in which the director, a woman, re-created her mother's madness. In the lobby of the Tel Aviv Cinematheque, Vera and Sara had circled each other, throwing out attentive-seeming questions, each growing infuriated as the other willfully misunderstood perfectly clear responses. Or was that just Vera?

"Why you didn't get off the bus?" The soldier is yelling at someone closer to the back of the bus.

Vera and the others crane back. She can't make out the person being yelled at.

"Why you didn't get off?" the soldier yells again, for some reason in English. Then, "*Btehki arabi?*" You speak Arabic?

The response is mumbled.

"Yalla, get down, get off," the soldier says.

Vera goes back to her phone. Since meeting Sara, Vera has undertaken an obsessive binge of the American journalist's oeuvre. Sara writes frequently about her sons, currently in Israeli elementary school, in a way that's unsettling but, fuck, so effective. Sara doesn't so much toe a line as maintain a contradiction, in which she's a liberal who bemoans the loss of any human life, and yet also a Zionist willing to make the sacrifices that a Jewish state requires. This maudlin gunk generates tens of thousands of retweets and shares. Vera's editors constantly remind her that this kind of "engagement" really does matter. In one article, Sara wrote about summer camp, how she was a camp counselor in Vermont the summer before she went to college, but how her young Israeli sons, when they come of age, will be in basic training not long after they turn eighteen. *I don't believe in weapons*, she wrote, *but my sons will sleep with M16s under their twin beds.* Sara closed that article by saying she wasn't sure she was a believer, *but like every mother whose sons are fighting, I will pray.* The image this sentence conjured for Vera was Sara as a giantess, looming in a ragged toga, gobbling up her blood-pulped children as in the walls painted by Goya in his blindness.

Finally the two soldiers leave. As the bus pulls back onto the highway, Vera is aware of her hangover pulsing down from her temples into her empty stomach. She briefly considers going back to Tel Aviv. Just an hour by bus from Jerusalem to get back to her mattress on the floor, her clean white sheets, her dried lavender in an old beer bottle. But she worries that if she returns to her apartment, she'll activate some greater irony, and Salem Abu-Khdeir will die without her there to witness it. She's gotten superstitious, as if she and not Amir were the professional athlete.

All day, she has been waiting for him to respond to her texts with the one text she hopes to see: *Come over.* He had physio today, and sometimes he likes to nap after. She hates that she knows his schedule, can recite the days he's got futbal practice in the mornings, his game days, his off days. His hours are etched into her own, but the reverse is not true. He'll go for days without responding to her messages. Each time, she promises herself that she'll ignore him when he stops ignoring her. But when he finally does send her some indifferent sentence fragment, she replies right away. If she could only ignore him long enough to make him feel something.

By the time Vera gets off to East Jerusalem, it's late afternoon. When she pushes through the grand wooden doors of the hospital, she recognizes Sara immediately. *This bitch.* These are the first words she thinks—in English, oddly—when she sees the American journalist and peddler of emotional porn in the marble lobby. Wide-hipped with her hair in a wispy braid, Sara sits on a wooden bench, typing something into her cell phone. It's obvious that both women are here to write about Salem. Fuck.

Sara catches sight of Vera and stands to greet her—flowing over in some flattering, expensive-looking caftan in a neutral color that disguises her body. Vera is aware of her own cheap harem pants, bought for a few shekels in Tel Aviv's central bus station.

"Vera, right?" Sara says as she approaches. Men would shake hands, but the two women merely stand in front of each other, close enough to throw a punch, or to hug.

Vera nods. "Sara?" she confirms tentatively, as if she hasn't read everything Sara has ever published, repeating especially indulgent sentences aloud to herself in a voice brimming with gleeful disdain. She picks awkwardly at a torn cuticle.

Sara nods then gets right into it. "Any idea when the director is coming out?" she asks. She breathes heavily through meaty nostrils. On the intercom, a doctor is paged. Vera doesn't catch the name.

And of course Vera has no plans to meet with anyone. She didn't think—what an amateur!—to reach out to the hospital director, but she says, "Soon, I think."

"I hope so," Sara says. "We need an update." Her hair is in a long braid that falls over her right shoulder, gray hairs peeking out from her part. It's girlish in a way that is entirely unerotic on a woman who is at least forty.

What's more repulsive than a woman who doesn't act her age? When Vera was maybe twelve—this is among her least favorite memories—she watched her mother try to sit on her father's lap. Almost fifteen years ago. She remembers Mother talking in a baby voice, but can't remember what she said as she flung herself into Father's lap, maybe something about Santa—all this in front of Vera—before he gently pushed her off, saying something along the lines of, "Come on now, dear, that's enough." What Vera remembers clearly is his reaction before he spoke: his thin face contorting in disgust.

"Well," Sara says, "nothing to do but wait." She returns to the wooden bench where she was sitting before, and Vera hesitates uncertainly until Sara gestures for her to join. They sit together. Afternoon's fast-draining light spills across the clean marble floor. A tall, lean doctor clips by, speaking hurriedly to a nurse trailing behind him. Sara and Vera follow him with their eyes. They are the only white women in the room. The women behind the administrative desks wear hijabs.

The waiting room has all but cleared out; the light has faded. The receptionists are shutting off their desk lamps when Sara exclaims, "Shit!" She is reading something off her phone. Then, presumably in some sort of gesture to Vera, says, "Scheisse."

"What?" Vera asks, seeing no alerts on her own phone. Could Salem have died already?

"Did Kareem just blow you off, too?" Sara asks.

"Who's Kareem?" Vera responds, picking up on it too late and hating herself. She presses at the tender crease on her thumb, the little patch of living skin revealed by all her picking.

"Oh, the hospital director." Sara eyes Vera appraisingly. "He texted, *No improvement. Talk tomorrow.* That's it."

It's early enough that Amir might text yet. "Beer?" Vera asks tentatively. The hospital is famous, Vera knows, for a small café run by German church volunteers. Actually, she's avoided it for that reason—too close to home, too much to get away from. And yet.

"They'll have wine, right?" Sara asks, tucking her phone into her shoulder bag—an orientalist affair with tassels and beads. She explains she's keeping kosher for Passover, meaning no bread, no beer, no grains but that unleavened matzah-bread.

Vera nods. She knows about the holiday from Amir. "They'll have wine," she confirms, not knowing but assuming. A bottle of house red that's been open for a few weeks, rancid and warm.

They exit the grand hospital building, through the lobby, down the white steps into the vestibule and out the double doors. The grounds are quiet as the sun continues to sink. You could run to the café in less than a minute, across the wood-chipped path, but they walk slowly, turning around to see the hospital, the incongruous bell tower, white and looming. Neither woman speaks.

Vera wonders what Sara will write about the hospital itself. Augusta Victoria—such a dramatic setting for this inevitable tragedy. Have they both noted the stately white bell tower, so European and misplaced? Who will work in the detail of the preposterous bell, installed by the hospital's founder, Her Imperial Majesty Augusta Victoria, the last German empress? Who will linger for a moment on the early, rosy days of the twentieth century, before all its teeth were ripped out? Did they both scribble notes as they wandered the sequestered hospital campus, dry pine needles crunching under their feet, noting the picnic tables filled with Palestinian parents eating packed lunches? Surely, Vera hopes, Sara had no need to mention the banner draped above the entrance: EASTER BLESSINGS FROM OUR FAMILY TO YOURS, written in German, English, and Arabic. No Hebrew.

Vera enters the café behind Sara. The music playing from the speakers swells with heartfelt guitar chords. The only person in there is a pimply teenager hand-washing glasses—"A Lutheran!" confides Sara. Vera takes a bottle of Palestinian beer—brewed clandestinely in a Christian village—from a fridge filled with Evian and Fanta, no Israeli brands. Sara orders her glass of wine at the bar.

Vera picks at her cuticles. "So what's your . . ." She hesitates here. She knows the word in English. Not *approach*, but kind of a synonym in this context. "What's your angle?" That's it: *angle*.

"Well, my work probes the emotional reality," Sara says, taking a small, reluctant sip of her wine. The damp wooden table where they sit wobbles.

"The reality of whom?" Vera asks, intending the question to be harsh—a critique on Sara's trite navel-gazing.

"Sorry, I don't quite understand." There is no apparent edge in Sara's voice. "What do you mean, 'the reality of whom'?"

Vera feels a wave of embarrassment. She thinks of her English as perfect. "I mean, whose reality do you probe?" She takes a long pull of her beer. Bitter bubbles.

Vera wants to tell this woman that she speaks three languages. She wants to say it in German and watch Sara's stupid face contort in confusion. Mostly, she wants another beer, but feels weird fetching one in front of Sara, who has barely touched her wine.

"Give me a second?" Sara says. "I'm going to find the bathroom."

As soon as Sara has disappeared, Vera gets up to grab another beer from the fridge. She begs herself not to check her phone, then checks it anyway to find, of course, no messages from Amir. She begs herself not to text him again, but she does that, too.

When Sara comes back from the toilet, she's wiping her hands dry on her caftan. The way Sara's eyes shift to the bottle, it's clear she's noting Vera's new beer but deciding not to say anything. Vera flicks the dry tail of her thumb cuticle; Sara picks right back up, talking about her *angle*. "I'm focusing on the mothers," she says, touching the stem of her wineglass.

"Which mothers?" Does Salem have more than one mother?

"I'm starting with Yael's mother."

It takes Vera a beat to place the name. "Yael is the settler who was murdered?"

"She was fourteen," Sara says. Now her voice is not without an edge. "Like Salem."

Already, Vera can anticipate that Sara is going to write about cycles of pain and revenge. She will focus on these two mothers; she will make their lives symmetrical, and in that way, she will avoid the complication of acknowledging the disparities in power that define their respective lives.

"I'll work in the mothers of Passover," Sara continues. "It's a story filled with lost sons, after all."

Vera can also anticipate that Sara's article will be almost unbearably poignant—dripping with meaning. Politics simplified into feelings. Passover. Dead children. Spots of red wine on a white plate, blood of the firstborn son.

Vera wonders if Sara knows how lucky she is to have sons. What an atrocity it is to have a daughter. It was not long after Vera's father pushed Mother off his knee that Vera made a show of sitting in his lap while her parents sat reading in silence on the couch. "You're too old for this," he cried out, but he was joyous, overflowing. Vera's delightfulness told him something he wanted to know about himself.

"Anyway, what about you?" Sara asks.

"My angle?" Vera clarifies, unnecessarily.

"Yeah."

"Bodies," Vera says. "The symbolism of bodies. It feels like the right fit for my readers."

Sara doesn't ask who those readers are, which annoys Vera because *Der Spiegel* still carries weight and actually pays pretty well, almost as well as the in-flight magazines she spends long days writing for each week: fluffy, adjective-heavy write-ups of restaurants, yoga retreats, all of it—this is Vera's stipulation—without a byline. But Sara asks, "Were you all day at the hospital?"

"No," Vera says, "I was in the West Bank most of the day, in Bethlehem."

"Oh?" Sara hasn't drunk more than half a glass of her wine.

"Yeah," Vera says, "I interviewed a professor at Bethlehem University. She writes about nationalism and violence." What she doesn't mention is that she found Samar by searching *nationalism violence Israel Palestine* on Google Scholar, then clicking around until she found someone who had published in German.

"Oh, wow, academic," Sara says, which makes Vera cringe, thinking of her editor.

Vera begins, "I'm not saying that Salem's body is like the body of Jesus, but . . ." She stops herself. Sara is not looking at her, she's texting something on her phone. Vera suddenly feels embarrassed, or maybe exposed, like she's too sincere, like she's the only one who is letting this kill her. "Who are you writing for?" she asks abruptly. She has to know.

"The *Times*," Sara says. "The *New York Times*."

Well, fuck. It makes it worse to know that Sara can't read the German article Vera will write. Even if they do translate it for the English site, Sara still probably won't read it. Neither will Amir.

Sara's thumbs hover over her screen a moment, then she starts texting, mouth vibrating in a private little smile. There's only one reason for that expression: a woman knowing that a man wants her. Does Vera look like that when she's reading a message from Amir?

Imagine this: it's Amir that Sara is texting with, Amir sending Sara a photo of himself standing in his bathroom mirror, cock in his hand. Revenge of the mothers.

Vera wants another beer, doesn't feel these two—three?—as much as she would like, but has to be careful about overspending the story advance. Who still gives a story advance? A luxury. But she wants more. She wants to feel good, or maybe just not shitty. She wants a lot of things. She wants to be valued, to be read. She wants to touch people, touch everyone, but can't quite bring herself to admit it. Is this what holds Vera back from being a real writer? That she writes not to seek after the truth, but to be loved, or at least admired? She wants all of her ex-lovers, all the men who let her go, to read her work—never mind that Amir doesn't know German and may well be illiterate—to read her and in that way, to know her, to really know her, from an inside that even in sex she couldn't communicate.

She can't bite down close enough to get rid of the last bit of cuticle skin, so she takes a risk and rips the cuticle off her thumb. Immediately there is blood—a vibrant moat filling the space between her thumb and nail. Under cover of the table, she presses her thumb into a damp napkin, hopes that Sara doesn't notice.

"Well, your angle," Sara says leaning forward, putting her phone screen-down on the table, "about bodies and how they are, maybe, exploited? It sounds very brave."

And maybe it's the flush of goodwill that beer cracks open from her heart, or maybe it's the way Sara's face seems old and unfuckable and tender, but Vera wants to be known by this woman, to say something sincere rather than always thinking one thing and saying another. Vera says, "Nothing here means what I think it means, yeah?"

"I think I know what you mean, but what do you mean?" Sara says.

"Like, the first time you went to a refugee camp, didn't it seem misnamed, somehow?"

"I've never been."

"What do you mean?"

"Well, I took Israeli citizenship, so—"

"But Shuafat camp is around the corner from this hospital," Vera says. "It's between us and the university."

Sara nods, like she's interested.

"His camp, Salem's camp, the dying boy's camp," Vera says, unable to stop her voice from raising. "Sara, it's inside Jerusalem. It's right here." She gestures vaguely behind herself.

Sara presses her lips together.

"You really haven't been?" Vera is almost pleading.

"Like I said, I focus on motherhood," Sara says, her mouth hard.

You can live inside a place and refuse to see it; you can live inside a marriage like that, too. Her parents tell themselves a story about themselves. Whatever doesn't fit, they ignore.

"What I was going to say," Vera takes a breath, "is that a Palestinian refugee camp isn't what you picture." She is trying to push forward, not to lose faith and give up on this entirely. "UN canvas tents, bags of rice, yeah? But it's not. Imagine the southernmost slum in any Mediterranean city."

"A crumbling maze?" Sara asks, leaning forward.

Who let this dumb cunt write anything other than YA novels? Vera truly wants to know. "Yeah, exactly, a crumbling maze." Already, she has lost the stamina to try and explain what it's like being in a room filled with young men, lean powerful bodies, telling her a story and watching her, watching the way her body moves, deciding which kind of woman she is; there are exactly two. How part of you is listening and the other part has separated, aware of the knife on the dish, put out by some young Palestinian wife when she came in with the juice and fruit. Don't narrativize the facts, but establish them, keep them handy. The father comes down now, shows you where the Jews came in, the soldiers. You move from room to room together, him having you picture the screaming women, the breaking lamps. The young men all follow behind like a chorus, watching. Where are the women? Invisible. Stop at the bedroom, when he enters the bedroom, stop at the threshold. Keep taking notes, look up, look down, but do not enter the bedroom with the man. Don't let those facts—your body, the bed—be correlated. Stand on the threshold, while he stands by the twin bed, and tells you about his three sons in zip ties, led off into the harsh lights of the IDF jeeps, led to a room where the Shin Bet guys were waiting. One son came back with his jaw broken. He is not even in high school yet.

To Sara, Vera says only, "They are weird places, is all." She picks at an imaginary table splinter. She checks her phone to find that Amir hasn't responded to her most recent text, the one promising that she was *a little tipsy*, and all that entails. Remember this, she begs herself, please remember this: the acid shame of someone not wanting you. Remember. But even as she begs herself, she is forgetting, she can feel herself forget, feel it slip away. She can see that Sara might be making moves to go, slipping a notebook into her bag, probably texting her husband that she'll be home soon. If she leaves, Vera has to leave. How else would she get a ride down the hill at this hour, down to the corner where the shared taxis huddle, shuttling people to and from Tel Aviv.

Sara scoots her chair back. "What time will you get here tomorrow?" she asks. The pimply teenager comes over to clear Vera's bottles and Sara's wineglass, still half-full.

"Early," Vera says. What to do now? Back to Tel Aviv? Is there anyone in Jerusalem she could stay with? The only people she knows here have been her subjects—a trio of Israeli leftists who recently got out of military jail for refusing to serve in the West Bank, some PR contacts, and an Orthodox Jewish teenager named Rachel whom Vera interviewed for an article she never wrote about American Zionism—no one she could call a friend.

"Will you stay in Jerusalem tonight?" Sara asks.

The question is like an incantation that makes Vera's phone vibrate. If it's Amir, don't respond. Remember, she begs herself.

Amir: *Come over.*

Grief, joy, maybe even hope. "Yeah," Vera says, "I'm staying with a friend."

Sara gets up. Standing over Vera, she smells like rosemary. "Do you want a ride down the hill?"

They drive down from the hospital campus, through the shuttered shops of the village, down past the Mount of Olives, past the unforgiving settlement block there, past the Israeli flag the size of a dump truck, past the silent graves like teeth in the moonlight. Sara's car is something clean and white and compact, as Vera knew it would be. Near the dip before the gas station, their windows are lit up by an army jeep, the kind with metal grilling over its windshield to block the stones Palestinian boys throw. Vera knows what they see: two white women. Nobody stops them.

The first time they slept together, Amir asked her why she lived in Tel Aviv. She lay in bed as he dressed to leave. "Why not live in East Jerusalem?" he asked. "Why not live in Ramallah or Bethlehem?" If she was going to spend all her time writing about them (about *them*) anyway? At the time, watching him buckle his belt with his back to her, feeling bereft and empty already, yes, already desiring his little pig grunts on top of her again, she answered something convoluted about needing to experience life on both sides of the conflict. Bullshit, he said. Bullshit. "You're scared of Arabs." She had responded by saying something along the lines of, You're too beautiful to be such a bigot. But who knows. When she first got to the area (*the area*, so euphemistic), armed with a few assignments and a solid set of contacts, she had briefly lived in East Jerusalem—in a cheap apartment with high ceilings not far from the hospital. She hated it. She hated the pressurized scrutiny, the walk home looking straight ahead, straight ahead, because only a whore would turn to the toothy hisses made from darkened doorways, the men muttering next to her, walking alongside her, their eyes on fire. She hated the restrictions, the secreting of wine empties into black plastic bags discreetly left in public trash bins. She hated the shame her body brought. Maybe most of all, she hated that nobody had to teach her to think this way. It didn't matter that as a child, she had splashed naked in ponds and lakes, never questioning the tuft of her mom's pubic hair, the floppy dark below her father's navel. Despite how she was raised, some part of her knew, by instinct, how to fear her own body. As soon as she came to Jerusalem, she understood something she had always known, always felt, ever since she became—she hates this word, even today she hates this word, a word that is dripping and fleshy, a punctured word—ever since she became a *woman*.

Vera watches Sara, who has her own thoughts, keeping her eyes on the twisting road as she drives. All is quiet as they pass the high walls of the Old City, the dark loomings of the Lion's Gate, Herod's Gate, Damascus Gate, then up past the ancient fortified walls, cut deep with slits for archers. Vera loves these landmarks. She loves them because they replaced her childhood bedroom, the cold quiet of her parents' living room, the lonely slope of the playing field outside her elementary school. The longer she stays, the farther she feels from home.

The first time a boy called the house, Papa slammed the telephone back into the receiver. Not just once, again and again until the handset smashed, bits of black plastic on the kitchen floor. Mama watched from a doorway in fear but also, Vera saw, in a shuddering excitement—this was new. A new possibility was taking form. Whatever was missing between her parents, they could plug it up, stuff it with their daughter's body, Vera's body.

Once they reach the Jaffa Road intersection, the women have passed the invisible but undeniable border that separates East Jerusalem from West. Vera tells Sara where to pull over. The car idles under the glossy, unlikely complex of Mamilla Mall, so much like an airport but so close to the mess of things. Why would he choose to live here? It's a building of pied-à-terre duplexes, a glossy, empty palace where half the apartments sit vacant most of the year. A few months ago, she reviewed a decadent hotel nearby.

Vera unclicks her seat belt, turns to Sara to say, "Thanks." She opens the door. Warm nighttime air, filled with promise, and something else, something Vera can't name, swirls around them.

"Do you want me to text you tomorrow," Sara asks, "if I hear anything? In the morning, I mean?"

"Sure," Vera says over her shoulder. When she gets out of the car, she sees herself the way Sara might see her: a girl disappearing toward a dark room where a man is waiting for her.

Vera opens her eyes to a room filled with too much sunlight, heavy midmorning light that tells her it's no longer early. Shit. Her phone is vibrating. Shit. She gropes the sheets, her hands sliding around the inexcusable red silk material—no, silk*like* material, like something out of a lusty paperback for housewives. Next to her, the mass of Amir heaves, sinks heavily into the mattress. He groans and pulls a pillow over his head, revealing Vera's phone underneath. Please, she begs, don't let the message be from Sara. Don't let it be about the boy.

She unlocks the screen. Sara. Shit. *He's dying.* Shit, shit. Get up, you stupid slut, get out of bed. Amir rolls more tightly toward the wall, the muscles on his back and arms adjust, shifting those absurd tattooed gashes—or are they supposed to be thorns? Scratch marks? She wants to cling to him from behind. The more he turns away, the harder she wants to hold on. But no, she has to get up; she has to get to the hospital.

She stumbles into Amir's pristine bathroom, into the shower with its absurdly good water pressure, the small, high window overlooking the steeples of the Old City. How different from her damp, dim apartment in south Tel Aviv—drain clogged by long hair, dead cockroach Vera's roommate smashed on the kitchen floor, a trail of ants leading from the dead thing into the wall. She hurriedly scrubs herself with a bar of perfumed black soap. She hopes the scent, earthy and robust, expensive-seeming, is enough to overcome the smell of last night's drinking. After a few seconds in the hot water, of course she has to pee. She knows she should climb out of the shower to sit, dripping wet, on the toilet, but she doesn't, and all at once she's peeing in the shower, her hips jutted out into the hot water. Relief, immediate. The pee is bright yellow on the tastefully mismatched mosaic tiles of the shower. She thinks, You're dehydrated. She washes off the dried blood flaking from her thumbnail.

She dresses without toweling off, clean underwear from her backpack, the clothes damp on her. She pauses in the doorway of Amir's bedroom. She is late; she needs to rush down the stairs, to catch a cab to take her back to the hospital, but she stays inside this moment, watching his back, feeling and resisting the pull toward him. She thinks, This is what I'll remember—a gesture that excludes me, him facing the wall.

On her way out, she grabs a bottle of fancy water from the fridge, her hand almost slipping. It's clean and orderly in there: just rows and rows of bottled water, a few kosher-for-Passover hard ciders, and a stack of plastic food containers from, Vera just knows, his mother—a woman Vera will never meet.

She's out the door and down the clean staircase, adjusting her bag on her shoulders, squeezing past an elderly couple who coax a small dog down the stairs, out the door clutching her bag before realizing that, shit, shit, shit, she didn't brush her teeth. An acidic boozy smell is no doubt festering in her mouth, but what is there to do?

She runs. Her billowy pants and linen top cling to her damp body. She speeds past a café. A middle-aged tourist couple with coffees lean over an unfolded map. Is it? Yes, they are speaking about church service times in German, from the north, it sounds like. They look up at her as she passes. Once she hits Sultan Suleiman Road, she begins to swivel her head back as she runs, looking for a cab to hail.

She's confronted with the sudden, shocking memory of Amir's orgasm last night. How he sat up while she straddled him, riding him but also kind of cradled by him, his huge arms supporting her to intensify the motion of her moving up and down on him, him in and out of her, a rocking motion. When he came, he pressed his forehead into her shoulder, and she touched the back of his skull, the way you'd comfort a child. Amir is fastidious about using condoms, which she generally appreciates, but now, all at once, she feels empty, and she wishes he had come inside her and was dripping out.

A honk startles her into a stumble. A cab! The driver has slowed to trail behind her. The cars behind him honk. He pays no mind. The driver, bearded, manipulates prayer beads in his right hand as he leans across the seat to shout out the passenger-side window at Vera, "Where to?"

She hurries out of the taxi without bothering to wait for change. The grounds of Augusta Victoria Hospital are quiet: empty picnic tables under silent windows. Vera pushes the heavy, arched doors, her sandals squeaking on marble. She's panting. She slows to a walk. The second set of hospital doors are—somehow this is not surprising—locked. Something has changed. She stands in the clean, well-lit foyer under signs in Hebrew and Arabic and English. NO SMOKING. Enormous thirst grips the back of her throat. She finds the water bottle in her backpack, sucks down a third of it in deep, rhythmic gulps.

Shut up. Listen.

She forces herself to hold her breath so she can hear. Cries from out back. Behind the building? Possible. She doesn't want to run anymore, her whole body feels heavy. Still, she runs out of the hospital's entrance and toward the back of the building, into the sound that you might confuse with sirens. What it is, she realizes as she takes out her phone, ready to record, is not the sound of sirens but of women screaming.

It takes about thirty seconds to reach the back of the hospital, where there is a small paved lot for overflow trailers and, beyond that, an empty field buttressed by a cement wall. Vera looks up to the hospital's third floor—so that's where his room was—to see the women are leaning out the hospital window. Women in hijabs. No sign of Sara. The women have torsos out the window, are pointing toward the wall beyond the lot, where, Vera sees now, a scrum of young men are moving around something. There are no police here, not yet. She does not know what the young men are doing, down by the wall between the hospital and the Palestinian village on the hill.

She runs toward them, the screaming of the women growing distant, the shouts of the men growing louder. Past the empty office trailers, the lone olive tree in the dry lot. As Vera approaches the men, she sees they are pressed up against the wall, an unfinished cement thing with metal rebar protruding. A few of them are straddling it, the hospital wall, which is taller than any man, over two meters high.

The men on the ground surge up against the wall. Surely, they are not trying to escape, because if they were, the men straddling the wall would simply jump over. So, what? On the other side of the wall, men and women from the village on the hill lean out the windows of unpainted cement houses to watch, saying nothing. Steady, she tells herself. She needs to keep her phone steady as she films—needs this footage to be actually usable when she sends it to her editor to put up on the feed. The young men cry out, and behind Vera, from a hospital window, the screaming of the women emerges at a chilling pitch. She remembers learning how the Roman emperor Augustus prohibited the ululation of women, for fear it would bring back the dead. And maybe it's this very thought that allows her to hear, to really hear, the voice inside the screams, the single pitch repeating, *Ibni, ibni, ibni.* "My son, my son." Her son. The body. They are trying to hoist the boy's body over the wall. They need to smuggle the corpse away before the police come. This is the only way he will receive a timely burial.

The men cry out in one voice. Because she's using her phone to film, she can't take notes, so she mentally recites the observations she'll put into the article later. How many young men? She is trying to count. At least fifteen young men, yes, fifteen shabaab, maybe twenty.

A young man in a red T-shirt falls to his knees, his head in his hands, pulling back at his hair, his mouth opening grotesquely in a private grief.

The body is wrapped in what looks like sheets. White with a delicate floral pattern. Perhaps his mother brought them from home. You can't see the body itself, just the outline. Is there a body bag beneath that? Or do they not have those at hospitals? Vera doesn't know. But it seems like maybe not, because you can see the outline of his feet under the clingy fabric; you can see the place where his head is. She's never seen a corpse before. It's bleeding, or at least, it's bloody. A woman's son. *Ibni, ibni, ibni.*

The way you'd hold up a child to wade through flood water, that's how the shabaab hold up the boy's body, trying to will the thing toward the wall headfirst. The patterned sheet has a splotch of blood that is growing. They lift him up to the waiting hands of the two men straddling the wall—jeans and T-shirts—who try to take up the body but can't seem to hold on to it right. They lose their grip. It shudders, flops, would fall but for the men on the ground who catch it. It tugs a memory in Vera, a body moving like that.

One of the two men on the wall turn and yell down to the other side, so there must be people there too, waiting to receive the body.

Where are all the reporters? Usually in East Jerusalem, you have so much as a tire fire and there are five news outlets filming it. Here, Vera is alone. Sara must be back in the hospital, in the room where the mother is screaming out the window. She is sequestered there, making her own mental notes. Maybe watching Vera. Maybe livestreaming the whole thing. Does she see Vera stepping closer? She is so close that now, when the men farthest from the body fall back, they must sidestep to avoid bumping into her, which they do without looking at her, like she's a post or a tree. When someone bumps into her shoulder, she doesn't fall down, she withstands the impact. She is at the center of something—something horrible, something that matters. She thinks, to Sara she thinks, Watch me.

When the body bangs against the wall, the blood at the head grows. Red smears against the concrete. She didn't know a corpse would keep bleeding. On her phone, she switches from the camera to her own feed and starts a live-stream. This is too good to wait. She needs everyone to know that she is here. That she is at the center. She needs them to know that this is her story.

The men adjust their grips, struggling with the body. What is this weight that only the dead have? She can ask that question in her article. The situation is profound enough that she will be able to get a little literary with the prose. *Every part of us wants to return to the ground.* Yes. *Earth is calling us home.* She recalls something the professor said that will be perfect to use in this scene. We forget, the professor said. It is so easy to forget. We forget that they are, we are, all of us sacred. Each one of us. Never to be replaced, never ever.

Another man falls, maybe praying. Or has he been hurt? But no, he's kneeling. Now the boy in the red T-shirt stands on the kneeling man's back, one hand against the cement wall, to balance himself as he supports the body from underneath, acting as the critical intermediary stage between the men on the ground and the men straddling the wall, lifting the body up, up. Vera feels herself gasp as the bloody sheets lift over the wall, wail of sirens in the background now.

At some point, she stopped filming. Her phone is hanging by her side as the exposed, pale feet disappear over the wall, into the arms of someone waiting below, somebody none of us can see. This is my body, this is my body, this is my body.

And then he is gone.

In the absence the boy's body leaves, the sound of sirens is suddenly enormous, coming from all around them, other sounds too, cries of a woman, boom of a teargas canister. As Vera heads back toward the hospital, she quickly ends the live feed and uploads the recorded video to the cloud, then hides her phone in her bra, where, she hopes, it will be safe from a search. She does this by instinct, although she's never done it before.

The young men, cut loose from their mission, head back toward the action, prepared to get their noses broken, or worse, maybe today is the day; those who can't afford another arrest try to scramble over the wall to the village. Soon soldiers in body armor will come bursting out the hospital doors, too late for the body they sought, and charge into this dusty field, this place between places, this no-man's-land high above Jerusalem, high above the village, so high that you can see, in the distance, bare hilltops where the villages and settlements end and the desert takes over, the sweeping red hills of Judea, out of which men continue to stream, mad with love.

Sisters

Mai and Leila are sprawled out on the living room couch, just the two of them, with the TV on. Mama is upstairs napping. The boys are outside playing futbal with neighbors in the grasses between villas. It's nearly noon on a Friday. Mai and her brothers spent the morning cleaning—Mai directing the boys to push around the sudsy water on the balcony and in the kitchen, making sure it drained properly, making sure they swept up the bits of hair and trash around the drain (a job that makes them squeal like the little boys they are) while she herself scrubbed down the counters, bleached the sinks. The activity is familiar—weekly for the whole neighborhood, everyone splashing soapy water out of windows and doors, bubbles accumulating in the gutters as the muezzin sings them through Friday. Leila isn't having morning sickness anymore, but Mama went over anyway to help her clean her own home, and after, they both came back here. (Mai still finds it weird that when Leila says *my home* she no longer means home-home but Tariq's home.)

Now the sisters are lounging in matching pajamas—soft sweater-y gray sweatpants and tops. Leila leaves a pair here; even in her second trimester she can still fit into a lot of her old clothes.

"This woman is nuts," Mai says, eyes on the TV.

"I know," Leila says, hand on her belly in the standard pregnant lady pose, "it's amazing."

They're watching one of those fashion design reality shows where contestants create clothing with various restrictions. Some Indonesian girl with pink streaks in her hair is having a meltdown because she's run out of the fabric for her ball gown—a Scottish-looking tartan that Mai said reminded her of Alexander McQueen but Leila said that was a stretch. The Lebanese host is trying to calm her down.

Mai's head rests on a pillow in her sister's lap; the windows open to the first of the warm spring days. They can hear the boys, brothers and neighbors and cousins. "Goal!" someone yells.

"Should we get up?" Mai asks. They'd told Mama they'd take care of lunch.

"Five more minutes," Leila says.

Always it is this dynamic—Mai a little deferential to Leila, adjusting herself (without being asked) to the parameters that Leila establishes.

When Mai and Leila were young girls, Mai was Leila's little shadow. This was back before Baba spent so much time in the U.K. growing his business—when they were a family of four, without any little boys yet. Mai trailed everywhere after Leila, in the garden, through the house, into the room they shared. If Leila wore red, Mai had to wear red. If Leila ate a plum, Mai wanted one, too. Predictably, Leila spent most of her time avoiding her younger sister.

It might have been Baba going away that brought Mai and Leila closer. Now he's back once, maybe twice a year, returning enough that his residency status won't be revoked by the Israelis. The money he sends home pays for the upkeep of a villa older than the Zionist state, a remodeled kitchen straight out of *Bon Appétit*, the mosaic in the fountain out front, the garden out back. In his absence, theirs became a house of women, a gentle loneliness pervading each afternoon they spent brushing Mama's hair or picking up the boys from school when Mama felt overwhelmed or when she needed help with chores. If before the sisters had been like rival states, competing for the commodity of their parents' attention, now they were something else, almost like coparents to their mother and brothers, to each other, and there was something blissfully enchanted in it. Up until Leila got married last year, they were princesses tending to the castle. They were intimidating, Mai knew. Haughty sisters—impenetrable and discerning as they walked home from school together, trying on each other's rings and holding them up to the light.

Leila told Mai she was pregnant the day that settler died. It was night when it came on the news. The blood, the EMT crying. Mama made sure that their gates were locked, the front door bolted. All around Jerusalem, they knew, Jews were watching the news and deciding to make someone pay. Maybe they were already circling the neighborhood in cars with the windows rolled down. Maybe already spray-painting those four Hebrew letters on Palestinian homes: נקמה. *Nekama.* Revenge.

Leila wasn't home. Or, she was at home with her husband, so she texted Mai to check in. *Are the boys inside?*

Yes, Mai responded quickly. *Yes, we are safe.*

She isn't sure why Leila decided to tell her at that moment, but she did. *I'm pregnant.* Pause. *Six weeks.*

Mai's first question after the obligatory hearts and exclamation points: *Does Mama know?*

No, Leila wrote, *you're the first.* Although she meant the second, of course, after Tariq.

A few days later, Leila came over to tell Mama and, over Skype, Baba. By then, Salem Abu-Khdeir was in a coma. The Jews had found their victim. On Al Jazeera they kept showing a still from the security footage: the blurry image of Salem's body, the way they left it in the street. It was a Palestinian taxi driver who took him to Augusta Victoria Hospital. "Why not Hadassah Hospital?" the news anchor asked him.

The driver was older than Mai's father. "He was so light," he said instead of answering the question. He covered his eyes with a hand pressing into his brow bone. He tried to say something but choked on the words. The news anchor touched the man's shoulder gently.

Leila hopes she will have a girl.

The Indonesian contestant has made a frankly stunning comeback just in time for the final judging when Leila hits mute on the TV. "What's that?" she asks, straightening to attention. "Do you hear sirens?"

Mai sits up, reaches for her phone. "I'm not sure." She goes to the window that faces the nearest street. She hears them now, faint sirens. How did Leila hear that? "Maybe something is happening over in the camp?" She lets the curtain fall back and is about to sit back down when she hears the unmistakable boom of a teargas canister and, almost simultaneously, an alert to her phone.

Leila is already rushing toward the door of the house. "Muhammed," she yells from the threshold. "Muhammed! Farouq!"

Mai looks at her phone. "Salem Abu-Khdeir is dead," she says, "and they are coming for him." But when she looks up, Leila isn't at the door anymore.

Mai cries out for her sister, crossing the room and running down the front steps. Outside, the day is bright. Across the garden, she can hear her aunt calling to her cousins. "Come home," she shouts. "Come inside!" There are more sirens now, and the booms from teargas down the hill. There must be soldiers close by, although she can't smell the teargas in the air yet. "Leila!" Mai calls.

"I'm here," Leila yells, closing the gate behind her. She's coming up the driveway with the boys. Little Farouq, in khakis and a striped red shirt that Mai picked out because it makes him look Parisian, holds Leila's hand, but Muhammed keeps trying to free himself. He wants to go with the older boys, Mai knows, to see what is happening.

There's Mama in pajamas at the threshold of the house. "Yalla," she yells to them. "Get inside, get inside." Her hair is covered simply with a kerchief like an old mother-in-law.

Mai is the last one in. She closes the door.

They're all on the couch watching the news. None of them wants to cook, so Mama brought out bread and slices of cheese. They eat while they watch. Mama in the middle, Leila and Mai on either side, the boys lying on the floor with blankets. The news shows the scene from a distance. The shabaab down the hill at the hospital, trying to lift the body in the sheet over the hospital wall. "God rest his soul," Leila says. She's rubbing her belly in circular motions, as if she could protect the baby from the unfolding atrocity.

"Why are they doing this to him?" little Farouq asks, adjusting his glasses.

"The Jews want to steal his body," Muhammed answers quickly, "to degrade us." Sometimes he seems older than ten.

There are shots now. Hard to tell if it's from the TV or from somewhere outside. Muhammed runs to the window that faces the street. "Come back here," Mama says sharply, and he does, although he doesn't sit so much as lean against a couch armrest until Mama pulls him into her lap. He protests mildly—listlessly pushing her away with his lanky arms—but eventually settles into her lap.

Mai uses her knee to nudge little Farouq, who's seated in front of her on the floor. He absently elbows her back. Delicate bodies of their boys, their little men, so vulnerable with their bruised shins and dark, uncombed hair. She kisses the crown of his skull fiercely, never taking her eyes off her phone, which she finds gives better news than the TV. On her feeds, everyone is posting about it like crazy. Ever since she made the decision to study biochemistry at Bethlehem University—crossing the Tunnels Checkpoint every day to come home—she has found herself more connected to the news, more aware. Her closest friend at school was born in an actual refugee camp in Bethlehem. Noor. She has a brother in Mejiddo prison, and even though Mai doesn't ask about it, this fact animates their friendship—Mai can feel the knowledge of Noor's brother pulsing under the surface. It makes Mai feel that she is doing more to resist than anyone in her family—more than Baba, who is away earning money, more than Mama, who sleeps all day (sorry, but it's true), more than Leila, who would have been willing to study at the Jews' university. Mai does more and she is proud of this. Having a friend like Noor makes her proud.

Online, Noor has reshared cell phone footage from someone who is clearly at the hospital. What it shows: Salem being slammed into the wall again and again as the shabaab try to lift him—his corpse—over the wall of the hospital. All this so he can be buried like a human being. Mama leans over to look at Mai's cell phone. "God rest his soul," she gasps when she sees Salem's body in the sheet, the bloody sheet. A single pale foot dangling out. On the TV, the news anchor is repeating the same information that everyone knows—about Salem being beaten to death at the Pisgat Ze'ev mall, about how no Israelis were ever charged. They don't show the image of him in the hospital bed, his head swollen and bandaged, his mouth mangled. In the video Mai is playing on her cell phone, a boy in a red shirt turns to yell at someone behind him. He is holding up what looks like Salem's shoulder. "Brother, help me," he cries out. Then the video cuts.

"Let me see," Leila says, but Mai hates handing over her cell phone, so she copies the link for Leila.

"I sent it on WhatsApp," Mai says.

Leila watches the footage. "God rest his soul," she says, her hand still on her belly. Mai can hear the small, distant voice of the boy in the video: *Brother, help me*. Then her phone starts ringing. "It's Tariq," Leila says as she stands to take the call. "Allo," she says into the phone. "Yes, we're fine. All of us, yes. We're inside. Okay." Pause. "Are you sure?" Pause. Mai can't hear what Tariq is saying. "Please be careful. Yalla, bye."

"Everything is okay?" Mama asks.

"Tariq will come by," Leila says. "He'll take me home."

After Leila was married, Mai found herself trying to observe Leila without Leila noticing. She was looking for signs on her sister's body—the way she moved, the way she adjusted her hijab—signs that she was not a girl anymore. This is a stupid thought—such a stupid, super-weird thought she would never say aloud—but why can't Mai be the baby growing in Leila? Why does growing up mean pulling apart? Why can't it mean coming together, becoming closer and closer until they are entwined like a single braid woven from two girls' hair?

"Are you sure it's safe?" Mai asks. "Are you sure you don't want to stay over?"

Leila smiles, her hand still on her belly—does she ever take her hand off her belly? "I need to go home," she says.

Mejiddo

Hussein's lawyer will have to come back another day because the entire prison is on lockdown. When you hear the siren, you know what to do: on your knees, hands behind your head, as if you were being arrested all over again. He'd been waiting—lying on his bunk, reviewing questions he wanted to ask his lawyer—for one of the guards to escort him to the area with the phones—blue metal cubes with glass partitions, talking into a phone, the whole thing. You sit on white plastic chairs during your phone calls. When Hussein tries to imagine an Israeli home, what he imagines is the Jews all sitting around on those white, plastic, Keter-brand chairs—all of them in prison guard uniforms—eating hummus under a portrait of their wife-of-a-dog prime minister. But anyway, there would be no visit with his lawyer today.

He's hungry. He's hungry, and the cement floor is hard against his knees, but he doesn't get up. He can hear the echo of the gates opening and closing, the yelling of soldiers in Hebrew. They are maybe three cells away. It's not the regular guards—the chubby, listless brown Jews who are almost sincere in trying to make small talk, bringing up Israeli futbal teams like, "Shibi. You like Shibi?" As if any of them would ever watch an Israeli league, would watch some collaborator playing with the Jews—no, it's the soldiers in black with their faces covered. For all Hussein knows, the same guys who came to arrest him that night, that long night—Mama and Noor in the driveway screaming, trying to fight the soldiers off him. Noor is a brave girl, a good girl.

Without meaning to, he is imagining minced lamb and rice. Bowls of yogurt for dipping. Real food, food of his family. Mama and Noor, scolding the little ones who run in to steal a taste before they sit for the meal. Hunger. Does he have any of those crackers left? Maybe better to wait until the chaos has passed.

It's just him and Said in the room right now, almost everyone else out in the yard walking around, stretching their legs. Hussein stayed behind because he was waiting on the meeting with his lawyer, and Said was . . . who knows, whatever Said does. He naps a lot. When the siren began, Said climbed down from the bunk above Hussein and they both knelt on the floor. Now Said turns to Hussein, his hands still behind his head. "Any more of those crackers?" Said asks. Said is older. Everyone who bunks in this room is older than Hussein. It was, actually, kind of a fluke that put Hussein in this room, which should go, according to the hierarchy, to someone here for something substantial, someone who has been here for a long time, will probably die in here. Hussein should be out in the yard, in the overflow tents the Jews put up. That's where most of the teenagers are, kids even younger than Hussein—eighteen, fifteen, eleven—who are here for throwing stones at soldiers. Some of them learn to read here.

"One moment, uncle," Hussein says. "I will check." He is careful to speak respectfully to Said, to all the older men. Keeping his hands on his head, kneeling as if in prayer, he turns to his bunk and, yes, he's got a packet of crackers there. It's a Jewish cracker, their holiday of unleavened bread. All week, there is no real bread in the prison, just this burnt, bubbly cracker. It's oddly satisfying to eat. Hussein has heard of guys who buy it even when they get out. Said told him that the Jews eat it to celebrate their freedom. Hussein grabs the packet and hands it to him: "Tfaddal."

Said nods, takes the packet, still back on his heels, and eats some of the crackers. White crumbs on the gray sweater he wears over his brown jumpsuit. There is yelling from another cell. Closer now. Sometimes shots, but sometimes it's a metal door being beaten in, for reasons Hussein does not understand. Hussein has learned to keep breathing even when it's going crazy. Said eats his crackers. He's an unassuming guy, slight and dark. He stabbed that settler-girl in her bedroom. What was her name? It doesn't matter. The miracle was that Said made it there—past the settlement's security, all barbed-wired and motion-detected. A miracle the window was left open. In he went, carrying a kitchen knife. A miracle that he survived even though the Jews shot him, even if he'll be in prison forever.

Hussein has been here for five months and hasn't been charged with anything yet. At least, as far as he knows, and he won't get to see his lawyer today. She's a Jew, his lawyer. A Jewish woman with a huge, appealing mouth, tired eyes, and wild hair. Hussein has no idea who pays her. The guards call her a Communist.

The metal door flies open, and the Jews with their faces covered burst in. Said is still eating the crackers. *Matzah*, that may be what the Jews call it. Said looks unfazed, puts his hands back behind his head. He leaves a jagged piece of matzah half-eaten in his mouth. It dangles there while the Jews scream and grunt at one another. Hussein's knees are on fire, the floor so hard. They are pulling down books, they are looking under posters of Real Madrid, they are squeezing out a tube of toothpaste—Rami is going to be annoyed when he comes back—looking under mattresses. There are collaborators everywhere, informants everywhere. Who knows what information they are going on.

Hussein hasn't heard the long-term guys talking about what they did to get here, but he knows anyway. The knowledge kind of seeps into you. He knows Said stabbed that settler-girl the same way he knows that Rami drove the car into the bus stop. Killed two of them. He knows but isn't sure how he knows.

Sometimes, at night, Hussein will feel Said's dreams drip down from the upper bunk. He'll dream about the mess of it, of his body, of her body, the knife. For every good hit Said got in—for every time he stabbed her chest, her neck, her arms—he missed and skidded off her thin shoulders, her forehead. The knife was slick with her. A girl's room on a settlement. A bunk bed, but no one in the top bunk. Everything in the room pink and girlish.

He cut himself, stabbing her. Her blood, his blood. His hands. Stabbing the Jew, stabbing and stabbing the Jew. She was fourteen. It never seems like enough. No matter how much you stab, no matter how dead she is, her face a cavity of blood, her arms flung useless in front of her, no matter how much, she can't be dead enough.

None of this Said has told him, but Hussein has felt, has dreamt.

Knees slipping on the blood-slicked floor long after she has stopped screaming. By the time her parents made it into the room, the floor looked like a child's finger painting, all in red. Said doesn't remember much of the arrest and subsequent interrogation except that he lost a tooth and has not had full range of motion in his arms since because of what happened to his shoulder blades.

The Jews are out of the room after no more than twenty seconds. Everything tipped over, spilled. There will be so much to clean.

By the time Rami and the guys come back from the yard—"Haram, look at this mess"—Hussein has wiped up the toothpaste from the floor. There are eight of them crammed in this narrow room. He can't believe how well he has come to know the others: Said by his naps, Hashim by the way he farts in his sleep, Rami for his patience, which is not to be confused with softness. Hussein has watched him choke a guy out because he was suspected of stealing. The eight of them, all bumping into one another, pick up their torn-apart cell until it is time for Dhuhr. Rami is the one who leads them through the midday salah.

"Will they let us out?" Hashim asks, tucking in the corners of his bed. They have all learned to clean here, to cook here. They are their own wives.

The cell is barely big enough for all eight of them to stand by their bunks, never mind to carry out the prayers. And anyway, this room is filled with images: posters, photos. Instead they go out into the hallway.

"*Hakol beseder*," Rami says in Hebrew. It's fine.

The cell door is indeed open, and they shuffle out into the hallway, arranging the flattened produce boxes on the ground in lieu of actual prayer mats. Hussein is proud to be in the Hamas block, how good it feels to stand together in proud rows behind Rami, eyes closed, setting their intentions on prayer. How good it feels to move together, to lean forward with flattened backs, to fall to their knees, to sit back on their heels. He is proud to be Hamas. Fastidious in prayer. He has seen how some of the other factions pray, rushing through the obligations as if they had never heard the hadith about the worst of all thieves—the thief who steals prayer from himself.

Hussein is on his knees, kneeling on cardboard. All noses tending downward in the position of seven bones: feet to the earth, hands to the earth, face to the earth, and knees to the earth—yes, knees to the earth—all day, Hussein has had his knees to the earth.

Samar in Chicago

As Samar watches her mother flash across the face of the red-haired woman in front of her, what she feels isn't horrified so much as annoyed. Or maybe she means exhausted. This white woman, some English adjunct at Chicago, is talking about "whiteness as pathology," and—there! There it is again. Something in the red-haired woman's mouth: the way her upper lip sticks on her dry teeth, glint of canines, like she's trying not to smile or she's getting ready to spit out an accusation, you can't be sure. That's Mother.

Not Mother as she is now. No. Not Mother who hobbles from the bathroom to the sitting room, who falls asleep watching reruns of Egyptian soap operas with her swollen hands folded in her lap. Not the old woman who grows sweet in her decline, on the phone with her eldest sister in Jordan, speaking about Samar as "my sweet Samar, my professor." No, not that woman. But Mother as Samar remembers her: young and terrified, wearing a look of surprise, a kind of pleading in the eyes, gentleness and fury.

Why are we still doing this? Samar wants to ask the ghost of her mother, her mother who is very much alive and napping—Samar's younger brother has informed her via text—across the ocean in Bethlehem. Why does her mother come to her this way, haunting her in the stricken faces of foreign women every time she goes abroad?

Samar is standing by a cheese table, clutching rubbery cubes and a glass of sparkling water. Reception fare. Less than half an hour ago she was presenting a paper (new work!) at this hodgepodge conference—sociologists, philologists, and cultural theorists presenting alongside geneticists, biologists, and physicists, all under the auspices of "Memory Studies." By all accounts, she should be feeling good; she should feel like a woman for whom doors are opening. Late, yes, fine, maybe late. She is forty—barely, but she is forty. It is true. It is all happening late. But it's happening, isn't it? She remembers the quiet, chestbursting joy of getting the email from the conference organizer—a woman, a medievalist—inviting her to present. She was at the home office she has made from what was her father's study. She was sitting at a desk that felt too big for her. After she read the invitation email, she closed her clunky laptop. She closed her eyes. She said to herself, *Remember this. Remember this feeling.*

The red-haired woman looks at her expectantly, waiting for a response. Is she Jewish? Hard to tell.

"Say again?" Samar says.

"How can you critique whiteness within a white institution?" the white woman asks.

Samar's presentation was on narrative and memory in Palestine. Ask me about my work, she thinks. About *my* work. "That might be a question for someone else," Samar says, careful to say it gently, arching up the statement into a question—gently, gently—lest she hurt this woman's feelings and be left to deal with the ensuing hysteria. She awkwardly shifts the plastic tumbler—lemon-lime seltzer—and the napkin of cheese cubes into her right hand. There is a pressure in her lower back, radiating down her legs and into the arches of her feet. She wants to double over, release the tension in her spine, but knows that this is impossible until she returns to her room. She's felt stiff ever since she got off the plane two days ago—a long wait to leave Jordan; a long layover in Istanbul where she slept fitfully on a faux-leather chair, clutching her purse; then an hour or maybe more in the windowless Chicago airport room where she waited to get her passport and paperwork back from the American border control— "Ma'am, we simply need to confirm a few things." The only other traveler in that room had been a man who remained in a far corner, throwing up into a plastic bag.

"I mean, because, you know, us white folks can be so defensive," the red-haired woman says, spilling over her words, her eyebrows are in alarming arcs. A familiar expression, Mother's expression: a woman who has lost control of her shopping cart, a woman who is scared of what she'll say next.

"Right," Samar says, "of course," trying to smile in a way that says, *But not you, no, no, not you.* All around them are white academics in sweaters and blazers, holding on to cubes of cheese, plastic glasses of wine. And yes, she could excuse herself from this conversation if she did it gently (gently, gently), but her other concern, aside from the white woman's feelings, is that tactically speaking, it might be better for Samar to be seen talking to someone rather than to be seen alone, which always seems to lower one's value in a crowd, such herd animals are we. The red-haired woman is now explaining to Samar that she is aware—so, so aware—of her privilege. Samar will give this until she finishes her seltzer.

What she wants is to find the medievalist who invited her to this conference in the first place. She seems kind. Frizzy hair, gummy smile. Samar will find the medievalist, and in that way, get introductions to helpful contacts who are here at Chicago or elsewhere. *Networking.* The word gives her a creeping feeling, but what can she do? Everyone does it. If she thinks about her situation too much—her age, not on a tenure track, teaching lower-level classes for the English department at Bethlehem University, and yes, publishing, but no, maybe not enough—she feels some combination of grief and panic. She hears, in her mother's voice, a nagging refrain that she is too old, that it is too late. Although Mother has never said such a thing to her. Those aren't Mother's words. They are words Samar says to herself in her mother's voice. Enough. Stop it. Enough. She'll find the medie-valist. White face in a white room.

It was a successful morning. Samar must hold on to that thought. She presented a paper in progress. It was tempting to wait, to hold back, to present something else, something more finished, but Samar knows that more good comes when you let the ideas be tested be-fore they're sealed up, before they are varnished into place. It takes a certain bravery to let people touch the insides, to expose the inner workings—the gears or stuffing or maybe (why not?) the guts of the paper. When it was her turn to present, Samar sat at a table onstage, behind a microphone and two bottles of unopened water, and she read a few pages aloud.

The conference is on memory, which is perfect for Samar because for years she has been writing about national narratives as forms of codified misremembering. When it was her turn to present, she spoke about forgetting. "In the memory economy," she said, "the ultimate luxury is to forget." Empires forget; their walls let them forget. Imag-ine, she said, an empire that memorialized the names of the people it killed in its invasions. Imagine the names of the Vietnamese dead on the American memorial wall in Washington. Impossible. It was satisfying, sure, to see approving nods as her audience scribbled notes on conference notepads. But mostly, the pleasure Samar felt came from articulating her own ideas clearly. Here are the concepts she has brought into the world. Here is the work she has defended against everyone, even herself. We live in a world of violence and chaos. No-body can argue otherwise. But in her writing, Samar finds a way, if not to order this chaos, then at least to make the chaos legible. De-spite the pressures that threaten to kill her, despite the checkpoints and water shortages, despite the liability of her own aging and child-less body, Samar commits—again and again—to imagine beyond her own survival. Her own voice will survive her, and knowing this is what keeps Samar alive.

Still, she was careful of how far she went. The last time she presented abroad it was at a conference on women and resistance, and the presenters were from all over the Arab world—Palestinian exiles, Lebanese scholars, brown women wearing kaffiyeh. There, she said things she did not say today. Today she did not say the words "BDS" or "Nakbah"; she did not read off the names of Gazan children killed in Israeli air strikes; she did not say the name Salem Abu-Khdeir, the teenager kicked to death by settlers. The way she spoke, you'd think she lived outside of history.

"I mean, I get it, obviously," the red-haired woman says, "the irony of, like, me playing the woke white lady." She says these last three words in air quotes with the hand holding her wine tumbler. Her other hand stays glued to her lower stomach, a self-conscious pose that Samar recognizes as nearly identical to her own. Mirror image. Didn't Mother have a theory about twins?

Samar drains the rest of her seltzer. Halas, social currency be damned. She would rather stand alone by the window and watch the snow fall. "Excuse me," she says, and at the exact moment she puts down her empty plastic tumbler on the cheese table, she is startled by a gentle touch at her right shoulder. Ah! Here is the medievalist, the very one she has been hoping to catch, smiling gummily.

"Deborah!" Samar exclaims. "It's so lovely to see you." She thinks they are the same age, she and the medievalist, who has two young children.

"What a marvelous presentation," the medievalist says, stepping toward her. The three women stand in a circle now. The red-haired woman sips her wine. The medievalist's hand is over her own heart; she smiles and nods at the red-haired woman, mouths *Hi* in a way that is friendly but also suggests no response is necessary, then to Samar, asks, "How are you feeling?"

And finally, at last, at last, the red-haired woman slinks away.

"It felt wonderful," Samar says, hoping it sounds bright and sincere, "such a wonderful room to be in." She is trying to enjoy this moment—a brilliant and, yes, well-connected woman admiring her work. But also, Samar must stay agile, must be sure she's moving toward something, that she is starting conversations that might lead to an offer to come lecture at Chicago, even if just for a quarter. Crazier things have happened. "I'm looking forward to hearing your talk on . . ." Samar hesitates, forgetting the exact nature of the talk—something related to the Crusades?

"That's so kind," the medievalist says, her palm still on her chest. "Do you have a moment to meet some colleagues?"

Samar discreetly slips the cheese cubes, folded in their napkin, into her purse. She spends the next half hour talking about dream work and, somehow, Air Canada with three tenured men-professors in the English department: one specializing in African American performance art, one in Sufi literature, and the third a doubled-over Chaucer scholar who did not extend his hand to shake Samar's. All white.

She wonders if in retrospect, this will feel like a kind of interview for some job at Chicago—even if it's not tenure track, some guest-lecturing position that leads to more, to more and more—and so she asks what she hopes are the right questions, not ones that show off her knowledge, but ones that give each counterpart a chance to show off his. She asks about diaspora; she asks about politicized bodies. The scholar of African American performance art, a trim middle-aged man with a cultivated almost-handlebar mustache, says he is thinking about exile and "misremembered pasts" as "the postmodern condition par excellence." He is wearing a plaid waistcoat.

"I can certainly relate to that," Samar says, and the man looks momentarily startled, like he was remembering something about her, and so that he won't feel bad, or like he said something wrong, and in that way have a negative memory of this interaction, which might cause him to later describe Samar as a difficult or aggressive person, she smiles in a way she hopes is gentle and good-humored, but that also doesn't create wrinkles in her forehead, as she's aware that her plausibility as a hire—if they are even considering her—has much to do with how old she is, meaning how much time she has left.

The medievalist is asking the Sufi scholar about his most recent monograph. It strikes Samar that none of the men has asked about the women's work, meaning the medievalist and Samar. Over her shoulder, she sees the red-haired woman pouring herself another glass of wine; Samar feels a sense of palpable relief to have made it out of that conversation. Her back is growing more and more sore; her bones feel heavy, soggy. She tries to discreetly shift from left foot to right foot to left again.

"By the way," the medievalist says, turning to Samar, "I so admired your remarks in the *Der Spiegel* article about that poor boy."

"Thank you." In truth, Samar was disturbed by the German journalist's article on Salem—specifically, how Palestinians were not permitted to represent themselves. Samar herself was one of two Palestinians quoted in the article, the other being the head doctor at Augusta Victoria Hospital. Everyone else was reduced to a state of animal noise: Salem's mother screaming out the hospital window; young men crying out in pain, in frustration; or Salem himself, nothing but the sickening sound his life-lost body made as it rammed again and again against the hospital's garden wall. She was wary of how this white journalist positioned herself—as a translator of these cries into language, as the one who made them legible, as if they didn't speak for themselves. Even Samar felt somehow reduced by the article. Her own quotes seem to her now like acts of ventriloquism: her words coming out of the white journalist's mouth.

"Well." The medievalist looks at her watch. It's a child's watch, Samar notes, plastic and pink, perhaps a gift from a daughter. "Shall we reconvene at six?"

The men nod. A look is exchanged that Samar pretends not to

notice, not yet knowing its valence, then the medievalist asks, "Do you have dinner plans? We're eating at a cute sushi place, I mean, if you . . ." She suddenly looks panicked, holds up her hands. "I mean, if you eat it. I mean, if you want."

"Oh! Thank you!" she exclaims. She's holding up her hands too. Both women hold up their hands, like they are assuring each other they don't have a weapon. "That's so lovely," Samar continues, trying to convey her sincerity with her eyebrows. Because it is lovely, it is lovely to be invited, and maybe this is the door. But Samar isn't sure. It may be expensive, the restaurant. And even though, yes, this is what the generous per diem is for, Samar knows she will feel guilty if she can't afford the probiotic pills she planned to bring home for Mother. And yet, Samar wants to say yes. Conversations are happening; ideas are being refined; she wants to be there for it. Perhaps she can go and eat only a soup? But also she is tired. She is so, so tired of being so, so careful. Perhaps it is time to go back to her room, to stay there. "I am a bit exhausted," Samar says, in a higher octave than natural.

The medievalist's hands are still held up, palms out. "No pressure!" she exclaims.

Samar feels herself deflating. "May I get in touch later, after I've rested?"

"Of course," the medievalist says, seeming relieved; she enters her number into Samar's phone. It might work. If she orders only a soup. It might work. She might have to leave early, if the dinner goes late. She likes to be by her phone, and she'll need Wi-Fi, at night, in case over in Bethlehem, nine hours ahead, her mother is having trouble in the morning, and one of her brothers needs to reach her. Oh, she doesn't know, she doesn't know.

At the coatracks, Samar searches for her puffy black coat. Next to her, two young women with ponytails are putting on hats and mittens:

"Since then, he's kept his door open during office hours," one says to the other, her voice low. Samar continues to rifle through the rack for her coat among various ski jackets, peacoats, and the odd sweater.

"But about myths of women's purity," someone says from the other side of the coatrack, and Samar looks up in surprise. The two women with ponytails are gone. Instead it's the red-haired woman, still carrying a full plastic tumbler of red wine, talking as if their conversation had continued in Samar's absence. "Such myths are, of course, crucial to myths of racial purity."

For a brief, alarming second, Samar wonders if the red-haired woman is real, meaning physically present. Or is she a phantom emanating from her own mind? Her own guilt about leaving Mother, her own ambivalence about wanting things, wanting to succeed?

"Your work," says the red-haired woman, leaning across the garments, "on the wall and the ethnic fantasies it invites—"

"I'm sorry," Samar cuts her off. She's searching for her coat again. "But I'm starting to feel the jet lag."

The lady is undeterred. "The wall, like any barrier, necessitates a gendered nationalism." She's speaking fast. Her eyes are like Mother's again, panicked and searching.

"The jet lag," Samar says, frantically riffling through all the black coats, so many black coats. Why does Samar have to have a black coat?

"On both sides, actually." The woman is gesturing with her plastic wineglass, which splashes a little. Red runs down onto her fingers.

"Right, right." Aha! She has found it. She hurriedly pulls on her puffy, black coat, careful of the tricky zipper.

"Over a meal!" the woman exclaims, walking around to stand in front of Samar.

"What?"

"Perhaps a meal, after you've rested?" Her breath smells acidic.

"I'm awfully tired," she says, her coat now zipped.

"But maybe later, a meal together?"

"Oh, we'll see." Samar adjusts her purse as she heads for the door, adjusting her trajectory to avoid a notorious scholar of Deleuze, who is towering over a thin woman with tattoos on her arms, perhaps a grad student, looking rapt and terrified. "Nice to see you," she calls out to the red-haired woman behind her, as she rushes through the wide, wooden door frame; she has one hand on the banister to guide her as she hurries down the heavy, slate staircase, her boots scratching and echoing.

The woman is leaning over the railing. "But when?" she calls down, her voice distant in the stairwell, her mouth a desperate shape.

"Okay," Samar shouts, unsure what else to say, then pushes the heavy fire door and steps out into the brutal, unfriendly sun.

Cold, the shock of it. How lovely. And how good it is to be out of that room. Cold. So cold, it hurts to breathe. From her bag she pulls out the accessories. Hat on, scarf around her neck, last of all, hands into gloves. Bought as a set: all purple with a silvery filament woven in. Kind of girlish, but why not? She walks quickly in what she hopes is the right direction. She walks with her hands bunched in the gloves, her periphery obscured by the scarf bundled around her neck and ears. She heads across a quad covered in a thin, filthy layer of snow, crunching along the salted path. She looks down at her feet, she looks up at the huge, Gothic buildings covered in dead ivy like stilled veins, then back down at her feet. The leather boots she wears are cute but not much against the cold. She grips and ungrips her toes as she walks, hoping that keeps some blood in them.

This is her first time in America. She has some distant cousins in California—years ago, they came to visit Palestine, but it's been a long time since the Israelis let them in. Before she flew, she sent a message to two of her California cousins with questions about Chicago weather and safety, if there were guns on campuses, white supremacists. One of the two wrote back: *I hear it's cold there*, she said. *Also, if you are alone, don't speak Arabic in public—not even on the phone.*

Off the quad and onto a sidewalk. Crunch, crunch, crunch. She passes posters taped up along a cement wall: Math tutor available, Black Lives Matter, 2000s-themed party at the student center, Campus Republicans meet next week, Study Korean, Rape Crisis Hotline, Vote in the student elections. A black-and-white photograph of a young black woman at what looks like a graduation ceremony has handwritten text underneath: *Say Her Name*. Next to it, another, half torn down.

She thinks about her own students, hopes that the grad student—not even a lecturer—who agreed to cover her classes this week at least takes attendance. She knows she is supposed to resent her students and the time they steal from her, but she likes them this semester, likes them every semester, really. They are young and bright. She knows, of course she knows, that she thinks about them much more than they think about her. They tug her away from her own work, her own research; she frets about their little ideas, the shortcomings of their work, which are of course her own shortcomings, the concepts she has failed to make clear.

"Professor, I know how to make buses materialize," one of her favorite students said to her recently. He was walking gingerly to her desk with two Styrofoam cups of tea.

"Let's hear it," Samar said.

The boy's name is Hamid. A bit naughty, but hardworking. The years he took off between finishing high school and starting university—working, saving money—have given him a certain hunger that Samar recognizes and respects.

"Yes," Hamid said, putting the cups on her desk and pulling up a chair so they could go over his most recent essay, line by line, together. "The trick is to light a cigarette."

"A cigarette makes the bus come?"

"Yes. Listen, I could be waiting for the bus for ten minutes, fifteen minutes, half an hour, it doesn't matter. The minute I light up a cigarette—yalla!—the bus arrives, and I have to throw the cigarette out or stink up my jacket by putting it back in the pack, half-smoked."

"So maybe it is time to quit smoking," she said, knowing it was expected that she prod him a little. A childless woman at her age is a mother to all.

"But, Professor," Hamid said, "if I quit smoking, the bus will never come."

In the Chicago cold, Samar holds her hands together such that her jacket sleeves meet and cover her wrists completely. She has seen monks walk through Bethlehem this way. She is walking in the direction of her room. Chicago is filled with things to see: the Art Institute, the giant Anish Kapoor bean in Millennium Park. But the university is in the south, and the conference schedule is quite packed, and Samar really hasn't gone anywhere in the city. It's not simply that she has obligations for the conference, although she does. And it's not simply that the cold makes wandering seem less appealing, although it does. Traveling consistently reveals to Samar how small she makes her own world, how she feels compelled to stick to the places that become familiar: the few buildings she knows on campus, the room where she is staying, the coffee shop between campus and her room. It was like this in Oxford, too—a constricted orbit.

When Mother called to plead with her to come home, to leave Oxford, it was the middle of the fall term, Michaelmas. How strange and enchanting the names of those terms—Michaelmas, Hilary, Trinity—like words from a secret runic language. It was evening, dark already. By Hilary, the days would be ending midafternoon, Samar knew, but most likely, she would not be at Oxford then: her twelve-month postdoc research was essentially finished; she had only two more months of funding. The evening Mother called, Samar had been sitting at the flimsy, pale plywood desk in the Saint Anne's graduate dormitory, reviewing a copy of the publication on which her name appeared. It was thrilling, yes, to see her name in the journal's table of contents, to flip carefully to page forty-seven, and see her name there again. But under the excitement was a tug of frustration. In both places, her name appeared under her advisor's name. She knew that this was the way things worked, and yet it was Samar who had furnished the central idea in a seminar paper that, initially, her advisor had been incredibly critical of, unconvinced, apparently, that the Israeli Apartheid Wall might be understood as a kind of war memorial. But something must have convinced him, because a few months later he asked her to help research a paper that "picked up where Samar left off," but that, as far as she could tell, was actually just her idea, expanded upon. She remembers the odd, exhausting mix of feelings: excitement and gratitude that her advisor involved her at all, didn't simply steal Samar's idea and call it his own; resentment and humiliation that she had to be grateful for scraps, as if she herself didn't believe she deserved more.

When Mother called, Samar was sitting at her desk, tracing over her name in the journal, and wondering, sincerely wondering, if she could handle this. Not the work itself, but all the battles one must undertake for the sake of the work. Did she have the strength to defend herself and her ideas in a climate where the stakes were so low that all the arguments—petty, academic, brilliant, self-referential to the point of irrelevance—took on a kind of hysteria? In a way, she is still answering this question. But that day at Oxford it was dark and cold already, and Samar was feeling the disappointment that comes with getting something you thought you wanted and finding you want more, when her telephone, a landline (although nearly everyone but Samar had a cell phone), startled her out of her thoughts.

One month later, she and her bags were on a flight to Jordan, where she stayed in Amman with her mother's sister until an uncle on her father's side had a permit to take the long drive from Bethlehem to Amman to pick her up, to take her and her three huge suitcases home. It was supposed to be temporary. That was a decade ago now. A decade ago. How does it happen? She was thirty years old and she was making good time. She had just finished her postdoc; she had begun to publish. She was earning, as they say in English, *a seat at the table*. She'd thought she had time, and then she came home, and it began to slip away.

But what Samar has been trying to remember is exactly what was said on that phone call. Did Mother ask her to come back? Did she demand it? Did she tell her that Father was sick, that he was fading away? Does it matter? Wasn't telling Samar about Father's weight, a ghastly number, a kind of demand anyway? But it matters. It matters to Samar. She wants to know how much she embellished the story, what she added, where she made assumptions, and what those assumptions have cost her. She wants to know but doesn't know how to start.

She continues along the sidewalk toward the room she's been put up in, past houses split in two symmetrically, one family in each half. Or not families, maybe, but student apartments with rotting couches on the porches and wind chimes everywhere. The sun is relentlessly bright.

She is within a boundary that the medievalist described to Samar during their conversations over Skype: a few blocks by a few blocks. "Those are the safest areas," she said, smiling. "I'll email a map." Samar knew this code, what "safe" meant in this context, coming from this woman. Safe meant not black. Safe for whom?

That was one of Mother's words back then. *Safe.* "I'm trying to keep you safe," she would hiss, with what seemed like rage to Samar at the time, but now seems to be more about fear. Love, fear, control, hate. It is so hard to distinguish.

What was it Mother feared when she stood in the doorway waiting for Samar to come home from high school, ready to interrogate her? Mother had no shortage of children to yell at, but it was Samar—the only girl and yet, no denying it, the most like her father—that Mother singled out, or so it seems to Samar. It always started the same way: "Let me ask you a question," almost sung to her, gently. Then it was a careful, strategic series of moves, establishing that perhaps Samar had not come directly home, but had stopped for a can of soda or an ice cream with friends, and then Mother could finally yell out what she wanted to yell out, which was something along the lines of: "Do you know what people will think of you?" These were the years that her father had spent in Saudi Arabia, earning money as a translator for American businessmen and sending most of it home. So maybe Mother was afraid of her own loneliness, her own isolation, and somehow, Samar's world, already opening up and expanding, terrified Mother, too. That might be a true answer, but it strikes Samar as an incomplete one.

Even today, the words "Let me ask you a question" freeze all the water inside Samar. Mother still says it, but when she says it, she's really just asking a question. "Let me ask you a question," she'll sing out, then ask about some neighbor's son, or whether the grocer across town has been caught weighting his scales yet. Samar has seen forty springs, but in those moments, at their slightly lopsided table in the kitchen, the apricot tree tapping its branches against the window next to the sink, she is thirteen again, and she is terrified.

Sound of footsteps. On the sidewalk behind Samar there is the sound of footsteps. No. Please. She tries to turn, but it's too hard in the puffy coat and winter scarf. Sound of footsteps, approaching, faster, a man because it's always a man. Hot coal at the base of her spine, moving up. She is trying to breathe deeply, slowly, but the breath doesn't seem to reach her lungs, not the deepest part that she needs it to reach. It's coming from behind. He's coming from behind and there's no time, no time, she needs to spin around but can't. There is no time. On the other side of the street, a woman with a furry hat is leaning over her baby stroller, adjusting an enormous blanket that must have a baby under it; ahead, a man in a long parka, jeans tucked into snow boots, is facing a brick wall, maybe against the wind to light a cigarette. These are the people who will watch when what happens happens. It is a bright, freezing spring afternoon. All these people are here and none of them are going to help her when he comes for her, closer now, oh my God, just let it happen, just let it be over. There is something worse than pain. It is the world itself crushing you, saying, You deserve this, you deserve this. It is believing it. Here it is.

The jogger says, "On your left," as he passes.

The panic evaporates and floats up into a clear sky. A man jogging, that's all. She wants to weep but knows she will not. The woman with the stroller is gone. The man in the parka leans against the building wall, smoking now.

Two blocks later, it's into the building using the plastic keycard hanging by a lanyard around her neck, up the linoleum stairs, unlocking the room door. There is a chill at the backs of her knees as she locks the door behind her. Safe. She sits on the bed, her coat on, everything on, trying to feel the word. Safe.

She's careful when she unzips her coat—warm, puffy thing she bought so many winters ago, back when she was still at Oxford, for a wintertime conference in Vienna. The zipper is a little tricky these days, but she hopes she can get another year out of it. Feeling prickles back into her cheeks and nose. Soon she will be hot. She remembers this. The incredible heat in places that were built for cold, against the cold. In places like this, there are no fire hazard space heaters, no tile floors like ice, no mornings sitting on your hands when you go to the loo—all the features of a Bethlehem winter. Instead the buildings have sources of heat like a central nervous system, or maybe she means cardiovascular system. Scalding hot pipes or dusty electric coils pulsing in the walls. At Oxford, back then, it was a radiator that took coins and got hot enough to melt a shoe. Here, in Chicago, it's a dial on the wall of the room and hot air breathed invisibly through some vent.

She unbuttons her trousers, then at long last allows herself to double over, drooping with her head heavy as her hands slowly tend toward the floor. She wants to groan aloud but won't. Her lower back elongates, a feeling like the muscles yawning. Plane rides get harder and harder. All throughout her thirties and, now, into her forties, she has waited for her body to return to normal. The stiffness in the morning, the unstable joints, uncooperative neck, clenched hips—when will it go away so that she can be Samar again? But this is her body now. She takes another deep breath then slowly uncurls to stand up.

Dizzy, she sits on the bed she slept in last night. The organizers of the conference have *arranged for her accommodations*, which is a civilized way of saying that they put her in a dorm room. It's not so bad. There is an adjoining toilet, private, and shared showers down the hall; there are only women on this floor. Samar has the whole room to herself, although it was built for two occupants—two narrow beds, two dressers, two desks looking out one big frosted window. White light plays brilliantly on the glass, on the delicate crystal flares left by the cold. The window glass is reinforced by wire, but why? What act of violence do the windows anticipate? Samar trained herself to think like this, to see the resistance that the State feeds its imagination on. On one desk, she has positioned the conference materials alongside the paper she is currently revising; on the other desk, she has stacked the student papers she needs to mark, and beside the papers, three green apples and an unopened bag of almonds. It is a nice arrangement, she thinks, to have two desks for two sets of work. It is good to have separate zones. The room answers itself. Left side, right side. She thinks, not for the first time today, about Mother's theory of twins.

Ah, the cheese! She gets back up, and leaning over the other bed, feels around her purse for the folded napkin. She places it by the apples. These are the foods she lives on at conferences: bits of reception cheese, crackers, almonds bought in a campus convenience store, apples from the breakfast table. No need to waste the daily allowance on food. She always loses a pound or two at these things, dreams of properly seasoned chicken, the right kind of rice—real food you get only at home.

Really, she should call home. Find out how Mother's doing, listen to her complain about her youngest daughter-in-law's cooking, although she's right, the girl does needlessly put sugar in everything. Samar flips open the welcome package, finds the insert about connecting to Wi-Fi, sits back down on the unmade bed, feet on the floor. She takes her phone from the bedside table and tries to follow the instructions, fiddling around. Keeps getting error messages. Well, anyway, it's late in Bethlehem now.

She takes off her shoes, puts a little lotion on her hands. Smell of cheap vanilla. She eases herself down to lie on the starchy white pillow, on top of the scratchy blanket. A heavy, delicious feeling pulls her deep into the bed. She closes her eyes. In another lifetime, maybe, she will be someone who can take naps, but lying in a room filled with afternoon sunlight, Samar knows that she will not be able to sleep.

Mother's theory of twins goes like this. It is always the case, Mother said, that with identical twins, one is left-handed and the other is right-handed. Therefore, Mother reasoned, all left-handed people were twins once, at the beginning, anyway, twins who lost their double at some point during gestation. Samar doesn't know if any of this is true, even the premise. What about triplets, then? Or do triplets not come from the same egg? She doesn't know. A geneticist would know. It would be so easy to check, but she doesn't want to know the truth about twins, she wants to know the truth about her mother.

What is her left-handed mother trying to tell her? What is the absence that living has left in her? Her mother was born in a house built from ancient stones, and now it's gone. The Zionists turned their fields into an airport. At ten years old, her mother fled with her parents to a cave, then a refugee camp, and then, at last, to a small house behind the bus depot in Bethlehem. Left-handed mother, forced to eat with the right, gesture with the right, never the left, the unclean. At sixteen, she left school to wed. What is her mother telling her when she talks about twins, her imagined twin, her disappeared sister, the right-handed version of herself? The correct version, the halal version, not the one living in this nightmare version of history, not the refugee.

Her father never doubted that he was the true version of himself. Never doubted his view of history moving toward progress. Never doubted the essential, prevailing human tendency toward decency. He insisted that the Jews would not build the Wall, and privately, Samar thinks this is what killed him: the loss of the fallacies that sustained him.

Uninvited, the red-haired woman's anxious face swims into Samar's thoughts. Leave me alone, she almost groans aloud. There are so many things she could have said to that woman, so many lines she thinks of now. Why is it, she might ask, that you can imagine anything but your own capacity for terrible violence? She's not sure if she's talking to the phantom of the red-haired woman or to whatever part of her is torturing herself this way.

Sometimes Mother comes close to apologizing. Samar's hand in her swollen hand, and she'll begin to say something, like, "When you were young, I was young too, I didn't know," but Samar will cut her off. "You took care of me, Mama, as best you could."

They'll sit with the TV playing low, Samar's head inclined to touch her mother's head. Mother is smaller every day, small enough to fit inside her daughter's body. They sit in blue-gray rooms, the day already over, these two women, each the thief of the other's girlhood.

Forgiveness is divine. God forgives us constantly, they say. Right now, for example. So why won't Samar let her mother apologize? What would she have to know about herself to know the answer to that?

Samar knows, by now she knows, that her mother is not the adversary. The woman who haunts her through the faces of unkind women is not Mother but is Samar herself, the argument is one she is having against herself—an attempt to expel an idea, or maybe a fear, that she has internalized, an idea that she wants to get out of her but doesn't know how. What's the idea? Something not quite articulable about her value, her odds. It is not the ghosts of her living mother she encounters, but emanations from inside herself. Perhaps, if Samar had married, if Samar had had daughters, she would understand. Mother used to say that. "When you marry, you'll understand." She doesn't say that anymore. It's possible that if Samar had married, if she'd had a daughter of her own, she would have, in some way, acted like Mother—wary and controlling, aware of the scrutiny their community casts on young women, how that can mark a girl forever. But Samar didn't marry and doesn't have children, so perhaps now, she treats herself like her own daughter—not letting herself stray too far, always calling herself home, or maybe better to say, calling herself back.

"She'll go when she's ready," Mother has always said to aunts to uncles to neighbors when they asked about Samar's spinsterhood, which wasn't—this is what nobody said but everyone knew—natural. Only the Christian sisters lived like that. "She'll go when she's ready." All the way until Samar turned forty. Did Mother want to keep her close? Afraid she'd run away again? Was it love or some form of punishment, and why, why, is it so hard to tell the difference?

She awakes to the knock at the door. The room is shades of blue and gray, dolorous light of early evening. She sits up in bed. Small knuckles, knocking at the door, not pounding, but urgent, rapid. She moves her feet to the floor, quietly, gingerly, so that the covers don't make any noise. She stands in front of the door, one hand holding up her trousers. The handle is shaking, harder, harder now. Outside, someone is trying to get in.

Rachel

"Look at what my friend wrote," Rachel says in English, holding her phone up to Miriam.

They are sitting in Miriam's kitchen with cups of green tea. There's another half hour in Rachel's lesson, and she's trying to distract Miriam so they don't have to go back to talking about the rabbinic basis for covering her hair after she's married. Every week, Rachel comes to Miriam's kitchen to prepare for being a wife—kosher sex, kosher living.

Miriam clucks with impatience but takes Rachel's phone. She puts on her reading glasses. Rachel likes that Miriam has a lively face and close-cropped hair that she covers in a spunky little beret. She's petite and pixie-like, although she must be about the same age as Rachel's mom. She has a son Rachel's age. Uri? Ori?

"*Aval zeh katuv b'Germanit*," Miriam says, looking up from the article.

They flow between Hebrew and English—mostly Miriam speaking in Hebrew and Rachel, who finds that kind of annoying, answering in English. "Yeah, it's in *Der Spiegel*, so it's German," she says, plonking her tea bag up and down in the steaming mug of water. "Don't you speak German?"

"A little," Miriam says.

"From your parents?" Rachel asks.

"From my parents," Miriam confirms. "And their parents. Although mostly, they spoke Yiddish."

"That's so cool," Rachel says. Yiddish strikes her as strange and lost, dusty and obscure. Everyone speaks English, everyone speaks Hebrew. Who speaks Yiddish? Black-hatters with twenty kids, and Holocaust survivors—the few that are left.

Miriam smiles. "*A bisl*," she says, returning to the article.

Rachel runs her finger around the rim of her mug. All of Miriam's mugs are super cheesy: covered in hearts and hamsas. This one has two cats on a tandem bike. It's stupid and cute.

"This is about the Arab," Miriam says, the phone impossibly close to her face. "The boy from the mall?"

"I think so," Rachel says.

"You know this journalist?"

"We're friends." Rachel can hear her own defensiveness.

"What, you're a leftist now?" Miriam laughs, handing Rachel's phone back to her.

"She's smart," Rachel says, struggling to explain what pulls her to Vera. "She's different." Everyone Rachel knows from back home in LA, everyone in her community there and everyone in her community here, in Israel, has different variations on the same opinion. Everyone agrees the Arabs are a problem, and they have different ideas about how to solve that problem. Vera rejects that premise altogether, which Rachel finds thrilling even if, deep down, she knows in her heart that Vera is wrong.

"Let's continue with the lesson," Miriam says.

Miriam is super popular with girls from Rachel's seminary because she makes sex sound so beautiful. How perfect that her last name actually means "heart." "You have to go to Miriam Lev," everyone says. They come back from lessons with Miriam in a state of divine horniness—ready for the bliss promised by kosher sex with their soon-to-be husbands. They'd stand under the chuppah that afternoon if they could.

Rachel will be barely twenty when she gets married in the fall. Vera—her German friend—can't believe this. Vera is older and a little slutty, which Rachel thinks is amazing. "But you're a baby," Vera said.

"I know," Rachel moaned, enjoying the attention. They were in Rachel's bed drinking wine. "I'm not even old enough to drink in America," she said, in the most childish voice she could conjure.

Originally, Vera interviewed Rachel about politics or something—research for an article that it seemed Vera never ended up writing. But since the interview, they've begun hanging out. Vera chews at her fingernails and tells Rachel about all her horrible dates. Once, Vera said she was making out with some guy at his place, straddling him, and when she felt his hardness on her thigh, pushing through his pants, she realized that he had a small penis—a tiny prick of a dick that, Vera said, wouldn't bring even a mouse to climax—so she pretended suddenly that she had a headache and ran home. "I needed a real fuck," Vera said, and Rachel spilled her wine laughing. What Rachel likes is that Vera is slutty but, like, cool about it. How many times has Rachel sat through some endless Shabbat lunch with a newly shomer negiah girl in an overly modest peasant skirt down to her ankles? These are girls who have sucked off half the graduating class at Yeshiva U high school, and then suddenly decide they won't shake a man's hand, as if, like, that reconstructed your hymen? Such bullshit. At least Vera doesn't pretend.

Rachel runs a finger around the rim of her mug again. Miriam is rifling through pages in a folder, no doubt searching for the next photocopied section of Talmud, when Rachel asks, kind of out of nowhere, "Why isn't a man niddah after combat?"

Miriam looks up with lively eyes. "You mean, why doesn't blood from a wound transmit impurity?" she clarifies.

"Yeah," Rachel says. "Men bleed all the time." Her fiancé—it still sounds so strange, that word, and soon she'll have to get used to another one, *husband*—comes home with dumbass injuries all the time. He got burnt on the chest with a contact radio overheating. He somehow managed to scratch his face on a bunk bed. They go for walks on Shabbat afternoons, before he has to go back to the army on Sundays. He talks about guys in his unit; he falls asleep in her lap. Some of it is horrible, but he never reacts to it much. "The stone-throwers hit a guy right in the face," he told her recently. "Split his cheek like a fruit. Blood everywhere." It had felt like a test, like she had to find the right thing to say, to comfort him, to be a good partner. All she could think to say was that it was horrible.

"You know this answer," Miriam says.

Of course Rachel knows: only blood from the womb carries niddah—not the blood spilled in combat. "But why is it all on me?" Rachel asks. She began this line of questioning just to prod Miriam a little, just to be a little difficult. But now she finds she's really asking. "Why is it the woman who carries something bad inside?" She thinks about her and Vera, drinking too much wine—far too much wine—and talking about sex while Vera rips at her cuticles.

The way that Miriam talks about sex, it's beautiful and important. Pleasure, she has reminded Rachel, is mandated by the marriage contract itself—an obligation that a man owes his wife. But the way Vera talks about sex, it's like the sex is a metaphor for something else, for some darker, stronger need that nobody can name. Vera tells Rachel about Amir, this loser soccer player who strings her along, spanking her, pinning her down. She talks about riding him hard, about hating him and that hate making the fucking—she actually calls it "the fucking"—better. Rachel wonders if she and Vera both carry the same darkness inside, and if, perhaps, they recognize that darkness in each other.

Miriam squirms in her seat. Rachel has seen this before, how excited Miriam gets when she's making an argument for the unspeakable beauty of the commandments. "What verb does Torah use for sex?" Miriam asks.

"'To know,'" Rachel says. At some point, they switched from English to Hebrew, but she can't remember when. "As in, Adam knew Eve." She tugs at her hooped earrings, embarrassed and annoyed at her own embarrassment.

"Good girl," Miriam says. "Listen, marriage isn't about rules. It's about coming to know. Within certain parameters, sure. But coming to know."

Rachel thinks about her fiancé's jawline, how it clenches when he's close to coming. She gives, she happens to know, amazing head. Her boyfriend in high school had a car. Once, she even did it to him while he was driving, accelerating up the PCH late at night. The car bouncing over uneven pavement, lights from the streets flashing into the window, as Rachel loved him with her mouth. Ira. He made aliyah to Israel too, she heard, and now he's in the army. Anyway, her fiancé's parents leave them alone in his room. They are engaged, after all. Sometimes they have real sex, although it's always quiet, tame, breathless. It doesn't sound like the sex Vera has—animated by an emotion that Rachel wants to call anger.

"Love is a state of knowledge," Miriam says. She is almost intoning at this point. "To know yourself," she says, "and to know him. Most of all, to know yourself through him."

Rachel closes her eyes. She wants to believe in the version of love that Miriam is offering. And yet, in some margin of consciousness, she has an image of Vera—fucking a man she does not love. Loving it.

Water

Oum Hamid does not have time to be waiting at this roadblock while the Jew-soldiers hold everyone up. If she's late for work again, that little brat Mona—the rich girl who doesn't even care about water sustainability, just enjoys the opportunity to travel for conferences—will have scooped more files off her desk. A long line of cars and vans curls up ahead of them on the highway leading to Ramallah. There is a fantasy version of her commute from Bethlehem that takes forty minutes, on a day without roadblocks. Not for the first time, the woman seated next to her sighs in frustration. Their shared taxi-van inches forward.

On the left side of the road, the settler cars are rushing by, unstopped by the soldiers. "Why don't we have our own roads?" little Fadi has asked her more than once. Oum Hamid is almost certain that when she dies it will be an innocent question that kills her—the heartbreak of explaining some mundane horror to a child.

Again, the woman next to her sighs heavily. She is wearing a nice pantsuit and her hair is not covered. "What's the holdup?" she asks, agitatedly trying to see outside. In another context, they might strike up a friendly conversation, but Oum Hamid doesn't have the energy to engage.

Nobody in the van answers. The woman is shifting in her seat. "Really," she says, "what's going on?"

It's the driver who replies. "The man, the one they say killed the settler-girl," he says, "the Jews are bulldozing his mother's house."

A Jew-soldier in a cruiser drives by, shouting out of a loudspeaker. "Hebron residents: go home," he says. "If your hawiyya lists Hebron as your residence, go home. You are not getting through today." It is almost nine. Oum Hamid has been in this shared taxi-van since just after seven in the morning.

"What about Salem Abu-Khdeir?" the woman asks, her voice verging on shrill now. She must be a visitor—a Palestinian who lives in comfortable exile in California or London or Argentina—someone who watches from the outside, someone who keeps score. She goes on. "Who will bulldoze the homes of the men who did that to him?" It's a rhetorical question. Nobody answers.

Oum Hamid takes out her phone to text Hamid. *Are you awake?* He has a lecture at ten.

No, he writes back, *I am asleep, I am dreaming.* His profile photo is of Salem Abu-Khdeir. Every time Oum Hamid messages her eldest son, she sees the dead boy's face, not bloated and cracked from the beating, but smiling and happy—a photo his family circulated.

Drop off the boys with Teta, she writes, *if Baba has left for work already.*

Hamid responds that he was thinking of leaving them alone at home. Then sends one of the crying-laughing emoji faces. *Just kidding*, he tells her. *Yes, of course I will drop them off.* He's a good boy. She had him at twenty and only took one semester off. Wrote undergraduate papers while nursing him, his father already spending long hours working at the bank. Baby Hamid never made a fuss.

She doesn't want to be one of those nightmare mothers for whom no one is good enough for her son—the kind of mother-in-law she herself has—but she knows she'll probably end up that way. Because how could anyone be good enough for Hamid? So tall and clear-skinned, so ambitious and able, so decent. He worked month after month, installing air conditioners who knows where; now he's earning a degree in the sciences; next, he'll be in medical school. He'll be a natural provider. His current crush—Oum Hamid has ways of knowing—is a classmate from East Jerusalem. "Don't be ridiculous," she told him, when he asked ostensibly hypothetical questions about marrying a girl with Jerusalem residency. He laughed: I know, I know. But did he know? This girl—Mai—is a princess. Her father works in London. She's a rich girl who is, probably, as bad as Mona: entitled and stubborn, someone who would never live in Bethlehem, who would try to wrestle Hamid away from her. Focus on your degrees, she told him. Then you can marry whomever you want. "You mean, whomever *you* want," he said in his teasing way. She was stirring tomatoes and onions in a frying pan, turned around to swat at him with a wooden spoon. He dodged it, laughed. Her sweet boy.

One of the settler cars in the left lane slows down so that he's idling right next to the shared van. Oum Hamid looks straight ahead. She keeps her eyes trained on a crack in the faux leather of the driver's headrest. The settler is yelling not at them but at the army jeep. "*Shalom!*" he says, his tone friendly as he leans out the driver-side window of his car. Then he asks a question in Hebrew, something like, What's going on? You can tell he's from America by how flat his words sound. They're mostly from America—the settlers who come here screaming about their birthright and tearing up the olive groves.

Oum Hamid and the woman next to her keep looking straight forward. Without understanding all the Hebrew, she can hear that the settler is making a big show of joking with the soldier. "*Achi*," he keeps saying, "my brother, *achi*." They are probably talking about the demolition today. Let it be a lesson to them, the settler may be saying in his tough-guy performative way. Is it for me, Oum Hamid wonders, for us, this performance? Would they even be Israelis without the audience of Palestinians? *I make you*, Oum Hamid thinks.

"Yalla, bye," the settler calls, and the soldier waves, and then the car drives off. The shared taxi-van hasn't moved yet.

Oum Hamid puts on her headphones. She tries not to think about Mona, snooping around her desk. Mona, young, plump, and venomous. Recently, she made a big deal out of Hamid's age—"A son already in the university! But I thought you were *my* age!" Such a brat. The kind of girl whose mother is supposed to open up a clothing shop for her, a little spot filled with junk jewelry from Turkey and polyester blouses that fell off some Israeli truck. What is she doing working in government? And why is Oum Hamid the only one who sees through her? Finally the taxi-van inches forward.

By the time she gets to the office in Ramallah, Mona is there, of course she is, poking around Oum Hamid's desk, which is really just a cubicle outside the director's office.

"Marhaba," Oum Hamid greets her, coolly. The girl is wearing an absurdly childish cardigan with embroidered flowers and pearl buttons. Grow up, she thinks.

Mona returns her greeting. Then she's peeking over Oum Hamid's shoulder at the director's office. "He's in there with some British man."

"Oh?" Oum Hamid makes sure no files are missing from her desk.

"A dignitary," Mona says. "Here to talk about water treatment." Mona's lipstick is incredibly pink.

Oum Hamid is about to ask a question when the two men walk out of the director's office. The director looking dignified, as ever, in his dark suit and graying hair; the dignitary much more casually dressed, without a jacket or tie. The director gestures to Oum Hamid and Mona. "These are my coworkers," he says in English. He makes the introductions.

"Tsharrafna," the guest attempts in Arabic, for some reason speaking in feminine. Nobody corrects him. He is young. Flushed, well-fed cheeks.

"Pleased to meet you," Oum Hamid says in English.

"Your director and I were just talking about peace," the British man says.

"As one does," Oum Hamid responds, pleased to note that Mona has not yet said a word.

"Yes, quite," the man says. And everyone laughs. "You know, I am always telling the Israelis—the Palestinians want peace as much as you do."

"Of course," the director says. "We all want to live."

"Both sides have suffered," the foreign dignitary continues. "But you know what they say." He looks around, as if one of them might guess. Then he covers his right eye with his right palm. "An eye for an eye," he says as he places the left hand over his left eye, "until the whole world is blind." He stands there a moment, his eyes covered. He is wearing a small gold cross.

Oum Hamid glances at Mona, who is looking down at her hands. The director clears his throat.

Finally the man uncovers his eyes. "And when will it end?"

"When they will it, I suppose," Oum Hamid says. Her boss glances at her. She knows he's thinking about the funding for the water treatment project.

"But we must all will it," the British man exclaims robustly. "Think about it, the Jewish girl is murdered on the settlement, then the Palestinian boy is murdered in the parking lot." He looks at all their faces. "On and on, for what?"

"Perhaps, think in terms of proportions," Oum Hamid says, keeping her voice friendly. "Who has power? Who has the water?" She wants to explain the basic facts of climate change to him. That one industrial Jewish settlement can contribute more to climate change than all of agrarian Palestine. But she finds herself exhausted before she can even start. She wishes the woman from the taxi-bus were here—someone who had the energy to yell about each injustice.

"Listen," the British man continues, "I tell the Israelis that the Palestinians don't hate you." He nods at Oum Hamid. "There is no hate in their hearts."

"About the treatment project—" the director starts to say, clearly trying to pivot away from this man's theories about peace.

But Mona cuts in. "It is impossible not to hate them," she says.

"What?" the British man turns toward her. The director's eyes are huge.

"I hate them," Mona says. "I hate them and you would, too."

The director rubs his brow in agitation.

Mona continues. "It's not an eye for an eye," she says. "An eye for ten eyes, an eye for a whole village."

"Look, I'm Scottish," the man says, looking pleased. This is his moment. You can tell. He's going to explain their own lives to them. He says that in Scotland, the people were tortured and oppressed for three centuries. "But we moved on," he says, "in the name of progress." He smiles sadly in the belief—it's all over his face—that this insight is beyond his audience. "Because if you hold hate in your heart, it will kill you." He repeats this last part. "It will kill you."

"Either way, the Israelis will kill me," Mona says. And Oum Hamid feels a surge of what can only be called love for this uncompromising girl.

Before Mona can say anything else, the director cuts in. "Please," he says to the British dignitary, "allow me to show you the model of the water treatment plant we are trying to fund." He leads him down the hallway, exchanging a quick *deal with it* look with Oum Hamid.

The women are left alone. Mona is fiddling with one of her pearl buttons in agitation. Oum Hamid reaches out, touches her hand. "They bulldozed his house today," she says.

"Whose?" Mona asks. She looks very young when she takes Oum Hamid's hand.

"The man that the Jews say killed the settler." Her hand is on Mona's hand.

"Is that why you were late?"

Oum Hamid nods. The women are not friends, but they are holding hands. "What about Salem Abu-Khdeir?" she says. "Who will bulldoze the houses of the men who killed Salem Abu-Khdeir?"

Mona shakes her head. "Nobody."

"Nobody," echoes Oum Hamid. There is a pause. Neither of them has to say what the other knows. That the Jews, deep down, are happy that the settler Yael Salomon was murdered in her room. They are happy for the excuse to do what they were going to do anyway, and now they can do it in the dead girl's name. "My daughter," Oum Hamid says to Mona, and it is the first time she is referring to her this way. And then, just as quickly, the moment is over. The women retract their hands simultaneously. "What did I tell you about snooping around my desk?" she snaps.

Mona shrugs and walks away.

Foudah

Miriam's phone lights up on the nightstand. She'd been dreaming—lightly, thinly, close to the surface—of a crowded room. I am all these people, she thought, shouldering her way toward some invisible center, saying, "Hello, hello, how are you, hello." But as soon as his message came through, she was up. She knew it was Ori before she checked. She knew it was her son.

You up, ima? His chat icon is a photo of his army boots. Miriam remembers when he sent that photo to the family group chat. The girls had cooed appreciatively—"Thank you for guarding over us!"—and little Tovah insisted Ori make it his profile photo.

Yuval, beside Miriam in bed, is long asleep. His breath is childlike—rhythmic and oblivious. The room is dark but for the light from Miriam's phone.

What happened? she pokes into her phone. *Are you okay?* If Ori were going out on a mission, he'd have sent her a golden heart emoji. That's their system. No words, just the heart. And only to her: nothing in the family group chat, no need to upset his sisters.

She'd call, but knows he can't answer. It's well past midnight, nearly one in the morning. No matter. Tomorrow isn't such a long day, only a few appointments with her brides—the newly engaged who come to her for the required learning before marriage. Her youngest client right now is a girl Ori's age from Los Angeles. Rachel. A moody, difficult bride—Miriam's favorite kind. She likes having someone to convince. It gives her an excuse to fall in love with her own observance, again and again.

She sends another text message to Ori: *Where are you?* She rubs her foot gently against Yuval's leg. It's almost like touching her own leg, touching the leg of her husband. The windows of their bedroom are locked; the curtains press out against the dark. Little Tovah's room is reinforced as a bomb shelter. Ever since that Arab boy died in the hospital—the one who had been in a fight—there has been talk of revenge attacks from the nearby Palestinian villages. Death and honor. Over the sound of her husband's gentle sleeping, Miriam can hear periodic pops of gunfire from over there. That's how the Arabs mark weddings. Even this late at night, it could be a wedding.

Ori kicks another pebble. He checks his watch, again. Not even 01:00, cus emek. With him are all the familiar pricklings. Boredom edged with exhaustion and a bleak, low-grade horniness that never quite goes away. He's posted inside the closed gate of the base, guarding the big tinny shed that is the armory. He can't see past the gate's camo netting but knows that outside, the road is badly paved. Really, this is less of a base than an outpost—not even a real mess hall, just some big pots to boil pasta.

Night air cools his cheeks and neck, but it can't reach under his vest, packed heavy with extra clips and stun grenades, rubber tubing, unexplained stray bullets he doesn't know what to do with, a notebook, and a dead pen. His right hand secures his Tavor in a gesture so ingrained he does not know he is doing it.

Here's a typical army atrocity: The armory is empty. Empty! It's locked and guarded and completely empty. Under the pus-yellow light of the empty armory, his shadow is long. It wouldn't be so bad if there were someone else with him. But everyone is either asleep or out on patrol.

On guard duty, you're not supposed to have your phone, but obviously he does. With his free hand, his left hand, he maneuvers to his chats. Ima has responded to his bored and desperate messages. She's asking if he's okay. But the girl he's been messaging with has not responded. He took his shot an hour ago: *Awake?* He knows by the little blue check marks that she saw the message and is ignoring him. Still, he thinks he might have a chance. The photos she posts are invitations, according to Danny, who grabbed Ori's phone when they were killing time between rotations. "Achi, look at the filter she's using!" Danny pushed Ori back with his fingertips so he could keep scrolling through the photos. "Do they teach you what that means in yeshiva?" Ori laughed as he sat back down on a cot, not minding the gentle ribbing about his background. They were all hanging out in a trailer. Danny and fat Moshik shirtless, bouncing around to some mindless dance-hall track that had the tiny speakers in seizures. "Yalla, Moshik," said Danny, still looking at the photos on Ori's phone, "she's almost as pretty as our Ori."

On guard duty, you're also not supposed to close your eyes, but he does that, too. Senses heighten. The air rushes in through his nostrils. A squeal of acceleration floats up from Highway 60. Arab or Jew, impossible to say. Pop of a rifle. Village wedding. There's another sound too, or it's not exactly a sound but a vibration underneath all the other sounds, the kind of buzz you'd expect from a live high-voltage wire. He opens his eyes.

Since that Palestinian kid died over Passover—Salem Abu-Something—things have been hot. East Jerusalem was insane for the funeral: Arabs waving around their shitty AKs smuggled in from wherever, dumpsters burning in the streets, the body wrapped in a flag, bricks through the glass of light-rail stops. He saw all of this online. Bethlehem is quieter, but still it's hot. You can feel it on patrol, knocking on doors in the camps, thick hijabis pushing you back, screaming, "There are no shabaab here," like, Okay, lady, sure. He'd rather be on patrol than stuck in a static position. Who's out with Alon tonight? Moshik? Not Danny, since it's Danny replacing him at 04:00 in cus emek more than three hours.

Tomorrow, he and Danny both rotate to washing dishes in the afternoon. Danny will put a huge tinny pot on his head and say something like, "Achi, this is real combat." Later this week they'll be backing up the Tunnels Checkpoint, which is boring but not as boring as this. Really, anything is better than being alone. He checks his phone again: nothing. Responds to Ima that yes, sure, he's okay.

This base isn't even that far from his settlement. So close, yet he's released to go home only every other weekend for sleep, hot shower, sleep, clean socks, sleep, TV, sleep, Ima's food, a bed with sheets, a pillow, and sleep, sleep, sleep.

Even when her son is close, he is in another world. And he is so close. Miriam could walk to Ori's base from home. Theoretically. As the ghost walks. If Highway 60 were safe at night, or safe on foot, ever. If it didn't wind past Palestinian villages and camps, if it weren't haunted by rusted-out sedans cruising silently, headlights turned off, waiting to kidnap a Jew. Basically, if everyone in the world froze for an hour, everyone but Miriam, she could walk to Ori's base. Out the front door in her long, fuzzy nightgown, which is decorated with hearts and coffee mugs. She'd cover her hair—simply, with one of her berets maybe, but she'd cover it, even if she were invisible to everyone but HaShem. Barefoot in the silent street. Past the Drors, past the Farbers, past the Chabad family that just moved in, past the Levis. Silent houses of white stone walls, red tile roofs, just like her own. The road curves down toward the settlement gates, widens. The gates would open silently for her, close silently behind her. Left on the highway in the silver-lit dark, past scrub brush and bullet casings, past the gates of the next settlement over. On Highway 60, she'd pass bus stops reinforced against car rammings, guard towers along the road, closed gates of communities like her own. She hasn't been to this particular base—they don't open it for Parents' Day like on bigger bases—but she can picture the way the water jugs begin to turn black as you curve up the road toward Palestinian homes. From photos that Ori has sent, she knows that once you get inside the base's camo netting, it's nothing more than a dirt lot scattered with a handful of trailers like shipping containers. Her son, she hopes, she prays, is bunked safe and sound in one of them.

Mostly, he wants her to worry about him. Then, when she's worried, he wants her to leave him alone. He can feel himself doing it—sending her texts that make her concerned about how he's eating, sleeping, if he's safe. Then, when she calls him or threatens to call Commander Alon, he gets annoyed. Annoyed and something else. On the Friday nights when he is home, she holds his head between her hands for the blessing of the children. She closes her eyes. All around them are the candles that she and the girls have lit and blessed. Her smell is familiar. So familiar. It's the smell of rooms that she's been in all day with the windows closed. Suffocating, comforting. Mother. When Ima blesses him her eyes close hard, but she holds him gently, and he knows, of course he knows, that she's thinking about stabbings, car rammings, stones to the back of the skull, shots to the gut with a secreted rifle. She's thinking of all the ways there are for him to die. She kisses his forehead forcefully, like she's trying to reach his brain, or maybe his soul. That's what he hates. It's her fear that makes him feel insane.

She's only called his commander once, as far as he knows. This was back before the final rotation of their training, which meant, wow, almost ten months ago, back when he was not even a year into his service. He was a new soldier, and Ima called Alon to ask why her son kept falling asleep at the table, falling asleep in the car, falling asleep on the toilet. And why was he losing weight? Wasn't he eating and sleeping right? Alon relayed all of this to Ori, in front of the guys. She wasn't the first mother to do it. Their first rotation was a tough one, everyone running on two hours of sleep. Alon decided to make an example of Ori.

"I told her, 'No, Madame Lev, he's not eating right, and no, he's not getting enough sleep, do you know why?'" Alon had one leg up on a rusted-out tank when he told this story. With his face cut up from shaving over his acne, Alon looks like a kid even though he's at least twenty-two. They were all sitting around the skeletal tank, waiting for something, Ori can't remember what. In one base or another, surrounded by dead things, waiting. Alon said, "'Because he's in the army.'" Then he turned to Ori. "Nu, tell your ima this isn't the fucking scouts." He gave the same little speech a few weeks later, when Moshik's ima called worried about his constipation.

I'm fine, he writes. *Go to bed.*

Something feels wrong, feels off. Miriam texts Ori: *Where are you? You're on base?*

You are supposed to get ugly with a girl in your belly, because, they say, she steals your beauty. But Miriam was pretty and glowing when pregnant with each of her older girls. It was Ori who drained her, sapped the color and glow from her cheeks, clogged her pores. She was swollen and lethargic. She took offense at everything. It must be a girl, people said, for her to take so much from you. She heard a smugness in their comments: *You're ugly and you can't give Yuval a son.* But it was Ori. Beautiful boy with such fine features. So sweet-faced as a toddler that you had to squish him to you, like something out of an old German fairy tale, yellow curls and dimpled apple cheeks. Now he is tall, broad, erect. He cuts off the necks of his T-shirts in the kibbutznik style; it shows off the new swell in the muscles of his shoulders, so at odds with the soft, full mouth. Little Avital's seminary friends giggle and whisper around him. Young teenage girls in long jersey skirts, all wearing T-shirts from their brothers' combat units. Over Passover—she loves to think about this—one girl dropped a plate when Ori walked into the kitchen. She looked at him and dropped it. The thing shattered.

From his shadowy side of the bed, closer to the window, Yuval lets out a small cry. He rolls toward her, and because she's sitting up, his nose smooshes against her belly as he flings his arm over her lap. A tuft of his hair, so gray now, sticks out to the side and she tucks it behind his ear with her free hand. Her phone light dims automatically. Yuval is breathing. Miriam is breathing. The room is dark.

Ori is startled at a low growl behind him. He spins around to see a border police jeep—the sound is the crunch of slow tires on gravel—coming at him from the heart of the base. Headlights killed. Could it be Alon? He can't see into the windshield, protected as it is with metal grating against stone-throwers. A grille like bared teeth. From here, under the uncertain light of the armory, the jeep looks like a dark mouth approaching him.

"Ahlan." He waves, but the vehicle curves by him, not stopping.

Inside, he can just make out the figure in the passenger seat, but not the driver. It's not Alon, he sees now; it's nobody in his unit. It must be one of the guys from the intelligence team that also uses this base. Cherries, they are called. They specialize in disguising themselves as Arabs.

The Cherry in the jeep does not wave. Nor does the jeep stop. It disappears behind the trailers where soon—but not soon enough—Ori will be sleeping. Maybe they are doing some kind of surveillance.

Not even Alon knows much about the Cherries or where their orders come from. They lean against the backs of trailers, smoking, growing quiet when anyone approaches. Maybe the weirdest part is that they don't wear a uniform. The Cherries dress like civilians: jeans and T-shirts. Either they're never in uniform or they're always in uniform. It depends how you look at it.

Ori is not exactly scared of them. But it's weird how much the Cherries look like Arabs, talk like Arabs. They cover their faces and join in on the wrong side of demonstrations, or a mob of stone-throwers, and then—it's so crazy to see—they are on either side of an Arab, a real one, before he can even throw the stone, lifting him up, pushing his head down. The guy never gets it at first, like, "Who are you? Who's your father?" The Arabs can't believe there were Jews among them, looking like them, speaking Arabic like them the whole time. Ori and Danny have watched this at demonstrations, when they're shooting teargas and sound bombs in arcs over crowds of villagers who wave olive branches, scurry like bugs, duck from the sound of it. But the Palestinians aren't really scared of flash-bang or even a little live fire. It's Cherries who really freak them out, who cause a panic to rise up. Ori thinks the Arabic word for the chaos sounds cool: "*foudah*." It's a word that sounds like what it is. *Foudah*.

Sometimes Miriam becomes aware of a ringing in the silence. Not a ringing like a telephone, and not an alarm for a fire or an air raid either. More like the sound a spoon makes when circled again and again around the rim of a full glass. An accumulation of vibration. She can't tell if the sound comes from inside her, or from something out in the silence, or if that is what people mean when they talk about silence. How could she ask anyone about this? What would the question even be? "Does your silence buzz?" Impossible.

There is death all over the settlement. Yael, of course Yael. And others since. One of the Weisner twins committed suicide when he was home for Passover from a yeshiva near Hebron. Nobody got close to the truth except to say that he'd had a funny walk. Yehudit's son was shot by an Arab who wrestled away his handgun at a bus stop near the junction. You were always going to funerals, to and from funerals, in cars filled with grieving mothers.

Ori presses his boot into the dry earth, lifts it up carefully to see the imprint of his tread. Then he kicks it all away. Sometimes he sees himself as he appears on the shuddering green surveillance screens monitoring every inch of the country, or at least anywhere it's hot. He knows there are rooms, isn't sure exactly where they are, but in these rooms girls with long hair and flat voices stare at screens. They are watching for disturbances, watching for the kind of thing you know only when you see it. They monitor the footage from heat sensor cameras, all over the checkpoints, all over the security wall, all over the north all over the south all over the Old City. All of it is monitored at several angles by these girls, who legally—like, by an actual law—are forbidden from taking their eyes off the screens where he and a thousand other soldiers count off the hours of long afternoons, of empty nights. This is the only job in the army closed to men. The watchers are always, always women.

A few girls from his scouts group ended up in green rooms. They say it isn't a bad job. Their shifts last only a few hours a day, then they are free. But it sounds crazy to him. To be forced to stare. If a girl looks away from her screen even for a second, she'll go to military jail. That's what he's heard. Actual jail. Because in the second she looks away, anything can happen: a soldier stabbed, a bomb affixed to the bottom of a bus, a body over the fence, all while the girl is tying her boots or texting her boyfriend. You hear stories about cockroaches scurrying over the girls' feet: everyone in the room is screaming and jumping up on chairs, but their eyes never leave the screen, not for a second. You hear other stories about guys who visit their girls when they're alone on a night shift in the green room, and one thing leads to another, as they say, but all of it happens with the girl's eyes staying fixed to the screen.

Ori tries to imagine how he looks on the green screen. A small figure in the dark. He wonders who she is, the girl whose job it is to watch him. To watch *him*. Who are you? he wonders. Who is the girl watching me? *Hello*, he thinks. *You up?*

A moth beats itself against the armory light, creating a convulsion of shadows.

Ori doesn't really think about the night at the mall with Meir and Liran. When he sees photos of the dead kid's face, Ori doesn't say to himself, Meir did that, my friend did that, I watched him do that. He doesn't, not really.

Sometimes he'll get an image of Meir walking away from him and Liran. The three of them were in the mall that night, wandering around kind of aimlessly, looking at window displays of the same headless mannequins in the same sweatshirts, half-heartedly checking out girls. Were they thinking about Yael Salomon? Butchered in her own home? Fourteen years old? Yes and no.

They got frozen yogurt in little paper cups with baby-sized spoons. Ori was out of uniform but carrying his Tavor, his lockbox broken again. All night, Meir had been eyeing it like, "Oh, wow, you got the new night-vision scope," like, "Yo, I hear the shoulder weight is really good." This from a guy who got an army exemption to play sports. Liran didn't let it go, like, "What online review did you read that in, achi?" Liran ended up in a tank, which is kind of lame, but he's cool about it. Says it is what it is. They were leaning against a wall or a counter. Ori and Liran talked about their commanders and their rotations while Meir looked around trying to find something else to talk about. He was the one who noticed first, Meir. He noticed that people were hurrying toward the exit, that there was movement toward the mall exit. Meir walked first, and they followed him, but it wasn't exactly following him. It was as if they were pulled, all of them, pulled out of the mall, past the revolving doors, past the dinosaur security guard with his useless handgun and his reflective vest, out into the well-lit street. There was a crackling in the night air, invisible but palpable. It reminded Ori of the rapid-fire stun grenades they use to control protests, the way they make the air snap with their vicious intelligence. Every wall, every tree, everything bounced and echoed a single sentence: "They've got an Arab." They were moving toward that sentence. Later, he read that it had been planned by a few guys but the crowd was drawn in spontaneously. When Meir went in, Ori and Liran held back, a quick shared glance was all they needed to confirm, because they weren't kids. They were soldiers.

What Ori returns to, sometimes, is Meir's back as he walked out and away from them that night, as he stepped into the crowd already undulating around the Arab kid on the ground. He joined his body into the frenzied activity that went on for long minutes, long after Ori and Liran had turned together to leave. They didn't see much. They didn't see what went down. They heard about it later. Ori heard enough to know that while he and Liran were walking toward the car, Meir was still there, kicking the kid with the others, kicking him until his organs began to bleed.

Back at the car, Ori and Liran waited in silence until Meir came and sat in the back seat, breathing heavy.

When Liran turned on the car some whiny, cheesy Mizrahi music started to play. Ori cranked the volume loud so none of them could talk. *My beloved, my beloved, my beloved*, the song screamed.

It didn't upset him. He sees a lot of things, nu. Like fine, when Arab kids throwing stones get arrested nu, fine, some of the keener guys—Moshik especially, that fat psycho—will want to smack them around a bit before handing them off to Shin Bet or to the Cherries, whoever is beating up junior terrorists that day. The guys in Ori's unit will talk about it later, and Ori will listen and shrug, like, Nu, so you broke his jaw.

He texts Ima: *I'm guarding the armory.*

Miriam saw on Facebook that the Arab, the one from the mall, might have actually been gay—it's possible his own family murdered him. An honor killing that they are blaming, of course they are, on Israelis. Any excuse they can get for revenge.

She pokes out a response to Ori: *Who are you guarding with? Is that the problem? Talk to me.*

Again, the slow crunch of the jeep startles Ori. Again, the moment of panic—Who is it? Who is coming?—before Ori understands that it must be the Cherries again. They are circling around the base, either on some mission of their own, or because they are fucking with him. This time, the jeep headlights are on as the vehicle approaches, slowly, slowly.

For a few miserable seconds, Ori can't see anything but white light. He feels helpless, pinned by the headlights, and in a way it is a relief. There is nothing he can do but wait for this to pass. Sounds magnify. Tires on the gravel, hum of the motor, Ori's own breath.

Slowly, the jeep arcs by him. The headlights no longer in his face. He can almost touch the windows of the vehicle, and although his vision is spotty from the headlights that were a moment ago in his eyes, he can see inside the vehicle enough that he's sure that it's the same two Cherries from before. This time, the one not driving gives a slow wave. It seems like he's laughing even if he's not smiling. Then he's gone.

Ori watches the jeep drive away to once again disappear behind the trailers. Even after he can no longer see anything, he hears the tires' soft crunch. He's breathing harder than he should be.

When he looks down at his phone, he sees that Ima is lighting him up with messages. Ori feels the tug of her concern. Using the voice recorder function of the chat, he records a quick message to her: "Ima," he says into his phone, "I'm fine." His voice sounds weird, too young and small. As if his voice couldn't travel in the darkness, couldn't go beyond the ring of light he stands in, by the bolted doors of the vacant armory. He imagines the Cherries in the jeep imitating his voice, laughing. He erases the recording and tries again, speaking low: "Ima, I'm fine. Go to bed." He sends it. Then immediately after, because she'll just keep asking unless he tells her, he sends a second recording: "I'm guarding alone. It's fine."

Miriam shakes Yuval awake. "I'm going to kill that commander!"

"What? What happened?" His face is scrunched and sleep-blind in the light as he rolls to his nightstand and gropes for his glasses.

"He's guarding alone." She's not yelling lest she wake the girls, but her voice is strained and the octave high. Guarding alone. Where? Where is he? When she tries to picture a Palestinian village, what she sees is a rock overturned to reveal scurrying, leggy insects burying themselves deep in damp, dark soil. They are looking for revenge. For that Arab boy's death, for history itself. They are going to take her son.

"What? Where?" He's putting on his glasses.

"Guarding alone," she repeats. "Patrolling alone, can you believe it?"

"Hold on. Is he guarding or patrolling?" They are side by side up against the headboard.

She ignores the question. "He's out there," she says. It feels true and urgent so she says it again. "He's out there alone." She adds, "He could be near a camp. Alone!"

"But, Miriam." His glasses are greasy, his hair tufts out to one side. I love you, she thinks, she can't help it, even though it's not what she should be thinking right now. He smooths down his hair. Takes her right hand in both of his and presses his thumb firmly on her wrist, like he's checking her pulse. He says, "That can't be true."

Already she's scrolling through her phone contacts: Alon Mechanic, Alon Neighbor, although they moved years ago. There! Alon Commander. "I'm calling." But she doesn't, not yet.

"At this hour?" He checks the alarm clock beside him. "Nearly two in the morning and you're calling his commander?"

She shifts to face him. She can see the young man obscured by his swollen features, just as she can see the child lingering in Ori's cheeks and browline. "Yuval, they want revenge for the Arab at the mall. They want revenge, and our son is alone."

"Miriam, if he's guarding alone, then it must be in a secure area." He's using army-talk.

She shakes her head. Guarding, patrolling—the distinction isn't the point. "Everything is changing," she says. There's panic leaking into her voice. Ever since that Arab boy died, something has been creeping out from her peripheral vision, almost like being haunted, some horrible price waiting to announce itself. She says to Yuval, "I have a bad feeling." Yuval is still holding her hand, so small in his. He rubs his rough thumb over her knuckles. He taps twice, nods. A concession, she knows, to her domain: the children.

Alon is crazy. No, not crazy. He's the kind of guy that the army saved. Poor family, absent father. He said as much himself on Parents' Day: "The army saved me." Miriam knows the kind of house Alon got out of because she used to visit houses like that, thirty-odd years ago—that doesn't sound long enough, it should be longer—a lifetime ago, when she was serving as a social worker in the army. Eighteen years old on the bus with her clipboard. That long olive-green army skirt swishing as she climbed filthy apartment building stairwells in the southernmost parts of cities, the smell of rot and damp cigarettes. She was a child, but they were all children. It had been her job to help soldiers from difficult homes get the special accommodations they needed. She advocated for these young men—got them safe housing, pro bono dental operations, reduced army hours. Nobody taught her how to do this. She figured it out along the way.

She knows before she calls that Alon will pull typical commander power moves, knows the phone will ring five times, knows he'll answer in the deepest voice he can muster, "Allo," never inflected with a question mark.

"Alon." Say it sharp, but not too sharp. "This is Miriam Lev, Ori's mom. How are you?"

"What is it?" Curt, efficient.

"I just talked to Ori."

"And?"

She plows ahead: "Did you know he's alone?"

"Listen," Alon says.

Yuval pats her knee. He heaves out of bed and walks, a bit stiffly, to their bathroom. Miriam watches him close the door behind him.

"Listen," Alon repeats.

But he doesn't say anything, so she says, "He needs someone with him, Alon. You know he needs someone with him." She is talking fast, she can feel the sharp wet dots of the letters, jabbing him over the phone. She is careful not to raise her voice too much. "Please, get someone else over there."

"I'm on patrol," he says. "Ori is in a secure location." The way he's reasoning with her, he sounds like the kid he is. How many springs has he seen? Twenty-two?

"And you, are *you* guarding alone?"

"Giveret Lev, I'm not guarding, I'm on patrol, so listen—" he says, showing his frustration with over-the-top formality.

"No, you listen! Ori is in danger. When I heard it, I thought there must be a mistake. I said to my husband, I said, 'There is no way that Alon sent Ori to guard by himself outside a camp filled with Hamasniks.'"

Alon clucks his tongue desperately. "Nu, Miriam."

She has to be careful about this one, but here it goes: "I didn't know that was legal."

Pause. In the quiet, she can hear Yuval on the other side of the door, peeing.

She goes on. "Really, I could have sworn that it was illegal."

"What you're asking me to do will affect all my soldiers," Alon starts. She lets him finish.

She's called Alon once before. Ori made her promise to never ever do it again. But everyone does it, everyone calls to complain. What kind of mother would you be if you didn't intervene? There's a joke that goes around: the Americans have an army of one, but we have an army of mothers. The new immigrants on the settlement have trouble getting over it. "It's so funny," Meir Klausman's ima, Susan, said to Miriam, breathy and chipper on one of their walks. "In the other armies, it's completely different." In her stiff-jawed Hebrew, she explained that an army mother in England would never get a commander's phone number, probably not even know where in Afghanistan her son was deployed. Miriam was bored, thinking, What do I care for some other army? Planning in her head what she'd put in the Crock-Pot when she got home.

On the phone, Alon is talking about the rotation, about who is closing Shabbat. Yuval walks out of the bathroom. She watches his lips move once he's in the bedroom. *Blessed are you who formed man with wisdom and created him with orifices.*

She keeps her tone low and tender when she says, "Alon." It's time to pull back. She's worked him up a bit; now she pulls back, makes an appeal to the soft spot she's exposed. "You're a good commander. You're fair. We know that Ori is lucky to have you. Please, Alon, help us out." Make him feel like a big man.

❦

When Ori checks his phone again, it's messages from his group chat with Tovah and Avital. "The Little Ones," that's what they call their group chat.

> Avital: Ima is calling your commander??!?
> Tovah: We can hear her from our room
> Avital: Tovah go to bed! Ori nu tell her to go to bed

What Ori thinks: Fuck, fuck, fuck.
What he writes: Both of you go to bed it's super late

> Avital: Why did she call him?????
> Ori: Because she's worried
> Avital: Are you ok?
> Ori: Yes go to bed I have to go

But already, Alon is calling. Ori doesn't pick up. Alon messages and Ori reads the preview so Alon won't get a notification that he opened the message: *I know you can see this.* Fuck it. Ori opens the message: *You explain to Danny why he can't go home this Shabbat.*

Cus emek, cus emek. Anything but this. Doing push-ups till your arms fall off, closing extra Shabbats on base, cleaning toilets even—anything is better than being the shitboy who steals sleep from a friend. He texts Ima: *Why did you call Alon?? He woke up Danny . . .*

The sound of feet on gravel pulls him out of his phone. Panicked because he thinks it's Danny, and what to even say? Sorry I stole your weekend at home? But it's not Danny. It's the jeep, idling a few meters away. Like a cat in the darkness. The jeep with the Cherries inside. Headlights killed. Ori has no idea how long the vehicle has been there, watching him.

The jeep begins to move toward him again. Again, a windshield like bared teeth moving through the dark. Again, faces he can't see, somewhere in there, faces. Only this time, the jeep does not arc past him. This time, the jeep stops just beyond the radius of the armory light.

Ori waits. He wouldn't have time to jump out of the way if they accelerated now—no, he'd fly into the gate of the base, broken legs, broken pelvis. *Just get it over with*, Ori thinks. Why would he think that? A crazy thought.

The passenger door opens. A Cherry gets out. His jeans are bleached a certain way, tight in a certain way. It looks so Arab, it's so Arab. He's got a brandless blue T-shirt with one thick white stripe down either side. He could be darting through an alley in one of the camps. He could be throwing stones to smash Ori's cheekbones. All he needs is a rag or kaffiyeh tied around his face and he could be one of them, crouching behind a dumpster in flames.

The Cherry walks into the light of the armory. From the dip of his jeans, Ori can guess he's got a handgun tucked in the back. Thin torso. He brings a hand to his mouth, removes an unlit cigarette to say, "We hear your ima called." He's standing an arm's length from Ori now, the jeep still in the background, driver invisible, engine rattling softly, ready.

"What?"

The Cherry doesn't repeat himself. Instead he says, "Do you have a light?" He glances down and kind of laughs. Ori realizes he's been standing with his weapon ready. Standing with his weapon held across his chest. Both hands in position. He's bumbling now. Brings the rifle down to his side. Pulls out a lighter from his vest, almost pulling out some stupid loose bullets by mistake. The Cherry is the same height as Ori. He leans in to light up, and Ori can smell him. Cologne and sweat. What is that cologne they all use? All of them. He even smells Arab.

The Cherry pulls back swiftly on an inhale. "So you're the beauty," he says.

Ori thinks for one full second about smashing his own face in.

The Cherry draws a quick figure eight with his cigarette in a gesture that Ori has never seen before, but which he understands immediately as the Cherry offering him a cigarette. Ori makes his own gesture, hands held up like, Don't shoot, which he means as, No thanks.

The Cherry shrugs. For the second time he says, "We hear your ima called." He draws out the words *your ima*—a challenge that they both know Ori won't take.

Ori is trying to focus on the Cherry's face, but finds himself following the ember of the cigarette. He believes that the Cherry knows all about Ima's phone call to Alon. He believes him. He believes this guy has seen every text Ori has ever sent. To his mother, his sisters, his friends. He'll believe anything this guy says. They are the same age, but they are not the same at all, not even close. Ori says, "Isn't Danny coming?" and his voice sounds pleading, childish. The Arab is smoking. No, the Cherry is smoking. But so Arab. Even the way he holds his cigarette is Arab.

"Don't worry about Danny," the Cherry says.

In the army, there are real Arabs. Bedouin tracking units, Druze warriors up north. All honor and carnage. When one of them speaks Hebrew, you can hear that they are Arab; you can hear the throaty gargle of Arabic haunting all the words. But the Cherry sounds normal. He sounds like Ori. Ori is about to ask his name. He wants to know if it's an Arab name or a Jewish name. But somehow he knows that the Cherry won't answer him. The way the Cherry smokes, he inhales before he is done exhaling. The smoke leaks out of his nose. Or maybe he would answer Ori. Maybe he would answer and say, "My name is Salem Abu-Something." Ori wasn't there. Ori didn't see. He didn't see what Meir did to the Arab. He feels like he's saying this to the Cherry, like he's being interrogated. Shut up. "Where are you from?" Ori asks, just to say something aloud.

"The north." He's facing the jeep.

"Like, a village?"

The Cherry turns to Ori. "Are you trying to find out if I'm Arab?"

"No," Ori says. Pause. The Cherry doesn't look away. "Yes," Ori says.

The Cherry moves his tongue around in his mouth like he's looking for something there. "I'm a Jew." Pause. "Brother, brother of mine."

Ori keeps talking like an idiot. "Why do you speak Arabic so well?"

"When did you hear me speak Arabic?"

When did he? "But you do, I mean, *yanni*, you can." He's talking fast, Ori is, talking like he can talk his way out of what comes next. But what comes next?

The Cherry laughs. "*Yanni*," he repeats. "Why do you speak Hebrew so well?" But he doesn't wait for an answer, shrugs with an agitation that feels familiar to Ori. He says, "You want me to speak Arabic." It's not a question.

He yells something in Arabic in the direction of the jeep. Ori hears the word "*jeish*," "army." The sounds of the foreign language creep along Ori's shoulders, like spiders down into his ear. Arabic. And suddenly Ori knows that he is wrong. He was wrong. Danny is not coming. These are not Cherries. These are Arabs. These are Palestinians from some Hamas village. Danny is dead. They got Danny already. He is bleeding out in the dirt behind their bunk trailer. He has been dead this whole time.

The Arab is going to stuff Ori in this stolen jeep and drive him into the night through the gates that Ori, yes, Ori himself will open for them when they force him to. The Arab turns to Ori, smiling, says something fast, but Ori is sure he is so sure he catches the word "Salem." The dead boy. They have come for revenge. Finally it's happening.

The Arab waves the lit cigarette at the jeep, and it must be a signal, because the headlights flash on. Ori is blind. Ori is frozen. Run, he begs himself. But he does not move.

Okay, fine. Okay, fine. Okay, fine. Ori did see. He saw more than he tells himself he saw. He saw the Salem kid covering his head with his hands, cradling his own head. They were walking away, but he turned back. He saw Salem trying to crawl away. He saw that. He did see that. He does not know if he wishes he had stopped it or if he wishes he had done it. *Please*, Ori begs inside. *Please*. He can't see for the light. Please get here, Danny. "Danny?" he finds he's said it aloud, not exactly a question. A plea.

He has learned what he's supposed to do in a kidnapping. Kick him in the balls and run. If he gets you in a choke hold, you use your weight to disable it. Wrists are weak. Joints are weak. But he doesn't move. All of this is happening in less than a second. In the time that remains, what Ori is thinking about is the girl in the green room. What does she see now? What does she see on her green screen? What will she do when Ori is taken away? Is she already crying, screaming into the contact radio as a yet-to-be-identified infantryman walks toward the hijacked jeep? From the stolen jeep he'll be hustled, bludgeoned, into a rusted-out Subaru then into a Hamas basement, and that's it. His face on posters, on bumper stickers. His face, a national wound. Which photo of him will Mom use?

The second figure is moving toward him out of the jeep. Here it comes. Here he comes. A figure in the darkness. Not now, Ori begs. Please, not tonight.

∽∾

Miriam falls asleep with her phone in her hands. Yuval gently leans over her to turn out the lamp on her nightstand.

∽∾

Ori's eyes are closed. Ice water in his gut. He is trying to remember his mother's hands.

"You piece of shit," the Arab says.

But it's a familiar voice.

"You piece of shit." That's Danny's voice. Danny's voice. Of course it's Danny.

Danny is greeting the Cherry with a handshake, turning to Ori to say, "Yo, did you hear this guy's Arabic? It's wild." Ori is breathing heavy. Danny is saying to the Cherry, who's throwing the rest of his cigarette to the ground, "Have you met Ori Lev? The shitboy I'm about to murder?" Danny laughs. It's too loud, like there's an echo bouncing off Ori's cold skin. Somewhere outside the gates, somewhere out there, is the deafening slam of a car door. Ori feels his guts clench, and he knows without any doubt, just pure knowing, that if any one of them—the Cherry or Danny or the third guy, whoever he is, still in the jeep—had touched him or made a move to grab him or even just pulled at his arm, that Ori would have shit himself.

"You heard how he stole my weekend?" Danny says, still to the Cherry. "He's as stupid as he is beautiful, this shitboy."

"He's about to piss himself," the Cherry says to Danny, nodding his chin toward Ori, who is trying to will his mind—beating like a moth against the armory light—to come back into his body. The jeep flicks its headlights and with that cue the Cherry heads back. Danny raises his hand to wave as the jeep drives off.

Only when they are alone does Danny give Ori a pitiful little shove. "Achi," he says, his voice truly plaintive. "Why?"

Ori knows with all of his heart how precious those three lost hours of sleep were to Danny. All of them can fall asleep like zombies: at the bus stop, leaning against a wall, tying a shoe. All of them are empty and holding on until they are released to go home for a few days to sleep and sleep until they are human again. Ori stole those hours from Danny. He fucked up the schedule, and now they'll both be trapped on base over the weekend.

Ori can't look at him. "I swear," he says, "I swear I didn't know she'd call."

Mornings are almost always chilly, even after Passover and closing in on summer. With her free hand, Miriam wraps her light, loose cardigan closed. She loves this gesture, how self-contained it makes her feel. She uses her elbow to lever the heavy-duty garbage bag against her hip. She loves the gray glow that fills the sky before the sun. Lit indirectly, everything around her—the flowering palms in the street median, the cars parked on either side, the dumpster she's walking toward—seems a slightly softer version of itself, more open to possibility. Perhaps Miriam is softer too, in this early hour before the people who need her can ask anything of her, or maybe better to say, before she can begin her obsessive monitoring for signs that they need something she can give them.

This morning, like every morning, Yuval rose first. How Miriam loves to lie in bed, soaking in the last sleepy moments of dawn, listening to the murmur of her husband's prayers. Modeh Ani, a prayer said even before you wash, and because of this, one devoid of the divine names. The prayer is, then, an imperfect offering—one made without the right words. Yet it is no less precious for it. There may be a metaphor there. Yuval's voice is deep, assured. When they were newly wed, lying together in an empty house, one not yet filled with children or even a dishwasher, he could make her cry out in pleasure just by speaking, lowly and sweetly, into her ear.

When Miriam rose, she hurried right to the toilet. Another blessing in her life: unshakable regularity. It's always in the morning after Yuval goes downstairs that she has her bowel movement. Always, an inexplicable thrill of terror as she sits on the toilet seat: *What, what, what will come out of me?*

The routine is that Yuval puts water in the kettle while Miriam takes out the trash for a few moments to herself. When she comes back, Yuval will have finished his coffee; her tea will be waiting. He'll kiss her forehead, then head to the office, stopping by shul for shacharit minyan; she'll herd Tovah and Avital to school. That forehead kiss is the result of a negotiation during which Miriam told Yuval she felt neglected when he left so quickly, as if he couldn't get out of the house fast enough. The kiss is their compromise. Is the gesture less satisfying because she requested it? No. Voicing desire does not dilute fulfillment. She teaches her brides as much—that communication is a mark of goodwill, of bravery, of love. She uses a parable of her own invention. Imagine your favorite part of the chicken is its dark thigh meat. You save this most delicious part for your husband, yourself eating the dry white breast—a sacrifice you've made for him without him asking you to do it. Only, you'll never know it, but he too is making a difficult sacrifice: he hates dark meat, which reminds him of a bruise. He craves the breast meat that he gives up, every time, to his beautiful wife. Two unhappy people, and for what? Just last week, she told this to Rachel, her youngest bride: there is no marriage built on suffering. Rachel had a cup of green tea in front of her, sitting back to tug at one of her earrings—a large pink crystal cube, the kind of gift a boyfriend buys in a remote bus depot on his way back from base. Yuval used to buy Miriam tinny bangles that made her look like a Yemenite bride. She still has them. Miriam knows Rachel's type: from a good, kosher home, yes, but filled with questioning.

Last night, Ori sent her whiny messages. He sounded annoyed, but he was grateful, she knows. She fixed the problem. She kept him safe.

Miriam opens the lid of the dumpster and heaves the trash bag in. She is at the end of the street. That's how it works here. Streets end, and then you're overlooking the hills of Judea. White rock and sparse evergreens, looking tentative and distant, unfolding below her.

There are doves everywhere, in every olive tree. Each year, Palestinians come to harvest the olives. A pretty sight.

The houses are not stirring yet. Here again is the gentle hum that animates Miriam's silences. It may come from the settlement's fence, which is electric, or was. They keep changing it to make it safer. Razor wire, motion sensors, lasers, cameras.

The settlement is always growing. From here, she can see not just the olive trees beyond the security fence, but the curve of the new developments, inching down the hillside. She's lived here for twenty years, and always thought of it as a village. Suddenly it is a sprawling place. New houses, new faces she doesn't recognize: young couples from Russia or America, here to take advantage of the government incentives. So many Americans. She remembers when they built the basketball court. She remembers Ori no more than eight years old coming home from basketball, thin-limbed and delicate, crying. She thought someone had hurt him, but he was crying because he had inhaled teargas, although he did not know it. The stuff floated up from the valley below when the police were dispersing the crowds of Arabs. He came home red-eyed, smelling sour, and Miriam had to laugh a little when she washed out his eyes with milk. "Oh, my love," she said, "I suppose we can't keep everything out with our fence." She tried to explain: "The police were shooting at bad men." She had him lean over the dairy sink so she could gingerly trickle milk from the carton into his red eyes. "Blink, my sweet," she said. The milk made white rivers down his precious face.

All at once, the doves let out their trills and flutter up from the lonely olive grove, which Miriam has been staring at with no intention for who knows how many minutes. The sun is up now, brightening the world and filling it with shadows.

Inside

Hamid monitors Muhi's face. Muhi has been silent—eyes downcast, engrossed in his own thoughts—ever since he began streaming the news from his tablet. Any second now, Hamid can feel it coming, any second now Muhi is going to look up with his tragedy eyes, his thick furrowed eyebrows, and begin on one of his hopeless rants. Death and injustice. Oslo. The Jews. Both of them are sitting on low plastic stools in the storage room, peeling MADE IN ALBANIA stickers off of wooden crosses. Muhi's legs are so long that he looks like a crouched insect. On the news, a kid is being interviewed at an East Jerusalem protest. "They take our lives, our bodies, our homes," the kid says in a village accent. "We have to protect what is ours." Muhi looks up. He is about to speak, Hamid can feel the moment coming. What else can he do? If Muhi goes off again, Hamid will die of agony. What else can he do? He needs a distraction.

"Believe me," Hamid says, before Muhi can get a word out. "Believe me, I think I made progress with Mai today."

Muhi's full eyebrows contort, but all he says is, "Oh?" He takes another cross out from the cardboard shipping box in front of them.

They are in the souvenir shop storeroom. All around them are cardboard boxes stacked on cheap metal shelving, piles of crosses, plastic bags filled with Palestine key chains, Virgin Mary icons. Muhi has the news streaming from his tablet, propped up against the legs of an empty plastic chair.

Hamid watches as his friend uses a pink plastic wedge to push off the incriminating MADE IN ALBANIA sticker. Muhi has boyish features—long eyelashes, mussed black hair—especially striking given how tall he is, standing at almost two meters. "Believe me," Hamid says, playing up his own deluded buoyancy for comic effect. "After class, I asked to walk her to the bus, and she said—" He pauses here, holding up an index finger, waits for Muhi to look at him with his dark tragedy eyes, and when he does, Hamid delivers the line: "She said, 'Maybe next time.'" He lets his hand fall in defeat.

"Oh?" Muhi repeats without much interest. His hands work off a sticker. Muhi is wearing one of his suits, or at least the dress pants. But whereas in the past the snappy clothes made Muhi look sharp, ambitious, now they seem a bit big on him. Hamid wonders if he's lost weight. Maybe he should ask. There are probably a lot of things that Hamid should ask his friend, but it's too hard to listen to the answers. Every time Muhi starts talking about his trip to Norway—freedom in Norway, that friend in Norway, can't stay in the West Bank, can't live like this, got to get back to Norway, Norway—Hamid needs to cut him off. He can't help it. He starts talking over Muhi, drowning him out with a pointless little routine about Mai, the rich girl who is breaking his heart.

Hamid wants it to be like it was before, when Muhi in his crisp suit used to dispense advice and all matter of aphorism. *Don't say, "If I . . ." Say, "When I . . ."* Hamid searches his friend's face for signs of an old Muhi that might be coaxed out, like kneeling down to the burrow of a small, nervous animal. *Come out*, he thinks.

The news anchor has moved on from the protests for Salem (Allahyerhamo) and is now covering an old story that Hamid already saw on his feeds: an American TV chef had an "Israeli food night" in which she made hummus, maqluba, falafel, and never once said the word "Palestine." The news lady is reading tweets aloud. "'They are erasing us, one bite at a time,' tweets Shab47 from Ramallah," she says. She's paid an actual salary to say that.

They have two more boxes of crosses to rid of MADE IN ALBANIA stickers. When Muhi acquiesced and finally agreed to let Hamid come hang out at the souvenir shop, he was clear on this: the ALBANIA stickers come off, but the GENUINE OLIVE WOOD ones they leave on.

Hamid doesn't let up. "Wallah, love is going to kill me," he says, then theatrically grimaces and puts his head on his forearms. Honestly, it's not a total lie. Even as he fools around for Muhi, Hamid really can see Mai flitting across the back of his eyelids. She is soft. In speech, yes, but physically too—neither fat nor thin but soft. And regal! So elegant when she turns away to smile into her hand or whisper something to Noor, that hardmouthed sidekick (and one to be careful of, Noor, with a brother locked away in Mejiddo). Mai is always walking away, walking toward a bus that takes her out of Bethlehem and across a checkpoint that Hamid, with his green hawiyya and no chance of a permit, can't ever hope to cross. At least not legally.

"Man," Muhi says at last. Finally speaking.

Hamid looks up, expectant, nervous. Will Muhi play along? Or will he pull them into another black hole?

"Man," Muhi says again. "What is it with you and these unattainable girls?"

Relief, because it's fine. It's fine. This time, it's fine. "I know," Hamid moans miserably. "Remember the girl from Nablus?"

"Wallah, I thought her brothers were going to kill you."

"How was I supposed to know?" Hamid gestures with his cross. "Who would know they were that high up in Hamas?"

Muhi makes a show of beating Hamid on the head and back, but really just giving him little baby taps. Hamid fends him off, making his own show of flailing his arms, of grabbing the back of Muhi's neck to pull him into a hug. The hair at the base of Muhi's skull is cut short. Hamid can hear the relief in his own laughter as they pull apart. They have been friends since before they were born.

It's late in the day, a Thursday. Each of them has a paper cup of black coffee at his feet, undrunk and cold now. Hamid came here straight from campus; his book bag is under his chair. They've opened the small door of the storage room to let in the still air, which at this hour is almost cool, spiked with the coming evening. Soon the maghrib call will waft in, and Hamid will stiffen alert, because he knows from Facebook that this is another one of Muhi's hopeless threads: *This year on Isra' Mi'raj the Jews are coming for Al-Aqsa Mosque, coming to raze the golden Dome of the Rock and rebuild their temple.* But for now, it's back to peeling stickers.

Hamid doesn't understand what he's doing in the dingy storeroom of a souvenir shop. No, that's not true. He's here because he's worried about Muhi and wants to stick close. Really, Hamid doesn't understand what Muhi is doing here. He's supposed to be at university in Ramallah, studying law, leaving them all behind. But suddenly now he's taking a semester off—we all know how that goes—to work for a cousin by his maternal uncle who is the manager at this souvenir shop, whatever it's called, one of the interchangeable joints dotted around the Church of the Nativity. Hamid hates the idea of Muhi working the sales floor: wearing a stupid Santa hat on his stupid head, stooping for commission from fat tourists, all *Yes, yes, locally sourced olive wood, yes*, with his hands folded. He hates the thought of him servile, feminine even.

Better to take the risk and slip inside the Wall if it means real work. Hamid made good money installing air conditioners for Segev the Russian Jew, who paid good cash to his small crew of workers, all of them inside without work permits. He paid at the end of the day, every day. Can't do much better than that. It was tuition money. Segev was funny, cigarette dangling from his mouth, sweater pattern like bus upholstery, saying in Hebrew that even Hamid recognized as slightly off, "Arab, Jew, what difference for me?" He kind of got off on giving Hamid advice. "Nobody to tell you your price." That was a favorite of his.

"Nobody but you, you mean," Hamid finally shot back in his ever-expanding Hebrew vocabulary. He was hunched with the weight of two air conditioners on the seventh flight of stairs in a building with a broken elevator in Ashdod, or was it Ashkelon? Some southern city. Segev was carrying—what?—a toolbox maybe, if that.

From behind Hamid on the stairs, Segev the Jew laughed in a single syllable, tapped on the boxes Hamid was carrying, but not too hard. "You're smart," he said. "Learn Russian, or better, learn English." Hamid remembers the building had no glass in the windows, just holes where the glass would go. That was a year ago, last Ramadan, a hot one. Hamid fasted with the others while they worked. He remembers looking out at the sea, looking south and wondering if he could see Gaza—the battered city, surrounded by the Jews on all sides.

He's hoping Segev will take him back to work during the summer vacation, although whenever he texts him the responses are noncommittal. *Good, good, talk to me when you're free.*

Hamid peels off another ALBANIA sticker. It leaves a slight residue on the wood of the cross, which is otherwise smooth and swirling with browns. He thinks about making a joke: *You're lucky you're so crazy-depressed that I come here to peel stickers with you.* But he decides not to risk it. Instead he asks, "So you'll come tomorrow? To lunch, yanni?"

"What's Oum Hamid cooking?" Muhi asks, without subtext.

"Whatever she wants, but come. Everyone asks about you." Once again, he finds himself searching Muhi's face, as if another Muhi were hiding in there.

"I'll probably come."

"Come, come," Hamid says. The news lady is on about a not-so-secret partnership between the Saudis and Israelis, which Hamid fears might set Muhi off, so he makes a quick grab for the tablet. "Yalla, enough of the news," Hamid says, fumbling to close the video. He searches for songs from the guy who won the last *Arab Idol*.

❧

The problem is that Muhi got away and then he had to come back. He's smarter than Hamid, it's fine, it's true. All of last year—the year Hamid spent working inside, the year he spent in the inky pre-dawn waiting for the guys who take you down south to smuggle you through the unfinished parts of the Wall, past the sights of the snipers, around the army patrol routes, all the way to the pickup spot, yanni, the year Hamid spent installing air conditioners for Segev—Muhi was already studying in Ramallah, well beyond the reach of Hamid's test scores. So yeah, he'd been jealous of Muhi in his businessman-looking shoes as he showed Hamid around a campus that wasn't just Palestinians but also international students, guys in hiking boots and white girls in enormous, flashy earrings who wanted to talk to you, with meaningful, pleading eyes, about *the occupation*, the word sharp in English, like four hard knocks on the door.

That year, all Muhi talked about was how he was going to do a semester abroad. His plan, he said, was to write to a bunch of the schools that sent their students to Ramallah on study-abroad, assuming these schools might host a Palestinian. Hamid and Muhi were rock-throwing by Rachel's Tomb the first time Muhi explained all this. It was winter, and the Jews were bombing Gaza again. It was all they watched on the news every night. The week of the bombardment, there was no work, too risky to get inside. Instead Hamid spent his days at Teta's with the boys. Mama and Baba came after work. All of them stayed up late every night, watching the buildings crumble, watching Jewish snipers pick off Palestinians at the Gaza border fence, Baba shaking his head and leaving the room then coming back, Mama and Teta clucking dolorously, all of them huddled around the space heater.

At the demonstration in solidarity with Gaza, Muhi tugged down at his hat excitedly, raising his voice slightly to be heard over the shouts of the shabaab throwing stones at the invisible soldiers on the other side of the Wall. A static of imperatives was coming down from the loudspeakers affixed to the army guard tower, a mix of Hebrew and Arabic. Soon the fog of teargas would rise, and everyone would scatter, which meant that the Jews might come out from behind the Wall. They only come when the crowd is scattering. Shots in the back. Muhi was explaining—raising his voice so Hamid could hear—that once he found out which foreign school would take him for a semester, he'd petition his administration to give him credit. He bent down to pick up a nicely shaped chunk of concrete. The group that day was small, maybe a few dozen kids from the camps. Their attention was lasered on the Wall, on the place from which the canisters would come. Muhi and Hamid moved with the group, tentative surges forward, pedaling back. Behind them, a boy was yelling up toward the guard tower, "Come out, dogs, come out."

When the first teargas canister popped itself about three meters in front of them, a kid with a red T-shirt tied around his face, maybe the taxi driver's kid, came running to kick it back in the direction of the soldiers, the thing streaking a noxious white. It's familiar, less a smell than a burn in your throat that brings on nostalgia. Years ago this had been them—Hamid and Muhi—stringy-armed youths from a nicer part of town who came down to the camps to do their part. Back then the Wall wasn't finished. The settler army had less to hide behind, and you had more chances to watch as your stone sang your name into a soldier's face. Hamid is pretty sure the Jews use more live fire today than they did even a few years ago. Or is that just nostalgia? After all, Hamid wasn't much older than thirteen the first time he held a friend's skull together, felt the plates shifting in his hands under the thick blood.

That day last year, Muhi adjusted his grip on the concrete chunk in his hand, as if they were teenagers again. Just before Muhi let it fly—long limbs configuring to snap the thing over the barrier (he's always had an amazing arm)—he shouted to Hamid, "It's about building your own destiny."

That was winter. Hamid spent the spring and summer working extra for Segev—things really pick up in the hot months—and by the next winter he had saved enough money to start at Bethlehem University, maybe not the most prestigious, but a degree is a degree. By then, Muhi really had done it. He was away. For the first month, it was all selfies from Norway: Muhi in a wool hat holding up a meatball on a stick, smiling with a bunch of blond people; Muhi posing in the snow with an Asian guy, his roommate in the dorms. *Is he Chinese?* Hamid asked over text. *He's Norwegian, he was born here,* Muhi wrote. *But yeah, he has family in China . . . if that's what you mean.* Hamid wasn't sure why this answer made him feel so far from Muhi, so left behind, but it did. Maybe it was that Muhi's life over there seemed capable of carrying more nuance and care than anyone was allowed over here. Hamid has never traveled, unless you count Jordan, which he does not, or Saudi, which he was too young to remember.

Sometimes it seems his entire life has been worn down to the few city blocks of Bethlehem between school and home, each inscribed in him: each dip in the road, each dusty corner, each dumpster, each double-parked car, each misspelled and off-brand store filled with junk from Turkey, from China. He wonders if that's a version of love—familiarity so deep it awakens dread.

As the months passed, more and more time went between messages from Muhi, and more and more of Hamid's video calls went ignored. He didn't give it too much thought. He was busy himself at the university now, catching up on premed courses, struggling through the yearlong Writing in English class, which was where he first saw Mai, carefully lining up pencils on her desk, carefully ignoring the men in the class, careful, careful, clean, and careful. A good girl.

Hamid had assumed Muhi would be back in Palestine for the winter semester, but he stayed away. Hamid wrote to check in: *You coming home?* And in the chat screen, he could see that Muhi spent a long time typing and pausing, typing and pausing, until he wrote only, *It's hard.*

At some point, he's not sure exactly when, he couldn't see many of Muhi's photos anymore. It meant either that Muhi had taken down a bunch of posts or, possibly, he was hiding more and more from Hamid, from everyone at home. You can do a lot with your privacy settings. *What are you hiding?* Hamid wondered and then immediately stopped asking.

Some things you have to force yourself not to see or forget as soon as you see them. Going inside Israel to work for Segev taught Hamid that. The scariest part wasn't the soldiers, he learned. Because the soldiers are everywhere, and after a while you realize they are fat and lazy and stupid, eating cheap sandwiches and draining blue cans of the same energy drink that Hamid favors. They only bother you if it's their job to bother you, on Highway 60 for example. No, the scariest part is seeing how permanent the Zionist state looks from the inside. It's the highways, the glittering stacks of skyscrapers, the trains, the car dealerships, the malls—everywhere you look, malls with American brands, malls like the one they killed Salem in. It's fortified with money, so much money. American money. Saudi money. It's permanent.

Once, when he was inside working for Segev, Hamid fucked up in a big way. He rushed onto the wrong bus. Turned out, this bus went direct to the Central Station in Tel Aviv. There's nowhere more dangerous for a green hawiyya without a permit. The place is legendary—a massive concrete maze crawling with soldiers whose job it is to catch you. Three arrests and your life becomes one long interrogation.

The day he got on the wrong bus he'd been so sure it was the end for him that it really was a bit like dying as the bus pulled in. But a small, bitter miracle: he slipped by the women soldiers guarding the exit while they were busy brutalizing an old man dressed with painful dignity, someone who came in from a village, you could tell, someone's grandfather. When Hamid saw his chance, he slipped by and into the bright afternoon. It was like being reborn. Stupid as it was to linger, he'd actually spent a good twenty minutes wandering in a vague circle around the slummy blocks filled with stolen DVD joints, filthy-looking butcher shops, kiosks selling calling cards, calling cards, every place advertising calling cards in an alphabet that Hamid did not recognize. He passed thin black men, silent in doorways. Refugees. Hamid was almost back at the tinny lean-to of shared vans that shuttle people between Tel Aviv and Jerusalem when a woman in her underwear tumbled onto the sidewalk in front of him. She seemed to have come out a side door of the bus station itself. He peered in. Wisps of smoke and flashes of yellow reached out from the darkness in there, he could hear a beat. A club? She looked up from the sidewalk, her face a blur of colors. She really was in her brightly colored underwear. It was the middle of the day. Hamid remained frozen as two other women rushed out the yellow door, picked up the woman from the sidewalk, one under each armpit. They were wearing long silky robes and pants but no shirts, just black Xs taped over their breasts, their nipples. Garbage. That's the word that came to him. Garbage, used up and rotting things. "She had a bit too much," one of the girls said in Hebrew but with a foreign accent. They'd thought he was a Jew maybe. The underwear girl's head was lolling. They brought her back into the yellow light, the curling smoke. As the door closed behind them, Hamid thought: *Nobody will believe this.*

When Muhi got back from Norway, Hamid heard about it not from Muhi but from Mama, who has been friends with Muhi's mother since before they were born, back when both their fathers were away in Kuwait earning money. Hamid had been sitting at the plastic table in Teta's kitchen. How is Hamid always with his mother in her mother's kitchen? Teta was having a lie-down. Mama adjusted the dials on the stove, pots steaming with, he would soon learn, chicken and the last of the summer maluchiya from the freezer. Mama hadn't even changed out of her work clothes yet, the dress shirt with the ruffly neck, the business slacks. She comes home tired from the long back-and-forth to Ramallah, slowed down in the afternoons by the Jews stopping traffic again and again on the roads that the Jewish settlers use. She said Muhi's mother was worried about him. Hamid should have been doing his composition assignment, but always he finds himself drawn to the kitchen once Mama gets home.

Outside the kitchen window, the nameless white cat was pacing, gangly and filthy. At the first sign of spring she'd busted out kittens under Teta's lemon trees out back. Hamid's little brothers torture the poor things with their love, carrying them from cushion to cushion. The kittens cry out as the boys hold them up by what Hamid wants to call their armpits, hind legs dangling, white torsos stretched beyond reason.

"Mama, is Muhi ever coming back?" Hamid asked.

"Yaa Mama, this is what I am saying," Mama said, rinsing cucumbers. "He's been back for a month." She used her free hand to massage her left temple, a gesture of exhaustion not related to Muhi, Hamid was fairly sure, but to the length of her day, the demands of it. He hates that she works. She doesn't have to; everyone insists that she doesn't have to, even Teta. It's like she has two jobs, one at home, one at the water sustainability office. When Hamid was very young, he remembers his parents arguing about it. He remembers Mama closing them in the bedroom while Baba yelled outside, "I am the man." Again and again. *I am the man.* Sometimes they slept at Teta's. But that was a while ago. Now, if things haven't resolved, they have in some way mellowed.

"I'll see him," Hamid said. "I'll see Muhi soon."

He could tell by the way Mama turned down all the burners that the food was ready. All she could do now was keep it warm until Baba came over. He stops at home before coming to Teta's. Hamid suspects it is a subtle protest to being stuck so often at his mother-in-law's. The boys were in the salon. Hamid knew without looking how they melted down the couch, their bare tummies exposed, each of them holding a screen up to his nose, one of them on Mama's tablet, the other on her cell phone. The one real conversation he ever had with Mai was about having younger brothers.

"A martyr," Fadi called from the salon.

Mama glanced up at Hamid, raised her eyebrows with a certain resignation, so he rose to go see. "What is it, yaa kitten?" he said, sitting down on the couch next to Fadi, the littlest. Fadi wriggled up so that he was lying atop Hamid's thigh, a tiny leg bouncing against his own. Hamid could see the screen from where he sat. It was hard to tell what it was, a blur of shapes.

"The Jews killed him," Sami said from across the room on the couch, not looking up from the tablet. Sami isn't yet twelve, but he's determined to attempt the full Ramadan fast this year.

"Who?" Hamid asked Sami. "Yanni, where?"

Sami ignored the question, engrossed, long thin limbs flung all over the couch.

Fadi, next to him, pointed at the screen, into the crowd. "He's in there." A body raised up, a bloody sheet. Then Hamid's phone buzzed in his back pocket, and he took it out to see the alert that, yes, early that day Salem Abu-Khdeir had died in Augusta Victoria Hospital. His corpse was smuggled out for burial, before the Jews could take it.

In the video little Fadi showed him, the hand that held the camera (a cell phone) was shaky. A foreign woman was saying again and again, *mein gott, mein gott*, as the corpse banged again and again against the garden wall that they were trying to secret him over. The sheet covering the corpse became bloodier and bloodier. For some reason, the video made Hamid think of Professor Farha, the unmarried woman who teaches composition. "All boundaries are porous," she once said. "It is this porousness that excites violence." He hadn't bothered to write that down, but he remembered it anyway.

When Hamid took the phone away, Fadi complained but only

for a bit, only until Hamid ruffled his hair and stood to throw him over his shoulder, saying, "What do I do with this kitten? What do I do with this adorable kitten?" He was terrified by Fadi's lightness, the soft vulnerable tummy, the twiggy spine, the shoulder blades like chicken wings, and Fadi oblivious to his own delicacy, laughing as he pretended to be a kitten: Mew, mew, mew. Later that night, after Baba came over, swirling his harsh, glossy energy through the door and into the house, talking loudly about his day and asking prodding repetitive questions to his sons while scrolling through his phone—"Ahh? Oh? Yalla"—barely listening to the answers, after cups of tea, after they piled into Baba's car to go home, after sitting at his own desk in the quiet house, attempting to do the writing exercise that Professor Farha had assigned, after the lights in the house went out, Hamid lay in bed and rewatched the shaky cell phone footage of Salem's corpse being smuggled out of the hospital. And actually that night it was Muhi who messaged him first. *Did you see what they did to him?*

A few days later, Hamid and Muhi met for coffee. It was night. All around them were guys their age drinking small coffees before moving on to hookah places. Muhi chose a café that Hamid hates. It has a phony French vibe and insists on serving espresso instead of normal Turkish coffee. Muhi sat low over some weirdly tiered cappuccino thing and sucked down cigarettes with an intensity that Hamid had not expected. In the street below he could hear cars driving by, blasting wedding music into the night. Hamid was surprised by his own nervousness. "So, how was Norway?" he asked.

Muhi laughed unhappily. "Life," he said. "Over there, it's life."

"When are you going back to school?" Hamid asked.

Muhi shrugged, winced.

"For summer school?" he offered.

"Have you seen this?" Muhi asked, not looking up from his phone.

"The Jews are spreading a lie that Salem didn't die from organ failure, but that his own mother suffocated him."

Hamid had seen reports of that particular lie, yes. The Zionist propaganda said that Salem was a homo, that it was an honor killing.

"How can I go back there?" Muhi said. It took Hamid a second to understand he was answering the question about his law degree. "Go back to Ramallah, back to pretending we have a state?"

Please shut up, Hamid pleaded silently.

Muhi kept going. "This isn't living," he said. He said it again and again throughout that afternoon, as the power flickered on and off in the café. "This isn't living." Suddenly it was all intolerable to him. The soldiers stopping you to check your hawiyya on the highway, no matter where you were in the West Bank, no matter that you were going from one Palestinian city to another. He tried to go to Ramallah yesterday, he said, and the journey should have taken forty minutes, but it took three hours. "Believe me, the Jews have their wall," Muhi said, "but they are pushing farther and farther in. What is left?" He was talking to Hamid as if Hamid were some Norwegian, some Chinese, some American, whatever, that needed to have this explained to him. They check our papers on our own highways. They come into homes in Areas A, B, C, and believe me, if there were an Area F, they'd come there too, they come and take whoever they want, do you understand, do you understand how your grandmother's lemon trees are dying, you are taking one-minute showers but up there (waving toward the settlement of Efrat, which creeps down the hill toward Bethlehem more each year) up there they have swimming pools, actual swimming pools filled with our water, with our water, have you ever been in a swimming pool? Of course you haven't. Because believe me, believe me (shaking his head bitterly), this isn't living.

Hamid watched the rage and desperation leak out of his friend's long-lashed eyes, he watched it drip across the table toward him. Even then, he knew that Muhi's voice, his refrain, would remain lodged in him for the weeks to come. Because Muhi was right. He was right that the Jews had cut water off to Hamid's zone, that the already-low cistern grew lower after an already-dry winter. Muhi was right. He was right about Teta crooning over her drooping lemon trees, about Hamid taking thirty-second showers and Mama calling out to him the second he went over: "Habibi, our water!" Sitting at the table with Muhi, under the café's flickering lights, Hamid knew that each time he rushed to rinse his hair, each time he stood under the nozzle of hot water begging for a minute to himself, just a minute more before Mama called out to hurry him, Hamid would hear the words Muhi planted in him that night at the café. *Believe me, this isn't living. This isn't living. Believe me.*

At the café, Muhi talked about water shortages, about Oslo, about jurisdiction over Highway 60, about collective punishment. He talked about the Israeli prime minister, the American president, the careers built on compromises in bad faith. A panic threatened to choke Hamid. Every sentence he'd ever thought and suspended was back, spilling out of Muhi's mouth and tightening around Hamid's neck.

"They know everything. They see everything. They control everything," Muhi was intoning. To the beat of his sentences he brought down an open palm on the table, causing the small dish of sugar packets to convulse. "What protest happens except that they let it? If they want to shut it down, what do they do?"

Hamid knew the answer: *They send in their secret police, disguised as one of us.*

Muhi said it as Hamid thought it, word for word: "They send in their secret police, disguised as one of us."

Hamid needed to go, wanted to go, but stayed seated.

"Have you ever written a Facebook post they haven't read? A text message? Have you taken a shit they don't know about?"

Now he's going to lean over and show me Salem's photo, Hamid thought.

And that's what Muhi did. He stuck his phone in Hamid's face.

On the screen was the famous hospital image. It was taken the day after the beating. Oum Salem holding open the boy's mouth, a dark wound in there, the head swollen beyond recognition, yanni, beyond being recognizable as a human.

It's true, there are martyrs all the time. In a single week: boy shot point-blank in the face by a border guard, elderly man at a peaceful protest asphyxiated on teargas, teenage girl with a knife at a checkpoint gunned down by five soldiers before she could get the thing out of her bag. They tore off her hijab, they tore at her dress. All of these came as alerts to Hamid's phone. But Salem stuck with Hamid in a different way, something about how he died—buying a hamburger at the mall.

"This is us," Muhi said. "This is them erasing us." Hamid felt a surge of hate rise up in him, not at the Jews for doing it but at Muhi for saying it. And wasn't there something else? Something else in Muhi's rage. Something that Hamid could not name, could not let himself name. It was Salem, but it was not Salem. It was the Jews, but it was not the Jews. It was Norway. The answer lay in Norway, and Hamid did not want to know it.

"How old was he?" Muhi said, lighting up another cigarette. A waiter approached their table, then, halfway there, paused and turned around back to the espresso bar. "Not much older than little Fadi, no? Sami's age?"

In that moment, Hamid could have flipped over the table. He put his head into his hands and made fists of his hair. He pulled hard. If Muhi had kept talking, Hamid really might have hit him, or at least walked out, but Muhi stopped, perhaps aware that he had gone too far, or maybe preparing himself to go one step farther.

"I had a friend," Muhi said, quiet now, almost soft. "A friend in Norway."

He said "friend" with a strange, implied significance that Hamid tried to ignore.

"I explained to him, this friend, about my life in Palestine. I explained to him the raids, the checkpoints, the fucking Wall, the lack of water. I explained that I had to fly to Spain to see my own sea."

Hamid was scrolling through his feeds trying to be anywhere but where he was. Here was a post from Mai's friend Noor, so typical for a religious girl: an image of a rosebush with, like, twelve of her cousins tagged, one for each rose. Muhi kept going. "The more I told him, the less it sounded like my own life." He paused. "I learned things." He paused again. "I learned things about myself there."

Hamid couldn't bear it, couldn't bear to let Muhi go on. He smashed through. He slapped the table, sugar packets jumping, and said, "Have I told you about this rich girl? She's killing me."

Muhi slunk back in his chair as if he'd been unplugged. No more talk of the friend in Norway as Hamid detailed his failed attempts to get Mai's attention. And that's how it started—the dynamic that continues to play out between them today in the souvenir shop. Hamid stuffs his doomed obsession into any space between them. He's got a whole routine about her, the rich girl, up there in a villa, tucked away in the hills of East Jerusalem; the rich girl who comes down, yes, she comes down, to study biology in the West Bank. Then she goes back up. She ascends. She's up there, dressed in white. She's a cartoon princess. Birds are feeding her pomegranate seeds.

In performing his obsession for Muhi, Hamid hears how he protects Mai from himself with distance and money. The Lexus in her Instagram photos, her villa, her father with an office in London. All of these boundaries are as real as the checkpoints between their houses. She is above him. In his most private moments, what he imagines is pulling her down. The fantasies aren't specific. There is a vague sense of desecration, something elaborate and procedural. It is at odds with what he believes he likes about her. A good girl. A pure girl. It is too complicated to explain.

He's caught himself being mean, or at least unkind to her. Recently, she was telling a group of classmates about the soldiers making two little boys at the checkpoint unzip their coats and lift up their shirts, all to see if they had knives on them. Mai had a hand over her eyes like a visor against the harsh afternoon sun as she told this story. Next to her, thin, brittle Noor squinted into her cell phone. Something about what Mai said allowed for some transference. She didn't have to say, *Next, they'll be making me do that*, but you could hear it, you could hear the threat of her violation hinted at in the story.

Hamid said something stupid and jokey like "We'll have to get you a suit of armor," smiling idiotically at sweet Mai, at terrifying Noor with her brother in Mejiddo. But Hamid could hear in his own voice the strain, the hostility.

Sometimes he lets himself imagine defending her. Some Jew-soldier tries to rip off her hijab, to pull down the shoulder of her shirt, everyone knows what they want. He imagines punching one of them so hard his fist breaks the Jew's face—a punch that surely would break his hand, but in this version, he smashes his fist into the dog's face and feels it all cracking, the nose bone, the plates of the cheek, all of it making a sickening, bloody crunch, and Mai seeing him now as someone strong and powerful. But mostly, he wishes she could see him as he really is. How he is with Fadi, for example, holding his brother's squirmy body in his lap, saying sweet words so that Fadi will hold out a palm for Teta, who needles chopped parsley into the tiny wart they are treating.

Hamid never met his great-grandfather, Teta's father, but knows from Teta's stories that in the years before '48—before the Nakbah, before the slaughters, before the displacement—the family's lost land had been adjacent to a so-called kibbutz. His great-grandfather had taught them how to work their fields: pale Jews being punished by the sun, the women all in underpants-looking shorts, struggling to speak in their non-native tongue. They watched Hamid's great-grandfather carefully. How to till like him, how to tie a kaffiyeh to keep the sun off. Like animals imitating a human. Later, they would chase the family off their land, shoot Teta's uncles in the fields and leave them for the flies and dogs beneath the olive trees. But before all that, Hamid's great-grandfather taught them to till. "I saw them up close," he said, or Teta says he said. "I saw them up close, and I can tell you, they did not come from God."

Hamid thinks of this sometimes when he's inside installing air conditioners for Segev. He's seen men walking close, not like friends or brothers, the arm carelessly flung over the neck like he and Muhi used to walk home from school. No, not like that but like a man and a woman. One hand in another's back pocket told you that these men had been inside each other. One of them had become a woman, had let himself be a woman. They'll be out in public, like, on a street in the middle of the day. *They did not come from God.* When Hamid thinks about it, it doesn't make him angry so much as terrified.

At the souvenir shop, he and Muhi are finishing up the last of the merchandise. Hamid doesn't know how much Muhi gets paid for this work, but can't imagine it's more than a few shekels an hour. A joke. The crosses are ready to be sold tomorrow. Fifty shekels each. It's evening now. Hamid can't see it, but he can feel it, the way time has shifted and something has drained away.

He finds that he wants to tell Muhi one true thing, an offering to replace whatever he can't let Muhi say. "I hate how I act around her," Hamid says.

Muhi is texting with someone, doesn't look up.

"Mai, I mean. I try too hard, I'm a clown." It's true. He does everything wrong. He knows you're supposed to give the girl only a little at a time, to hint toward interest but make it uncertain, so that it could just as easily be her own imagining. You make her want an idea that comes from her own head. But Hamid goes too far, always too far. He's nodding at Muhi, who's nodding back at him. It's an understanding. That's the lifeblood of survival, isn't it? Being understood?

"I get trapped inside how I act," Hamid says. "I can't stop."

Muhi shakes his head. "Believe me," he says. "I know. I know this so well." He rubs a hand hard through his hair. "I'm always performing. It's never me but a version for other people."

"Wallah," Hamid says, "exactly." He isn't sure he knows what Muhi means, but he thinks he might. It has something to do with the way he laughs too hard whenever Mai makes some inane remark, yes, but also, it has to do with how Baba spreads his knees on the couch while Mama serves tea to company, the way he talks about his wife's work like it's an indulgence he permits her—the hours on the highway, the thankless office job, the negligible pay barely covering the cost of transportation. Everything his father says really means this: Don't think for a second that my woman earns more money than I do. And everyone always laughs, nods their heads, agrees. Everyone tends to the fragile blossom of his father's dignity. Everyone. Even Hamid.

The music streaming from Muhi's tablet is interrupted by an ad for hand soap. "A clean family, a safe family," says a woman's smooth voice in Fus-ha.

Muhi grimaces, like he's remembering something beautiful or horrific, it's impossible to tell. "My friend, my friend in Norway," he says. He's careful with each word. "He tried to, I mean, he said if I wanted, I could stay."

"What do you mean, stay?"

"He'd help me stay."

"Without papers?"

"Yeah," Muhi says. "That we could live, like, I could live, you know, with him." Muhi breathes in. "When I say 'live with him,' I mean he and I—"

But Hamid can't let him. *I'm sorry*, he thinks, but even as he thinks it he's forgetting. He's forgetting what Muhi almost said. Hamid says in a too-loud voice, "But what if she wants to keep studying?" He cuts Muhi off.

"What?" Muhi looks like he's been woken up from a dream.

"Mai. What if she wants to get a master's degree, yanni, to work. I want my woman at home. A woman is a woman, you know?" Hamid wants to stop talking but can't. "A woman is a woman, and a man is a man."

For a second, Muhi's eyes are panicked, drowning.

And then they're not.

Muhi sits back, slaps his thighs as if a decision has been reached. He says, "She's from Jerusalem, yeah? A rich part?"

"A rich neighborhood, yeah," Hamid says, relieved. That was easier than it might have been, distracting Muhi again.

"Not from Shuafat camp?"

"Definitely not." No rich girls in that camp.

"But nearby."

"Not far from there," Hamid says, warming up. "I'm telling you, she's in a rose garden right now, white roses, she's—"

"She's in danger." Muhi cuts him off.

"What?" Now it's Hamid's turn to feel smacked awake.

"The Jews are going crazy," Muhi says. "They won't let anyone into Al-Aqsa."

"Well, I know, but . . ." Hamid pauses.

"The Jews are shooting people in the street."

"But she lives in a villa," Hamid says, a weak protest.

"She's just now on her way home," Muhi says, looking at his watch. His voice is rich and assured as if he's announcing this on the news.

"Probably."

"Taking the bus to Checkpoint 300."

"No, she goes through the Tunnels Checkpoint."

"Ah yes," Muhi says, his eyebrow going up. "She's allowed to use that checkpoint."

"Yes," Hamid says, mesmerized by this answer-and-response he's fallen into with Muhi.

"And now she's getting off the bus."

"Maybe."

"Yes, now she's at Damascus Gate, where the fighting has begun in the streets."

"I don't think—"

"And there are snipers there already."

Shut up, Hamid thinks, but only starts to say, "We don't know—"

"There are snipers there already, and the girl you love is alone."

"What?"

"You've seen what they do to girls."

Hamid stands up. All of him hot.

"You know what they want." Muhi is rising slowly too.

It feels possible that they might fight; something is snapping in the air. "This is what you want?" Hamid says, his voice thick. "This is what you want?" Everything is about to end. All of it. Or it was already over. It was over from the first time Muhi mentioned his stupid fucking "friend" in Norway.

Standing, Muhi is taller, thin and taller, thinner and thinner. "Let's go there," he says.

"What?"

"Let's go there."

"What?"

"What? What?" Muhi mimics. "Isn't that love?" he says. "Protecting what is yours?"

"What, like you have a special permit to get inside?" Hamid says, casting his eyes around the room for anything else to focus on. Brown boxes filled with crosses. Prayer rug. Light bulb. Filthy gray utility sink in the back. "Hi, yes," he says in a sardonic voice into his hand, held like a cell phone. "What's up, Jews? Listen, give me a six-hour permit so I can go bodyguard an unattainable rich girl."

"You know how to get in," Muhi says, quiet, unwavering.

This is, of course, true, but it's true in a limited way. Sneaking in to work for Segev, Hamid was always part of a group. It wasn't so hard if you knew people down in the camps, learning what corner to meet at, what abandoned bus stop. Men huddled in the cold dark before dawn, sweatshirt hoods sheltering cigarettes. Hamid liked being among them because he knew it was temporary; he'd be educated; he'd get out. Then all of them filing through a gap in the Wall, somewhere the construction wasn't finished or somewhere it could be undone or even, a few times, a tunnel. The spot changed, you weren't ever sure where you'd cross, but once you did, it was doubled over and running through some neglected olive grove until you hit the place where the car was waiting, driven by a man who drives with a lookout on speakerphone. That's how he knew where to turn and avoid the army.

You don't do it alone, and you don't do it at this hour. What Muhi must want is for Hamid to say, No, it is impossible. Because it is impossible. All along he's been right. Just because Hamid couldn't bear to listen doesn't mean Muhi wasn't right. They are trapped. That's the truth. They are trapped. If they attempt what Muhi is suggesting, getting arrested is literally the best-case scenario. Most likely, they wouldn't make it more than a few meters before the Jews shot them down.

"Yalla," Hamid says. "Let's go."

Out the back door and into the soft night. For reasons known only to the logic of this insanity, they avoid the well-lit main street and take the side alleys, smooth stones glowing gray. Neither is saying anything. Hamid can feel Muhi towering behind him, waiting for him to crack and say, *Look, it's impossible, you're right, we're trapped in these shitty lives.* There's no way for them to get down south at this time of night, not that it would even matter, not that any of this even matters, so instead Hamid leads them down to the Wall by Rachel's Tomb, as if this weren't the first part of the Wall the Jews finished, as if it weren't the most, like, heavily guarded segment within a kilometer. Down through the long grasses by the Wall in the moonlight, down through the sharp smell of burning, the chop shops and construction lots. It's a Thursday. Where is everyone? Where are the souped-up Subarus cruising low at night, blasting American music until their speakers fritz out? Where are the wedding parties honking their horns after one another? The road is silent, badly paved and cracked, curving against the Wall. A single stray dog hurries into the shadows.

Hamid and Muhi pass eight-meter-high graffiti: grotesque cartoon of the Jew prime minister and the American president making out, tongues lapping at each other like dogs; stenciled graffiti of soldiers firing bouquets of flowers into a crowd. Tourists take photos by these images, holding up peace fingers. Then they leave.

Hamid doesn't remember picking up his backpack, but he's carrying it. Muhi trudges behind him. A few meters up, he can see one of the guard towers lighting up the darkness horribly, and beyond that, the piss-yellow gate the settler-dogs come through.

He turns back to Muhi. "Listen," he says. The plan is to say something like, *There used to be a crossing spot here, but it looks like it's gone*. If he does this, it's as good as admitting to Muhi that he's right.

But Muhi is pointing, a long arm that reaches past Hamid's ear. "There," he says. In the dark, Muhi is distending. He seems to be growing taller and more fibrous, as tall as his own shadow stretching out in the light from the guard tower.

Hamid is afraid that if he turns his back to Muhi, his friend may disappear entirely, but he follows the pointed hand along the Wall and there, wallah, there really is an opening. He's heard of this happening, although never here, never this close to one of the army bases, never this close to the city. It's that one of the eight-meter-high concrete slabs has shifted so it's at the wrong angle, like a crooked tooth. The result is a slim gap in the Wall, a place where a child's body could slip through—someone smaller than Hamid or Muhi.

Still, Hamid floats toward it, or it toward him. He kneels down to peer into the dark gash. He's trying to be cautious. He brings his face close to peek through, like some pillager of an ancient tomb. He's waiting for a Jew's gun in his face, he's waiting for the sound of the shot, the sound of his own screaming, the end of this unnatural silence. But it's quiet. Muhi's hand is on his shoulder, Hamid's own hand steadying himself against the concrete as he presses his face into the harsh light on the other side of the Wall.

"What do you see?" Muhi whispers.

For a long second, the answer is nothing, because his eyes are adjusting.

And then it's trees. All around him. Lemon trees, enormous and fragrant, waxy and electric with color, in the impossibly bright night.

Green Room

Trailer H is cold. You've heard that it's the coldest, although they're all cold. Cold keeps you awake, keeps the girls from dozing and the monitors from overheating. You are in a cold room, dimly lit by thirty screens. You watch your screen, not the whole screen, but the points you've been trained to designate as anchors for your vision. Guard tower, parked car, house door, bottom right corner. Today, you're monitoring a shitty house built into the Wall, or bisected by the Wall, it doesn't matter. What matters is that you see it in parts. What matters is what you are looking for: a change.

The first times you monitored alone—after shadowing the older girl with perfect eyelash extensions—you were convinced you'd miss it, whatever it was, when it happened. You'd shift your eyes away, or zone out, or fumble with a water bottle cap, and then—right then—a terrorist would plant a bomb. An Arab would slip through with a knife, with a gun. You learned how the infrared only picks up on a gun when it gets hot, meaning when it fires, meaning when it's too late. Someone would die and it would be your fault. You were nervous— nervous you'd get diarrhea, that they wouldn't let you leave, that you'd poop in your chair. None of this happened. Now, three months later, it's as if you've done this your whole life. You watch the screen in a state of numb readiness, alert and steady. Guard tower, parked car, house door, right corner. You can point out changes to an intelligence officer whose shaved face is level with your cheek, a voice in your ear, and you do not even think about turning your head to him. Guard tower, parked car, house door, right corner. You are good at your job.

Guard tower, parked car, house door, right corner.

Guard tower, parked car, house door, right corner.

A private variation of these words loops in each girl's head. Each of you have a loop of four points that you review over and over. Guard tower, parked car, house door, right corner. You know that later today—when you're in the mess hall, or texting in your bunk, or hanging out with Chen at the picnic tables, or on the phone with your mom while she's on break at the nail salon—part of your mind will continue to loop around these words, these points of reference.

Guard tower, parked car, house door, right corner.

In Trailer H, there is a hum, a machine hum, that nobody in the room registers anymore, not even you. When you first started out, you noticed it—the sound underneath all the other sounds. You wondered if it was coming from the girls, from you, as each of you hummed along in your synchronized surveillance. Guard tower, parked car, house door, right corner. Now you do not notice it unless you try. If you force yourself to hear it, then you hear it, like saying a word again and again until the ending and the beginning become indistinct. Guard tower, parked car, house door, right corner. You're not allowed to close your eyes, and you won't, but if you did, you'd feel the machine glow of your screen penetrating your eyelids. You don't let yourself calculate how many hours you have left in the green room. The Green Room. That's what the boys call it, the warriors who come in to review an irregularity, to be updated or appraised. They call it The Green Room. You and the rest of the girls you work with call it simply The Room. Of the four girls you bunk with, you are the only one who has not been touched by a man, a boy, a man, and you wonder if that's the kind of thing people can tell without asking you.

This room has no windows. The only light comes from the machines. Thirty girls in Trailer H, all of your backs toward the center of the room, all of you facing the wall, facing your monitors. You wonder how many of you are virgins. Guard tower, parked car, house door, right corner.

Here, it is either never night, or it is always night—you're not sure how to think of it.

Everyone has heard the stories. Legends, really. A girl who twists around to crack her back and misses the suicide bomber who sneaks through; she kills herself. The story is that she killed herself in her bunk, dripped blood on the girl beneath her. You sleep on the top bunk because Chen wanted the bottom.

Other stories: the cockroaches running over boots (that really happens), the boys coming in at night (you wouldn't know). Guard tower, parked car, house door, right corner.

You don't think about what happens beyond the frame of your monitor. Your job isn't to provide context. You know this. Your job is to see what happens and to report it to someone who will know what to do with the information. You watch. Of course, you do know a bit about the context of what you see. You know that your section is at the top of the curved road that leads to the Tunnels Checkpoint.

Chen sits at the monitor immediately to your left. Today she is watching an area closer to Rachel's Tomb. You are not allowed to talk about what you see, but that's fine because outside of this room it is the last thing you want to talk about.

Your nail polish is chipping.

Chen has gel polish because it stays longer, but your mom warns it will weaken your nail beds. Guard tower, parked car, house door, right corner. You've known Chen since you first got placed in this unit, because the two of you had to take additional Hebrew classes. During coffee and cigarette breaks, the two of you quietly spoke Russian together, when the *morah* wasn't around to scold you back into Hebrew.

Chen said that she and her boyfriend—a *jobnik*, an office soldier—were going to wait, but that didn't last long. Once a week, you let yourself think about Chen and her boyfriend having sex. You picture her face, contorted in that distinctly anguished pleasure that even you can recognize. Sex face.

Guard tower, parked car, house door, right corner. Guard tower, parked car, house door—movement.

Movement.

Movement.

You know it's a dog, your brain tells you it's a dog, but you force yourself to visually confirm: four legs, placement of the heart. You say it to yourself. You say, "Dog," only you say it in Hebrew. *Kelev.* Everything in Trailer H happens in Hebrew, even when it happens in your own head. Russian is for outside. *Kelev.* Wild dog. The Arabs won't keep dogs. Unclean, they say. At home, you have a little white dog as fluffy as a cloud, rancid breath worse than his farts. You love him. You love him even though your mom named him Nikki. Stupid name. On the screen, the dog sniffs at something you can't see. Now you toggle: guard tower, dog, parked car, dog, house door, dog, right corner. The dog sniffs himself.

The door to Trailer H opens, but none of you look away from your screens to see who it is. Sometimes you have dreams that you are trying to see what's on your screen but the image flickers and you can't focus.

"Hi, girls." The voice is immediately recognizable as your *mefake-det*, a heavyset girl from the south who enlisted for officer's school and an extra two years. The dog leaves the frame. The image on your screen shifts in a digital shudder. You do not know why it does this, but sometimes it happens.

It's Chen who speaks up to say, "Target is moving." The *mefake-det* comes over. When she leans over Chen's shoulder, you can smell her breath—meaty-sweet, like a condiment, or maybe beef jerky. No more dog. Guard tower, parked car, house door, right corner. Your eyeballs move in a rhythm, flicking from one quadrant to the next. It's easy to focus, pleasant, even.

"Not alone," *mefakedet* says.

"No," Chen says. "Target is not alone."

Guard tower, parked car, house door, right corner.

"Hum-tel expected that," *mefakedet* says.

The human intelligence girls read Arabs' Facebook posts all day. All day on Facebook, which they say is so much more boring than you can even imagine.

"Target is the tall one," *mefakedet* says. "No backpack."

Chen grunts an affirmative in a way that means she already knew that.

"They're at the barrier," Chen says. The click of her controller tells you she's zooming in on something, isolating an image. Guard tower, parked car, house door, right corner. The dog is back in your frame. *Kelev.* Wild dog.

Mefakedet speaks into her contact radio. "This is control H, we have target at the barrier, over." Then, to Chen, "Stay on them."

"I think they're kneeling," Chen says.

"Target static, over," *mefakedet* says into the contact radio.

You don't wonder what is happening—you don't wonder if they are going to call it in, dispatch a jeep to intercept these guys—because you are back inside your screen, monitoring the dog that has come back onto your screen, looking, you assume, for scraps.

Later, when the two of you are taking eye drops and sharing a package of sugar-free licorice under the startling morning sun at a picnic table outside, Chen will break a rule to tell you that there were two Arabs, that the target just got back from Norway. How are the Arabs vacationing in Norway, Chen will ask, while we're stuck here? So did we get him? you'll ask, and Chen will say, Yeah, we got him. Sometimes when Chen is talking to you, you'll realize after a little while that she's not looking at your face but at her own reflection in a mirror or pane of glass behind you, or even in your own sunglasses.

You take turns rubbing each other's scalp in her bed. Not every night, but many nights. It drains away the tension of watching, of waiting for it—whatever it is—to happen.

Checkpoint

Emily tells her husband that she wants to go to the West Bank. "Jeremy invited me," she calls out to Ido, speaking loudly so he can hear from the bathroom where he's brushing his teeth. "It's a tour group," she says over the buzz of his electric toothbrush.

"Are you kidding?" Ido comes out of the bathroom. He's ready for work at the animation studio, dressed in a white tee and perfectly fitted jeans that Emily picked out. "The sixteen-year-old?" he asks. "This kid wants to take you to the West Bank?" Emily has told him about Jeremy, the American leftist from her Arabic class. *Little Jeremy, sweet Jeremy, hopeless Jeremy.*

"Jeremy is twenty-three," she says, trying not to smile.

It's morning. Emily is lying on the big bed curled around Mayan, both of them nearly naked: Mayan but for her teething necklace, a string of honeyed, amber beads; Emily in simple white underwear with a tiny bow on the waistband. Mayan lies belly up, experimenting with her fist. Open-close, open-close. She turns her incredulous unibrow (Ido's contribution) in Emily's direction. *Can you believe this?* Open-close-open. *It's me doing this, me!* It's happening so quickly, too quickly—Mayan learning the world, learning her body in the world. Mayan finding her voice. Recently, her babble has begun to coalesce into words. "Mama," she cries out when Ido comes in the room, when she reaches for Emily, when she reaches for her bottle, when she reaches for a toy. Anything she wants is "Mama!" As soon as she gets it, she wants something else.

"So what do you think?" Emily says to Ido. Then to Mayan in the sweet voice, "Can I go? Can Mommy go to the West Bank?"

"Emily, come on." Ido is buckling his belt. "*Maspik.*" Enough.

"But it's not just Jeremy," she says, a little whine in her voice. "It's an organization. West Bank tours for Americans. For Jews!"

"Emily, he's a kid," Ido says. "He doesn't know what he's doing."

The choice is Emily's to make, and she could say as much to Ido, but she doesn't. Instead she pulls back. "Come here, Daddy," she says. Careful to say it softly, careful to keep her voice light, not to clog it with suggestiveness. Her husband gets nervous when she tries to act sexy. He wants it to be something she's not aware of, something he sees that she can't. Or is that Emily? Is Emily the one who needs that?

Ido remains in the doorway with his face in his hands. In a moment of what feels like panic, Emily imagines that he might be crying. She waits a breath, and in that breath understands that he's not crying, just rubbing his tired eyes with his palms. "Daddy's coming," he says.

He leans onto the bed to make a farting noise into Mayan's belly, and she screams with delight. He does the same thing into Emily's butt. She makes a show of protesting. "Ido! *Maspik!*" Then he's out the door and off to work.

After Mayan gets her breakfast—whipped organic turkey (a newfound favorite of Emily's meat-hungry baby)—Emily fixes herself a concoction of juiced greens and powdered collagen and brings her laptop to the couch. Mayan is at her feet, chewing idly on her teething necklace. Soon she'll be walking on her own; already she is hoisting herself up—butt first, adorably—with the help of chair legs and door frames. But like her mother, she prefers slow and sleepy mornings, becoming hyper only in the afternoons, when she crawls madly about for a few hours before the naptime crash. Strange how quickly Mayan is becoming distinct—her preferences, her mischief. A human emerging. Come out, Emily thinks. Also: Slow down. Sometimes: Come back, please come back to me.

Emily is writing a memo for a new client—another Tel Aviv health and wellness guru—about how to brand her social feeds more effectively when a text comes through.

Jeremy: شو هو قال لك؟

Very committed to practicing his Arabic, this kid. For a moment, Emily doesn't recognize a single letter of the script, just sees something foreign, threatening. Then the letters organize to sounds, *shu hu 'allik?* Finally words: *What did he say?*

He could be texting from the West Bank or from East Jerusalem. That's his job. He leads tours for a nonprofit that "fosters Jewish-Palestinian encounters." At least for now. Jeremy's life here is nothing more than a glorified gap year that will end in the summer, when he starts some urban planning master's at MIT.

She responds to Jeremy's text in English because she hasn't bothered to download an Arabic keyboard yet: *He said no way . . . too dangerous*

Jeremy, switching to English: *Hmm. Let's talk in class tomorrow.*

Their Arabic class meets on Monday and Wednesday nights. They aren't learning literary Arabic, but rather the local dialect, which the language school, deferent to Israeli sensibilities, refers to as the Levantine (as opposed to Palestinian) Colloquial. Jeremy is the class baby. He's the only student under thirty and the only man at all in a room filled with mothers who are all older than Emily—middle-aged potters and acupressure masseuses with wild gray curls and piles of hand-dyed indigo scarves. All Jewish. Like Emily, these women live in stately, Ottoman-era homes with leaky pipes and year-round drafts. Rarefied discomfort. A few of them are native-born Israelis, but many are Americans or South Africans—women who married Israelis or who immigrated here with grown families. Sometimes one of their daughters will drop by during a lesson—diligent, plain-faced girls who come straight from the army bases where they train boys to disable bombs or jump out of planes or snipe. Then Emily will elbow Jeremy and mouth, *Ask her out*, while Jeremy gives her pleading eyes that say, Please! Stop! It! But usually Emily and Jeremy are the two youngest in the room, despite over a decade between them.

They sit side by side in chairs with tiny desks affixed, always in the first row. It's easy around Jeremy. Nervous and affable, he seems more Jewish—more familiar—to her than any Israeli. They take breaks together, perched on a bench in the language school's leafy courtyard garden.

There are many laudatory reasons to study spoken Arabic, but none of them are Emily's, not really. In some ways the language itself is incidental. What she loves is that for a few hours each week she must give herself over completely to not knowing. She's a baby who must learn it all again, must learn the world through language. These are the only real hours that she spends apart from Mayan. Teething, fussy Mayan. True, her baby is blessed by late-afternoon naps during which Emily rolls out her yoga mat in the living room for her practice, sometimes with a private teacher, often alone, but the fact remains that before Arabic class—all winter, for example—Emily was never more than a few feet from her daughter. At a certain point she began to scare herself, desperate for two contradictory things: to feel like her own person and to have Mayan be part of her body again. While Ido spent long hours working at the animation studio, Emily might lie with Mayan on her belly, this belly she has worked so hard to smooth back down into a beautiful shape, a shape that excludes Mayan, warm and chubby. All winter, Emily was obsessed with the thought that Mayan would never fully return to her. All winter, she held Mayan against herself in a state of without. Never again, never again would they share a body.

And sometimes the opposite. Sometimes Emily needed to pull back against Mayan. Sometimes Mayan would be screaming from her crib, hungry, always fucking hungry. Emily alone in the house, Ido at the animation studio all day. Emily working, yes, but doing social feeds from home now, not even going into Tel Aviv to meet with clients, keeping it all to Skype, keeping it all contained to their home, stuffy and containing, but somehow cold, always cold. Mayan was screaming. Emily felt every cell in her body lurch toward her child. But she stood at a threshold, stood under prayers folded and hammered to the doorway, under crystals lining the shelves, under feathers hanging from the ceiling, under all these promises of love, Emily pulled back from the maddening octave of her child's scream-ing, just to feel, for a moment, separate from her. "Cry," Emily would whisper. "Cry, you bitch."

So when their bright-eyed neighbor, a famous choreographer with a house full of daughters who all got out of army service on notes written by compliant doctors, ran into Emily (with Mayan strapped to her) at the shuk, sifting through burlap sacks of organic lentils, and told her about the Arabic classes that met twice a week in the evening, Emily said, *Yes, yes*, even before checking with Ido that he could get home in time to watch Mayan. "Of course, yes, yes," he said later in bed. "It's a great idea." Emily was almost certain she detected relief. He kissed her nose, her eyebrows. "It will be great," he said. "You'll be brainwashed by the resistance. I'll have more time for my comic strip."

His online comic strip, a side project, is becoming a little fa-mous. *Emily and Ido.* Sweet vignettes of them, or a version of them, and their domestic life. A burly man with sardonic eyebrows who trails after his impossible, irresistible woman-child wife—she of the tiny waist and long eyelashes. He's always drawing cartoon-Emily in boy shorts that let her butt cheeks peek out the bottom. In one of his most popular scenes—available as a postcard, a print, and even a mug (who would want such a mug?)—Emily is slung over Ido's shoulder the way soldiers carry each other, her cute butt up by his ear. She's holding a wineglass. The swirls around her head show that she's dizzy, drunk. The caption says, "Once a year, I let her have that second glass of wine and . . ." In another, Emily is wrapped in a short towel; her impossibly long hair piles up, filling half the comic's frame; Ido is pulling the stuff out of the shower drain. Not rotting and matted with skin and snot—the way hair actually comes out of the drain, the way it did when she was losing handfuls a day after giving birth—but shimmering and untangled. Flaxen gold. Caption: "Life with Rapunzel." In another, cartoon-Emily is in underwear and a T-shirt, held like a baby, like Mayan, in Ido's arms. He sits on the couch. The TV is on, its glow lights up his face, but he's watching Emily, his sleeping wife, with all the wonder and terror of a parent. Caption: "Night watch."

Cartoon-Ido and Emily don't have a baby. Mayan is never in the frame. At first, Emily kept waiting for her to show up. It seemed inevitable: the three of them on the big master bed, big spoon, little spoon, littlest spoon. Something like that. But nothing, not yet.

Emily hasn't asked about it, but her mother-in-law has. Ido was complaining about how much tax he has to pay now that he's making real money as a small business. His mom was holding Mayan, singing a song about a butterfly, a cute word in Hebrew: *par-par.* "Nu, when are you going to give them their baby?" she asked.

"Who?" Ido asked.

"Emily and Ido!"

Ido laughed. "Nu, one grandchild isn't enough for you, Ima?"

His success has made their lives easier. The cartoon brings in money, sure, but what really matters is that Ido now finds he's respected at work—new title, better projects, a seat in the right meetings, whatever those are for animators. It's a change; it's a relief. As recently as this past winter, Emily had wondered if they hadn't reached their end. They took a trip up north for a night—their first night away from Mayan. It was tense, miserable. They picked up some

German girl hitchhiking whom Ido tried desperately to impress, talking about the shows he'd worked on, as if he'd done anything other than draw backgrounds; he was trying to make himself look big, feel big. This was before the *Emily and Ido* comic, before the balance started to tip back in his favor. Emily had sat in the passenger seat, silent, as Ido talked to the girl in the rearview mirror; in her grew the unspeakable fear that her husband was pathetic, a loser. That was the fear that haunted their winter.

Funny how something so small as a comic strip could shift it all back into place. Now, just a few months later, Ido is—Emily doesn't know how else to put it—Ido is a man again.

The next night, in Wednesday Arabic class, Jeremy leans from his desk toward Emily's before the lesson starts. "So, wait, what exactly did your husband say?"

"He said it's too dangerous," Emily answers.

"But the group is all Jews," Jeremy says. "Rabbis! Did you tell him it's a bunch of American rabbis?" He's speaking in a hushed tone, even though all the other women are chatting as they wait for the instructor, Mary, to arrive. "We're not going into Area A. Did you tell him that? The café is in Area B, not far from the tunnels."

"I'll tell him." Emily has her phone out to check how many people have liked the photo she recently posted to her personal account: an overhead shot of her Arabic notebook lying open, an olive branch from the language school's garden taped to the page, her illegible writing in black ink working its way around the branch. At the bottom of the page, two words are large and legible, one in Arabic, one in Hebrew: the words for peace, *salaam*, *shalom*. She deliberated over a caption but went with: " . solidarity . sister tongues . tikkun olam . " Barely a thousand people have liked the post, which shouldn't annoy her but does.

"I really think you should come," he whispers. He fiddles with the corner of his textbook.

"I know," Emily says. "I just need to convince him." She would never admit it, but she likes this tug-of-war—Ido and Jeremy—over her.

Before Jeremy can ask her why she has to convince her husband at all, Mary enters and greets them: "*Marhaba*."

"*Marhabtain*," they all respond in unison.

Then they begin their lesson.

Jeremy calls Mary a Palestinian. Ido calls her an Arab, sometimes, an Arab-Israeli. She comes from the Galilee, a Christian. She teaches in the evening. By day she's finishing coursework for a PhD in Arabic literature at the university in Jerusalem. During the unit on family, Mary told the class about her two children (eight and ten, girl and boy). Her children and her husband live with her in-laws up north. Mary drives up every weekend to spend time with her family. To clean the house, to do the cooking for the week. Then she returns to Jerusalem. A pretty woman, probably Emily's age, pale and dark-haired like Mayan.

Sometimes, instead of waiting for Emily after class, Jeremy will walk Mary to her car, talking politics maybe—a topic Mary avoids at all costs in the classroom. Emily thought poor Mary would faint the day that Jeremy brought up the murdered Palestinian boy. It was around Passover. At the time, their class was completing a unit on hospitality and greetings. To practice, they pretended that they were an extended Arab family at a meal. They pulled their desks into a circle and served one another imaginary cups of tea, heaped invisible spoonfuls of rice and meat onto one another's plates. Mary's suggested topics for mealtime conversation included current events, entertainment, and family updates. They were talking about an imagined wedding in the family when Jeremy, in his flattened-out Arabic—his is by far the worst accent, somehow even more American-sounding than his Hebrew—asked the dinner party: "Did you hear what the police did to Salem Abu-Khdeir?"

Emily, who at the time hadn't quite understood all of what Jeremy said, asked, "*Shu?* What?" Her accent is better, but her Arabic remains rudimentary.

"They *sara'u* his body," Jeremy continued.

Emily didn't know what that word meant, and it appeared the other women didn't either, because they looked to Mary, who kept glancing at the classroom door as if she expected someone to charge in. Then Naama, who improved the quickest because both her boys serve in something called "human intelligence" and learned Arabic fluently through the army immersion program, said in Hebrew: "*Lo ganavu et ha-gufa shelo.*" *We didn't steal his corpse.* What are you talking about? Her silver earrings swung clackily as she turned to frown at Emily, as if Jeremy were Emily's responsibility.

Still in Arabic, Jeremy was trying to explain that it's true, the Jews hadn't succeeded in stealing that corpse, but they had stolen others—this was their new tactic (a word he said in English).

What did he expect? That they would stay in character? That this classroom of Jewish women would talk about the event, about Israel, the way that the Palestinians talk about them? "*Al-yehud, al-yehud.*" *The Jews this, the Jews that.* And what next? A conversation about the Yael Salomon, blaming that girl for her own murder just because she lived on a settlement?

Mary spoke up. "Allahyerhamo, zichrono l'vracha," she said. A bilingual pleasantry to bless the dead boy's memory. Then she suggested, in Hebrew so that everyone understood, that they discuss something more familiar—"easy" was the word she used—like the results of *Arab Idol*, which they have been following as a class.

After the lesson, Emily and Jeremy sat on their favorite bench in the garden. It was night. They were lit by streetlamps. Heady scents of jasmine and tuberose in the air. He was disappointed that the discussion about the dead boy had been cut off. Trying to comfort him, Emily spoke, maybe inanely, about how he should try to find the gift in every situation, even difficult ones, try to find the lesson.

He made a face. In his nasal voice—a voice made to haggle over the price of fish in some shtetl, to yell out pro-union slogans in Yiddish—Jeremy said, "What? Like the world was created for the sake of your own self-understanding?" He gripped and ungripped his pale hands. "Emily," he said, so earnestly that she wanted to kiss him, "we killed that boy. We desecrated his body. There is no lesson there."

She didn't know what to say then, so she chattered on about messages from the universe, about how she had known she was pregnant (after a year of trying, finally pregnant) before she peed on the stick, because that was the week she dropped and shattered three water glasses in three days.

But later—after she and Jeremy said good night, and Emily walked home to her leafy, wealthy neighborhood—she found herself pressing Ido about Salem Abu-Khdeir's death, like suddenly she was playing Jeremy and Ido was playing her, playing Emily. She perched on Ido's knee while he sat at his computer, coloring in some background for his comic strip. Mayan was next to them in her crib, lying on her back, huge eyes taking in the world, determined not to sleep, not yet. Ido had a mug of chamomile tea, made from the loose, dried flowers that Emily buys from the Arab vendor in the shuk, who carefully packages each purchase in plain, waxy paper. Outside the night wind moved through the flowering willows that line their street, planted, the story goes, by a widow of the Six-Day War. That week, Mayan would begin to crawl, but she hadn't started, not yet. The room was still.

Emily and Ido had never talked about the dead boy before, not even after the mall footage of his lynching—that's not the right word, "lynching," so why does it feel to her like the right word?—was released. But now, she brought it up, the beating, the lack of criminal charges, the perversion of the army trying to steal a dead boy's body. For what? To avoid a protest? To silence a cry? "Aren't you ashamed of this country?" she asked.

"What can we do?" he said in English. "Sometimes the tactical move is horrific. That's our reality." He'll say this sometimes. Racism isn't ideal, but it's the reality.

"We killed that boy twice," she said, getting up from his knee swiftly, wanting to go outside but knowing she had nowhere to go.

She disagrees with both of them. She needs both of them. It's as if she's cast each of them, Ido and Jeremy, Jeremy and Ido, to voice opposing elements of the dilemma within her. She'll echo Jeremy's words to Ido, yes, but just as quickly echo Ido's words to Jeremy.

"Racism might not be ideal," she said to Jeremy not long after, "but maybe it's our reality." Class was over. Everyone had gone, but Emily and Jeremy remained seated—two students at their little desks in a classroom decorated with Hebrew and Arabic letters, all written out in ornate calligraphy.

"You don't know what you're saying," he said.

"I know exactly what I'm saying," she said, and because it would give her an edge, added, "I'm a wife here, a mother, not just someone passing through."

"Don't get mad at me just because you're seeing things you don't want to understand."

"Maybe I do understand," Emily said. She knows a lot more than people expect her to know. She knows Israel was founded on a series of colonialist atrocities, yes, and that she perpetuates them, fine. "Maybe I understand perfectly. Maybe I just don't care."

She had startled him. He of the concave chest, of the pale, studious arms, the family tree of Hasidic rabbis and Derrida scholars. Finally he said, "I don't think it's true that you don't care."

They turned their faces away from each other. Emily was burning, but she didn't want to get up and leave. That's when he asked her. That's when he planted the idea about the West Bank. "Please come," he said. "Come on one of the counternarrative trips I lead." He touched her shoulder lightly, so lightly.

"I don't know," she said. She began to doodle the word "counternarratives" in the margin of her notebook, open to that day's lesson on the Arabic verb system, nearly identical to the Hebrew verb system. She knew that later, when she described the scene to Ido, she would contain Jeremy in her descriptions: his youth, his size, his delicacy. This is how she makes him seem lesser. Less what? Important? Forceful? Does that mean masculine, in Emily's world? She's not sure. *Little Jeremy, sweet Jeremy, hopeless Jeremy*, as if talking about a pet or a child, never mind that he's taller than she. In this way, Emily also contains the opinions that he's come to represent, dismissing her own misgivings about the life she's choosing, day after day, for herself and for her daughter.

"Please," Jeremy said, pleading. "Think of it"—he interrupted himself with something between a laugh and a sigh—"I don't know, think of it as a gift. For Mayan, for a different future."

Sometimes she tries to imagine the size of Jeremy's penis. He's such a frail boy—there she goes again, but it's true. His wrists are even thinner than hers! And she is strong, hoisting herself into backbends, upside down on her hands, heart open against a wall. He seems to be made of an eraser, pale and pliable. And yet she's heard it said— where did she hear this?—you never know who is going to get one. She likes the idea. You never know! She herself has seen so few: one, Ido; two, the man she dated briefly before Ido; three and four were her attempts at one-night stands, and in both cases, the condoms were rolled on before she really had a chance to look at the things; five, her college boyfriend; and then there's six, if you count the old man in the nearly empty Michigan bus station who, with the most pained expression on his face, brought out his flaccid penis (uncircumcised! a first for college freshman Emily) and stood plaintively in front of her until she found her voice to scream. She doesn't know how the ratios work, if they hold: hand to foot, foot to cock, that kind of thing. But she likes imagining that Jeremy has a huge one, that this explains his loose, ill-fitting jeans. It's so big, nobody has ever sucked him off, not really, just run a tongue up and down like a cat at milk. Why does she think these things? Who knows, who cares? There are worse things to think. And anyway, she's giving him a mythology, giving him what everyone wants, which is to be more than meets the eye.

That Wednesday night after Arabic class, Emily tries Ido again. All the elements are the same—the big bed, Mayan, Emily in her underwear, Ido in the bathroom—only this time, it's night. Ido is peeing with the door open. "It's in Area B," she calls out to Ido. Mayan is, with Emily's help, standing up on the bed, clutching Emily's fingers with her tiny hands, an expression of fierce joy on her face as she totters. Emily coos to her, "Yes, yes, yes."

The toilet flushes. Emily's not sure if Ido heard what she said, but when he comes out, zipping, he says, "Baby, what do you know about Area B?"

"It's safe," she pushes on. "Safe for Jews. Just me and a bunch of American rabbis."

"Emily, Area B is still dangerous," he says, "still hot." He gestures impatiently, his thumb touching his middle and pointer fingers like he's holding something invisible and delicate—a feather, a grain of salt. "Do you even know where, exactly, this kid is trying to take you?"

"Some café. I forget the name."

"Nu, give me this Jeremy kid's number," Ido says.

Not wanting to let go of Mayan, Emily nods toward her phone on the bureau. "It's saved under 'Jeremy Arabic,'" she says.

Ido knows her pass code, of course. Emily watches from bed as he calls Jeremy from her phone. She thinks of Jeremy picking up the late-night call, wonders what he was about to say before Ido cuts him off in curt Hebrew, the vowels short: "*Lo*," Ido says, "*zeh ba'alah*." No, he's saying, this is her husband. Although in Hebrew, the word for husband is *ba'al*, literally "her master."

"*Az, l'ayn atah rozeh lakachat et ishti?*" Impatient, forceful question: Where are you trying to take my wife? (Literally, "my woman.") She knows she's not supposed to, but Emily likes the way it sounds in Hebrew. *My woman.* She likes the possessive urge this scenario is bringing out in Ido.

Ido waits for an answer, but after a few seconds (probably annoyed at Jeremy's slow Hebrew) he switches to English. "Okay, but where, exactly?" It will go on like this for a while, until Ido discovers what Emily has been trying to tell him: that the group will go to a café in Area B, beyond the Tunnels Checkpoint but not inside Palestinian-controlled Area A. Does it matter, Emily wonders, A, B, or C? Aren't Israeli settlements everywhere, anyway?

She lowers Mayan back down to her hands and knees. She whispers sweetly, softly, "Enough? Enough for one day?" This is around the time that Mayan gets sleepy. Blessed with sleep, sweet baby.

Ido is quiet, apparently listening to something that Jeremy is saying on the phone. He raises an eyebrow at Emily, shakes his head. Emily laughs into her hand so that Jeremy, speaking earnestly on the other end about Palestinian self-determination, doesn't hear. Who will win control of Emily? Ido will win. Of course Ido will win. He'll pull her back to his side. Ido will win, and it will feel good.

She feels the stirring of wanting him. That old ache, blooming up from the muscles in her cervix, the root chakra.

Recently, they've been getting into anal. Ido is funny about it. "The year of butt stuff," he'll say, unloading more plant-based, perfume-free lube from a canvas tote bag. The first time they tried it, it was her idea, and it was horrible. Mayan had just started sleeping through the night, and Emily was, hard to say, maybe just hungry for something to feel intense and new. Plus, they had all that lube lying around from the difficult, tentative months after the birth when Emily was still healing, when the stitches were still dissolving. Anyway, horrible. She was expecting it to hurt, so it did. We receive what we're prepared to receive, she knows that, but couldn't help it. She was afraid. Her muscles clenched up before he was even halfway in. *"Aud?"* said Ido softly in her ear. *"Ou sh'zeh koev mi di?"* His whisper was heavy, wet, shuddering with effort as he asked her if it hurt too much. Almost always, their sex comes down to this: two languages, two people reverting to two mother tongues.

"No more," she said, elbowing him off her. "Get off me." Then she rolled into a ball and waited for the soreness to pass.

Later, she soaked herself in a hot bath scented with lavender oil, the tub lined with candles and tumbled rose quartz for what she's read is its soft, healing energy. Ido has given up asking if she really believes in all that new-age crystal stuff, has come to understand that what Emily likes is the ritual of it. In her bath, she guided herself through a breathing exercise, not seeking out an answer but preparing herself to receive one. It came to her, in the heat of the bathtub while Ido anxiously fumbled around the kitchen, making—it turned out—a mushroom frittata for her, rich with cashew milk and spiced with cumin; he brought it carefully to her in the bathroom. Really carefully, easing the door open as if she were Mayan asleep and he was checking on her. He came into the bathroom, thick-calved in boxers, her hairy husband. She saw him enter as if he were his own cartoon. He placed the frittata on the closed toilet seat, a kind of table. Exotic smell. He's good with spices, better than she. He squatted by the tub, his wrist deep in the water. He took her foot, little bells of her anklet ringing; he held it, held her, in his hand, wondering at her smallness, she knew. When he kissed the bridge of her foot, lavender water dripped down his chin. "We don't have to try again," he said. "I don't need it. There's nothing special, I mean."

"I love you," she said, closer to crying than she had expected.

One second later, Mayan began to cry, and rather than talk about whose turn it was, Ido motioned for her to stay in the bath and went to their baby.

But the next time it was better, so much better. Part of it was the online research Ido had done. He kissed her kneecaps beforehand. "The internet says, however much lube we think to use, double it." Part of it was her breathwork, part of it was the sprinkling of weed that Ido's intern from work had given them. They rolled it into a cigarette with tobacco, neither of them experienced with how this worked, both of them giggling and fumbling with the rustling, translucent rolling papers they kept tearing accidentally.

They had talked about it before, and decided that at first, they'd use a condom. Emily felt she needed to do more research on enemas before she cleaned herself that way; it sounded to her like the kind of practice that could mess with natural flora and bacteria. But at the same time, she explained to Ido, she didn't want to worry about him being disgusted if, for example, she got him dirty. He'd been there at the birth, Emily holding the jagged chunks of rose quartz the doula gave her, screaming and covered in every fluid her body had to give, the slick of her insides—blood, piss, shit, snot, all of it—and yet, she was too embarrassed to say anything more direct than that: *In case she got him dirty.* She had been readying to feed Mayan when they had this conversation, rubbing the baby's gums so that she didn't teethe on a nipple, a trick Emily learned from Ido's mom.

"Whatever you want, baby," Ido had said, tugging first Emily's earlobe then Mayan's. "But just remember, I love everything about you." Pause. Another kiss, this one a little more forceful. "Including your poops."

"Ido! Gross."

"I do, I can't help it," he said. Then singing in that Mizrahi style he affects sometimes, "*Habibti, habibti*, your poops like roses, your poops of gold." Then back to his own voice. "Okay, no problem. Condoms, yalla."

Sometimes she's moved by his decency in a wave of something that feels like sadness.

She echoed him. "Yalla." When Mayan latched on, it startled her, as always, just for a moment, before they settled in to the rhythm of feeding.

The next time, it worked. Ido was whispering to her the whole time he eased in. Not asking if she was okay, but telling her how beautiful she was, how good she felt. As Emily relaxed into the blurry terror of having someone up her actual asshole, strange pressure in her spine, she found herself thinking of the cartoon version of it, not that Ido would ever. But how this moment would look in the cartoon, his body covering her, thick and hairy, her slimness under him, her flushed face, hair in her eyes. She thinks about it sometimes, how Ido must have women fans who want to be Emily, or to replace Emily, or think they are more Emily than Emily. Usually, it makes her anxious to think of Ido's female fans, but as Ido pushed deeper into a part of her that had—strange thought—never before been touched, she found herself thinking of those other women, how he could hurt her, of course, but he wouldn't. And yet, if he fucked one of those other women in the ass, he might. He might not care whether he hurt them. The idea excited Emily—that her husband's tenderness was reserved for her alone. Ido was steadying himself over her with one hand, the other cradling her chin, breathing into her ear. Doesn't that always feel the most thrilling, the most intimate, his breath tickling its way down into her? She was wedged over her own forearm so that she could reach down to rub herself. She imagined the women were watching, the women who left comments on his page and ordered prints and T-shirts. She imagined them watching from the doorway, silent and agonized. "Say it," she said, hearing the desperation in her voice, liking it. "Say it."

"You're mine," he said, she made him say.

Then the collapse of coinciding orgasms. When they finished, she was still crying out—no, that wasn't right, it was Mayan. They'd woken up Mayan. Ido kissed Emily on the forehead before wrapping a towel around himself and running to their daughter. Emily lay on their bed and carefully touched the soft puckering of her asshole, its new tenderness.

Emily rouses herself from dreams of physical love to find that Ido is still on the phone—asking Jeremy how many times he's made this particular trip to this particular location—and Mayan is now asleep, her legs up in the air. Carefully, Emily gathers the sleeping bundle of her baby into her arms. Carefully, carefully, walking through the quiet house—Ido's voice receding—and into the nursery. Yellow curtains. She double-checks the monitor to make sure that it's on.

When she returns from the nursery, Ido is finishing up the call with Jeremy. "*Beseder, achi,*" he says. He winks at Emily to say, *Just one more minute.* "*Beseder,* my wife is crazy, but *beseder.*" The goodbyes run their course. Ido ends the call.

Emily knows that he's going to tell her that it's insane. That it's crazy. That she can't do it. She can't go into the West Bank. The West Bank! No way. She hugs him from behind.

"Nice kid," he says.

"He's sweet," she agrees, playing with his belt buckle.

"So he'll pick you up tomorrow around eleven," Ido says. He turns around to kiss her forehead. "I'll stay home from work, no problem." Tomorrow is Thursday, Israelis' Friday, and a lax day at Ido's office.

"What?" she says, sitting slowly on the bed.

"You should be back in the afternoon," he says.

"Back from where?"

He laughs like she's joking. "I'll get takeout sushi for dinner, *beseder*?" Not a trace of malice in his voice as he goes back into the bathroom. No spiteful glee.

"What?" she says again, as the bathroom door closes. It never occurred to her that he'd agree. But he did. He did. And now she's going.

Out of the tunnels, Emily is taken aback by the size of the checkpoint. They drive by the looming steel overhang. In the shadows stand soldiers weighed down by weapons, bulky in combat vests. "We won't go through it?" Emily asks Jeremy. He's driving. When she got in the car, she asked him if he was even old enough to drive, prompting one of those wounded smiles he specializes in.

"What, through the checkpoint?" he says, looking out the window. "No, not now. Only on the way back in." Actually, Emily knew the answer about the checkpoint—of course the traffic is only monitored one way—but asked anyway, because it's calming to have simple things explained.

She's sitting up front; Jeremy's charges—three rabbis—are in the back. The other eight or so rabbis are in a hired van. Earlier today, as Jeremy maneuvered out the small side streets of Emily's neighborhood and toward Derekh Hevron, Emily introduced herself to the two woman rabbis in colorful kippas and a man in a sharp suit whom Emily would have pegged as Sephardi Orthodox, but who was, he explained, the first trans rabbi hired by a synagogue in Maine and currently at work on an updated gender-neutral siddur.

Perhaps trying to appear unfazed by the checkpoint, the rabbis continue their conversation about the movement of women who risk arrest by bringing a Torah to the Western Wall for a Rosh Chodesh prayer service marking the start of a new lunar month, a privilege reserved for cis men in Israel. Emily has the sense that it's a performance for her benefit: Oy, none of the rabbis in the car practice a Judaism recognized by the State. Oy, if they lived here, they would not be permitted to officiate weddings, and oy, their conversions would be invalid. The larger of the two women, who wears a billowy dark green linen tunic and pants, leans forward into the space between Jeremy and Emily to say, "Israel is the only country that persecutes Jews. Reform Jews! How crazy is that?" Something cloying about the way she needs Emily to confirm for her that yes, it is unfair, yes, you suffer.

"That's crazy," Emily agrees, already worried that perhaps this day is asking too much of her.

Last night, after Ido got off the phone with Jeremy, Emily laid out her clothes with care: jeans and a loose mint-green tunic bought at some yoga studio in New York, modest but not in a way that made her look too Jewish, as in, like a settler. It had all felt so important, so weighted with consequence. These were the clothes she'd wear in the West Bank. *The West Bank.* When she imagined the words she saw them jagged and cast in shadow, strange and hard to place. But they won't be in the real West Bank—no ancient markets with twisted alleys, no village composed of junky trailers, all the women hiding in a single room. No, they'll be in a restaurant listening to a Palestinian activist talk about his life. Emily hopes—Jeremy would hate this, but she hopes that the restaurant sells Palestinian handicrafts. Soap from Nablus, painted ceramics from Hebron—souvenirs she could bring back home, touches of another world. (Here, she imagines an interjection from Jeremy: *Another world, yes, because it is separated by the violence of our state.*)

Emily doesn't post many selfies; if she posts her body, it's an abstracted hand, a foot. But she might post a cropped selfie—eyes and forehead?—with her gossamer head scarf, a pale blue, which she last-minute shoved into her bag on the way out the door earlier today. She was rushing around after getting Jeremy's *outside* text, but despite being late, she lingered a moment in the kitchen with Ido and Mayan. "Tell Ima, 'Don't go,'" Ido said, ostensibly to Mayan. "Tell Mama to stay home with us."

Mayan steadied herself with one hand on her daddy's shoulder, the other hand waving jaggedly. She wore only her teething necklace. "Mama," she cried out, joyful and forceful, naked and blameless. "Mama!" The room was shrapnelled with rainbows, the result of a many-faceted crystal pendant in the window, a gift from Ido. One of Emily's most popular posts is a close-cropped photo of Mayan clutching the crystal in her tiny, perfect fist.

With the rabbis' permission, Jeremy takes a slight detour so that they can drive by Rachel's Tomb. "It's a kind of pilgrimage site by way of a bunker," he says. They drive along the Wall, enormous, as close as Emily's ever been to it; the automated metal gates, ugly; the towers for snipers, or probably snipers, who in the car would know? "The way they built the Wall here," Jeremy says, pointing out Emily's window, "they cut off the trees from their ancestral owners." The car loops around without entering the tomb complex, not having time for that, Jeremy says, but the truth, Emily assumes, is that the Orthodox Jews who run the shrine would freak out if they saw a woman in a kippa like the two in the car. And maybe it's the specter of that exclusion that compels the rabbis to turn their attention to Emily, to begin quizzing her on her people. Did she go to the same socialist Jewish summer camp as Jeremy? Did she come from Yiddish-speaking Labor Zionists? Habonim? Hatzair? Or something else? Jew by choice? Egal-Orthodox? "We went to a Conservative shul twice a year," Emily cuts in. "Although since my dad's dad died, he's been going more."

"Zichrono l'vracha."

"Right, thank you, it was a while ago," Emily says. "Anyway, I always had the sense my parents were rooting for Israel, even though we never talked about it."

"What do they think of you living here?"

"It's been years, and they are still a little shocked," Emily says, thinking of her mother's last visit, just before the last Gaza invasion, trying her best to look plucky as they waited out an air raid siren in the apartment hallway. But, Emily continues, she found her husband here, an Israeli, yes, and had her baby here. She glances at Jeremy as she says, "The land redeemed me." At this, the rabbis sigh, richly, deeply.

At the café, Emily picks at the wooden table. The middle-aged Palestinian man addressing the group is holding up a laminated map as big as his torso. He's referring to violated borders, to international crimes. They are the only people at the outdoor café. The seating— mismatched wooden tables contrived from barrels and planks, haphazard rugs heavy with dust—is orchestrated to overlook a rocky incline dotted with determined olive trees and shrubs, all unfolding toward a dry wadi, which will remain, for Emily, nameless. So this is the West Bank.

From here, you can't see the Tunnels Checkpoint, but it's close, mere minutes driving down the steep road out back. The Palestinian speaker—what's his name?—is pacing in front of the seated group. Jeremy is hunched over, legs crossed, and rapt. "I am from here," the speaker says, his finger nearly in the map's pale blue sea, somewhere south of Tel Aviv. "I am from here, but we were chased from our land." He's showing the expansion of the settlements with a red marker. At first, he was drawing imaginary lines with his fingers, but sweet Jeremy ran up with a handful of dry-erase markers. "You think of everything!" Omar exclaimed—that's his name, Omar— and since then he's been making lines and hasty shadings to show the steady creep of boundaries pushing Palestinians farther east.

Emily spells out his name with her finger on the table, the grain rubbing against her phantom script: guttural *ayin*, *meem*, *raa*. Omar. It means "age."

"Today," Omar says, his finger in the interior of the map, "I am also from here." For three generations, his family has lived in a village south of Hebron. It took him four hours to arrive to this café today.

Omar spreads two fingers on the map: his village and the café. "It's so close," he exclaims. "Look how close!" He speaks English from somewhere deep down in his throat. It makes the language sound older than it is, at least to Emily. Yet, he continues, it took him hours to get here: checkpoints, random searches, rifles with their safeties clicking off, guard towers with snipers manning the roundabout where their army has killed seven Palestinian teenagers this year alone. "If only," he says, "I could drive my car as the crow flies." Pause. "Or maybe," now speaking with the practiced cadence of a showman, "better to say, as the dove flies." The rabbis sigh, always sighing, these rabbis.

Emily looks again at Jeremy, sitting with his clipboard on his knee, face crinkled in attention as he listens to Omar. She knows it's stupid, but she is jealous of his attention. She imagined—this is so dumb, but she imagined that he'd be looking over at her, monitoring her to make sure she absorbed what she was supposed to bring home. Now, here at the café, sitting at a table across from a young rabbi with wild, curly hair and her freckled wife (from Chicago: the weather! yes, the weather), Emily feels oddly alone, adrift. Phone out, she checks on her head scarf selfie, finds that the post is doing pretty well. *Your eyes!!!!* comments a fairly famous mommy blogger. Emily hearts the comment.

Omar started his presentation by talking about the Nakbah, a word Emily knew and assumed the rabbis did too: "the disaster," meaning the ethnic cleansing at the founding of modern Israel. His thesis statement, if you can call it that, is that the Nakbah isn't a distant historical event but an ongoing one. On the laminated map, his Xs mark the spots of destroyed Palestinian villages in 1948 and in 1967, yes, but also earlier this year in Palestinian village lands that the army commandeered for drills, a practice Emily had been only vaguely aware of. The story of Omar's life, the story of his family, is in a way the story of this whole place. "It cannot go on like this," he says.

A hand goes up from the table next to Jeremy's. It's the rabbi working on the gender-neutral siddur, the one in the smart suit. "Where did you say the checkpoints were?" he asks, serious and diligent. Emily finds herself wondering how gender-neutral pronouns work in Hebrew or in Arabic, where every form is gendered, even the plural ones.

Omar re-explains the concept of floating checkpoints. "The Israelis control all the highways. They can stop us, arrest us, even when we are in Palestinian areas." He says "Is-ra-el-is" in four distinct syllables. Emily wonders if he had to practice saying that instead of saying what he would say in Arabic: *al-yehud*, "the Jews."

Text from Ido: *How is it? You beseder?*

I'm beseder, she writes to him. Then, because she knows he'll like it: *Kind of boring*

Ido: Don't tell Jeremy

Emily: Can we make coconut milk ice cream for dinner?

Ido: Only if you and Mayan sing the Israeli national anthem first

In Ido's mind, everything is the simplest version of itself, the cartoon version. Emily knows, for example, that he's made Mayan a zero-sum game: she either waves an Israeli flag on Independence Day, or she rolls in ashes and mourns the Nakbah. She either learns about the Holocaust or she learns the names of the villages the Jewish fighters erased in pursuit of a state. For a while, he was convinced that Emily wanted to send Mayan to a bilingual preschool when the time came—one where the students come from Jewish and Arab homes, where they learn in both Arabic and Hebrew, side by side, hand in hand.

At so many points, Emily had the chance to correct him. "Where did you get the idea that I have this plan?" she could have said. Sure, it's true, she does have friends who send their kids to such schools, but it's also true that she's not sure those kids get the *best* education, despite receiving the most ideologically sound one. Because sound ideology won't get you decent SAT scores, and if Emily has a long-term plan, it's that Mayan could, if she wanted to, make a life in America, make a life somewhere less pressurized and limiting. Anyway, many times she could have told Ido that he was mistaken, that she and he weren't as opposed as he was imagining. But she didn't. She let him cast her in this role.

Just before Passover, they went down south for two nights. Mayan stayed with her grandparents for the second time in her life. Two nights. The longest Emily had ever been apart from her. She and Ido stayed in a desert bungalow; the quiet was like wine. They were celebrating. *Emily and Ido* was now a success, had been featured on multiple websites, and was getting the kind of traffic advertisers are interested in. That was the weekend the hand-in-hand school was firebombed. Not during a day with classes, thank G-d, but on a Saturday night. It was hard-core settlers who did it. They waited for Shabbat to go out, then they bombed the bilingual preschool. They did it without violating the Sabbath.

"You see," Ido had said. They were in the rental house's kitchen— tiles of burnt orange and bright blue. Emily was cutting vegetables. That's all a vacation is: same chores but in someone else's kitchen. Ido was leaning against the fridge, reading from his phone. "You see? It's not safe, these schools, they aren't safe." He sounded like a child. *You see, you see?*

And instead of saying, *What has convinced you I want to send her to this fucking preschool?* Emily said, "Okay, Daddy, you're right."

"Say it again," he said, something joyous breaking through his concerned face. He was behind her at the cutting board. She had put down the knife.

She turned to him, his body pressing her against the counter. This is what they wanted, what both of them wanted. For a moment then, she understood why she had not cleared up Ido's confusion, why she had not shown him that they didn't have the opposing positions he had imagined: it's because of this, because she knew they would both feel good when she acquiesced, that they both need him to feel powerful, and sometimes it's her job to orchestrate moments when he does. "You're right, you're right," she said. "Are you happy?" She sounded pouty and miserable, but she was overjoyed. Something had been restored. She was once again his hippie wife, hanging prisms in their windows, bringing feathers home from walks in the Judaean hills where they took Mayan after it rained, with the sunlight cracking through dark, low clouds in scenes that made you say, Oh, of course the Bible came from here, of course a man walking in these hills after rain could imagine G-d coming down to walk among the tents of Abraham.

At the café, Omar is taking more questions. A voice from the back, a New Jersey accent, asks with frustration, "Isn't it illegal? What the army is doing?"

Omar shakes his head, a sad, quiet laugh as he fiddles with the dry-erase marker. "It is legal because they write the laws," he says. "This is the undramatic heart of the occupation." Pause. Then, making a gesture with a marker like a wand: "Bureaucracy."

The New Jersey voice speaks again: "So what do you want?"

The other rabbis shift uncomfortably. Emily does, too. Hard to tell how aggressive that question was meant to be. *What do you want?* Jeremy turns to eye the person who asked, a concerned look on his face. Emily is ashamed of the question, the indelicacy of the question. But also she wants to know the answer. What does he want? What do they want?

Omar says, "I want to drive without being stopped. I want to build without being destroyed." Pause. "You see this checkpoint?" He points toward the Tunnels Checkpoint. "You know I cannot cross it even with entry papers for Jerusalem? I must go through Checkpoint 300, like a dog in a cage."

The man from the back won't let up. "So let's say the Israelis get out of Area C settlements. Is it enough?" he asks. "Will that be enough?"

"No," Omar says, his face hard to read. Amused? Or maybe strained. "No, it will not be enough. Because Jerusalem is not free."

A quiet murmur from the rabbis. Jerusalem, Jerusalem. It's always about Jerusalem. Femme fatale. Jerusalem—the city where Emily lives in a gorgeous, pillaged home that she will never, never ever, give back. She feels the flexing of a possessive muscle she did not know she had. She wonders if the rabbis feel it too. A coursing in them that says, *She's ours, it's ours, Jerusalem is ours.* These thoughts surprise Emily, but also, they do not surprise her. It's Ido's voice she hears inside her. *Mine.*

"But surely, the real problem is the settlers," another rabbi says, a large, avuncular-looking man with a colorful kippa. "The settlements in the West Bank."

Omar waves his hand in annoyance. "Israel is all settlers. Jerusalem, Tel Aviv, it's all settlements."

"No," another voice says, "like, you know, the illegal settlements."

Omar says, "Well, for some people that is all of Israel."

The possessive muscles in Emily surge again. She can feel it in the others, the arguments coming: The land we bought, we paid for! The swamp we drained to build Tel Aviv! The blooming in the desert! And what of the refugees? The boatloads of survivors, tattooed with concentration camp numbers. These are settlers? We are settlers? Impossible, Emily thinks, and all the rabbis think. She hears someone whisper, *the right to exist.* And aren't they the good ones? Emily, Jeremy, and all of these nice rabbis? Here they are, listening to this Arab talk. They don't have to be here. Surely, they are different from the wild-haired extremists who set fire to Palestinian schools, who take and take and take. That is not them, no, not them, not them, no, no.

Jeremy stands up quickly. "This may be a good time to break for lunch," he says.

Right now, more than anything, Emily wants to go home. She is tired of how complicated things feel here, how uncertain she is of her own moral superiority. It's easier with Ido: he's the right wing, militant and unsympathetic; she's the left wing, charitable and good-hearted. Two wings. Who is she here, listening to this man talk? A settler, apparently. An aggressor. It's too much, it's too complicated. She wants to go back. She wants her bed, her baby. She wants her husband's body—that familiar, loving expanse. Her husband wearing his boxers in the kitchen, cooking eggs. Her husband dancing around their house with their baby, Israeli folk music blasting. Her husband spreading her, moving his tongue over her clit for as long as she needs. Her husband with his finger in her asshole, making her move. Her husband, her man, her *ba'al*. A comforting thought: soon, she and the rabbis will pile into the two vehicles they took over and head back onto Highway 60, through the checkpoint, waving curtly to the soldiers who will think they are Jewish settlers coming in from a settlement block in Area C. They'll drive through easily; they'll go home.

Jeremy continues, speaking to the group. "These are difficult conversations and important ones," he says. "But they're a lot harder on an empty stomach."

For lunch, the restaurant is serving a vegetarian meal. Rice and lentils. It has a name, this dish. Emily learned it in Arabic class—hospitality unit—but she can't quite remember. The Chicago couple are eating boiled eggs out of a Tupperware container, presumably because they are observant enough that they don't eat food from nonkosher kitchens, vegetarian or otherwise. Then again, who knows? Maybe it's not religious at all—maybe the couple is afraid that Palestine is rampant with dysentery. Jeremy is still seated with Omar.

Emily has taken a few bites of the lentils—"Nice but a bit greasy," she told the two Chicago women—when she gets the terrorism alert to her phone:

Stabbing, Damascus Gate, one fatality, attacker neutralized.

271

These updates are sent by the army. She and Ido get them all the time, and usually ignore them, but already, he is texting her: *Where are you?*

Then: *Come home.*

Then again: *Where are you?*

Jeremy seems to have gotten the news too, because he's scrolling intently through his phone. The rabbis are oblivious. The rabbi in olive-green linen is standing over Omar, speaking animatedly. Others are eating or taking photos of one another standing next to olive trees. Finally Jeremy glances over at Emily. She holds up her phone to indicate that she read it, too.

Jeremy jumps up on a table. "Excuse me," he says. His voice, unaccustomed to yelling, strains. "Because of an incident in Jerusalem, we're leaving early."

"An incident?" the freckled Chicago woman asks her wife, who is already tugging a blue baseball cap over her curly hair, then to Emily, "What kind of incident?"

"A terrorist attack in Jerusalem," Emily says.

The rabbis are suddenly alert, electric. Hurrying toward the cars, conferring with one another, yelling updates from their cell phones, checking the army Twitter account for confirmation. As if they have a clue, as if they are from here and know how any of this works.

Emily texts Ido: *Baby I know. I'm coming.*

Where are you? He's insistent. *Eifo at?* He wants to protect her. He's calling.

"Hi, listen," she answers.

"*Eifo at*, mami?" His voice is edged with panic. Where are you? Where are you?

Usually, she would answer in English, but right now, she wants to be speaking Hebrew, she wants to be home, to be closer and closer to home. "*Anachnu adayn kan*," she says. We're still here. She's walking with the group toward the cars, parked precariously on the incline. "*Netzeh aud daka, beseder?*" We're still here but we're leaving soon.

The rabbis glance over at her as she talks. She likes what they see: a woman who has chosen to be from here, capable and bilingual. A woman loved by a man who knows how to protect what he loves. I'll update you, she says. I'll update you, and I love you.

They are in the car after hurried handshakes with Omar, who watches them drive away. How will he get home? Emily wonders, and then immediately understands that she does not care. Maybe later she will think about it, text Jeremy to see if he's heard from the man they met today, but right now she cares only that she is going home. Back to her familiar kitchen, her sheets, her baby, her husband, her objects, her place in the world. She texts Ido: *We're on our way.* Jeremy is driving. This time, Emily is in the back, next to the heavyset rabbi in a green linen tunic. The Chicago couple are in the car, too.

Down the hill toward the Tunnels Checkpoint. Wheels on loose dirt and stones—a soft sound. "So sorry, what exactly is the issue?" asks the rabbi in the blue baseball cap, trying to keep her voice level.

"Well, because of a stabbing," Jeremy starts.

"A terrorist attack," Emily cuts in. Ido has texted her details. "They killed an Israeli girl."

"A border guard," Jeremy says, looking back at her in the rearview mirror.

"A teenager," Emily says.

The rabbis tut-tut cluelessly.

Emily closes her eyes. It's a gift, think of it as a gift. Here's the gift: you get to go home. No more tragedies, no more maps, just the knowledge of your family, the bodies of your family, your baby, your husband, waiting for you.

They round a curve, and the highway unfolds below them, to their right, the metal overhang of the checkpoint. Jewish cars take the left lanes, whizzing through. They don't have to pull over to be inspected; they don't have to do anything. Rabbi Green Linen has put on a sun hat, and Emily feels a surge of gratitude toward the woman: she did it because the soldiers might have balked to see a woman wearing a kippa, would have assumed that something was wrong, something was up, would have needed to clarify: Are you a Jew? Are you one of us? She put on a sun hat so they could breeze through. Home, home, home.

On the far right shoulder, one of the ugly white-and-blue Arab buses pulls over for inspection.

Emily can't see the Palestinians getting out of the bus, one after another, but she can see the soldiers in their flak vests, leaning against the guard shack, speaking quietly to one another. She thinks of Ido, young and bored, on guard duty in Nablus, in Gaza, in hell, a lifetime ago, waiting for her.

Before she hears the sound, she feels it. The sound is enormous, less a sound than a vibration. Then movement. Then it's all movement. The car swerving drunkenly. The car smashing into the concrete divider. Jeremy's nose cracking against the steering wheel.

Inside the car, it's snowing. Winter of a childhood in Michigan.

When she opens her eyes, the car is gone. No, that's not right. The car door is open. She unbuckles her seat belt. She gets out. Up ahead, a burning bus. Car crash and a burning bus. In the car, Jeremy is moaning, his face smeared in blood. "I think it's broken," he says. The woman next to him is all white—the white dust of her airbag like baby powder. Emily is standing outside the car. She runs a hand over her face, her scalp. Adjusts the pale blue scarf. Nothing hurts. Even her clothes seem clean.

A minor crash. Poor Jeremy's nose. But up there—where the checkpoint is, or should be—a bus is burning. A suicide bomber? Has there been one since the '90s? Above them, helicopters now, circling and dipping.

Emily did not realize she was still holding her phone, but she takes a picture of the helicopters flying so low she can make out the sunglasses of a soldier up there. She isn't scared. Even now, especially now, because she has always felt—a feeling so true why bother putting it into words—that she will be an exception.

Thursday

Meir is hunting for a stapler because his own stapler, shit fuck balls, is broken again. This is the main function of his army duties—stapling reports to other reports, duplicates to other duplicates, all placed in one filing cabinet or another. For what? Don't ask that question. It's only taken a few months in the army for him to figure out that this is the one question you can't ask yourself if you want to survive the mindless boredom of it all: Why?

He's lucky, he knows. He's on base mostly half days, heads to practice in the afternoons, and some weeks, he doesn't have to come in at all. He shares a desk at an office in a trailer filled with papers, piles of papers. Most of them are soldiers' applications to greet Birthright trips, to be the Israeli soldiers that step onto the buses of American/Canadian/South African/French/whatever Jews and introduce themselves as real, live IDF soldiers. That's all this office handles: processing those applications, which, for Meir, means making duplicates, duplicates, duplicates. He glances at the applications sometimes. *How will you embrace your role as a cultural ambassador to diaspora Jews?* All of the answers are bullshit: about wanting to show the Jews of America that Israelis are normal teenagers with abnormal responsibilities; about helping them see how Israel keeps all Jews safe; about wanting to inspire young Jews everywhere to stand with us. Bullshit. Just say the truth, Meir thinks. You want three days' leave from your service to go hook up with American girls—notoriously easy—whose panties will drop when you show them a photo of you holding a Tavor, an M16—hell, a water gun, probably. All the guys want to do it. Why the girl soldiers want to greet Birthright trips is a little beyond him. Maybe they want to practice their English?

The girls in his office are plain and nervous, many of them religious in their swishy olive-green skirts and leather sandals. He imagines them shy and overwhelmed on a bus filled with American teenagers who are so free they have no idea how free they are as they roll into breakfast an hour late or demand an entire tour bus pull over because they didn't go pee at the last stop.

Right now, it's just Meir and Pnina, everyone else getting lunch. She doesn't say much to him, and Meir has decided it's because she's nervous. She parts her dark, oily hair in the middle and walks in the least inviting way possible, like she is leaning into the wind. "Hey, Pnina," he says, standing over her desk. It's piled in papers, manila folders, stamps, dead pens, empty coffee cups with brown sticky residue. All their desks look like this. "Can I use your stapler?"

"I'm using it," she says, not looking up and also not using her stapler. She's making notes on a form.

He leans over more, trying to make his arm muscles pop. Meir has a habit of rolling his uniform sleeves up as much as they will go, which, Amir told him, makes him look like he's running a gay car wash. "Come on," Meir says. He says it the way he imagines Amir might say it to a girl, like, *Come on, I know you want to,* the way that, probably, combat soldiers say it to American girls after telling them about the friends they have that died in Gaza or were stabbed to death while waiting for the bus. Meir has stories like that too, but nobody is sucking his dick about it.

Pnina looks up, her sallow face annoyed. The room is stuffy and badly lit by a dirty fluorescent. Everything smells vaguely damp. "Fine," she says, handing him a stapler decorated with her name in sparkles. A functioning stapler is a precious commodity. Someone even made a movie about it.

"Thanks," Meir says. He winks, but she's looking at her phone now. Her phone case is elaborately pink.

"I don't believe this," she says.

Meir is halfway between their desks. "What?"

"Have you seen this?"

"What?" he asks, more impatient now. The impatience in Meir has been building ever since the guys who planned the attack—that is, who planned to attack a random Arab at the mall that night—were arrested and tried. They each got maybe a month in juvie, which Ima says will be mostly counseling anyway. At the trial, there were protestors every day in support of the guys, along with a few Arab-lovers protesting against them. Nobody else was named, which was good, of course, because Meir might have been kicked out of the league—you never know when there will be some politically correct gesture or whatever. And yet, he wants everyone to know what he did that night. Everyone. Ori, Amir, Ima, Pnina, the American Jews who flood into Israel to fuck a warrior and then go home. He wants everyone to see him as he is.

But whatever is on Pnina's phone, Meir doesn't get a chance to see it, because all at once the base sirens are going. Rising and falling like a baby screaming, like a cat in heat. Pnina looks at him, panicked. Is it rockets? Do they go to the shelter? Or something else? The red lights are flashing, and now, over the speakers outside, someone is telling them what to do. "This base is on lockdown," the voice says. "Until further notice, this base is on lockdown."

Ido has just gotten off the phone with his wife. "I'm coming home," Emily said. "I love you. I'm coming home." Ido sits at the kitchen table, holding Mayan above his head, saying, "Ima will be home soon." Mayan squeals, her eager, chubby legs motoring in the air.

Maybe she'll be a swimmer. He lowers her to the ground, where she stands unsteadily by gripping on to his calf. He picks up his pencil, taps his sketch pad.

For a while now, he's been trying and failing to draw Mayan for the web comic. *Emily and Ido.* The way he draws himself and Emily is almost realistic. Her tits a little bigger, waist a little smaller; his chest a little broader, arms a little hairier. It's fine; it works with the feel of it—a glossy domesticity. But he is not sure what trait of Mayan's to exaggerate. Does he make her eyes wider, anime style? Or play up the chub of her cheeks? He finds himself unwilling to distort her. When he attempts to draw Mayan, it's in a more naturalist style, like a sketch you'd make before filling in with watercolors. It won't work in the script.

"Mama," Mayan cries out, from where she is now sitting on the floor. "Mama" means everything. Pick me up, feed me, I've shit myself. Mama, mama.

Ido picks her up again. Up and down, up and down. "Your crazy leftist ima will be home soon," he says. Mayan is on his thigh now. He bounces her up and down gently, the way she likes. With one hand steadying her, he continues sketching out the scene he's been attempting all afternoon: Emily curled around Mayan, Ido curled around Emily. Three concentric bodies in a bed.

Mayan babbles.

Ido keeps bouncing his knee. "That's right," he says. "Ima is done with the Hamasniks." He speaks to Mayan in Hebrew when they are alone, always in Hebrew. He likes the idea that as Mayan begins to grow up, he and she will eventually get into good-natured arguments in Hebrew about a novel Mayan is assigned to read for class, a novel that Ido read years ago, and whether it is—whatever—too ideological or if the Hebrew feels too stilted. But what he likes to imagine is Mayan and him going back and forth, and Emily struggling to follow along, because her husband and her daughter are speaking a Hebrew too fast for her to follow, and anyway, she hasn't read any books in Hebrew. Ido can picture Emily's head turning to him and then to

Mayan, then back to him, back and forth. He's not sure why he finds the prospect of excluding her so satisfying.

A breeze moves the white curtains of the kitchen, and somewhere, the minor notes of a wind chime and a police siren sound in the distance.

Mayan grabs his pencil in an eager fist. She's wearing a diaper and her teething necklace. "You want to draw? You want to be a cartoonist?" he asks, in the voice he uses just for her. "Yalla," he says, and forms his hand over his daughter's to help her draw a heart. Outside, another police siren.

"Mama!" Mayan screams, shrill and joyful.

There are more sirens now; he can hear them outside, nudging the wind chime as they float in the window. Three, four. Four sirens is too many sirens. Five sirens, six, and then more than he can count. What now? If Ido got up to look out the window, he would see only the quiet order of the front garden and the tall cypress trees that shield them from the street. He is careful to put the sketching pencil out of Mayan's reach before he checks his phone. No new messages from Emily. *Where are you?* he types. She should be through by now, right? She should be back in Jerusalem by now. He waits a long beat. The sirens are everywhere; the whole city is sirens. Mayan is reaching for the pencil. Looking on his phone, he sees that there is nothing new from Emily, not even the blue marks to indicate that she's seen the message. Ido opens Twitter: if there's been an incident, the army will post there first.

Shibi and his wife have taken little Nasir out grocery shopping when the news begins to spread. Amal is inspecting each cucumber before she puts it in the bulging clear plastic bag. Shibi is consistently amazed at how much produce they buy, and then how much they eat, apparently, over the course of a week. Now that he is four, Nasir is allowed to pick out one treat each time they come to do their weekly

grocery shopping. He has run off to the candy aisle—his paradise—
and is no doubt looking for the biggest chocolate bar commercially
available.

"Are you craving cucumbers?" Shibi asks his wife as she continues
to fill the bag, which is now as big as Nasir's torso. "My little wife
wants cucumbers?" The more pregnant Amal becomes, the more he
needs to adore her.

"Not cucumbers," she says, fake pouting. "Chocolate. Godiva."

"Oum Nasir wants chocolates? You little sweet?" He can't stop
talking to her like she's a baby.

"Shibi!" she scolds him, embarrassed that he is so affectionate in
public. But what can he do? She *is* a sweet. He wants to eat her! He
wants to eat his precious wife.

They are speaking Arabic in the Jewish supermarket, which is
generally fine, maybe a few looks, but nothing they haven't learned
to ignore. At first, they tried to go to a Palestinian grocer in East Jerusalem, but wallah it was inconvenient. It was farther now that they
live in West Jerusalem, and anyway, the vegetables all come from the
same Israeli farms. So week after week, they come to a big Israeli
supermarket to do their shopping.

A Jewish woman and her teenage daughter, both of them in heavy
makeup with too much jewelry, are looking a little too hard at his
wife. The woman who must be the mother has her phone to her face.
She is shaking her head, saying something to her teenager, and Shibi
is suddenly aware of a strange energy in the grocery store, a tension
that goes beyond the threshold he has developed for low-grade hostility. Long looks from the settler men comparing bags of sunflower
seeds. A young woman holding her baby close and turning to leave
the store when she sees Amal in her head scarf. It's only like this
when something is going on. When a boy had been kidnapped. When
a soldier has been stabbed. When a bus has been bombed. Where is
Nasir? Panic rises. His eyes are dry. "Where is Nasir?" he says aloud,
and Amal, bless her, picks up on everything immediately.

"I will find him," she says. She puts the cucumbers in the cart, not bothering to knot the bag before running off. "Nasir!" she cries out, but not too loud, more like a strained call. "Nasir!" She is heading toward the candy aisle in the back. They abandon the cart. Shibi heads past the dairy fridges, toward the checkout line, because sometimes Nasir gets distracted by the junk there. He doesn't know what has happened. He doesn't have time to check his phone. He needs to find his son.

Miriam is kneeling on her front lawn surrounded by her daughters. "Ima, we don't know!" they cry out. "B'ezrat haShem, b'ezrat haShem." They don't finish the sentence, just repeat the phrase. G-d willing, G-d willing.

Miriam heard the boom faintly but didn't connect it to the checkpoint—the Tunnels Checkpoint, where Ori is stationed this week—until the text alerts began coming in. Explosion at the checkpoint. Explosion at the Tunnels Checkpoint. Then she ran outside; she ran into the lawn, her daughters running after her. She would have kept running out into the street, but the little ones clung to her legs and the bigger ones grabbed her from behind. "Daddy is coming home," they said, but how will he get home? The roads will be blocked.

"My boy," Miriam is moaning on her knees.

The neighbors cover their faces to pray.

She could run to him. If they would let her. She could run on Highway 60, run toward Jerusalem until she reached the checkpoint, run all the way to her baby, her baby, her baby. What have they done to her baby?

Cunts! Vera could have been at the checkpoint today. Like, it was not inconceivable that she would be at the Tunnels Checkpoint today.

She runs to the front gates of the church to see smoke rising up from Highway 60, down toward Bethlehem. Cunts, cunts, cunts. Something is happening, and someone else is getting there first. She had to come to this stupid church to write a stupid sidebar for a stupid in-flight magazine, and, like, shit, she could have gone to the Church of the Nativity. She chose this church because it's closer. But if she'd gone to the Church of the Nativity, she might have been at the checkpoint right now.

Police cars race toward the tunnels. Army jeeps, too. All lights, all sirens. The civilian cars pull over to the side of the road, their drivers getting out to watch the emergency vehicles fly by. Vera takes some photos on her phone because she might as well try to get something. The nun she was interviewing comes out to the threshold to see what the fuss is, looking past Vera toward the highway. Vera stands by the church gates—pulled toward the action yet separated from it—scrolling through her phone, desperately looking for an update.

Already, a location tag for "Tunnels Checkpoint" is active online. Photos of a burning bus. Suicide bombing? There hasn't been one of those in a few years. And on a Palestinian bus? Maybe Israeli settlers? A revenge attack? Or something else entirely? An actual accident? The IDF Twitter has not posted anything helpful. *Developing situation*, they tweeted. *Explosion on Highway 60.* This stands in contrast to the usual snark of the Israeli army social media presence, which reads like it's run by a bunch of teenagers (it is), who have been known to post videos of air strikes in Gaza with a bull's-eye emoji. Vera scrolls through civilian-uploaded photos of the explosion. More photos of the burning bus. Ambulances with the red Star of David (no crosses here). The sirens continue to scream down Highway 60. Vera finds a photo of helicopters circling through the smoke, unbelievably close up. She "favorites" it so she can find it later—maybe she'll use it in coverage of the explosion. Not that she has anything to say except that she saw maybe thirty police cars and some smoke. She refreshes her feed. Cunts.

᠔᠂᠒᠑

"Go home," a soldier is saying through the megaphone. "This highway is closed. Turn around." There are more army vehicles than Oum Hamid can count, blocking the road toward Bethlehem. Squat and green. Fifteen? Twenty? Everyone in the Bethlehem-bound van has gotten out. They were near the front of the queue when the soldiers shut everything down—a few minutes earlier, and they would have made it past this roadblock and home to Bethlehem. But now they are standing in the sun, held back by soldiers in combat vests and the knee pads, some of them talking into walkie-talkies, and from the cars next to and behind Oum Hamid, the shabaab begin to emerge from the vans and cars in line—"What's the holdup?"—their agitation mounting.

"Stay back!" a soldier yells into a megaphone as a man approaches, not a young guy in jeans, but a man in a suit. The man continues toward the soldiers. Everyone watches as he approaches the soldiers. What does he think? That he can explain his way through? The soldier yells something in Hebrew at him. The man is gesturing. He says he needs to get through. "This is inhumane!" the man exclaims. Maybe he knows someone at the checkpoint, someone hurt in the explosion. Oum Hamid texts her son again. *Where are you? Tell me you are home.* No responses yet. But there's no reason for Hamid to be at the Tunnels Checkpoint. There isn't, is there? Then why does she feel dread pressing at her throat? She dials Hamid. The man in the suit is yelling. The soldier pushes him back, pushes on his chest. A young man behind Oum Hamid cries out in anger. Hamid's phone is ringing, no answer. Another young man, this one in jeans, younger, runs forward to help the professional man up off the ground. The other soldiers have become alert, are beginning to step toward the two men. She dials Hamid again. One soldier is speaking into a walkie-talkie; another has his weapon raised in the air. More young men are emerging from the line. Hamid's voice mail again. A stone flies up, over the rest of the traffic, and lands among the soldiers. Then, that horrible sound that nobody should ever get used to: a warning shot.

Samar is at her office desk, her fingers hovering above her keyboard as she searches for the right word in English—the word she has been looking for, one of those four-syllable English words that comes from Greek and conveys something unbelievably specific. The word is about to come to her. She can feel it—emerging from the folds of her mind.

She's alone in the office. The three other professors who share desk space here have left for the weekend. Samar relishes the quiet of the empty office; soon, she'll go home to check on Mother and countenance the constant, invasive presence of her youngest brother's young wife, meddlesome little Fatima. But not yet. A soft breeze comes through the window left ajar, playing with Samar's hair. Outside, she can hear the murmur of students calling to one another. Voices of young men, laughter of young women. She remains stuck in the sentence she is composing. What is that word? She feels it hovering just beyond her, like a dream receding. She closes her eyes. She doesn't think about what the word would be in Arabic or German or French. She waits for it to come in English, because she's writing this paper in English. The word is elusive by its nature; it means to draw attention to something by downplaying it. Talking around it. Yes, here it is. One of those rhetoric terms. Here it is.

Even before the students begin to clamor and phones begin buzzing with news, it is a distant, percussive sound that jars Samar out of her concentration, eyes open. Her first thought: They are invading again, like they did in 2002. Tanks storming the Church of the Nativity, artillery echoing across pink marble, and all over the city, bombs falling. The campus is up on a hill, and, surely, that makes it vulnerable. Should she get down? To the floor, yanni? The room is eerily still. Her fingers are still hovering over her keyboard. If it were close—whatever it was—she'd surely hear car alarms going off. So something far. Now, outside, she can hear students calling out to one another. "Are they here?" a boy shouts. "Have the dogs come?" You never know when the Israeli army will fight their way onto campus to arrest one teenager or another.

"What does it say?" another boy is shouting. "What have you heard?"

The wooden door of Samar's office flies open and Noor, a reticent and terribly thin girl from her writing seminar, appears at the threshold. "A bomb at the checkpoint," she says, almost pleading.

Samar beckons her in. "What?" she asks. "A bomb? Can it be?"

Noor comes to her desk, all angular and cheekboned. "A bomb at the checkpoint," she says again. "And Mai is there."

Samar is frozen in her chair. *Paralipsis.* That's the word that she was looking for. Paralipsis.

Three Seconds

Hamid runs down the hill toward the Tunnels Checkpoint. Smoke in his throat. He trips over a twisted sheet of corrugated metal, maybe part of the checkpoint overhang, or maybe just an old scrap, who knows. Even as he's stumbling, he's asking himself what Mai is wearing today. Blue, right? He saw her after class. Image of Mai turning away from him, always turning away. And yes, blue. Some kind of blue dress-shirt thing with ruffles.

When Hamid heard the explosion, he was in a place he goes to be alone—a secluded old ruin in Area B, a grassy stretch of nothing just off the road that leads to the checkpoint. The past few days have been unbearable. Ever since the night when they took Muhi—the vicious jeeps sweeping in, pushing Muhi to the ground, and, maybe this was the worst part, letting Hamid go, not even arresting him, letting Hamid go and driving off with Muhi—Hamid has felt the stranglehold of despair that previously gripped Muhi. Like he contracted it.

At first, he'd assumed the explosion was a missile. He was so close to the checkpoint, it was almost as if he'd been expecting it. As he ran, he prayed, or something like praying. *Please, not her too. Please.* He ran down the hill toward the checkpoint, ran to where he thought Mai might be, making her way home from school. Words from Muhi—Where are you, Muhi? What are the Jews doing to you?—echoing in his head, *Love means protecting.* Hamid ran through the barbed wire to the Tunnels Checkpoint. The chaos of the explosion kept him safe. If they shot at him, he didn't hear it. By the time he reached the checkpoint, the Jew paramedics were already loading their people onto gurneys, inserting IVs, shouting into cell phones too fast for Hamid to understand.

Now: sharp smell of smoke at the back of his throat, burning bus where the highway to Jerusalem should be. Now, he understands it was a bomb.

He's tripped into a soldier. Wait, no, a large woman in green, the same ugly green of the Jews' uniform, but this is a big woman in long, flowing clothes, like a dancer or a cartoon witch. Her back is to him, and when she turns to face him, Hamid sees that her face is falling off. There's no other way to say it. Both of her hands are held up to a curtain of blood coming through her fingers. Hamid lets out a cry, but the woman doesn't say anything as she continues her unsteady walk toward the Jew paramedics.

Sirens, smoke. If Mai is conscious, she might get in an ambulance going into Jerusalem; if she's unconscious, the Zionists will probably send her to a Bethlehem hospital. He passes a compact settler car, new-looking, all four doors open, people gone like in a zombie movie.

Mai, where are you? He finds himself backing away from the center of the fray, into an area more peripheral. He steps back onto something soft, please not a body part, but no, it's a kid's backpack.

The white lady comes out of nowhere. She's in front of Hamid, about two strides away, dressed in greens and blues. Weirdly clean-looking. Untouched. She's holding up her cell phone, taking photos or maybe even live-streaming the destruction. When her phone rings, she answers it. "Ido, baby, I'm okay," she says in English, her voice breathless. "I don't know, but I'm okay, I promise I'm okay. Hold on."

Then—and Hamid cannot believe his eyes—she holds out her phone and takes a selfie. What the actual fuck?

Men are hosing down the burning bus. He takes out his phone to check for messages. Just Mama. *Where are you?* Twelve missed calls. He rubs his thumb across the long crack in his screen.

He doesn't know what else to do, so he does something stupid: He searches through a group chat containing everyone from his composition class. He finds Mai. He dials her number. Ringing, ringing, ringing. He's about to hang up. Then: "Hello?"

"Mai!"

"Hello?"

"Mai, can you hear me? It's me, it's Hamid. Where are you? Near the ambulances?" He does that thing that fathers do when they take phone calls, pressing his hand over his free ear so he can hear what she's saying better.

"What should I do?" Her voice is at once clear and floating.

"I'm near the ambulances," he says.

"The ambulances," she echoes. "The ambulances." Then the call ends.

Hamid pulls a handful of his own hair. Focus. She sounds like she hit her head, which must mean she was close to it when it happened. Maybe, then, she's near the place where the buses pull over for the soldiers. He thinks he knows where that would be, where that was, before the explosion.

He sees Mai from a distance. He knows it's her without having to get close, just from her shape—womanly, something elegant in the hands. She's helping someone, getting them to safety, and he's about to call her name when he stops. Ugly green, and this time it really is a soldier. He's wounded, the soldier, and he's taller than Mai. A settler. A dog who hops on one leg, while Mai, please no, stands with him, supporting his weight so that he can keep moving toward help. Her body is small under his arm. The two of them aren't farther from Hamid than—what?—maybe the distance across a wide street, but somehow it seems at once closer and farther, distorted as through warped glass. He can see how their bodies are pressed together, almost rubbing as the soldier hops forward. It is disgusting.

"Oh my gosh," says a voice to his left.

He turns to see the white lady, the one he saw taking a selfie, brandishing her phone. She crosses in front of him. She takes a few pictures with her phone held above her head. She's standing right in front of him. Hamid wonders if he's invisible or maybe dead. Standing behind her, he can imagine the frame of the photo she is taking, how it must appear on her phone. He stands and watches the living image. For a second, when the soldier's head pauses in its bobbing, the two of them, Mai and the soldier, look straight ahead. He sees the image they will make, the two of them. He sees it the way it will be seen not just by people he knows, but by strangers to this place, by tourists, by Jews, even: a torn uniform, a bloodied head scarf, two bodies in support of each other, four eyes focused in the same direction. He could stop it. He could run and smack the phone from the white lady's hand. He could stand in front of her, blocking the view of Mai. He could grab Mai's hand, pull her from the danger of being seen this way. But he does not move. He stands still and watches as the image is minted, the image that will (surely it will, won't it?) ruin this girl's life.

SUMMER

Match

Vera's sometimes-fixer Mo is pointing out sniper positions on Highway 60 when Vera catches sight of Rachel—the Orthodox teenager she's been getting drunk with recently. In an effort to put some distance between them, Vera's ignoring Rachel's texts, or at least lengthening the time between receiving the text and responding.

She and Mo are in a communal van, an "Arab bus," driving by an illegal Israeli settlement that juts out onto the highway. Humvees idle around the settlement gates. The homes inside seem pretty. White stone, red tile.

"Sniper," Mo says, pointing to the junction ahead.

Vera is, like, not entirely certain whether Mo is trying to get her killed. She's taking an optimistic tack. In the version she's telling herself, Mo doesn't want her to actually die today, just wants her to feel how easy it *would* be to die, meaning how it feels to have your life treated as expendable, meaning like a Palestinian, like him. So fine, yes, Vera is riding around in a communal van imagining all the ways there are to die. All this in the name of a more expansive empathy. The van's other passengers, eight people, pay no attention to Mo or Vera. The men, all in work boots, may be coming from construction sites. The only other woman is a young mother seated next to Vera with her son on her lap. When Mo first began to point out snipers, Vera looked around her, anxious that such talk would disturb the other passengers. But of course, even if they had understood the German, why would it shock them? This is their life. This is their commute.

Vera is wearing the dorky press vest, which Mo likes to point out probably makes her a sniper target. He's looking his full seventy years in a cargo-pocket vest and a bucket hat getup that seems, to Vera, like something you'd wear fishing out on a lake in Bavaria. Get this guy a canoe. But no doubt he's right in his tactic: dress like a tourist, (probably) don't get shot.

Nearly a week after the explosion but no word yet on which side was responsible. Palestinians or Israelis. Arabs or Jews. Each claims the other did it. Some theorize that it was actually an engine fire on the bus. From the dismal strip of Gaza, Hamas, for once, has not claimed responsibility, but that hasn't stopped the Israeli army from conducting a crackdown on what they call Hamas operatives in the West Bank. Their latest tactic is a disturbing one: posing as journalists. The undercovers who took away two student leaders from the university in Ramallah yesterday presented themselves as press; Vera suspects this is a two-birds move, in that (1) it allows even non-Arabic-speaking army operatives to maneuver with relative ease in the West Bank and (2) it screws over the despised international press. Now Vera keeps a digital portfolio on her phone: screenshots of articles, links to YouTube videos of interviews. She has anxiety daydreams about her phone dying, leaving her unable to prove to a group of desperate, enraged men that she's not a spy.

For now, Highway 60 is still blocked off at both checkpoints serving Bethlehem: the Tunnels Checkpoint, what's left of it, is letting only Jews through, and Checkpoint 300 is shut down altogether. The Palestinian workers who commute inside must cross elsewhere, lining up as early as two in the morning just to make it to construction sites by eight a.m. Vera has tried and tried to pitch a story on the aftermath of the explosion for Palestinians, but all any editor cares about is the photograph—the image that emerged from the wreckage and quickly went from some Instagram mommy's live feed to every screen on the planet: the Palestinian Girl and the Israeli Soldier. Who is she? Who cares? Most Palestinians assume the photo was faked. Resigned paranoia of a people who live under the heel of an empire. But elsewhere, the photo has become the obsession that Vera knew it would. From the first time she saw in her feed—standing by Highway 60, watching the police cars scream toward the checkpoint—she knew the photo would take on a life of its own.

"Sniper," Mo says, pointing out one of the van's windows at a metal guard shack crouched by the side of the road. Everything here is painted an ugly shade of military yellow. Next to Vera, the boy seated on his mother's lap is asleep.

Mo doesn't like the angle of Vera's new assignment, and to be fair, he's right: the story she's been hired to write is garbage, more sensationalized junk hyping up the Girl and the Soldier. Mo has been pushing her to write about something more substantial—the water shortages or the nearly daily raids by Israeli special forces, who seem to be working through the camps with a systematic vigor. How to explain how hard it is to get editors interested in the same news always coming out from here: oppression, power, and irony. But the image of the Girl and the Soldier is fresh and promising. Mysterious, suggestive. Hopeful.

All last week, Vera had been waiting for it to fade but it grew and grew. The internet has christened the photograph with a caption: *This is what hope looks like.* If Vera cared to, she could read a variety of metamedia articles about the origins of that phrase. *This is what hope looks like.* Yesterday, the actual president of France tweeted the photo out to his several million followers: *Voici l'espoir.* And so Vera caved. She wrote to her editor at *Der Spiegel* and said, Look, I'll go around the West Bank and ask people what the image means to them. He bought the story on spec. Two dollars a word. She needed the money.

Mo is looking up something on his phone now. The van is quiet but for the prayers coming from the radio and the woman sitting next to Vera who whispers softly to her toddler son, waking groggily from his nap.

They drive slowly past another settlement gate. There are bus stops, heavily fortified against missiles, against car rammings. All around them are soldiers with scraggly forelock curls, women in head wraps, men in jeans with tasseled *tzitzit* (as Vera has learned to call them) and handguns tucked in their pants. These are the settlers. Religiously devout, undeterrable. And there, among them, in a knot of settlers, is Rachel. There. Rachel waiting for the bus. She's leaning against the cement bunker of a bus stop talking into her phone, gesturing with her free hand. Vera feels a dirty pull at her throat. Her heart is too loud.

The van is close enough that Rachel, if she looked in expecting to see someone she knew, might recognize Vera. If this were Jerusalem or Tel Aviv or even Berlin, Rachel might peer into the slow-moving van, just out of curiosity. But here among the Palestinians, Vera is invisible to Rachel, who is—Vera sees now—not Rachel at all. That woman isn't Rachel. Of course she isn't. Vera doesn't know what she was thinking. For one, this lady has her head covered in a wrap, which Rachel will do only after she is married, if she actually goes through with it. Also, this woman is too old to be Rachel, who is still, technically, a teenager. All the details are wrong. How could Vera have gotten it so wrong? The settler woman at the bus stop is heavier than Rachel, and though her features are similar—those striking eyebrows—they are less pronounced, less beautiful. Vera can imagine Rachel's complaint: "That's what you think I look like? That??" *Tsk-tsk.* That's the sound Rachel makes. *Tsk-tsk.* A kind of exasperated punctuation. *Tsk-tsk.* A sticky and irritating sound, like Velcro being pulled off the back of your neck.

Vera has known Rachel for the better part of the year. They met when Vera was researching an article (never published) on the so-called modern Orthodox American Jews of Jerusalem, how their military zeal and their money have reshaped Israeli politics. But in the last month, since Vera broke up with Amir—really, for the last time this time, really—she has found herself almost inseparable from Rachel. Vera stays over at least once a week with Rachel in Jerusalem. It's easier to stay with Rachel at her apartment in Jerusalem than to take the one-hour bus all the way back to her own apartment in Tel Aviv. But more than that, it's easier than being alone, than drinking alone. Here they are. Two girls, afraid of the dark.

Leave me alone, Vera thinks.

As if the words are a spell, some summoning magic, Vera's phone starts vibrating. Rachel's name on the screen. It's Rachel calling. Calling, calling, calling.

Vera doesn't pick up, but she sends a text message with a lot of exclamation points, which is meant to convey, I'm not mad at you (!!). *I'm reporting!!* she texts to Rachel, *I'll call you later!!*

Wifey, Rachel writes back. This is how she refers to her. *Come over tonight. I have too much wine.*

No, Vera thinks. But she knows she'll end up going.

In the van, Mo begins again. "In the last year, nine Palestinians have been shot at that intersection," he says. "Two in the last week." He looks out the window as he talks. He's old enough to be Vera's grandfather. Most of his life he worked in government. His wife likes him to keep busy, he told Vera, so in his retirement he tours around journalists and aid workers. His German is superb; his accent, lovely, almost a lisp. He quotes Old Testament verses ironically. "Love thy neighbor as thyself," he might say, when describing for Vera the recent settler attacks on Palestinian schoolchildren. He's been working with the magazine for years.

"Sniper," he says, pointing to more metal trailers crouching by the road. "Sniper." His voice is joyous, triumphant. "Sniper," he says, now pointing to the road back behind them, where the woman who isn't Rachel is waiting for the bus.

The danger past, they fall into silence again.

"How can they say they love this land," Mo asked her back in the spring, "and yet they do this?" It was just after Easter, not long after Salem Abu-Khdeir died at Augusta Victoria Hospital. Vera and Mo were following a farmer through his ruined olive grove, ancient trees the villagers have tended for generations, trees older than any living community member, hacked and burnt by the settlers. Mutilated arms, charred limbs. Mo was translating for the farmer, whose rural Arabic was tricky for Vera to follow. "We have named these trees for our mothers," Mo cried out, echoing the farmer. Then, in his own words, to Vera, "Vera, is this love? What these settlers do, is it love?"

And Vera nodded, wrote it all down in her notebook. But privately, so privately it was in a space she wasn't sure her mind would let her touch again, she thought, *Yes, of course that's love*. Because this was how her parents had loved her, or what they called love. What other people would call control, her parents had called love. Vera unable to leave the house. Vera unable to take a phone call from a boy. Vera barred from movie theaters, which her parents imagined as places where all kinds of dark gropings might happen. Her parents weren't religious. Their fixation was more private than that, harder to explain. Vera's body was as regulated as the contested ground she writes about, or so it seems to her. Today, despite knowing that her parents were wrong to conflate control with love, Vera finds she can't quite unlearn the conflation.

Later, after the van arrives without incident in Hebron and after Vera has done her man-on-the-street interviews there—walking around the contested city split down the middle, ancient residences now used as army posts, after she is done holding up a cutout of the Girl and the Soldier from an Israeli newspaper and asking beleaguered Palestinian merchants and children, "What does this mean to you?" and getting mostly bewildered answers like, "No, I'm sorry, I don't know who she is," or, "That photo is a fake," or, mercifully for Vera's copy, a child who laughed out in English, "Hope! Hope! Hope!"— after all that, Mo asks Vera if she has eaten.

They are sitting on the steps of the towering Ottoman-era Tomb of the Patriarchs. Like everything in Hebron, it is split. One entrance for Arabs, one for Jews. For hundreds of years, the Ottomans forbade Jews from entering the holy place to pray; now Israeli soldiers stand around with knee pads (snipers) and stun grenades (police), speaking clipped Hebrew into walkie-talkies. "Have you eaten supper?" Mo asks, watching the soldiers as Vera flips through her notes.

Vera recognizes the invitation. "I need to get back to Tel Aviv," she says, hoping she sounds regretful. She has eaten at Mo's home before. A small and lively home. White stone on a hill. Plastic chairs in a garden tended carefully with rationed water. A sturdy wife who delights in her grandchildren, a strong-fingered woman with whom Vera can speak only in Arabic. Sons and grandsons older and younger than Vera who eye her with interest, ask her opinions on Brexit. A beautiful place. A tiring place. A place that requires Vera to be at her best—her most present and generous. And tonight, Vera wants to be at her worst. "I'm sorry," she says.

"Another time," Mo says, his hands on his knees, sounding neither surprised nor disappointed. Then, ever the fixer, he says, "The name for this city comes from the word for 'friend.'"

"In which language?" Vera asks, knowing the city has two names: Hebron, Al-Khalil.

"In both languages," Mo says. "Put that in your notes."

They are sitting on the steps of a resplendent site of worship. Underneath the shrine is a cave—a burial cave. Once, they say, it held the body of Abraham, root of the Abrahamic faiths. Down there, deep below, his body turned to dust along with his wife, Sarah. Isaac and Rebecca were buried there, too. Jacob and Leah. Only one matriarch is missing. Jacob's favorite wife is buried elsewhere: Rachel. Rachel is not here.

໑໑໑

Later that night, Rachel is on Vera's phone and Vera is on Rachel's tablet. Vera is checking her email. Rachel is talking to strange men, pretending to be Vera, so, pretty typical as far as their nights together go. It's the dating app that everyone uses, grim and unavoidable: a few profile photos and a one-line bio. "The meat market," Vera calls it. She hasn't used the app in months. Isn't that what made her ill-fated obsession with Amir a kind of relief? No more compulsive checking of the app to see who chose her; no more setting out to explain herself to strangers, or maybe better to say, to articulate a version of herself that they might want. But Rachel is delighted by the whole setup. "Look at all these guys!" she exclaimed the first night Vera showed her how it worked, how when a match's picture popped up, you tapped here to show you were interested, tapped there if you weren't. "They are everywhere!" Rachel said, tapping out approvals on every match that came her way. "This guy is 250 meters away, and he has a motorbike."

Vera doesn't fully understand why she has started spending so much time with Rachel, why she craves their time together even as she finds Rachel immature and annoying. Before Vera broke up with Amir, Rachel was just another overly friendly, lonely girl who texted Vera more than Vera texted her. They went from zero to sixty, as it were—from seeing each other for coffee once, maybe twice, over several months, to seeing each other a few times a week. Surely, Vera thinks, the sudden intensity must indicate an instability. How long can this last?

But for now, they're in Rachel's bed, Vera up against the headboard, Rachel stretched feline over her feet. Vera sends off another email to the travel website that still owes her for months of copywriting. *So sorry to be a pest!!* she writes, which she hopes comes across as Fuck You, Pay Me. This is her life, isn't it? Begging for her little scraps. Small consolation: it's delightful to finger-tap out emails on Rachel's tablet. Tap, tap, tap. It makes Vera feel rich, spoiled. Safe.

She taps to her feeds. Right away, there it is: the photo from the explosion, the Girl and the Soldier, the photo that launched a thousand shitty, derivative think pieces on war and violence. A girl in a hijab helping a wounded soldier, her so-called enemy, to safety. Every time you see it you notice a new, poignant detail. Her hand is clutching his waist, his ruined leg is bent—he must be hopping. Around them is the explosion's smoke and rubble. You look at it and you think, *War*, but also you think, *Future*. You think—goddammit, you really do—*Hope*. This is what hope looks like.

Neither the girl nor the soldier is looking at the camera, but somewhere beyond it—toward wherever they were trying to go. This creates the effect of them moving past the viewer toward some distant, hopeful future that only they can see, that they will lead us to. The soldier is fair. His body dominates the frame. You can't see much of the girl but the hijab. It is white, perfect, or rather perfectly defiled with a dark patch of what is either dirt or blood, his or her own. Her face, in profile, is almost entirely obscured; you see the suggestion of the nose, the mouth. You project expressions onto her. A smile, a grimace, a cry. She might be wearing jeans. There are, amazingly, no other clear photos. Nobody knows who the girl is.

Vera has forty-eight hours until her deadline. She taps to an article published earlier today by someone she used to work with at the university newspaper. It's a feminist hot-take on the gendering of the image, the fetishization of the hijab. It's wise and insightful, and nobody will read it. What Vera does learn from skimming through the vaguely condescending article (written by a white woman who does not wear a head scarf) is that an American pop singer with a huge following posted a photo of herself wearing an oversized T-shirt with the photo silk-screened on and what looks like no pants, just knee socks. Her caption: *This is what hope looks like, y'all.* She has over one hundred million followers. One hundred million. That's more than the population of Germany. *This is what hope looks like.*

"Fuck me," Vera says.

"We're working on it," Rachel replies cheerfully.

Because Rachel is engaged to be married, they keep up certain pretenses, namely, that Rachel is looking for potential matches for Vera. And yes, okay, it's a little weird to have Rachel talking to strangers pretending to be Vera, but Vera can't help it—she feels bad for Rachel. The girl is nineteen and engaged. Nineteen! Rachel's fiancé—whom Vera has never met—is barely twenty-one, Israeli-born son of South African parents on one settlement or another. He's finishing his army service—a "warrior," Rachel says, who uses a night-vision scope to go raid Hamas safe houses. Rachel's complaints about him have an indulgent ring: "He comes home, smelly and exhausted. He's away for ten days, for two weeks, the whole time we're talking about how badly we want each other, how we'll do this, we'll do that . . ." Duh, they have sex, she said when Vera asked, What, like, you think I'm Mormon? "But when he gets home, do we make love? No! Of course not, no. He sleeps the whole time." Vera has the sense that Rachel is reading off some sort of army girlfriend script.

You're twenty-six, Vera scolds herself. So why do you spend so much of your time with a nineteen-year-old Zionist? Fresh from high school, Rachel came to Israel last summer to do a few months of volunteering at some day care. She met her fiancé at a friend's party; he took her home that night, not to fuck her but to meet his parents. They all sat around a well-lit kitchen eating coffee cake. By the end of the summer, Rachel was engaged. She hasn't been back home to LA since. What is Rachel running away from? Vera wonders but doesn't ask, because then she'd have to answer the question herself.

The day before the explosion, Vera blocked Amir's phone number—not so much to prevent him from reaching her, but to stop herself from hoping that he might. The space he left behind has given Vera a breath of almost divine clarity; she sees herself as she really is. She is a scraggly and helpless planet, flinging itself from the gravitational pull of one obsession to the next. There she is. You can trace her trajectory back, all the way back before Amir, before her college boyfriend, and all the lovers in between, all the way back to her mother, the one who broke her heart first and irreparably. Mama, her rival in Father's affection. Vera won—of course she won, lovely and clever, brilliant and thin. Vera won her father but lost her mother, who does not—no other way to say this—particularly like Vera. There she is. Mama, burning, as Vera's father smashes their house phone into little plastic bits. A boy has called the house for Vera. Mama watching, Mama behind a closed door.

The day of the explosion, Vera wasn't at the Tunnels Checkpoint, but she was just up the highway, at an obsolete church, for a pointless magazine assignment, and as the smoke rose and the sirens colluded toward a point down the highway, she wasn't thinking about reportage or even survivors. She was thinking, joyously, really, *This*. This is the perfect excuse to text him, to text Amir. But she didn't. She was good. She's trying to be good. She's trying to remember that you can't convince someone to love you, not if they don't want to.

"Stop it."

Vera looks up. Rachel is up on one forearm, pointing at her. Rachel with dark, curly hair and strikingly full eyebrows; Rachel in an expensive, loose T-shirt, and diamond stud earrings. Real ones. Rachel says again, "Stop it." She wags a finger. "Your nails! Stop chewing them."

Vera has been at her cuticles again. They are rough, and where she has peeled the dry skin away there is a tender pink, obscene and new. "Okay, okay," she says, annoyed and happy every time Rachel nags her about it.

Rachel rolls back onto her belly, engrossed in all the formulaic exchanges that talking to strange men entails. *Let's adventure together*, the messages say. *Let's go to Iceland, to Nepal, to Berlin. You could show me around Berlin.* Always the same.

Since Amir, Vera has been on a few dates. The most successful one, if that's not a ridiculous thing to say, was with a recently divorced guy from the Belgian embassy in Tel Aviv. In his company Volkswagen, she straddled him as they made out, and when he pressed his fingers up into her, he had such a dopey, blissed-out smile on his oblong face that immediately and viscerally, Vera missed Amir, missed the molten center between them—a wanting so heavy it came out like anger. She made a quick retreat, hurried out of the car and walked home to South Tel Aviv to masturbate in peace.

Rachel has chosen new photos for Vera's dating profile, insisting on the kind of slutty-looking one where she's holding a glass of rosé in a low-cut gown. The photo was, actually, taken at the embassy gala where she met the divorced Belgian. Vera explained all this to Rachel—why not? "Your life is so stupidly cool," Rachel said. That is, of course, plainly untrue, but Vera liked that it might look that way to a repressed teenager.

They are in Rachel's bedroom in Jerusalem, avoiding the flat-mates that Vera has seen only fleetingly in the common areas. Rachel's room is filled with marvelous, gilded details: sugar body scrub in a glass jar on the edge of the dresser, the obscene price sticker still on; rich, heavy-smelling candles on a mirrored tray next to bottles of perfume. Her floor is covered with laundry—jeans crumpled and inside out, lacy thongs curled like dry leaves. Some dumb reality show is streaming on Rachel's laptop. A woman in a gorgeous gown is weeping. "I thought I'd have more time," she moans. Vera drinks deeply from an expensive wineglass. This is what she has chosen over dinner with Mo and his family. Instead of long discussions about life in the West Bank, Vera chose this. Wine-drunk and watching bad TV. Familiar.

"Shoot, this guy is texting me in German," Rachel says, looking up. Clear skin, full eyebrows. Her hair is a gorgeous waterfall of tight ringlets, always clean and soft.

"Wait, you gave him my number?"

"No," Rachel says, making the impatient *tsk-tsk* sound. "No, I mean on the app. He's texting me in German."

"Tell him you're practicing your English," Vera says, going back to searching for additional images of the Girl and the Soldier. What she should be doing is typing up her notes from earlier today. Fast turnaround. Two days. She takes a sip of wine. Then a gulp.

After a few seconds, Rachel lets out a frustrated sigh.

"What now?" Vera asks.

"This is just so"—she hesitates—"so fun. It's fun to do this, to be like this."

It strikes Vera as a bit too cruel to explain to Rachel what she means: that it's fun to act her actual age. "Have you seen this?" Vera asks, turning the tablet to Rachel to show her the image of the Girl and the Soldier.

"Yeah, obviously," Rachel says. "We talked about it in my Hebrew class." Twice a week Rachel takes lessons in a language she refuses to practice. Vera has heard her on the phone: *Excuse me? English, please, yeah, English, Anglit, English.*

"And?"

"And what? They are going to kill her," Rachel says. *Tsk-tsk.* "Hamas, or someone."

"Kill the girl who helped the soldier?"

"Yes," Rachel says, "I mean, they kill traitors, don't they?"

"A lot of Palestinians think it's faked," Vera says.

"Hmm," Rachel says, already back on her phone.

The exchange strikes Vera as fairly representative. When Jewish Israelis see the image, they see a "good" Palestinian doomed by the brainwashing of their own leadership. "We fear an honor jihad," the Israeli minister of culture said recently, inventing a phrase that doesn't exist in Arabic or Islam. The minister is an unsettlingly beautiful woman who kohls her eyes. That phrase—"honor jihad"—was later repeated by the American envoy to the UN, while night after night, young Palestinian men in zip ties were brought out to Israeli jeeps in their pajamas. Conversely, Palestinians look at the Girl and the Soldier and see a faked image, and in that way, they see confirmation of Israel's total control. Only foreigners see hope—two sides, both alike in humanity. Romeo and Juliet, but with semiautomatics.

This may be what makes Vera so uneasy about the image. It says whatever you need it to say. This was the crux of the *New York Times* article not written, thank God, by someone Vera knows—she couldn't handle the jealousy if, say, that American cow Sara had landed the byline—but by the head of the paper's Israel bureau, an elderly white woman, Jewish, with chunky bangles. Vera has unsuccessfully pitched her a handful of times. "An Explosion, a Uniform, and a Head Scarf: Image from Israel Inspires and Incites." The article reported that on *both sides of the Wall* (Americans love this turn of phrase) there is suspicion about the photograph. A well-designed graphic reproduced the paranoid deconstructions found on Facebook in Hebrew and in Arabic—ones that magnify the photo until it's pixelated, mark it with red circles and arrows, pointing to the supposed digital traces of photoshopping. Mossad did it! No, ISIS did it! No, the Jewish media did it! No, the girl isn't helping the soldier—look closer!—she's trying to kidnap him.

"What about the soldier?" Vera asks. She sometimes uses Rachel in her magazine stories; it's truly half-assed reporting—quoting Rachel man-on-the-street-style, filler stuff.

"Ori Lev?" Rachel looks up again. "I know his mom!"

"Wait, what?"

"Yeah, she's my *kallah* teacher."

"Your what?"

"Someone who helps brides prepare for marriage."

"Your marriage counselor is the soldier's mom?"

"She's not a marriage counselor, but yeah."

Vera is so close to asking, *So, like, you all know each other?* But realizes in time that it might come off wrong, so instead says, "What a small country."

"Totally," Rachel says, rolling onto her back, still engrossed in Vera's phone. "I mean, I don't know Ori, but yeah, Miriam is great."

"Can I get her number?" Vera has to ask, right? She might be sick to death of this dumb, fluffy story, but a connection is a connection.

"She's changed her number," Rachel says, rolling back over to her tummy. "But you know she's already done, like, a bunch of interviews, right?"

This is true. Vera has seen video clips of a woman with her hair covered in a vibrant blue wrap, saying to the camera, *We're grateful he is alive*. Vera isn't sure she believes Rachel about Miriam changing her number. Then again, she's not sure she really cares. She doesn't want to interview Ori Lev's mom. She doesn't want to cover this story at all. Still, she's curious. "Wow, well, what do you think will happen to him?"

"To Ori?" Rachel asks.

"Yeah, will there be consequences?" Is the kid a traitor to Israelis now? How would that work?

Rachel shrugs. "He's safe, *baruch haShem*." She hasn't looked up from Vera's phone. Tap, tap, tap. "Oh, look! An engineer!"

Vera feels herself letting go of the conversation about the Girl and the Soldier. She drains her wine and leans over the edge of the bed to pour more, coming up with a full glass in one hand and the bottle, which she extends toward Rachel, in the other.

The night will continue like this. Wine and strange men on the internet. All of it a kind of foreplay for when the girls lie in the dark and make confessions. They have to wait; they have to work up to the point when their hearts spill over. Whispering, whispering, lying still on Rachel's bed, hiding from her flatmates in the closed room. This is how it works. They tell each other stories in the dark. Scary stories. Stories of themselves. They alternate, like children: your turn, my turn. Who threw up all through high school, whose father consistently introduces her as his wife then stammers an apology, whose mother shook her till she blacked out, who is begging an unkind man to fuck her, whose body was punished, by whom, how. They crack themselves open; they convince themselves that they love each other like sisters; they say it, again and again—"I love you; you're my sister," which is something that, surely, no sister has ever had to say.

Rachel tells her about the religious lessons for young brides. "Miriam, my *kallah* teacher, says that love is a state of knowledge."

"Your what?"

"My marriage guide, remember?"

"Right," Vera says. "Miriam says what?"

"That love is about knowing someone," Rachel says. She talks about the verb "to know" in Hebrew, how it's also a verb for sex. Vera feels a pang of jealousy, that Rachel has this framework—this ancient framework—for understanding what happens between her body and another.

"So what's wrong?" she asks, cutting Rachel off.

"My fiancé thinks I'm disgusting," Rachel says. "There's so much we don't know, and I wanted, I mean, I was just curious . . ." She pauses here.

Vera: "About—"

"I mean, what it would be like, you know? If he came on my face." Her tongue sounds swollen in her mouth.

Vera nods. It must be nice, actually, for everything in sex to be so illicit, so charged. Rachel lives in a world of boundaries, all of them waiting to be crossed. Once, it was like that for Vera. When she made it to the university in Heidelberg, free from her parents' obsessive surveillance of her body, everything was new. She woke up in a series of strange rooms. Then it wasn't so new.

Vera lifts her chin to manage more wine, puts the glass back down on the nightstand.

They are lying facing the ceiling, heads almost touching. Vera lets her head loll sideways to watch Rachel as she talks. Rachel is rich, and therefore Rachel is beautiful in the sense that she's well maintained. Facials, hair masks, eyebrow sculpting, whatever. But the closer Vera looks, the uglier Rachel gets. Two thick black hairs sprout from her chin. Vera wants to lick them. Why not? She's asked herself this, of course. Why not? Rachel's complaints all come down to this: she wants more from her fiancé. More sex, more desire, more kink, more orgasms. By Rachel's telling, her future husband is content with quiet, sleepy, lukewarm sex once a week or so. Middle-aged pacing. It sounds pretty nice to Vera, at least in theory. Anyway, the question: Why not? Why not have sex with this girl? Why not split her open? But that's a mean way to say it. Also, self-aggrandizing—as if Vera gave such life-ruiningly good head. Here's a kinder question: Why not bring each other some comfort, some pleasure? Why not?

Instead she asks, "Is coming on your face, like, not allowed religiously?"

Rachel lets a hand drop to the bed in frustration. "Technically it's not, like, ideal," she says, *tsk-tsk*. "But not forbidden the way some things are."

No period sex—Vera knows this one. "It gives me privacy," Rachel said when she first explained it, as if the pussy-terrified rabbis who wrote these laws set out to empower teenage brides, as if a woman were even a human being to them. Ask Miriam the *kallah* teacher about that.

Rachel says, "It's like, they think you're either a virgin or a whore."

Vera has thought this exact same sentiment herself, but somehow, hearing Rachel say it makes it seem stupid, sophomoric. And really, Vera knows precisely why she'll never kiss Rachel: because she doesn't want to be the one thing that makes Rachel happy. She doesn't want this sad, unfulfilled girl to become obsessed with her, to become her problem, to spill her sad, sticky feelings all over Vera. She doesn't want to deal with the disgusting overflow of Rachel's need. It is possible that this is exactly how Amir has come to think about Vera, why he's begun to ignore her so completely.

❧

When it's her turn to start talking again, Vera is sitting up against the wall. Rachel is drifting in and out of sleep, or maybe consciousness. "Do you know," Vera whispers, "how men talk about being tortured?"

Rachel's head is in her lap. Vera touches her hair. Soft hair, rich-girl hair.

"No," Rachel whispers. A single perfect sound that Vera wants to make her say again.

So she tells her about interviewing Palestinian men who were tortured by Israelis, interrogated in nameless prisons. The ones who get really fucked up, the ones with unhealable shoulders, the ones who look a little to the side when they speak to you—these men, they revere their torturers. Or maybe it's the pain they revere. They talk about pain the way you'd talk about a religion. It is a strange, impenetrable bond that develops between the body and its pain.

"You're scaring me," Rachel whispers.

What Vera says: "Shh, little one."

What Vera thinks: *Good.*

What Vera wants to say, but never will: Do you know how lucky you were? Your people, I mean. You went all those years, those hundreds of years, thousands of years, and never had a state, an army—never had the means to oppress. Do you know what you gave up? Now your fiancé is off shooting teenagers in a field; they're falling down right now, right now, the smoke from tires wafting past their perfect child bodies bleeding out in the dirt. You are the first Jews to do such a thing.

There are years never spoken of in the homes of Vera's grandparents, but once, Vera found an old photograph tucked away in an old Bible, of all places. A black-and-white photo of her mother and a young man. Or that is what she thought at first glance. But no, she realized after looking a moment longer, it was Oma, her maternal grandmother, looking young and bright with a face scrunched up in laughter, posing with a young man who must have been Vera's late granduncle. In the photo, Oma and her brother are waving little swastika flags. When Vera thinks of that photo now—the one she pressed back into the spine of the heavy, leather-bound Bible in her grandmother's sitting room—she feels shame, yes, of course, but also defiance. Because now she knows. Looking at Rachel, she sees it and she knows that anyone—anyone—can find themselves on the so-called wrong side of history.

The late-morning sun is hot on the top of Vera's head as she and Mo walk toward the entrance to the camp, which is built on a hill like a city in the Dark Ages, when the streets rejected the Roman grid in favor of something more tangled. There's dust and a faint smell of sewage. A young boy wheels a younger boy in a cart. They cry out to Vera in English: "Hello! Hello!" Her hangover is blooming down her spine; her tongue feels foreign. Dammit, Rachel.

Mo, looking plucky in his cargo pants with zippers and pockets galore, asks which families the boys are from, and in this way, Vera assumes, shows that he is from here, or at least used to be—was born here. The boys run off, maybe to herald their arrival. Mo turns to Vera, his face round beneath his khaki fishing hat, the drawstring long under his chin. He says in his whistling German, "Welcome, Vera, to my birthplace." Then he turns to walk up the hill and Vera follows. She's lucky he keeps making time for her. He doesn't have to; he's a great fixer and in demand, has been for years. His full name is, of course, Muhammed, but he is always Mo to foreign journalists. Without Mo, who was born in this camp, who made it out but whose brothers remain, Vera could never enter here to wave around a photo of the Girl and the Soldier asking, What does this mean to you?

Vera understands Mo's frustrations with the story she is writing; she shares those frustrations. She wants to write something urgent and true. It's possible that the success of the Salem Abu-Khdeir piece—her well-received (and now prize-nominated) coverage of the body-snatching from the hospital—gave her the false hope that all her future work would feel as important and consequential. But, of course, she can only write what editors want to buy. "We'll try to make it informative," she told Mo in the van yesterday. "Like tricking a kid to eat his vegetables."

Now she waits behind him while he knocks at a door in a well-lit side alley. "The man we will meet," Mo says to Vera, "is a father to me." He knocks again. Inside the house, a woman's voice—high, gentle, but slightly urgent—asks them to please wait a moment. Mo checks something on the ancient flip phone he uses. "I hope he is awake."

The heavy metal door opens, seemingly on its own, but no—it is a tiny boy, very young, with a backpack as big as he is, who opens the door and greets Mo with a terribly serious little handshake before running down the steps. Perhaps he came home from school for lunch. Mo laughs as he steps inside the home; Vera follows.

Inside, the curtains are closed against the daylight. A voice from upstairs, the woman's voice again, greets them, asking them to hold on a moment, please, to please sit, please and welcome, welcome, welcome. Vera is able to follow the Arabic.

She and Mo are in a sitting room of heavy fabrics and low tables. The young woman comes down the far stairwell, rushing. "Please," she echoes herself, gesturing toward the couches. "Please." Her long khimar frames her face and covers her torso, like a girl's cloak in a fairy tale. She pauses to exchange greetings with Mo and Vera. *Keyfak, alhamdulillah; w'anti, keyfik, kol ishi tammam, alhamdulillah.* She is harried, but there's something graceful in it, the way she disappears into what must be the kitchen and in an instant is back with a tray—little crystal glasses filled with fruit juice. "Just a moment," she says, as she puts down the juice on the low coffee table in front of them—"*Tfaddlu*"—then she's rushing back up the stairs.

"Not his daughter-in-law," Mo says, sipping juice, "but his granddaughter-in-law."

"How long have you known this family?" Vera asks.

"As long as I have known my name," Mo says.

The old man is descending slowly, with the girl's help. He's in a pale blue thawb.

Mo stands. "*Yaa haaj*," he says.

The men grasp hands. Mo moves to hug his elder—no, wait, not a hug but a deferent kiss. Mo kisses the older man's right hand. Their Arabic is too quiet and quickly spoken for Vera to understand. She is aware of her intrusiveness here.

Mo introduces Vera: "A journalist."

"Welcome," the elder man says.

"This man is as my father," Mo says to Vera, helping him sit. "Abu Rami."

"Welcome," Abu Rami says again, and Vera thanks him.

"He fled the village with my parents," Mo says in German.

Vera nods. She wishes she were writing a better story, had better questions to ask this man. This is, probably, exactly how Mo wants her to feel.

The soldier, Ori—what's his last name? Lieb?—was interviewed on Israeli TV for the first time today. A beautiful kid. Blue-eyed and full-mouthed, with a cast on his leg, sitting on his mother's leather couch, he said, "I'm grateful to the girl, whoever she is. I hope she's safe." This is the current line from the Israelis: The people want peace, but Palestinian leadership demands violence. The Israeli army's social media platforms—they are savvy, so savvy—released a series of announcements in English and Hebrew, promising to protect the girl if Hamas clerics issue a fatwa for her death.

Over the course of the next hour, men from the neighborhood trickle in. Some of them Mo recognizes instantly; some of them need introductions—this one's son, all grown up; this one's brother, back from Saudi. Each man shakes hands with all the others when he enters the home, and, when Vera rises, they shake her hand too, looking amused about it.

They drink strong black coffee and eat from plates of fresh figs brought in from the backyard by their host's great-grandson, a wiry boy who brings handfuls of the fruits—splitting with ripeness, revealing their own pink insides—to his mother in the kitchen, who plates them and brings them into this sitting room where the men talk about their children, the lack of rain, and the new roadblock. They show Vera photos of their dead. Shot unarmed, shot in a protest, here, a gurney soaked with blood, he died here. Phones out to show Vera, who has seen, at this point in her career, enough corpses to know it's not a peaceful expression that the dead wear but a look of exhaustion that not even death can end.

On the couch opposite Vera, her elderly host eats a piece of melon, slowly, nodding his head to something that Mo, next to him, is saying.

"My cousin," a man in a Real Madrid T-shirt is saying to Vera, pressing his phone toward her. "In Gaza, my cousin." It's a video, a man dying on video, lying on a stretcher, his hands reaching toward or past the camera, and all around him, Red Crescent workers hunched over, no IV in sight, nothing but some gauze. He's bleeding out from his side.

"*Allahyerhamo*," Vera says. The day's hot sun filters through the heavy curtains, the still air. Vera writes down the dead man's name. She glances at Mo, who won't look at her. There is something she is meant to do. She's being paid to ask about the Girl and the Soldier. She underlines the dead man's name. She is stalling. She takes a sip of dark Turkish coffee. She wishes she could ask this question to a woman, to the granddaughter-in-law, for example. But she is not here. The women are in other rooms, in anterooms. Vera takes out her phone. "May I ask," she says in her careful, overly formal Arabic, "what do you think of this?" She holds out her phone to the man in the Real Madrid shirt. She shows him the image of the Girl and the Soldier. "What does this image mean to you?"

The man with the dead cousin looks to Mo, evidently confused. "*Shu bid-ha?*" he asks Mo. What does she want? Then, to Vera, "Why are you asking about this?" The photo is a fake, he says, a trap by the Israelis. "It is to kill us," he says in English. The room is looking at them, at Vera. Doesn't she understand? He asks this to Mo in Arabic: "Doesn't she understand?"

Vera is trying again. Trying to ignore Rachel's texts. She's tired of being around such a miserable person, such a self-hating person. Also, tired of being so fucking hungover.

Her story is due tonight. She's in Jerusalem, riding the tram, riding along the seam that divides the city. East-West, Arab-Jew. The train is northbound now, just past Damascus Gate, with the gold crown of the Old City—the Dome of the Rock, how many have died to protect it?—disappearing behind them. She knows that at some point, between now and the next stop, the tram will cross the 1949 armistice line as it plows its way into East Jerusalem. A line will be crossed and nothing will change, except that technically, by the time she gets to the next stop, Vera will be in the West Bank. Every few months, someone publishes an article about this tram, about the divisions it both enacts and erases.

Vera is not here to get man-on-the-tram quotes from anyone. She sits in silence, watching the city go by. White sun, white stone, new condos, glimpses of old ruins. She'll ride the single line all the way up to Pisgat Ze'ev, to the mall where Salem Abu-Khdeir was beaten into the coma that killed him, then back down to the central bus station, where she'll catch the bus back to Tel Aviv. The ride serves no purpose, except that it gives her time to think about causality: one event leading to another, one act of violence necessitating another.

Most recent text from Rachel: *Are you even getting my messages?*

Vera doesn't answer. Instead she opens up her dating app—something she hardly ever does without Rachel. The most recent conversation is with a guy that she told Rachel not to message. Nimrod. This is, Vera has learned, an actual name that some Israeli men have: Nimrod. His profile includes two shirtless photos, both of them at the gym in front of weight racks, his shorts low enough to show the curve of muscle disappearing below his waistband. It's a photo that says: Message me if you want to fuck. Dammit, Rachel.

The most recent part of the chat:

Nimrod: So its just you 2 girls?

Vera: Just us.

Him: What would u do if I was there?

Her: What do you want?

Nimrod sent a devil face.

That's Vera. But it's not Vera. But it is Vera. Rachel's words, Vera's face. She wants to throw her phone away. She's sitting between the thick bodies of two elderly women who are, in the ways of their respective religions, entirely covered but for the face and hands. What would these modest women think, Vera wants to know, if she explained the situation to them? *Basically, I'm being pimped out by a child-bride to help her feel less trapped in her own life.*

Instead of heading back to Tel Aviv, Vera gets off the tram at Damascus Gate and takes a short bus ride to Ramallah, a city that Israelis call the "Tel Aviv of Palestine" without ever having seen it. Fantasy of symmetry. She wanders around Al-Manar square, a roundabout with low-slung buildings clustered nearby. Young men and couples circle the shops. The atmosphere is subdued. Weekday evening. In the center are four stone lions midroar, each facing one of the cardinal directions. Large green signage advertises the Stars & Bucks Cafe complete with copyright-infringing mermaid—a favorite of tourists because, Vera assumes, it suggests a certain inextinguishable pluckiness. Here she is, making a last-ditch effort at reporting.

She's a failure. That's how it feels. Tonight, she'll send the magazine a story she's not proud of. She doesn't know how to write a story worth selling, or sell a story worth writing. She passes a butcher, blood on a linoleum floor; she passes two cell phone kiosks next to each other. It came together for the last big piece: the body smuggled out of the hospital, the screaming women, the contextualizing interview with the Palestinian professor, Samar Farha. Vera has emailed the professor a few times in hopes she might do a quick interview about the Girl and the Soldier. No response yet. Now, as the day softens into evening and Vera faces the mortification of asking strangers about the image (The Image), she decides to call the professor again. Why not?

Two rings, three, four. The call goes to voice mail.

"*Marhaba*," Vera says in the recording, then switches to German: "This is Vera Baldauf, the journalist from *Der Spiegel* who interviewed you around Easter." She stops at a corner under a sign for an Arab bank. "I'm not sure if you saw my emails"—pauses as she moves out of the way of a business man who needs to use the machine. Vera hates leaving voice mails—"but I'd be grateful for your insights on the Girl and the Soldier." She recites her number twice, then hangs up.

What now?

She thinks for a shameful instant about texting a photo of the Stars & Bucks sign to Amir. But she can't; she knows she can't. So what now?

She goes back to Jerusalem via the Qalandiya Checkpoint, one that monitors the flow of workers, students, and families into East Jerusalem. She's always wanted to write about Qalandiya, but what is there to say that hasn't been said already? It is a horribly articulate place, a place that tells bodies that they are worthless, helpless. This message is conveyed in the narrow metal cages you funnel through single file, in the awkward turnstiles, in the waiting for the man ahead of you to take off his belt at the metal detector, and the bored-looking soldier watching the man, an older man, whose hands struggle with his belt buckle. Every second is the second before some horrible act of violence.

Or anyway, that's how it is when you get off the bus. Today, Vera doesn't have the energy to go through the checkpoint the way that a Palestinian has to. Once she promised herself that she would never take any of the privileges afforded to a white foreigner. But today, and not for the first time, she stays on the bus when the soldiers make their sweep, while those with Palestinian identification cards—*hawiyya*, she's heard them called—line up to funnel into the cages, to go through on foot so they can put all of their belongings through a metal detector, step through a scanner, bring their papers up to a bulletproof window, and wait, wait, wait. Vera accepts that she is an exception. She and a handful of white tourists stay on the bus as it winds past the Palestinians who are penned up, waiting to get through. She takes out her phone. She texts Rachel.

Vera refills her wineglass, or really, the water glass she's using for wine. The night is already soft around the edges. Rachel is making compulsive lists: pros and cons for getting married. The cons are mostly questions. "Maybe I'm just scared of uncertainty," Rachel considers. The pros seem to boil down to this: How can you go back when you've come so far?

At some point, Vera begins drifting toward sleep, her head in Rachel's lap. When she blinks, she can see Rachel's face scrunched in concentration, typing, typing, typing on Vera's phone. Messaging with Nimrod, maybe. Or someone else. Talking to Amir. No, shut up.

"I love you," Rachel says, talking to Vera but engrossed in Vera's phone. The room is dark. The air conditioner is blasting, and the down comforter crinkles when Vera rolls to one side.

"I love you," Rachel says again.

This is too much, Vera thinks as she swirls in and out of focus. This is too much. Why does too much feel so good?

She wakes up into the night, the room dark. Rachel is intoning. "You know he wasn't my first. My fiancé. He wasn't my first."

They lie side by side now. Vera tries not to move, tries not to show that she is awake.

Rachel continues, about the boy at the party. He pushed her up against the wall when she said, No, no more. She said, No more. "I said no," Rachel says. "I said no."

Stop, thinks Vera. This is too much, this is too familiar, this is too close. But she stays silent and Rachel keeps going. "He pressed his fingers inside me, this boy, he pressed his fingers inside me and said, 'Doesn't feel like a no.'" He didn't stop. He didn't stop. Vera hates how well she understands what it means to have a night inside you that never ends, that is always happening to you.

Rachel is sniffling snottily.

Don't, Vera cautions herself, but she rolls toward Rachel. She holds her—damp heat coming off Rachel's oversized T-shirt, her full cock-eyed breasts. "You poor baby," Vera whispers into her soft hair. "You poor baby." That is what she says. Here's what she's thinking, to Rachel, to herself: *You cunt, you cunt, you crybaby cunt.*

Amir has found a way to reach Vera, and it's oddly quaint: email.

Email from Amir Oved, waiting in her inbox, next to rejected pitches about refugee camps and e-invitations to weddings. She filed her story this morning, a few hours late, yes, but not too late. The professor never got back to her, but perhaps that's for the best—it might look unprofessional for Vera to use the same expert for all her articles. No word from her editor yet. But here is an email from Amir. An actual email. Turns out he uses a Yahoo account. The message: *Come over.*

She knows she shouldn't, but she writes back, *I'm in Tel Aviv.*

Refresh, refresh. New message.

So ill cum to you.

Vera responds immediately. *No.* Send. Then, *Leave me alone.*

She waits. She missed this. The terror of waiting. She missed this. Fuck, she missed this.

His response: *I don't think that's what you want.*

Her body betrays her. When he talks to her like this, she becomes some tropical flower unfurling. She can feel the heat and warmth in her blooming, her clit swelling. Why is it this she likes best? The moments when he overpowers her? Do I, wonders Vera, seek after the violation of my own boundaries? And does that mean, the logic continues, that I hate myself?

She writes to Amir: *So then what do I want?*

She can't even wait for an answer. She's too hot, too turned on. She rolls over onto her stomach to touch herself this way, likes how her face mashes into the pillow. He's here, she tells herself, he's here and he's too big for the room. He's filling the doorway. He's on top of her. With her free hand, she slips two fingers into her mouth, lets herself imagine they are his. It's something he used to do, and she remembers that he was, actually, fairly gentle in the way he pressed his fingers into her mouth. Part of her always wished he would go too far, gag his fingers down, down her throat, down, his hand disappearing into her, his arm, until he himself slid completely inside her. Come inside me and replace me. It's late and she's hot under the covers. Her roommate isn't home, but even as Vera gets close she doesn't let herself cry out. It's an old habit dating back to her first furious rubbings as a child, so young she couldn't name what she was doing, only knew it was forbidden, her own body forbidden to her. Amir understood this without needing it explained. An idiot, yes, but someone who understood by instinct how Vera fought against her own pleasure. When she kicked, he held her legs down; when she tried to shove her orgasm back into whatever vessel it sprang from, that's when he gave her his fingers, as you would to a teething child. Alone in her dark room, her horrible room, the muscles of Vera's stomach shudder. When she does come, it's a wounded sound smothered by her pillow.

Lying on her back, breath still heavy, she opens her email up again. Refresh, refresh. He hasn't responded.

Down at the Gaza border fence, nine teenagers are shot in one day. The boys are unarmed but for rocks. Vera isn't there. She's afraid to go down to the border fence, afraid to get permission from the Israelis to enter the dark prison of Gaza. Afraid they wouldn't let her back in. But she reads about the deaths through Mo's Facebook feed. He shares a post made by a teenager in Gaza.

"If I die at that fence tomorrow," the boy wrote, "I leave all my possessions to my friends, except my middle finger, which I leave to the Arab leaders of the world for abandoning us to the Jews."

Rachel is frantic, jerky in her movements, as she goes through Vera's shirts. "Which one," she says, her eyes bulging.

"It's really up to you," Vera says, not looking up from her computer.

They're in Vera's room. It's the first time Rachel has ever come to visit Vera in Tel Aviv. She showed up with barely any notice maybe two hours ago, possibly drunk already, pajamas and a toothbrush in her handbag, saying that she'd made a decision: she was going to end the engagement. Really, really. Vera handed over her phone the way you give a kid a video game to shut them up.

After, like, forty minutes, maybe less, Rachel spoke up. "Nimrod wants to meet." She was in Vera's bed; Vera was at her desk reviewing her editor's proposed changes. The headline Vera had suggested was "This Is What Hope Obscures." Her editor nixed that: *Too oblique.* The headline he's going with: "Palestinians Aren't Impressed with That Girl and Soldier Photo You Keep Seeing—Here's Why," because God forbid there be an ounce of dignity in this fucking enterprise.

"Sorry, who wants to meet?" Vera asked.

"Nimrod, the guy I've been talking to."

"Yeah, well," Vera said, looking up from her computer, "I'm not really up for it."

"No, I mean with me."

"What do you mean, with you?"

"I told him I wasn't you, I mean, that I was using your profile to meet guys." Rachel was fidgeting with Vera's phone.

"Are you for real?" Vera asked. Rachel didn't answer, which meant yes. Vera stood and crossed the small room to her bed. She reached out an expectant hand. "Give me my phone," she said.

Rachel pouted, handed back Vera's phone.

Vera clutched the phone protectively. "Rachel," she said, still standing over the bed, "what do you want?"

"I need this," Rachel said, eyeing Vera's phone.

Vera knew she was supposed to say, Okay, but don't do it this way, don't go out into the night and meet a strange man, at least, not until you set things right with your fiancé. But instead she said, "Okay, does he have your phone number?"

"Oh, right," Rachel said, "right. Can you write that?"

When Vera opened the app, she glanced at the revelation, the exclamation points and ellipses. She scrolled up and saw the back-and-forth between Rachel and Nimrod stretching back over a week. *Did you miss me, baby?* All of it coming out of her face, attributed to her face, her photograph, her name: *Vera, 26.*

"What's your number?" Vera asked. Rachel recited her phone number and Vera typed it in. She hesitated. Here was when she was supposed to ask Rachel if she was sure, really sure, that she wanted this, and did she want it with *Nimrod, 34.*

"Are you doing it?" Rachel asked, reaching for Vera's phone. "Let me do it."

"I did it," Vera said, and she sent Rachel's number to the man. Three seconds later, Rachel's own phone buzzed.

"He wrote, 'Hey, catfisher,'" giggled Rachel, joyous, enflamed.

For the next half hour or so Rachel lay on her belly, texting from her own phone, feet rubbing against each other sensually. Vera thought maybe it would end there—Rachel sated by texting. But all at once she jumped up and began racing around the room trying to figure out what to wear.

Now Rachel is pulling one of Vera's fitted black tops over her head, a little chubby in her bra. "How does it look?" She turns to Vera.

"Cute," Vera says. She's reading over the final version of the article one last time before sending it back to her editor. Soon Rachel will be out of Vera's apartment. *Please leave*, Vera thinks. Leave me alone. She asks, "Where are you meeting?"

"In the market. That's close, right?"

"Yeah, but take a taxi," Vera says. "Which bar?"

"Actually, his place. He's going to make me crêpes."

Jesus Christ, Vera thinks. She asks, "Crêpes?"

"Yeah, he swears he makes amazing crêpes," Rachel says, looking through Vera's shoes now. They are the same size. "He had the special pan thing."

You stupid girl, Vera thinks. You doomed girl.

"Can I wear these?" Rachel pulls out a pair of glittery faux-leather boots that Vera hates.

"Yeah," Vera says. If Rachel ends up in a freezer, no great loss on the boots.

Ten minutes later, Rachel is hugging Vera, her rich-girl hair soft on Vera's face. This is it. This is the end, even if she doesn't know it yet. When Rachel comes back tomorrow morning—somehow Vera knows it will be morning by the time the girl comes back—when she comes back in the gray-blue morning, having taken a taxi, she'll try to tell Vera about what happened. *He really made me a Nutella crêpe. We drank wine and then . . .* But Vera won't let her. She'll insist that she has work, too much work, that Rachel has to go, that they'll talk later. She'll hug Rachel. She'll say, "It's okay, it's going to be okay." That's the last thing she'll ever say to her face-to-face. Vera learned from the best how to ignore someone who is trying to reach you. Already, she knows how she'll tell this story, the one about the desperately sad religious teenager. Two girls, different in every way but alike in their loneliness. A friendship premised on the continual violation of boundaries, until it reached its inevitable, horrible end: Vera implicated in an act of infidelity, Vera bound to Rachel, who wore Vera's clothes as she set out to meet a stranger, to break a promise. She'll say that Rachel was like a drowning person, someone who pulls down anyone stupid enough to get near. This is the end. The end of a friendship that was, for a horrible month, something like a marriage. These are the last seconds of Rachel, before she becomes nothing but a story Vera tells. This is the last of a girl who has become, for Vera, the embodiment of something she hates in herself. *I'm sorry,* Vera thinks but will never, ever say, not to Rachel, not to herself. These are Rachel's footsteps, the clip of ugly faux-leather boots fading down the stairwell and into the night.

Vera's Room

Vera doesn't let herself think about the night back in college, but sometimes it tugs at her. She doesn't remember how she got into the room, but she remembers waking up in it and he was inside her. He was on top of her, over her, face-to-face as she woke up in a room of neutral tones, a symmetrical room. There was a word forming inside her. She could not let that word form inside her. She woke up in a room with generic landscapes on the walls, how many hours had she been here, she woke up with a man inside her, pumping inside her, and she did something she didn't know she could do, which was that she stepped out of herself and projected a series of contingencies, and in one, this is a story she has to tell about herself, and in another, she changes the story, forces it into a different shape. She woke up with a man inside her in a strange room, a hotel room, she would eventually figure out when she stuffed her bra into her purse and ran, split-lipped, down and down and down the stairwell, into the cold day, onto the commuter bus, where government workers looked at her and away, her eye makeup smudged and her face bleeding where, she knew without remembering, he must have bitten her. At the bar, someone had handed her a drink. And then? And then she came to with a man inside her in a strange room, Yeah, he was saying, Yeah, yeah. Her body was jerking, the way it would if you were dragging it along the ground. But she was in a strange room, neutral tones of a business hotel, scratchy sand-colored blanket. Yeah, he said, his face floating blurry above her. She had to make a decision. The decision was this: Do I tell myself what is happening to myself? If yes, then this becomes part of her, what's happening becomes part of her. If no, if it's a story she edits, that she presses into a place it's not supposed to fit, then she might not want to die after, and yes, the story might leak out, and yes, she might bite her cuticles till they bleed, she might drink until she gets sick, yes, she might develop a cruel edge, yes, yes, there might be consequences, but they are ones that, she thinks, she hopes, she can live with. In the room, under the man, she wrestled the moment into a new shape, one she thought would save her. She wrestled the horrible word out of her mind. Her lip was bleeding. It was years ago now, but it is still happening. Her lip is still bleeding. She is telling herself that this is not rape, that she is not being raped. She kissed him. She kisses him. She kisses the man on top of her.

Noor's Way

After the cut, there is an interval of time—no longer than a sharp inhale—before the blood comes. Inside that interval, Noor watches as the small slash she made across her own thigh opens like a mouth. Always a shock to see her pale, fibrous insides. Looking exposed—surprised, even. No red yet. The blood comes soon. But first this suspended moment when the cut is open like a zipper and each time—each time—Noor feels it might be reversible. Once the blood comes, the cut will be a fact. But now—on her bedroom floor sitting up against the door with her carefully curated kit of tools beside her—before the blood dots and pools in the cut Noor made on herself, on her own body, she feels it might be reversible, that this time she might undo the horrible thing she can't—can't—seem to stop doing to herself. The new wound might zip right back up. A moment—suspended.

Since Hussein returned, she's been cutting herself more often. The man who came back both is and is not her big brother. Something washed away, something else hardened. He coughs like an old man now. In the middle of a sentence, he'll begin coughing, hand to his chest. He says it's because of how he was interrogated—the cold room where they kept him. He looks off to the side when he speaks to you, like he's talking to someone else or to a different version of you that is standing just to the left.

Mejiddo. After the raid they brought him inside to prison. It was almost impossible to get a permit to visit him. "It's not so bad," he told them from his lawyer's phone, a Jewish woman who is, Hussein told her, a good person. "The men stick together. We make salads." He learned to chop vegetables with the edge of a tin can lid. He told them it was not so bad, but it was so bad. She could hear it in his voice—anyone could hear it—that it was so bad.

He doesn't speak about the interrogations, but he must dream about them. She dreams about them, too. She's in a room and there is a man slamming his hand down on a table in front of her, a man pressing a knee into her stomach, her hands tied above her head. She knows this is called a *stress position* but is not sure how she knows that.

The Jews held Hussein for months and never charged him with anything. They came in the night and took him into their truck, hands bound in front of him. Thank God, he was dressed at the time. Their faces were covered in black; they crouched when they walked, lit their way with the bright lights on their guns.

It is hard to say if her brother will ever get married. He sleeps a lot.

Sometimes when she's hurting herself—riding a wave of rage at her own body—she thinks about stabbing a Jew. Not doing it at the checkpoint itself, because that's what they expect, but doing it once she got inside. On the street, from behind maybe. Not with the razor she uses on herself, obviously, but something from the kitchen. Stab a soldier's face. The head, they say, go for the head, the neck. She's seen the videos. Go for the neck, the Jew's neck. You have to move fast before they shoot you to death on the street.

What would happen to her parents if she did it? They would be distraught and brokenhearted, of course. Also, proud.

It is beyond belief how the Jews multiply—the religious settlers especially, with their packs of vicious children, righteous and armed. They won't stop coming. They'll never stop coming, chewing up the land, building their new cities. The hills are choked with their construction. An infestation. Rats. She's seen pictures online of Jews drawn as rats, rats with their weird side curls, their vicious scrunched faces. Yes, she thought, those are my neighbors, my neighbors the rats.

Every year they inch down the hill, they inch down the hill and what are we supposed to do? Sit and take it? Let them take more and more until there is nothing left? Already, it is like choking. How many times has she canceled plans with a friend in Ramallah, said she was feeling sick or Mama needed her help around the house, because she couldn't bear the thought of the journey, because when the soldiers stop the car, stop the bus with one of their floating checkpoints and traffic has stopped, traffic has slowed, settler cars are zooming by on the highway but you are sitting there, you are waiting, and in the waiting you know, you feel that they control not just the roads and not just your body, but time itself. Often, Noor finds that the only way she can survive the waiting is to float away from herself—the soldier is shouting something, the soldier is walking away with your hawiyya, the soldier has wandered off and comes back with a bag of chips he's eating, you have to pee, you are drifting away from yourself. That's survival. That's something like survival.

On herself, Noor is careful. The razor blade is clean—sterilized each time with rubbing alcohol—and she cuts no more than once a month, hardly ever more than once in a month. But the knowledge that she can do this to herself (that she has, that she will) is a secret she carries with her everywhere. A threat, a promise. Precious.

It is a relief. Each time she makes the slash, the skin kissing open, the moment suspended between the wound and the coming of blood—each time, it is a relief. Even after—after the blood and the cleaning, the bandaging and the dressing again—the cut can take care of her for days. When she finds that she's not acting like herself, when she feels trapped in her own mask—amused and slightly bitchy, trying to impress Mai, a girl who shines brighter than she— when Noor finds herself hiding her own pain too well, hiding the desperate, drowning girl she thinks of as herself, as her true self— then it is her most recent cut she goes to touch. *I know you*, the gesture says. *I see you, I feel you.* Tender, sore spot. A threat, a promise. Sustenance. And maybe—is this possible?—maybe a form of love.

Before, she didn't feel particularly close to Hussein. She's always found him overbearing. He began asking her when she was going to veil when she was maybe ten, which was annoying, because obviously she was going to do it and she didn't even mind being the first in her year but none of the girls above her were veiling yet and it felt kind of ostentatious. She was eighteen when they dragged him to Mejiddo. When he came back, she was already a student at Bethlehem University and there was nothing he could do.

It was a relief to have created this space for herself. And yet she has consistently woven Hussein into her persona while at school. It feels good, complaining about his overbearingness to her classmates. She enjoys rolling her eyes when, walking arm in arm with Mai, they see maybe a Russian wife in a tight-fitting shirt; she enjoys whispering, "My brothers would kill me!" She feels precious in those moments, protected. Loved.

Sometimes she wonders if she has relied too heavily on this feeling.

She and Mai got along instantly. They always have the same read on situations. They understand each other without words. When the rich, unveiled Christian girl in their organic chemistry class is distracting the study group by going on about some gown that she is having made, Noor and Mai can exchange a single meaningful glance that says, *Can you believe this girl?* and then go back to reviewing their notes, and never have to say a word. But sometimes, Mai refers know-ingly to her brothers, about Hussein in particular, and that makes Noor feel used, even if Mai is just following the lead that Noor her-self established by talking about them that way first.

"What would your brothers say?" Mai might ask, when a woman tourist descends from the checkpoint bus in shorts.

And it feels unfair, somehow, for Mai to get to make these jokes when she has only younger brothers and a father who leaves it up to his daughters about what they wear. Noor wonders if this is what attracts Mai to her—that she is living a life that is more truly Pales-tinian, that she makes Mai more authentic, Mai who takes a bus back into Jerusalem, whose mother drives a black SUV—she's seen the photos online—who has gone on trips alone to England, where her father keeps a house.

Mai hasn't been to school since the explosion. Noor messaged her a screenshot of the Girl and the Soldier and wrote under it, "My brothers would . . ." waiting for Mai to finish the sentence, but Mai didn't say anything.

Hussein did genuinely freak out about that photo. "It's disgust-ing," he said.

"But it's faked, isn't it?" Noor said. It was after dinner. They were all drinking tea in the sitting room, the TV on.

"Who knows?" Hussein said. "The Israelis can get to anyone." Then he got up and went to his room. And Noor, very discreetly, pressed over her clothes into a cut place.

Obviously, she worries about scarring. That one day she'll have a husband who might ask, What is that on your legs? What happened? What is wrong with you? But she is careful. The blade is clean; the wound is tended to. No more than once a month, sometimes twice, sometimes twice. When it heals, she dabs the spot with vitamin E oil to help the skin recover. In the year she has developed this practice, only two puckered scars—each the length of a finger joint—remain visible on her upper thigh.

She wants to live. Doesn't she? She doesn't want to die by cuts. She doesn't want to die by Jewish bullets. Anyone who attacks a soldier gets shot on the spot. Stripped down by the Jews. If she ever managed to get the knife across—that alone, impossible—she would probably do little more than graze the soldier's ear before they shot her and let her bleed out after ripping off her clothes, her scarf. You see it all the time. Blurry images of a boy or a girl, stripped down in the street, limbs all wrong and blood smeared.

She wants to live. And yet it's true that what you do to survive can kill you.

When the little mouth of her new cut fills with blood—irreversible as it always was—Noor feels horror and disappointment but also pride, because she knows that nobody—nobody, not the Jews who tortured her big brother, not her brother—nobody can hurt her more than she has hurt herself.

Come Home

Every day is another day that Mai does not tell Leila what happened at the checkpoint. They are in Leila's bedroom, the bedroom she shares with her husband. Leila is looking through her closet for clothes that Mai might want, stuff that doesn't fit her anymore. "I've been trying to walk more," Leila calls out, her voice echoing from the closet.

"Oh?" Mai says. She's lying on Leila's bed, Leila and Tariq's bed, propped up by the astounding array of throw pillows. Where do they go at night? The pillows. On the floor? In a secret chest? Or do Leila and her husband sleep with pillows piled on top of them, like children hiding? It's late afternoon. Sunlight filters heavily through the rich, ornate curtains that Leila took forever to pick out. This is the softest, happiest part of the day—when the housework is done, before Tariq comes home from work.

Leila emerges from the closet holding up the ugliest blouse Mai has ever seen. It's pink, it's blue, it's splashed in silver sequins. Disco vomit. "How about this one?" Leila says. She holds the thing up to herself. It couldn't so much as fit over her shoulders now: swollen Leila, a cream puff almost in her ninth month.

Mai says her sister's name sternly, in two descending syllables. "Leila." She says it like their father used to when scolding them.

"Leila. I wouldn't wear that to clean the house. Never mind to a wedding." Their cousin Rania's wedding is tomorrow.

Leila sticks her tongue out. Pointy, pink. She looks so young, so familiar. Sister. "Why?" Leila demands. "It's cute!" She shakes the hideous blouse at Mai; its sequins tremble. So tacky, so offensively off-brand for Mai, who takes pains to dress elegantly: Audrey Hepburn–style pearl buttons and round Peter Pan collars with lace detailing.

"Maybe as a dish towel," Mai says.

Leila throws the hideous shirt at her. "Ungrateful girl," she says joyfully.

Mai has a feeling of lightness, like shrugging off a backpack after a long day. What am I forgetting? she wonders. What have I put down? Then it weighs her down again. She remembers. The explosion. The photograph.

When she sees the image—the girl helping the soldier stand—she says to herself, *That's you*, but she doesn't believe it. Every day she almost tells Leila. She almost says, *That's me*, and then she does not. In the image, she's unidentifiable. She's sure. She's almost sure. You can't tell it's her. So many times she has inspected the figures, tried to see them the way that Noor or Leila might. The soldier takes up most of the frame, hopping on one leg, yes, she remembers that, getting him to the ambulances that way. Even in the slightly blurred photograph you can see that he's beautiful, lips and cheekbones. The girl, meaning Mai, is eclipsed. Most of her body hides behind his. You can see her face, but only half of it. Most of what you see is the head scarf, smudged with blood. Foreigners love that it's blood, she knows, love that her head scarf seems white in the photo although it's not—another fact that obscures her—it's pale pink. She threw it out. Hard to tell what she's wearing. Her jeans could be a long skirt. Her ballet flats—also pale pink—are indistinct. She loves those shoes, but she hasn't worn them since that day.

Since the explosion, Mai has spent almost every day here, helping out Leila during the last weeks of her pregnancy and recovering from her injuries—the slight concussion, the relatively superficial cut on her head. Yes, she could have gone back to school already. But she hasn't, and maybe—who knows?—maybe she won't.

The first few days were an actual nightmare. Mai's head echoing, damp sheets in bed, hazy, dream-wake, checking her phone, knowing only that there was something she could not tell anyone, anyone, anyone. The image of her and the soldier was everywhere: on all her feeds, in all her group chats. She thought interest would fade, but it jumped the way a spark can—suddenly, the image was on the American news and all over her social feeds. There were girls with hundreds of thousands, sometimes millions, of followers posing in T-shirts silk-screened with Mai and the soldier; she watched in horror as the image became, for foreigners, a shorthand for the fantasy of a symmetrical conflict. Three stupid seconds, now somehow extended, given their own history and even their own tagline: *This is what hope looks like.* She dreamt about herself in the image, about the image walking toward her, about knocks on the door, about explaining herself to Noor, to Leila, to Mama. She would wake up unsure how much of it she had dreamt. She would dream she'd dreamt the image, that it was all a fabrication. And then she would wake up and it would be as it was before, only, in the time that had passed, the image's reach had grown.

She tries to assure herself that the power of the image—the fuel for the foreign obsession with it—is its very inscrutability. The girl in the image isn't a person to the people who see it—she's a symbol. And if there is a violence in that, it's a violence that keeps Mai safe. Nobody she knows thinks that the photograph is real. It's all part of the lie the Zionists created—like the explosion, which they planned as an excuse for the raids. Nobody knows it's Mai, except Mai. She's sure; she's almost sure.

She's been keeping up with her schoolwork from home. Noor texts about the assignments—new chapters twice a week in the organic chemistry textbook, all kinds of biology lectures to watch online—and takes photos of her own corrected assignments (balancing endless oxidation-reduction equations) so that Mai can check her answers against them. With her brothers' records, Noor is only very rarely granted a permit to cross from her home in Bethlehem into Jerusalem. Mai finds—here's a horrible thought—relief in the fact that Noor can't come knocking on her door. Mai doesn't know if she'll return to write her exams.

Noor was texting her today. *How are you feeling, habibti?* When you text Noor, no profile picture comes up. Instead it's an image of a butterfly. Her "about me" reads, "A girl should be like a butterfly: beautiful to look at, impossible to catch."

> Mai: I'm still weak, but better.
> Noor: Will you be coming back? For the exam?

Mai has wondered if Noor knows, of course. But it seems impossible. Noor is so principled, so unequivocal—surely, she wouldn't pretend if she suspected. She would call and if Mai didn't pick up, she'd leave a voicemail: "What is this? How could you? Who are you?" Or maybe just text her a single word, "collaborator"—the ugliest word—before blocking Mai's number. Something. So Noor must not know. Right? She must not.

After Mai got Noor's text this morning, she hesitated, shifting onto her stomach in bed. The family doctor, an elderly man with long, elegant limbs, has told Mama that Mai is fine to go back to school, but Mai keeps stalling. She tells Mama she doesn't feel well enough yet, but the truth is that she still fears she's misread the situation—that she'll be recognized. *I have to see what the doctor says*, she wrote to Noor. Then, *How is it there?* Then, *Yanni, what's the mood?*

Noor: *No raids today.* Mai saw the most recent one on her Facebook feed: Jews posing as journalists, dragging away the student union leader—a charismatic senior.

Mai knows she should go back. She knows. It wasn't so long ago that she convinced Baba to let her enroll in Bethlehem University in the first place. "You'll spend all day on the bus," Baba said, his face pixelated on the computer screen. They were Skyping; he was in his office in London. He had a point: not the getting there, which was easy, but getting back through the Tunnels Checkpoint, lining up off the bus to show your papers to the soldiers. "It's not even a top school," he went on. Implied in this comment, a question: Why not go for one of the Jews' universities, closer and so much more convenient? She didn't indulge the phantom question, but rallied on: "Their environmental science department is well regarded," she insisted, then began listing off the publication histories of various faculty members. He folded.

Between the two sisters, everyone had thought that Leila would be the one to go to university, and she had, at least for a time. Two semesters at the Jews' university up the hill—so close, a short bus ride away, and better than any Palestinian university. Leila's Hebrew was good enough to do it. Not just any degree program—the law one. Top of the top. So good they ignored the painful details, like how, technically, Leila had to register as an international student. Jordanian. "I've never lived in Jordan," Leila told the clerk, who shrugged.

Leila was friendly with her classmates, nearly all of them Israeli Jews. Why wouldn't she be? Sometimes she stayed after to study with girls from her class. Leila said some of the Jewish students ignored her while others seemed overly cordial, but for the most part, everyone got along. They fastidiously avoided political topics as they quizzed one another on the vestiges of Ottoman laws in the Israeli legal system. This is a part of Mai's life that she would never be able to explain to Noor: how normal it could all seem. In a Jewish restaurant, at a Jewish school, on a Jewish bus.

When Leila began her studies, Mai was still in high school. She used to bring Leila cups of tea alongside a few of their aunt's date cookies on a chipped plate, Leila's favorite, the floral one with no discernible provenance, part of no set in their house. Leila bent over her books—everything in Hebrew. Mai was proud of her sister. Then she came home one evening to hear that Tariq and his mother had been by. Mai expected Leila to be droll and dismissive, but her sister was flushed and nervous when she talked about the car salesman who had come looking for a wife. Mama was every bit the proud hen as she hustled Mai out of the room so that she and Leila could get on a video call with Baba to discuss. Two months later, Leila was engaged. She decided to drop out of school before the wedding. "I'll be back," she insists whenever Mai asks her about it.

Of course, since she got pregnant, Leila's body has changed. There is so much that Mai can't ask about, or is afraid to ask. She doesn't know how to talk about the details of marriage. Before, they were so good at being close. Of course, they had their own rooms, but how many times had Mai fallen asleep in Leila's bed, their hair braided together in imitation of something they saw on some fashion page? Soft R&B songs playing. They sang along to lyrics that sounded nothing like the English they learned in school, waiting for the words they recognized. *Baby, baby, love, love, love.*

Today, Mai and Leila get the news at the same time, hunched over their phones, scrolling. A new martyr. Not at the checkpoint, but at a train station in Tel Aviv. He was a construction worker from a village outside Ramallah.

"Sixteen years old," Mai says, reading off her phone. He secreted a kitchen knife across Qalandiya Checkpoint, slipped away from the construction site at lunch, and walked to the Tel Aviv train station, where, by reconstructed accounts, he sat on a bench for about fifteen minutes before stabbing a soldier in the neck.

Mai and Leila show each other images and updates on their phones. They martyred him in the station. Executed. The word the Jews use for this is "neutralized." On her feeds, she sees that Hamid has reposted cell phone footage of the Jews shooting the boy. In the video, which Mai doesn't show to Leila, but which she watches on her phone, he has already been shot, but he's alive—his head lolling side to side in pain or delirium.

Mai forces herself to watch the video. Recently, she's been forcing herself to watch everything horrific, even going back to rewatch the security footage of the mob attacking Salem. A kind of penance.

Hamid has captioned the posted video: *They shot him down like a dog.* He has currency at school, and the videos he posts always get at least a few hundred likes. Before, Mai would have left a comment under the video to praise the martyr. But not now. Something is off with Hamid. They aren't in touch over text, obviously—that would make her an easy girl. But before, when she commented on any of his posts, he always liked the comments, maybe even replied. But since the explosion, he's ignored her completely, and she wonders—is this paranoid?—she wonders if he knows something. If he's one of the few who doesn't think the photo was a fake.

"Halas," Leila says. "Let's go for a walk."

The day of the explosion, Noor and Mai had class in the morning—a not entirely unpleasant degree prerequisite on academic writing taught by an unmarried woman. Professor Samar Withered Branch—that's what some of the students call her behind her back. After, Mai and Noor walked around campus together, letting the late morning draw out. The weekend had already begun and it was the middle of the day. Such luxuries! Together, they walked under low-hanging trees with tiny, silvery leaves, their heads tilted toward each other as Noor whispered knowing little jokes about the sleep-deprived newlyweds walking side by side around campus. It had taken Mai by surprise at first, Noor's humor coming from a girl who seemed so careful, so traditional—natural makeup only, no loofah to volumize her hijab. But their friendship had been instant, as if they'd known each other since childhood, not met less than a year ago at a welcome lunch for biology and chemistry first-years. Mai fears a friendship that started so fast could end just as quickly.

"But what even is a calorie?" Mai was asking Noor as they made their way back from the snack vendor. Mai had bought a package of sweet-sour candy, because Noor said that each one had only fifteen calories. Noor knows the calories in everything. It's crazy. Probably actually crazy. Mai teeters between finding it kind of fun—feeling like a woman, reciting the grams of sugar in soda—and finding that she's edging closer to something along the lines of concern for impossibly skinny Noor.

"Units of energy," said Noor. "How does someone so good at orgo not know what a calorie is?"

"Hey, how did you do on the mass spectrometry quiz?" Mai asked.

Noor didn't answer. Instead she looked across the small square to a group of their classmates, the young men in their self-conscious little circle. She was watching them as she said to Mai, "That boy is suicidal over you." Hamid, slim and capable, was working up the courage to come over, looking at Mai then back at his friends, laughing too loudly, then looking again. "Suicidal," Noor repeated as she brought her phone to her ear.

"Don't you dare," Mai hissed in a whisper.

But Noor was already speaking into her phone as if there were someone on the other line. "Hello? Hello?" she said, sidestepping to answer it, creating an opening.

Of course Hamid sensed the moment; of course he began to walk toward her, hands in his pockets, body curved, boyish. Standing in front of her, he spoke hurriedly, almost mumbling when he said, "I'll walk you to your bus." No greeting. Just that: I'll walk you to your bus. His voice was raspy. She could smell his cologne.

"I'm walking," Mai said stupidly. He was an arm's length away, but she took a step back.

"Walking all the way to the checkpoint?" His hands were crammed into his front pockets.

"No, I mean walking to run an errand and then walking to the bus," she said, so obviously lying that she couldn't make eye contact.

He smiled like there was someone with a gun to the back of his head, telling him to smile. "Okay, so next time," he said.

It's not that she doesn't want attention, just that she doesn't want the consequences—the pressure to drop out that comes with marriage no matter what he promises beforehand, a mother-in-law demanding Mai move to Bethlehem, too far from Mama, from Leila. Or, if not, the exhausting, maddening bureaucracy of the paperwork it would take to make someone like Hamid into a legal resident of East Jerusalem, the impossible years living in a nebulous zone at the cusp of the Wall before permission was—or was not—granted to her husband to live inside it. Everything is so adversarial. Your will pitted against another's, again and again.

Mai helps Leila down the steps—going ahead to steady her sister on her forearm—and out the gate. It's cool enough now, the late-afternoon breeze arriving from the Judaean Desert. They're hurrying to avoid Leila's mother-in-law, a thin woman with a squished nose who always finds a way to make you feel fat. Her house is on the other side of a large garden almost identical to Mama's—filled with citrus trees and tangled mint, squash, tomatoes, and small, sweet cucumbers. They timed their exit by the pulling out of her SUV from her driveway. She comes by Leila and Tariq's place daily while Tariq and his father are selling cars. She brings foods that are good for the baby and side-eyes the dishes left in the sink. Leila said that the first month was the worst, Tariq's mama coming over to criticize everything about the way she ran a house, just because she could.

"Is she still driving you crazy?" Mai asks, closing the green gate behind them.

"Now, with the baby," Leila says, hand resting serenely on her stomach, "it's like we're on the same team."

"Right," Mai says, her voice heavy with skepticism. "Remind me, why are we sneaking out again?"

Leila laughs, a concession. "Maybe a little crazy," she says.

"Yalla," Mai says. "Before she can ask me what I've been snacking on."

They make their way down the street, almost clean—this is maybe the loveliest part of the neighborhood—past the gates to compounds, the mosaic tiles, the cheerful colors, down the sloping hill to the corner store, where they'll buy chocolate milk, an excuse for the excursion.

It feels like a lifetime ago, although it was just a few years that they walked home daily from school together. Leila's last year at the academy, Mai two years behind her. They walked home every day in their uniforms, ignoring the boys and ignoring the Jews, absorbed in each other's impressions of the French teacher, and unafraid. Always, they ended up a bit entangled. One sister's head on the other's shoulder at a stoplight. One tugging on the other's blouse, not to communicate anything specific, just to say, I'm here, You're here. It was like your own body, the body of a sister. Only you loved it more, or, with less reservation. There is nothing about Leila that Mai would change. Not even now that she has stretch marks scratching down her belly.

Easing themselves down the hill, Leila takes Mai's hand. They went together to get their nails done yesterday—matching sets in a subdued, elegant pink called "Bubble Bath"—for cousin Rania's wedding tomorrow. Leila's fingers are thin, all joints, all little knots. Bony fingers tickling her ribs, squeezing her elbow. Is that why Mai felt so immediately close to Noor? Because she's a thin girl with Leila's bony fingers?

It's true that in some ways, Mai has tried to re-create sisterhood with Noor—the tender exchanges, the conspiratorial laughter, the whispers in sunlight. Only it never quite works. There is no way for her and Noor to belong to each other so fully. Always a certain sizing up of the other, always keeping something close to one's chest. Always measuring words, your own before you speak, and after, hers—just to be sure, just in case a note of hostility was detected. Care, yes, love even, but also caution.

The street is quiet this afternoon except for two boys around their brothers' ages, running after a soccer ball, kicking it uphill then chasing it when it rolls back down the middle of the street. They are Jews from the nearby settlements, with the strings hanging from their pants and their prayer caps. Slowly—or not so slowly—they are taking over East Jerusalem, Palestine's last holdout in the city. Around the settlers, Mai is careful; she walks closest to the road to keep Leila on the inside. Two army jeeps cruise by slowly. The wiring on the windshield makes them look like they have gritted teeth. Neither girl looks at grimacing jeeps as they pass nor at the Jews inside. They are girls who know not to look. During the Al-Aqsa Intifada, there were tanks parked in their neighborhood. This was in the long weeks after the Jewish prime minister tried to claim Al-Aqsa. Mai doesn't remember, was a baby, but Leila told her how Mama would push baby Mai in the stroller right past the tanks. "We ignore the dogs," Mama would say, clutching Leila's hand and looking straight ahead. It's a phrase they love to repeat, Leila imitating Mama, who laughs and shakes her head. *We ignore the dogs.*

On the day of the explosion, Mai stood in line at the checkpoint. She stood behind two little girls, dressed like two little dolls, in red and white with hair ribbons and Mary Janes, both clinging to the wide expanse of their black-clad mother. Earlier, when they were waiting at the bus stop, Mai and the mother had exchanged greetings. Mai complimented the girls' dresses, and the woman complimented Mai's eyeliner, a painstaking feline wing tip. The woman was on her way back from visiting her own mother. At the checkpoint, the little girls tugged on their mama's long coat, shifted their weight from leg to leg until their mother gripped their hands to say, "Halas!" Mai remembers the shape of them, a trio, moving toward the soldiers when they were called up. Soft smudges of black and red. And then they died. All three of them. Mai learned about it after. There was a photo that Mai was almost sure was one of the girls: a tiny hand dangling from a stretcher. But that is not the image that became famous.

For a week after the photograph of Mai and the soldier was taken, Mai was ready, waiting for someone to ask: Mama, Leila, Noor, a cousin. Anyone. The answer was always on the tip of her tongue. No, that's not me, of course it's not me. But no one asked.

Baba came back for Leila's wedding, of course. He comes back when he can. Mai knows it's not easy for Mama, all alone. For months, they lived with a blue tarp flapping in the upstairs window because the contractor would not rush for a woman. (Tariq got it fixed with one phone call.) But that's the arrangement Mai knew best: the father goes away, the mother stays home. Had she thought that Tariq, like Baba, would go away? Would come back once or twice a year, to give Leila a baby, to dance at her cousins' weddings? But of course, it was Leila who went away. Not far—still in East Jerusalem—but away.

Even before the explosion, it was different. In some ways, the explosion didn't change anything—just pronounced the changes and, in that way, showed Mai what she already knew: you can't go back; Leila won't come home. Leila lives in her husband's house, tends to the plants of her mother-in-law's garden. When Mai comes here, she keeps her head scarf on, because she's in Tariq's home, even when he's not here. There are so many bodies between their bodies now. Tariq, the baby. Maybe, really, maybe the soldier too. Is that why Mai did what she did that day? She doesn't know; probably, she'll never know.

ᓂᓄ

The thing about the explosion is that it's always happening. Or no, it's always the second before it happens, the second before Mai's world splits open. This isn't new, not really. Her whole thinking life, she has thought of this fact as something she knew: that everything can change, all at once, in horrible violence. She thought she knew it, but she didn't know it, not really. She didn't know it in her body, it wasn't a truth that lived in her, and now it is.

It was a sound but also it wasn't a sound. She remembers this. The sound was so big she didn't hear it, only knew it was ripping her apart. One second, she was standing in line at the checkpoint, waiting her turn to go up with her hawiyya, careful with her hands, hands out of her pockets, Jewish cars speeding by as Mai and everyone else waited. One second, she was in the world, thinking about Noor or about Leila, thinking about fashioning her day into a story she could tell them, tell herself. One of the woman soldiers was wearing lipstick—red a shade too dark on lips in desperate need of exfoliation. It was almost funny. A dog in lipstick. *Oppress them, but make it fashion.* Those thoughts, or ones like them. Mai was wearing her petal-pink flats that look—they really do—like Chanel. She was thinking about how to make Noor laugh with the lipstick comment, or about whether she wants to complete her Audrey Hepburn aesthetic with a string of pearls. Those thoughts, or ones like them, second to second. She had her hands out of her pockets. Her hands were not in her pockets, and when the lipstick Jew called her, she went.

When it started, she thought she'd been shot. The rush of heat was monstrous. It turned the world inside out and sucked everything in then threw it up again in a rage against gravity. But not a bullet. No, it was a sound. A sound so big it was white, a sound so big it was erasing her. Those are the only words she has for it. That was the bomb exploding.

After, when she got home—bleeding in the taxi, the driver

refusing to take her money (would he recognize her in the photo? Mai has wondered, but after this much time she must assume he has not)—Mama and Leila came rushing out, enveloped her completely. All of them were crying, crying out. They took her inside to bathe, her brothers hiding behind doors, scared by Mama's fear. Someone, Mama or Leila, got her into the bathtub. It was Mama's fingers—strong, thick, able—that washed off the grime, used the pitcher they keep for the boys' baths to wash Mai's hair, gently cleaning away the blood from the cut on her head—"It's not so bad, my heart, my life, it's not so bad." They wrapped her in clean sheets, like a corpse, and laid her out on the bed to wait for the doctor.

"Who did it?" Leila asked from the doorway. Mai knew without seeing her she had one hand over her mouth.

"Let her sleep," Mama said. Her perfect body, thick and full, weighing down the bed. Strong hands, worried eyes.

"I woke up and I didn't know my name," Mai told them. "Then I ran."

"Rest now," Mama said. "The doctor is on his way. Rest now."

The story Mai told—that she woke up and did not know her name—is not exactly a lie. It is true that when she opened her eyes, she didn't know her name. That part is true. The first thought that came to her was a pure pronoun: *I.* Her second thought: *My legs.* She was certain that her legs had been blown off. You must sit up, she told herself. But she was scared of what she would see, so she remained on her back for another second, just another second. The sky was gray and pulsating with light. She ran her tongue around her mouth to check if her teeth were still there. Then, in a single motion and before she could think better of it, she sat up into a headache that bloomed out from her temples. She saw her body unfolding beneath her—tummy to legs, legs to feet. All of it whole, complete, Mai. She thanked God. She wanted to weep, but she did not.

Not an arm's length away was a huge cement slab with a tangle of steel wire sticking out like wild hair. Just a little closer, and it would have crushed her. *Here*, she thought, *here is something else that did not kill me today.*

In the kitchen, Mai finishes off her chocolate milk while Leila warms up the light evening meal for Tariq, moving gingerly. In a single impulsive motion, Mai hugs her sister from behind. "Mama," Mai says. She can feel the stretched orb of her sister's stomach, and sometimes can feel the baby kicking in there, although not now. Leila is so big that Mai can't enclose her fully in a hug. Sometimes Mai will let herself imagine. Imagine we came from each other. Imagine if there were nobody else, if nobody else ever touched us. "Mama," she says again.

Leila clucks, shimmies away as she fishes out olives from the massive jar she keeps under the sink. She hefts it up, a jar as big as a toddler, to hold the contents up to the light. The olives are starting to brown a little. Leila might add a lemon.

"What do you think?" Leila asks. "More lemon?"

"More lemon," Mai confirms, reaching for one from the basket on the microwave that Leila and Tariq leave unplugged when it's not in use. She cuts it into halves, then quarters, then eighths.

"Habibti," Leila says, "how's your head today?"

Mai hands Leila the lemon segments without looking at her. "Better," Mai says. Leila hasn't asked her when she's going back to school, but surely, she must wonder; surely, that must be the question underneath her question, so Mai answers that question, too. "I'm feeling almost ready to go back," she says as she rinses off the cutting board.

ᶜᵛᵛᵛᵛᵛᵛᵛᵛᵛᵛᵛᵛᵛᵛᵛ

She saw his feet first, his boots. After the explosion, as Mai got her bearings, it was his boots that she saw first. They were jutting out from the other side of the cement slab. She couldn't see the rest of him, only his boots. A dead body, she thought. She was lying next to a dead body. The two of them had lain side by side, as if buried together. Just as easily it could have been her, she knew, crushed by the cement block, lying dead next to a stranger. God is great, she reminded herself as she crawled toward the boots, past the tangled rebar clogged with chunks of dirt and asphalt. She needed to check. Why? Why didn't she run? She has asked herself this. Her only answer: because it could have been her, on the wrong side of the cement slab.

On the ground, bits of metal glinted. Please, she begged silently, don't let me see a headless body. Then she looked up. She saw past the boots—green uniform, no weapon. A soldier, a Jew.

Breathing. He was breathing, pants sticky with blood, arms obscuring his face in pain or delirium. It was quiet. Too quiet. It can't have been that quiet after a bombing, she knows, but that's how she remembers it. Silence in the smoke, him sensing her and slowly bringing himself up to sit, gingerly, the way less than a minute before, Mai must have done. A beautiful boy, almost sleepy-looking, tousled, like a child roused from a nap. She and Noor have joked about this, how some of the Jews are, like, objectively handsome. Beautiful monsters, they call them. He had no weapon that she could see. Her hands were up. That was a strange thing to realize. She'd been holding her hands up, as if he were about to shoot.

It depends on the day. Sometimes Mai will try to pull Leila into nostalgia, and Leila will resist. *Remember the French teacher?* she'll say. *Remember the girl with the buckteeth?* Leila will shake her head, tell Mai that it was years ago, years and years ago, and she can barely remember it now. As if it were a decade ago and not two years, barely two years. But today, Leila is game to re-create the past, which is why they are back in the bedroom now. Tariq's meal—covered to keep it warm—is waiting for him on the smaller table in the kitchen. They are playing songs from Mai's phone and bouncing on Leila's bed, on Leila and Tariq's bed. "Bouncing" is maybe too strong a word. They are wobbling on the bed, moving gently, letting the bed squeak, squeak, as they sing along to the indefensible pop songs of their youth, the ridiculous saccharine auto-tuning. "No, no, no." Leila's voice trembles as she waves her finger and her giant hips.

Mai doesn't hear Tariq come in, but she can feel everything in the room change. Suddenly it is drafty, the open door, yes, but something more, a sense of being exposed, like, fine, yes, like the wind that used to draft through the window with the tarp over it, until Tariq had the workmen fix it.

He is standing at the bedroom threshold, compact in a suit. Mai steps down from the bed. She watches Leila's eyes go over to Tariq, the music still playing from her phone. They watch each other. "No, no, no," Leila says, mouthing the words to him. Now it's teasing, now it's for him. He's in dark trousers and rolled shirtsleeves; his watch glints. A man who sells things; a man watching his wife on their bed. It is as if Mai isn't here. All at once, she knows that Leila has been waiting all day for this. All day, she has waited out the hours with Mai for this, for her husband to come home and want her. Mai feels betrayed, invisible. Alone.

Why? Why didn't she run? When she saw that it was a soldier lying there. Why didn't she run? The soldier had gotten himself up to a seated position, legs straight out. Something was wrong with his right leg, twisted up all wrong. The angle of the kneecap was revolting. He didn't speak, but he knew she was there. Her hands were up, as if he had a weapon, but he didn't. Smoke swirled around her, and far off now, she heard shouting.

He made a sound that might have been "Mama." His head was dipping and weaving.

In the story Mai tells about this day, she is already gone; she is not standing here doing something doomed and stupid. But she didn't walk away. She took a step toward him and bent down slightly, as if talking to little Farouq. She could have said anything. She could have spoken to him—this blue-eyed colonizer—in the Arabic that all the soldiers know, the phrases they repeat in clunky approximations: "Give me your ID." She wishes she'd said that to him. "Give me your ID" or "Open the trunk" or "Stop or I'll shoot." But she didn't. Instead she asked, in Hebrew, "Are you okay?"

He said, "Please," in Hebrew. That's all he said.

She knew then that she wouldn't walk away. She knew she was going to help him even if she hated him, even if he was a monster. She was not—is this the right word?—she was not *brave* enough to walk away, not even from someone who thought of her life—Mai's life, Mai's own life—as a problem.

She has no memory of answering her phone and no idea how it survived the explosion, but she was speaking into her phone then. "Hello?" she said. There was a distant voice on the line. *Maybe that's me*, Mai thought, *calling myself*. "What should I do?" she said aloud. On the other end was a jumble of voices. Later, she saw that an unknown number had dialed her, and out of fear that they would call her again, she blocked the number. But that was later. At the time, she only echoed the distant voice she heard coming from her own phone. "The ambulances," she said. "The ambulances," she echoed. Then she hung up.

On the ground, the soldier was trying to stand. His leg twisted horrifically. He cried out in pain.

"Hold on," she said in Arabic, then, in Hebrew. *Hakeh reg'a.* She hesitated then added, "I'll help you."

ᥭᥫᥭ

In the car, dropping Mai off at home, Leila and Tariq sit up front. Mai is in the back. Leila is talking quietly with Tariq about one of their neighbors—the one who keeps letting stray dogs into her yard. "I don't know what goes on in that house," she says. They drive past a Jewish settlement block, spreading out across the old neighborhoods. The huge, gaudy Israeli flag flies next to a huge, gaudy American flag, side by side.

"Still not back at school, ah?" Tariq says to Mai in the rearview mirror. Hanging from the mirror beneath his eyes: an air freshener and a pendant of the golden Dome of the Rock. He doesn't pray every day, but on Fridays goes to Al-Aqsa, often bringing the boys. Tariq smiles. He has perfect teeth. He does well at the car dealership, Leila tells Mai. That's why everyone—Leila, Tariq's mother, even Mama— drives new Volkswagens. Not a tall man, but powerfully built. He moves knowingly the way a cat lurks before pouncing.

"Not yet, but soon," Mai says.

He laughs. "Good, good," he says. Teeth flashing. She's never seen him angry, but she can imagine it: an affable rage.

Then to Leila, in a quieter voice, he explains that he'll be late to cousin Rania's wedding tomorrow. "Forgive me, my queen," he says.

Leila sticks her tongue out at him.

"What's this?" he exclaims. Looking at her, then at the road, then back at her, furious with joy. "Mai, your sister is a very bad girl, do you know this?"

Last year, Mai found a recent photo of Tariq and Leila on Leila's phone. It was of the two of them, taken by Tariq from a high angle. He had a shirt on, but it was kind of unbuttoned. Leila was in a tank top, the kind you'd wear as an undershirt, not a real shirt. She looked up at the camera, her eyes big. Leila's head came up to Tariq's chin, and her expression—this was on purpose, maybe—was girlish, wide-eyed. She looked like—how to explain this?—like she belonged to him. Mai wanted to throw the phone across the room, but also to keep it forever. Now, Mai supposes, she has a secret from Leila. The Girl and the Soldier. Whenever the image appears, Mai is there, hiding in plain sight. She has a secret from Leila the way Leila has secrets from Mai. The way secrets live in your body and alter it, Mai has that, too.

Once she got the soldier standing, they began to walk. Slowly, carefully. She kept him off his injured leg by having him hop, supporting him under his armpit and gripping his waist a little. He was thinner than she thought he'd be, thinner than Mai. He smelled like burnt earth. She had never been this close to a man who was not her father. She could feel something slip inside her—a sense of resolve leaking out from a newfound porousness.

They were only like that for a few seconds, a minute at most. She has no idea when the photograph was taken of the two of them. *The two of them.* She didn't notice anyone noticing them—just the opposite, actually. After a few careful steps, when they entered the periphery of the explosion—the bus burning, the Red Crescent ambulances to the right, Red Star to the left—she was struck by how close they had been to the ambulances the whole time, not much farther than the length of a playground. How weird, she thought at the time, that nobody stopped her. Though people only see what they expect to see. Hadn't someone said that? So maybe, she thought, she and the soldier were invisible together.

The Israelis had already detained a few shabaab, lining them up against a jeep. Young men, her young men, though no one she recognized, looking up at the border police—hands up, each with his hawiyya between his fingers. The boys were zip-tied, she could tell, by the way they held up their hands together, a gesture of supplication, a gesture that looks like praying if you don't know what it is. They were zip-tied, but the Jew shot one of the boys anyway. Mai didn't hear the shot, but she saw the boy collapse onto his side, then the other boys yelling, trying to inch over to help, the soldier waving his weapon, shouting at them too. "No," she said, she said it aloud. "No." The boy lay on his side. Not moving.

And then the Jews were running toward her, two paramedics in blue, running toward her with weapons. One of them a woman with a ponytail, one of them a man in settler clothes, fat, with strings hanging out of his pockets.

"Stop!" the woman yelled in Arabic. "Stop or I'll shoot."

"No," Mai said again. Then, "Please."

But they only pushed her. The woman paramedic pushed her, hard in the chest, pushed her away. She fell onto the ground coughing. Later, on the news, this woman would insist that the girl in white must have been trying to kidnap Ori—that's his name, Ori—because if she had nothing to hide, why did she disappear so quickly?

Get up, Mai said to herself, gasping on the concrete. Get up. She heard them speaking to the soldier rapidly in Hebrew, *My brother, what unit are you in?* Then, to each other, *Radio in, tell them we've got a flower.* She's still not sure if she misheard. A flower.

Then she really did run.

Back at home, the boys are finally in bed. Mama and Mai watch TV in the salon. All day, Mama was at her own sister's home, hollowing out zucchinis to be stuffed for Rania's wedding tomorrow. Mama, who gives and gives. Now, on the couch, Mama rests her bare feet in Mai's lap. The news is on. Saudi atrocities in Yemen, American atrocities in Iran, the winner of *Arab Idol*. Mai is rubbing her mother's feet with a lovely, thick lotion, scented with geranium.

"Worse and worse," Mama says.

Mai rubs her knuckle along the tender arch of her mother's foot, the lotion is slick on her hands. "I know, Mama," she says.

"Look at me," Mama says, "putting you to work on my old feet."

353

Mai runs her hand over the delicate bones of Mama's foot bridge. She wants to say, I'm trying to protect you. Instead she quotes a hadith. "Paradise is at the feet of our mothers," which gets a laugh from Mama.

The news anchorwoman, whose lipstick is a warm, purply brown that would look nice on Mai, says, "We now continue ongoing investigation into Israeli terror tactics." Today, they examine Israeli soldiers disguising themselves as civilians. Footage, now, of the disguised agents: video from Mai's campus of the "journalists" in their press vests, dragging away the student union leader; images of "aid workers" in Gaza handcuffing an elderly man in a wheelchair. "Recently, the Israelis have begun to use women as undercover agents, too." Then there she is. Mai on TV, Mai with the soldier. Rubbing her mother's feet, Mai thinks, *That's me, that's you.* Mai is too scared to look over at Mama, so she stays fixed on the screen, which has already shifted to footage of shabaab in protest. Now that the Jews are done terrorizing families with the raids, they have begun to claim that, in fact, it was a gas leak that caused the explosion.

"Yalla," Mama says, "time for bed."

In the morning, the three of them are together at home. Mai, Leila, Mama. They are folding sticky sweet cheese into cream wraps for halawet el-jibn to bring to the wedding this afternoon.

Mai is reducing rose blossom water to a syrup in the big, dented pan that her parents have had since they first married, so out of place in the renovated kitchen, the sleek stove range hood, black and soundless. Leila and Mama are lining baking sheets with plastic wrap. The boys are at school, the only traces of them are little figurines popping out of every corner—toy soldiers in the fruit bowl, behind the drying rack, in the deep sink.

Mai remembers the three of them preparing desserts for Leila's wedding. "This is the last time," Mai had said to herself then, stirring the same syrup that she is stirring now. That day, she knew, it would never be the same. And she was right. All she wants, all she has wanted, is for time to stop, just a little bit, just a pause. But the harder she tries to stop it, the more it hurtles her forward. She says, aloud, she says, "It's me."

Mama and Leila don't look up. Mama tells Leila to begin coating the trays with vegetable oil, but very lightly.

"It's me," Mai says again. "In the picture, it's me."

They pause what they are doing and look at her.

"The Girl and the Soldier. It's me. I'm the girl."

Mama and Leila exchange a startled glance in which they determine—Mai recognizes this exchange, has participated in ones like it—that Leila will be the one to speak. "You thought," tender little sigh, "you thought we didn't know?"

Mai: "How?" She's not sure if she says the word aloud.

"We knew as soon as we saw," Mama says.

Mai has stopped stirring the syrup. Could they tell from the wound? From the cut on her head? Had they deduced the connection between that and the photo?

Mama looks almost pained when she says, "I would know you from your shadow."

"I don't think—" Leila starts.

Mama finishes, "Nobody else can tell."

"Your face is hidden," Leila says.

"And the colors are wrong," Mama says. "The pink looks white."

What now? When Mai imagined this conversation, she imagined that it would end with her apologizing, asking forgiveness, begging even. She should feel relief. Instead what Mai feels is a loss so complete it is as if her legs really are missing. Everything has been changing for a long time. She has known this but hasn't wanted to let go of the possibility that they could go back, that time could reverse, that Leila would come home and the two of them would become girls again. But everything is always changing, and never again will Mai belong completely, perfectly and completely, to her mother, to her sister. Never again. Never again a child. Never, ever again.

Mama draws her daughters close. The three women draw together, as if around Leila's belly, as if the three of them were carrying Leila's belly together, as if the one inside were each of them, each of the three women, inside the others.

Brothers

Ori is the only one in civilian clothes, sitting in the special chair that lets him rest his leg, still in a cast that goes up past his knee. All the guys in his living room—Danny, fat Moshik, Commander Alon—are in uniform, all of them carrying weapons. And then there's Ori, in sweatpants and an old T-shirt with the neck cut off. So far, nobody has mentioned the photo of Ori with the Arab girl.

"So what's it like in Hebron?" he asks, not sure which guy he should look at.

Alon shrugs. "You know how it is, achi." He takes a cookie from the plate that Ima brought out earlier before squeezing Ori's shoulder then disappearing upstairs to give them, the boys, privacy. "A lot of action," Alon continues, "a lot of bullshit." His Tavor rests on his leg.

Ori assumes it was Ima who orchestrated this visit from the guys, even if she insists it was his commander's idea. Strange to have them all in his living room—on the couch, their boots on the carpet (Ima told them not to worry about taking them off). He hasn't seen them since the explosion. The initial handshakes were awkward, and not just because he was in a cast. It has been a month. A lot can happen in a month. A lot of distance can develop. And who knows if Ori will be allowed to reenter his unit when his leg heals. Who knows if he's still considered a fit soldier.

"The Arabs in Hebron are wild," Moshik says more to Alon than to Ori. "Always filming everything."

"And the internationals?" Alon says to Moshik. "Remember, Mosh, those Christians from Germany or Sweden or wherever?" He shakes his head.

"Nazis," Moshik says, his mouth filled with cookies.

"Exactly," Alon says. "Remember that old lady?"

"Achi, that was crazy." Moshik smacks Alon on the shoulder—a casual touch that makes Ori feel very far away from them. "She kept calling us the SS!"

Danny still hasn't said a fucking word. Ori tries to make eye contact but Danny won't look at him.

"Anyway," Alon says, turning to Ori as if he just remembered Ori was there, "how are you feeling, achi? How is the leg?"

"The cast itches," Ori says, directing his answer at Danny, "but it's not so bad." Danny is fiddling with the strap of his rifle and doesn't reply. Ori and Danny became close after the final march that initiated them into the unit—each pushing the other to keep going, keep going, achi, and when one thought he would drop dead from exhaustion, from despair, from fatigue, it was the other who placed a firm hand between his shoulder blades—*Yalla, achi, you can do it*, and they did. Only now, Danny won't look at him.

"Well, we miss you," Alon says, generously. Ori wonders if he had to force Danny to come. Soon, Ima will come down and tell Ori it's time for his physio appointment, and the guys will go back to being soldiers.

"It's weird being home," Ori begins. It's weird not having a weapon, he's about to say.

But Danny breaks in: "What did she smell like?"

"What?" Ori asks.

Danny repeats himself. "What did the Arab girl smell like?"

It takes Ori only a second to process the question for what it is: a test. Alon and Moshik shake their heads, but they don't tell Ori not to answer and they don't tell Danny he's an idiot for asking. They wait. Ori remembers so little from that day. Her voice coming to him as if they were underwater. Floating, soft. *The ambulances, I'll take you to the ambulances.* She didn't save his life, but she didn't *not* save his life. She helped him walk. Her body, so small, propping up his. Her hands gentle around his rib cage. *Slowly*, she said. Why him? That question, surely, is a boundary that now exists between Ori and his unit-mates. Is he some kind of Arab-lover? They all must wonder it.

Danny is waiting for Ori to answer. *What did the Arab girl smell like?* The question is a test, yes, also an attack, sure, but most important, it is an opportunity. It doesn't matter what happened. It doesn't matter what Ori felt—brought to safety by a girl with a soft voice and gentle hands. All that matters is right now, what he says to his brothers next.

"Like hummus," Ori says.

Danny looks up at him, hopeful and relieved. "What?"

"Achi, I'm telling you," Ori repeats, holding eye contact with Danny, "the bitch smelled exactly like hummus."

And then Danny is laughing, and Alon and Moshik are hooting in disbelief and Ori feels, for a beautiful second he feels, like maybe everything is going to be okay.

Meir's Mum Watches TV

Susan Klausman pauses in folding the laundry—she's waiting for Meir to come home from futbal practice—as she watches a BBC update on the recent terror attack over in America, and it's horrible, obviously it's horrible—twelve Jewish teenagers killed when a gunman walked into a JCC, bloody footprints on the sidewalk in the afternoon, Jewish blood—yes, it's horrible, it's horrible, just like all the American Jews crying on TV are saying, parents doubled over like they've just been kicked in the stomach. "It's horrible, it's so horrible," they say. "I never thought, we never thought," then not finishing the sentence, but Susan knows exactly what they did not think, which is that it could happen there, it could happen in America, in the northeast of America—not in the dark tangles of that country's fetid South but in the northeast—filled with liberals and smug ideals, the same way nobody thinks it could happen in London, and this is what gets to her, because of course they never thought it could happen to them, of course they thought they were an exception, but now they see, now they see, now they see, and look, it would be wrong—it would be incorrect—to say that Susan is happy it happened. How could she be happy that those babies were massacred? How could she be happy to see Jewish blood spilled? No. No, obviously Mrs. Klausman is not happy it happened. That's a disgusting thing to imagine, being happy it happened. But—at the same time—there is a fist inside her that is raised, that is vindicated. Watching those parents, those weeping parents, she shakes her head to herself and says, "Now you see, now you see, now you see." Who is she talking to? To those Jews who stayed behind in England, in America, in France. The diaspora. The doubters. Now you see that they hate us. Now you see that they will always hate us. Who is "they"? Everyone. Everyone who is not a Jew. The man who did it was white. No matter. The Arabs, the Muslims, the Nazis. The goyim. Now you see why we came to Israel, why we need Israel. Now you see what we have known, what we have always known, what we cannot forget because every day they try to kill us. Mrs. Klausman is surrounded by newly washed, unfolded dish towels, by piles and piles of Meir's boxers and compression shorts and futbal socks. Last week, the only news she saw on the BBC was about that photograph—the Arab and the Soldier. Who cares? Where was the coverage of the most recent stabbing? An Arab stabbed a boy Meir's age in the middle of Tel Aviv. Right in the bus station. Now it's all about this attack in America. On TV, the parents are screaming about gun control. Gun control this, gun control that. What they don't see is that you fight hate with power. You become powerful, so powerful that if someone hurts—hamsa, hamsa, hamsa—if someone hurts your baby, if someone touches a hair on the head of your precious boy, you can make them wish that they were never born.

Emily in Rechavia

Emily knows that she's better suited to live in Tel Aviv, in one of the gentrified neighborhoods with abundant Pilates studios, pop-up shops for crystals, and weekend-long probiotic workshops. But she and Ido live in Jerusalem, and this feels right, because (1) she and Ido have a car, of course, which means they can escape the claustrophobic shutdown that reigns each week for twenty-five hours from Friday night through Saturday night, and in that way, the city isn't too oppressive; (2) Ido's parents gave them a house, like gave them an actual house, where Emily tends a garden filled with kale and rosemary, breastfeeds her baby in rooms with high ceilings—an Ottoman house, some call it; others, an Arab house, because of who was chased out; (3) Ido's job is in Jerusalem, at an animation studio in an industrial zone on the outskirts of the city, and even if his web comic has kicked off in a meaningful way, and even if Emily's own posts have begun generating considerable revenue since she photographed the Girl and the Soldier, she knows that Ido will continue working at the studio for the simple reason that he likes having somewhere to go every day.

But (4) may be the most important reason to stay: Jerusalem is magic.

Or a kind of magic. Emily's acupressure masseuse, an Orthodox

Jewish woman originally from Florida, described Jerusalem's magic as "touching planes," which doesn't quite make sense but is also perfect. So for example, you'll hear a song, and it will make you think of a woman you knew only briefly. Or, no, you didn't really know her, not really; she was someone who sold tiny flower bouquets out of a nonkosher café on Fridays, before Shabbat came in. They were wildflowers, bound together in twine, and affixed to them, always, was an unbearably short poem in Hebrew that Ido, when Emily brought one home, would help her sound through. *B'stav*—"in the autumn"—*matok*—"sweet"—*hiyah pardes-i*—"was my orchard." Ido told her that the word for "orchard," *pardes*, was associated not just with fruit, but with learning to the point of a divine encounter that drove some to madness. Emily thought *pardes* sounded like "paradise," the English word, and looked online to find it wasn't a coincidence: the words sprang out of the same Persian root, *firdaus*, which in Arabic came to refer to a layer of heaven. Emily saved that particular poem, or verse, and even now, it is tied to one of the bunches of dried sage and rosemary she keeps hanging in the windows. How did it survive all those moves? That brown slip of paper? But it's there, though you'd never notice it unless you were looking for it, hanging in the stately bathroom window, the frosted glass overgrown with creeping vines that tremble pale green in the sun. *B'stav matok hiyah pardes-i.*

That was all a long time ago now. They were both students. It was the winter when they began, Ido and Emily, a rainy winter. Nearly every weekend, Emily, who was at that time in Tel Aviv for a master's, and who had no expectation of staying more than a year, took the forty-minute bus ride to Jerusalem, because Ido had a one-bedroom apartment, but she lived with a roommate whose small dog was always pooping in their living room, which was also their dining room.

Even before she moved to Jerusalem, she felt at home in the city, or at least, in Ido's gentle part of the city—a place that invited walks to and from cafés with mismatched tablecloths and slow service by barista–art students who were discussing a poet, a documentary, a feeling; a place where trees older than the state of Israel shaded crooked sidewalks and rain-blanched benches. Emily felt herself a bit more dreamy here than in frantic Tel Aviv, more quieted. She loved wandering with Ido around the bookshops of his neighborhood. Ido looked for old children's books, interested in the drawing style. Emily pretended to consider volumes of poetry while watching people come and go: old-world men with scholarly stoops and worn-out coat collars who inspected the volumes, or were hurried along by wives with plump wrists and thin gold watches, scolding their husbands in Polish, in Yiddish. The old men left trails of papers, shedding papers like dandruff: sheet music for violin, photocopies of rabbinic commentary, humanist critiques of Zionism in German. All the old men carried the heavy plastic shopping bags they took to and from the National Library, where bags of any other sort are forbidden.

The young men who worked in the bookshops were shy and helpful. Thin and overworked, in wire-rimmed glasses, they had the same bent posture as the old men. The Rechavia Stoop, Emily called it to herself. Rechavia was the name of the neighborhood. All the streets were named after Jewish writers and philosophers, poets, translators of Homer into Hebrew.

That winter, she and Ido fell into each other quickly, and right away, it was more than dating. They called it playing house. In their version, playing house involved cooking elaborate, beautifully seasoned meals together and making love—sometimes sweet, sometimes rough—on every chair, couch, and window ledge in the leaky, creaky apartment. That's how they imagined married life. Each week, Emily came in on Friday and left on Sunday. The café, the one where the young woman sold flowers, was on Emily's way from the bus station, just as she descended the hill that constituted Ido's neighborhood. She'd stop at the café so that she could knock on Ido's door bearing flowers. On Fridays, and maybe every day, for all Emily knows, the café was always playing Israeli folk music. One song in particular always seemed to be on rotation: a sleepy children's song about David and Goliath. The girl—the florist—was Emily's age. She wore an apron with many pockets, each of them with different types of scissors for different types of flowers. She sat at the table the café let her use; she fashioned bouquets from flowers in buckets at her feet. Because Emily came each week, the florist—Inbar, maybe her name was—began putting bouquets aside especially for Emily. Wild bunches of purple thistles and unnamed yellow flowers, filled in with sprigs of rosemary, plant of remembering. *B'stav matok hiyah pardes-i*. In autumn, my orchard was sweet. Sweet was my orchard in autumn.

But where is she now? Emily wondered recently, when she passed an open window and heard that particular song—that sweet, silly folk song that nobody plays anymore, a children's story, a murder, David and the giant—the one that was always playing as Inbar bound her bouquets, and in that very moment, eleven years later, on a street in Rechavia, there she is, as if the song summoned her. Here is Inbar, walking down the main street of Rechavia, not as she was, meaning not a mirage, but really Inbar, appropriately aged and holding the hand of a little girl, maybe five, who wears a sweater stitched in a floral pattern, vines and blooms all over the little torso. "Yalla, Stav. Yalla, Stav-chik," Inbar is saying to the child. She named her Stav, autumn. *B'stav matok*, sweet in autumn. And before Emily can say anything, before she can lift her hand to wave, to say, You know me, before any of that, the woman and child have rounded a corner, and they are gone.

To the Sea

They call it going to "The Sea." Hamid can't remember which of his friends came up with the name. Maybe Muhi? Poor Muhi. Finally out of jail, never leaving his house. This never ends, does it? What is "it," even? But it never ends. Hamid is alone. He has come here alone. The Sea. To get here, you ease yourself down the terraced slopes of Beit Jala, down among the shards of white stones like scattered teeth, like fragments of bone among the grapevines and olive trees. It may be fifty kilometers inland, but they call it The Sea because it's as close as they can get to the sea, this in-between place.

Hamid eases his way down. Behind him, the unpaved road curves toward the closed Tunnels Checkpoint. Maybe it was fate that put him here on the day of the explosion. From here, he was able to run to the checkpoint in just a few minutes.

The Jews forbid anyone to build here—in the sloping zone between the road and the checkpoint—although probably, one day, the Jewish settlements will spread to here, too. But for now, it is just the hills, sparsely green and farmed by Palestinian hands, dotted with a few crumbling ruins of old stone houses. Going to The Sea means perching up on a ruined roof, somewhere private—hidden from the road by the incline of the hill above, hidden from the wealthy

Christian houses that dot the ledge, hidden from the checkpoint, from the settlements. Hidden.

Hamid hoists himself up onto cool stones. The valley unfolds beneath him, hills and wadis flowing westward, all the way to the sea. In another life, a freer life, Hamid could walk all the way there, past settlements and army bases, walk into the past itself, through the ruined fields of his grandparents', the ghosts of villages, all the way, all the way to the sea.

In the years since high school, The Sea has become Hamid's refuge. He comes here alone as much as he comes with his friends, and has to assume that they do the same: that each of them has, in turn, come to sit on the ruined roof alone. Who built you? he wonders. And who was chased away? Who was murdered? Who is gone? The foundations indicate that it once stood at four rooms, at least, but most of the walls are gone. Now, as afternoon slips away, Hamid is alone with the gnarled trees, the blameless sky, and his own confused thoughts—Ramadan thoughts. The fasting makes all his thinking at once more spectral and more lucid.

Hamid is not sure he's religious anymore. Not that he thought of himself as religious before, just he never really thought about it at all. But still he fasts, because, well, that's what you do.

Recently, it's been impossible for him to hold on to a single thought, any thought, for more than a second, before some contradictory notion comes crashing in. He tells himself he's losing interest in religion, that what matters is people: humanism. But almost in the same instant, he feels a deep sense of betrayal by almost every human being he has ever known. At least the Jews are open about it. They are what they are, they kill who they kill, and they don't pretend otherwise. But then there are the Palestinian police, secretly collaborating with the Jews, or beating up shabaab at protests in Ramallah, just because it makes them feel like men. And Mai. She wasn't who he thought she was. She wasn't the girl he dreamt, wasn't anyone at all, and he won't tell—he'll let the story slip away, won't reveal what he knows about that day, but he won't forget. She didn't come back to finish the semester before the break began for Ramadan. Maybe she'll never come back. It truly does not matter. All he knows is that now, he is twice as alone as before. Hopeless. Everything feels hopeless. The animal of this place is eating its own tail. When it becomes too much, he comes to The Sea.

Hamid rests his chin on his knees. He is alone. Here, it is only the land. Hamid and the land. No people, no history, even. He closes his eyes. He lets himself imagine that from here, he can hear the sea, the crashing of waves traveling to him over the hills and wadis. He imagines he can hear the sea making its persistent promise, whatever that is—something about eternity, about oneness, about annihilation. He keeps his eyes closed. He can do that here, at The Sea, because he knows when he opens them again, there will not be another soul in sight—only a stray cat, too far from whatever dumpster it calls home, stalking tiny white butterflies in the blurry, nostalgic light before the sun begins to set.

Samar's Fast

No, Samar never called the German journalist back, did she? Lingering in the back garden, alone among her father's fruit trees, Samar is listening to old voice mails that need to be deleted—*Your mailbox is full*. And no, she never did call her back, Vera Something, the German journalist who, back in the spring, left three (a bit excessive) messages—"Marhaba, Dr. Farha; Guten tag, Professor Farha; Samar, hi, it's me"—asking if Samar would please (please, please, please) comment on the Girl and the Soldier, the photo that the Israelis may not have faked, Samar isn't as sure as everyone else, but that they certainly capitalized on. Now it's summer. Samar doesn't know if Vera is still here, or if she's off documenting war elsewhere—white supremacy in America, who knows.

The back garden is mercifully cool near the end of the day. Samar, hazy and dehydrated in the final hour before the fast breaks, lets herself weave in and out of the plum trees, the apricot trees, the lone almond tree, with its hard-won, fuzzy fruits. Her senses are precise, sharp with hunger. The flutter of bird wings ripples like the pages of a heavy book. Some of these trees are as old as Samar. The two olive trees are older. Siblings. Inside the house, her sister-in-law is in charge. Fatima. Sitting by Mama's bed, adjusting her IV, rushing back and forth to the kitchen to check on the Iftar meal.

"Welcome," Fatima said when Samar got to the door. "Ramadan kareem." Her pudgy little face was glowing. Playing hostess.

"Welcome?" Samar said archly. Then gave an insulted little cough. As if Samar had moved out already, as if Fatima and Samar's brother no longer lived in the apartment down the hill that Father bought years ago, as if this house were already Fatima's. "Ramadan kareem," Samar said as pointedly as she could, walking past Fatima, through a doorway that is more familiar to Samar than her own body, the dip of the threshold worn over by generations of feet.

Fatima trailed behind Samar, talking sweetly, eagerly: "The new IV is more comfortable for Mama." A girl, Fatima, her youngest brother's young wife—glowing with health, with youth, with yet another pregnancy, like a sweet little overstuffed confection. She has the look of a country girl.

"Is something burning?" Samar asked to get rid of her, and almost immediately felt guilty. *It's not your fault*, she wanted to say. *You're a nice girl, my destroyer.* The truth is that, well, the truth is that Samar is nervous. Nervous! As if she were the young girl here.

Everything has changed so quickly. Samar won't be teaching the composition class come next fall. This is good; this is new—the result of a campaign by Samar to get, if not tenure, better recognition by the school. In truth, the article by the German journalist—the one published in the winter about the body of Salem Abu-Khdeir—helped Samar make a case for herself as a kind of public intellectual, quoted, as she was, heavily in the piece. (The older professors, old men, always old men, had insisted that exposure in popular outlets should count against her, not for her, but the dean—increasingly obsessed with proving the humanities' relevance—brushed away these criticisms.) Now, Samar doesn't have tenure, no, but her photograph is on the landing page for the school as a featured faculty member.

Next year, she'll be teaching a course of her own design: "Novels of Resistance"—no more lower-level composition classes for her.

So yes, she could have called Vera back in order to do it again: to be interviewed about the Girl and the Soldier, to provide (as she did for the Salem article) a kind of cerebral center for the story. Yes, she could have exchanged meaning for exposure. In the case of the Girl and the Soldier, they would have spoken about the anxious intimacy between the oppressed and the oppressor; they might have spoken about the Western fixation on unveiling—revealing, exposing. How what they call progress is a series of commodifications. But she didn't call her, didn't give her the quotes—the meaning—that this white woman so craved, because why should Samar peddle out her insights to be quoted briefly in a German-language magazine? She'll write it herself. Indeed, Samar has started drafting a new article. She's saving the best bits for herself. She'll say it in her own words.

In the garden, Samar has plucked off a leaf from a plum tree and is sitting on a bench that Father installed years and years ago. She is under a canopy of grapevines, and the air is cool. Her thirst is less an appetite than a buzz, a hum, an animation inside her. She tickles her nose with the plum-tree leaf. She is, she knows, more sensual now than she has ever been.

Her phone is in her pocket. The messages from the journalist erased; the messages of congratulations saved. Mabruk, they say, mabruk, mabruk. That's the other reason that Samar never called Vera back. There's no time. It's all changed so suddenly: Samar is engaged to be married.

Married.

She still forgets sometimes. When she is home, when she is wandering in the garden that has grown her whole life, when she is bustling around in the kitchen with Fatima, when she is sitting by Mother's bed to hold her hand, or at her father's old desk trying to write, it feels, to Samar, impossible that she will leave, that soon she will bring her clothes and books to another home, the home of her husband. Her husband.

Husband. Fiancé. Groom. Abu Hashim. Yusef Abu-Hashim.

He is a widower. None of Samar's firsts will be his firsts. No matter, no matter. Samar knows enough to know that symmetry is a lie.

One of the hardest parts about getting engaged was how happy it made Fatima, that little full-faced weasel. Fatima's mother had been instrumental in the engagement, eager to get Samar out of the house so that her daughter could finally move out of the apartment down the hill and begin running the proper house, the grand house. Fatima's mother diligently monitored the whispers and nods, found out which men might be looking for someone like Samar, which aging men might want to marry (or marry again), not for children but for some housekeeping and companionship. It was an intrusion that maddened Samar—the names always being dropped, casually mentioned—how embarrassing. But with Mother increasingly frail, Samar felt vulnerable, scared. It was the street in Chicago she kept recalling—terror in the middle of the afternoon, the footsteps coming up behind her. Just a jogger, it had turned out, but the fear was real. An unmarried woman. What could she do? She could leave or she could marry. Didn't it come down to that?

"Did you hear the widower Abu Hashim has come back from America?" Fatima's crooked-toothed mother said, ostensibly to Fatima, one night as Fatima washed vegetables and her mother—not even bothering to hide what she was doing—used her footsteps to count the length across the kitchen, measuring out space for a new fridge, maybe. The weaker Mother became, the bolder Fatima's family grew.

"Ah," Fatima said, loudly. Her husband, Samar's brother, was napping in his childhood bedroom before dinner. His boys were watching TV. (Fatima is hoping for a girl this time.)

Samar was at the kitchen table with Mother, trying to get her to drink more water.

"Is he the one with the son in Atlantis?" Fatima asked.

"In Atlanta, yes," the mother said. "The son sends back a lot."

It was obvious that they had rehearsed this. Samar was burning up. She had told them to stop. She had told them to stop trying to set her up with all these leftover men. (*Then what are you?* She could see the retort in their eyes.)

"He likes books," Fatima said, glancing at her mother to confirm the line. "I hear he likes books."

Abu Hashim the widower. A gentle man, unhurried. His children are grown; his oldest, yes, lives in America with children of his own. His younger son works in Saudi, and a daughter who lives with her in-laws inside, yanni, in East Jerusalem. It took, he told Samar later, years and years for his daughter to get her blue hawiyya, and so much money. All that to say, when Samar moves into his home—her husband's home, *husband, husband*—it will be just the two of them. His home is lovely, one of the old stone buildings by the university. Not much land for a garden, but well built and vine-covered. Samar has a room for her desk—her own room to work in. And it is not so far from Mother, just a cab ride away, not so far.

A gentle man. Yes, he seems to Samar like a gentle man. Is it age? He is over sixty; she is barely past forty, although still bleeding, and she wonders . . . but no matter.

She doesn't know if she is making a mistake. It's true. She doesn't know. Nobody willingly gives up an entitlement, not even a gentle man. So she will cook, yes, and clean. But he will, she senses this, bring her cups of black tea when she is writing. Sugar and sage. She will have a room to write in—not her late father's desk dragged into her bedroom, but a separate room for writing. A desk overlooking the small, tangled garden that, at some point, Samar will coax into order.

"I admire your voice," he said to her during their courtship, fiddling with his hands when he came to see her at home. Mother sat in the corner—this was back in the spring, and she was not yet confined to bed—grinning away. "Your writing," he went on, "it sounds like you."

In this moment, she thought suddenly of Father and how happy he would have been to hear this man praise his daughter's mind. "Thank you," she said. Later, only when they became more familiar, did Samar say suddenly one afternoon when they were sitting some distance apart on the bench in the garden, "I wish you could have met my father." Her father reading his newspaper, her father at the window, waiting for history to right itself. Her father, killed by hope, by his own broken heart.

"I would have loved to meet him," Abu Hashim said. "Allahyer-hamo." Not yet taking her hand in his. A gentle man.

Fiancé. Husband. Widower. Abu Hashim. An engineer. He still works, although nothing full-time. For years, he lived away from home, on great ships that traversed the oceans looking for gas—an engineer in perpetually crooked glasses (her imagination here) sur-rounded by a tough and able-bodied crew who sometimes held box-ing matches belowdecks. Sweat and darkness. But now he is back; he is home in the home his parents left him. Of his late wife, Allahyer-hamha, Samar knows little except for the specter of a horrible and fast-acting cancer years ago.

Is the marriage a mistake? Does it matter? In the end, Samar felt she had two choices: to leave, to push and push until she got a one-year teaching fellowship elsewhere—Chicago held promise—or to stay and marry. How could she stay in her childhood home once Mother goes? Relegated to some back room in what will become Fati-ma's house? Unbearable. To go from berating the girl for her overly sweet tea, her unconvincing mopping, to go from that to being the withered branch with no rights, no power. No. Not that. So what, then? Leave here for good? Pull up her roots?

Sitting on this bench, the grape leaves trembling in the smudged light of gloaming, Samar tries to look upon her mother's house, the house her father built, the way a stranger might see it in passing. Solidly built, without the affectation of a winding staircase, so popular these days. Stone and high windows. A kind of fortress. This is the house where Samar has marked every Ramadan of her life, except for the years she spent at Oxford.

The wedding will be after Ramadan, of course, a few days after Eid. Quiet, quick. They would have done it before if there'd been time.

Abu Hashim made his quiet, self-deprecating jokes. "We could always marry during Ramadan," he said, adjusting his glasses. A tall man. Thin and elegant. "A bargain wedding!"

Mother was bedridden by then. Samar's brothers and an uncle sat with legs spread wide on low sofas in the salon. Abu Hashim had come to speak to them about Samar, to ask their permission. Her men. They had all laughed at his joke: a wedding without a meal. Samar brought in the tea on a tray. Then she left the room, left the men to talk. She went to hold her mother's hand.

"Mama," Mama said to Samar, delirious, distracted.

"Mama," replied Samar, tapping her mother's hand, avoiding the spot where her IV drip was needled into her papery skin.

"Mama," Samar's mama said again. There are days when that is all Mother says. Mama, Mama. To Samar, to Fatima, to her sons. Mama, Mama.

Later, Samar's brothers repeated Abu Hashim's joke to the whole family: a Ramadan wedding, a bargain wedding. Samar sensed—perhaps overly sensitive, she knows—that there was a glint of cruelty in it. Samar, a bargain bride, a withered branch. Samar over forty. Barely, but over. And all of this like some farce of a real wedding. Wasn't it?

"Halas," Samar said to her brothers, her voice so much higher and sweeter than the voice she thinks of as her own. She saw Fatima and her mother exchange a conspiratorial glance, and wondered if they would giggle about it the next day when Samar left for campus—how young Samar sounded, how nervous.

It will not be a big wedding. They'll host guests at home, meaning at Abu Hashim's home. The home she must now come to think of as her own. It will be a quiet wedding. No abduction rite, with Samar fake weeping—or really weeping; girls get very into it—torn from her mother. No enormous dress swallowing her, no pale face painted on her face.

A small party. They'll greet the guests as man and wife. No elaborate ritual around the loss of her girlhood. No ululations of women watching her be taken away to sex, sex, sex.

And yet.

He's a gentle man. He'll be gentle, she tells herself. He'll be unhurried. It is not his first wedding night. His children are grown. These are the ways she reassures herself. This is something extra for him—a bonus near the end. She is happy with this arrangement, because, she imagines, so much of herself will remain for herself. In this marriage, they will each have their privacy.

Samar is not scared of sex. Oh, no, she is anything but scared. To be touched! To touch! She has waited so long, deferred and deferred. Sometimes, sitting in the little room of her mother's salon, Abu Hashim telling them about some element of chemical engineering, she'll feel a kind of wild fire rushing up from her stomach, lower than her stomach, up to her throat. She'll see his hands, thick, able fingers, and want to press her deepest part up against him right there. To be touched, to be touched—this does not scare her. If she is scared—if there is a buzz of fear—it's when she thinks about being seen. To be naked in front of a man. To see herself through his eyes, to wonder if her breasts look as deflated as she fears, if the pudge of her loose lower belly is obvious. Samar doesn't think of her own body as wasted, but sometimes, she'll feel the places where what was full is now, in a sense, empty. Or she'll pause when plucking out the gray hairs from the part of her scalp. She plucks them one by one—gray baby hairs she hasn't dyed yet. But she has paused to ask herself, *Who has seen me? Who has borne witness?* Then, immediately, she feels embarrassed for having indulged such thinking. Is that why she said yes? To be witnessed? To be seen?

The day is gone. The sun has slipped. Soon the adhan will call the end of the fasting day. Fatima must be arranging the table, or sitting once again by Mother's bed to encourage her to sip a bit more tea, or perhaps, she is continuing her less-than-subtle casing—visualizing where she might put a new couch, or standing with her arms crossed in the dining room, assessing the table, which seats eight, and could she fit in an extra leaf? Then turning to the curtains, feeling the rich, heavy material in her tiny hand, unsure if she'll keep it as it is, meaning sumptuous, or will she go with something that lets in more light. The bedroom that Samar's brothers shared will become Fatima's sons' bedroom. And Samar's bedroom? The one that remained hers when she went off to Oxford, the one that was waiting when they called her back, when her parents called her back? That bedroom will become, Samar imagines, the nursery for the girl Fatima is carrying.

Any second now, the call will go up, and Samar's nephews will tear out of the house to fetch her back inside for the Iftar meal. Samar has known her nephews all their lives. Sweetness and terror: helping their mother mop the house on Fridays, chasing after pigeons in the courtyard. They are good boys. In her way, Samar is essential to them—her insistent questions about their homework, the quiet house she keeps with Mother, the treats she brings back from her travels. What will they think of Samar the wife? Do they think of her as old? Do they equate Samar with her own mother? Two old women in a house too big for them?

At Oxford, Samar thought of herself as old already, already too old. She was barely thirty, but she felt like a spinster. Foolish girl. If only she'd known how young she was when she was young. She tries not to think about Oxford too much. The early days, over a decade ago now, when she was finishing her PhD, she thought that she might never come home, although that's not quite right. She knew she would come back, but let herself imagine she might not. Oxford, Oxford. Lonely days. But lonely days that felt—no other word—important. She thinks of long afternoons in the student housing, unsure what to do with herself in those hard-to-place hours before sunset. Sundays in England were the worst—a nebulous, unformed day you had to get through while waiting for the week to start. She would sit at her cheap plywood desk by the window. She fed coins to the radiator. Often, she tried to read, but dropped her book at the sound of the plaintive cries, radiating through the wall—ragged, tinny sounds of a desperate coupling that filled her neighbors' Sunday afternoons. When she opened her window, she only heard them louder. Sometimes she wasn't sure. Sometimes it could have been weeping. "Please don't let me die of loneliness," she would whisper, closing her window again. At times, she wondered if it wasn't birds, playing tricks on her lonely ears. Crows, complaining to one another, or the thin notes of longing issued by the lone heron that flew from tree to tree in the commons. She might laugh then. What would Lacan say about such a desperate imagination?

Oxford, Oxford. When Ramadan came at Oxford, Samar found herself cheating—breaking the fast before it was time. Before, that had never been an issue for her. Even as a young girl, sitting with the older women to fold chopped, honeyed nuts into pastries, to tend to meat, Samar did not feel herself tempted. But in Oxford, she found herself taking water during the fast. She would wake up from a daydream and find that she was drinking a glass of water from the sink in her room. Why bother to stop? There was nobody there. Back then, Ramadan was falling in the winter. There was no need to take water: cold days, damp, she probably drank enough water through her skin. The thirst wasn't a question of hydration, she thinks, but of displacement. Who was she away from the dip in the step of her mother's threshold? Who is she? To tell her, she needs to walk where the driveway leans left, to walk under the canopy of pale green in the house's entryway, to come home to the smell of her mother's cooking, to nurse petty rivalries with her sisters-in-law, to abide the manic energy of her nephews. Sitting on her father's bench in the dying light, Samar feels—Samar knows—that she can't leave without losing herself. She can't do that again. Death to leave, death to stay. Is that free will? Choosing what you love enough to let it kill you?

And now and all at once, here it is. The adhans' calls begin to rise up from the valley and the hills. Voices blending and weaving, voices outdoing one another in an expansive, ephemeral symphony. For today, for now, the fast is over.

Acknowledgments

First and with my whole heart, my thanks to Hadeel and her beautiful family, without whom this book would not be: thank you, Hadeel and Shadi, for giving me a home in Bethlehem, thank you for telling me about your struggle and trusting me to hear it. Thank you to Caesar Hisham, the greatest tour guide in all the land and the one who opened the door for me. Thank you Hani, Sabah, and Mohammad, for treating me like a sister.

This novel was written almost entirely while I was a student at the Programs in Writing at the University of California, Irvine. That program is led by the brave and tireless Michelle Latiolais. Michelle, you believed in this book even before I did. Thank you for giving me the space and fortitude to write it. I love you. For the support and guidance, thank you to Sarah Shun-lien Bynum, Danzy Senna, Amy Gerstler, and Professor Julia Lupton.

Thank you to my wonderful workshopmates at UCI for your insights and camaraderie.

Thank you to my actual angel of an agent, Joy Harris. In you I have found a reader, a champion, and a dear friend—you're the best birthday present I ever gave myself! Thank you to Terry Karten at HarperCollins, whose insights and care touched the heart of this novel. My gratitude goes to Jonathan Burnham, president and publisher of the Harper division of HarperCollins, who gave his full support to Terry, and to Jane Beirn, who shared her enthusiasm with me early on. Everyone at Harper took such care with this novel. Special thanks to Amber Oliver and Milan Bozic (that cover!). Thank you Patrick Crean for bringing my book home to Canada.

Thank you to those whom I learned from in discussion: Omar Hmidat (teacher and friend), Farouk Yasseen, Karen Isaacs at Achvat Amim, Noa Levy and Tair Kaminer at Hadash, Aryeh Bernstein, Tal F., Elad ("Max" no more!)and Naama Ariel, Debbie and Yair Amichi, Inbal Oychon, Rotem Kahalon, Sunny Nagra, and especially the musician Muhammad Mughrabi (Jabid), who invited me to Shuafat camp and showed me a video I couldn't unsee. Thank you to Sarai and the whole Darmon family of Kibbutz Regavim—your home is a refuge.

I am indebted to the following books and articles: Adam Afterman on the Jewish theology of revenge; Svetlana Boym's *The Future of Nostalgia*; the poems of Mahmoud Darwish, especially "Ana min hunak"; Matti Friedman's *Pumpkinflowers*; Stathis Gourgouris's *Dream Nation*; Sayed Kashua's *Let It Be Morning* (trans. Miriam Shlesinger); the stories of Etgar Keret; Amos Oz's *Between Friends* (trans. Sondra Silverston) and *A Tale of Love and Darkness* (trans. Nicholas de Lange); Sherri Mandell's *The Blessing of a Broken Heart*; the works of Edward Said, especially *Orientalism*; Raja Shehadeh's *Palestinian Walks;* A.B. Yehoshua's *The Lover* (trans. Philip Simpson). I was fortunate to take Professor Liron Mor's incredibly rich course on the Palestinian novel in UCI, where I encountered Jabra Ibrahim Jabra's *In Search of Walid Masoud* (trans. Roger Allen and Adnan Haydar); Elias Khoury's *The Kingdom of Strangers* (trans. Paula Haydar); Adania Shibli's *We Are All Equally Far From Love* (trans. Paul Starkey) and "Out of Time"; and Helga Tawil-Souri's article "Checkpoint Time" in *Qui Parle*. Professor Radhakrishnan's course on Fanon, Said, and Humanism at UCI introduced me to Frantz Fanon's *Black Skin, White Masks* (trans. Richard Philcox). I also owe a debt to the films of Elia Suleiman, especially *The Time That Remains*; Hany Abu-Assad's *Omar*; Rana Abu Fraihah's